A F T E R M A T H

ALSO BY ANNE CAMERON

Fiction
Selkie
The Whole Fam Damily
A Whole Brass Band
Escape to Beulah
Deejay & Betty
Kick the Can
Bright's Crossing
Women, Kids & Huckleberry Wine
South of an Unnamed Creek
Stubby Amberchuk and the Holy Grail

Traditional Tales
Tales of the Cairds
Dzelarhons

Poetry
The Annie Poems
Earth Witch

Stories for Children
T'aal: The One Who Takes Bad Children (with Sue Pielle)
The Gumboot Geese
Raven Goes Berrypicking
Raven and Snipe
Spider Woman
Lazy Boy
Orca's Song
Raven Returns the Water
How the Loon Lost Her Voice
How Raven Freed the Moon

Stories on Cassette
Loon and Raven Tales

AFTERMATH

ANNE CAMERON

HARBOUR PUBLISHING

Harbour Publishing
P.O. Box 219
Madeira Park, BC V0N 2H0 Canada

Harbour Publishing acknowledges the financial support of the
Government of Canada through the Canada Council for the Arts
and the Book Publishing Industry Development Program
(BPIDP) and the Province of British Columbia through the
British Columbia Arts Council for its publishing activities.

Cover design and illustration by Kim LaFave
Printed and bound in Canada

Canadian Cataloguing in Publication Data

Cameron, Anne, 1938–
    Aftermath

    ISBN 1-55017-193-3

    I. Title.
PS8555.A5187A75 1999   C813'.54   C99-910676-4
PR9199.3.C2775A75 1999

THE CANADA COUNCIL   LE CONSEIL DES ARTS
FOR THE ARTS   DU CANADA
SINCE 1957   DEPUIS 1957

For me, life has seemed to be a collection of spirals, each leading into another, some off-kilter, some others more or less eccentric, and still others becoming dead ends, trailing off by themselves. Once in a while I almost convince myself that in this spiralling I see, or sense, a pattern. There is every chance in the world I delude myself into thinking there is some sort of reason to it all because daily life, up close, is often so untidy and so unreasonable.

And every now and again it feels as if I'm almost back to square one, all set to repeat one of the spiralling cycles. But before I can start it – again – I first have to finish things, tidy them up, get them in order so I can move on – again. I think the all-knowing shrink types even have a term for the tidying-up process, and I think that term is *cloture*, which seems to me to be from the French, meaning "closure." Or "fence." Enclosure. Which makes me wonder why they had to get esoteric and try for cloture when they could have as easily said closure or fence or enclosure, but I guess that's how you learn to do things if you stay in school long enough.

Fiction can grab a writer just as strongly as it can grab the reader. Writing is an odd occupation, a bizarre pastime, very similar to trying to grab a handful of water and then hang onto it. If it is true, as the song suggests, that "a dream is a wish your heart makes, when you're fast asleep," perhaps fiction is what happens when the dream your heart makes is grasped firmly and gently (and that's a great trick, try it sometime) and put on paper for others to share. Writing is similar to hypnosis, or self-hypnosis; you sit down at the word processor, or pick up your fountain pen or your ballpoint or your pencil or whatever your particular mechanics of the craft happen to be, and then you "concentrate," and the next thing you know, if it's a good day, it's three hours later, there's a nagging pain in the small of your back, your bum is numb and your bladder is sending out bright red warning signals that it's time to shift position or flood the house. And hypnosis, whether self-induced or not, brings with it almost total recall, which is, I believe, why so many of us appear to be so haunted. But hypnosis can be a way to dredge up the bogeys and frights and maybe this time put them to rest.

Way back in the sixties we all parroted, "what goes around comes around." Suddenly everybody capable of growing long hair and/or a moth-eaten beard was going on about karma and past lives and did you ever wonder why so many of them had to be pharaohs or kings or bishops or popes, and so few would admit to having been ditchdiggers or galley slaves? I have personally met at least half a dozen women who claim to have been Cleopatra; I have never met one who claimed to have been Ilse Koch, the Bitch of Buchenwald. A tall, skinny, bearded, long-haired, Scots-born professor once told me he had been an "Indian chief" in a previous life. Amazingly, he could recall nothing at all of the customs, mores, philosophies or life skills of any of the First Nations. An English-born professor confided in me that he had been a pharaoh, had even so named his son. I haven't met anyone who was a slave, dying of overwork in the construction of a pyramid.

But what pop/cult was blethering on about is very true for some of the darkest parts of our souls. What goes around comes around. Those who were abused become abusers, those who were damaged become damagers, those who were carefully taught not to give a fat rat's ass about others because loving hurts too much, teach others not to give a fat rat's ass, and we have become a culture which relates in just about every way except from the heart to the heart.

We don't need any more royal commissions, we don't need any more studies, we don't need any more statistics, we don't need any more bullshit from those without the spines to develop a political will. What we need is for those who get paid better money than most of us will ever see to stop playing with us and properly fund the rape assault centres, the transition houses, the group homes, the places where those who are being regularly crucified on that cross we call "love" can go for help, the places where those who are the victims of atrocity can find quiet, if not peace.

More and more of our children and grandchildren are committing suicide. They are murdering themselves and each other. Our jails are full. Rape is so commonplace a person from another planet would have reason to think we consider it normal. Sexual abuse of children is rampant and always has been. But it is not true, as some Christian credo would have us believe, that "there is no hope in us."

We're full of it. One of the most fragile things in the world and it grows in some of the most sterile soil. It's what keeps me breathing in and breathing out again.

I grew up right in the middle of a horror story even Stephen King couldn't imagine, and I thought all that nutsiness was normal. Instead of sanely deciding I wanted no part of any of that stuff I'd learned, I tiptoed into marriage, and if that wasn't as big a horror story as what had preceded it, it came in a close second. And I gave birth to kids who were born to parents who had no idea at all what life was supposed to be, and even less idea of how to raise children. Society taught me a lot of stuff – the names of the kings and queens of England, the year of the signing of the Magna Carta, and other things even stupider. Nobody taught me to mother.

Except my kids. I learned more from them than I can believe. Unfortunately for them, I learned it late and I learned it the hard way. And did them no favours.

And now I am a grandmother. And that is terrifying. Except my kids taught me well, and I think I am a better Gunga than I was a Mom. And I did not do as badly by my kids as was done by me, so there is some small improvement.

Just not enough, and not fast enough. We do what we did, over and over and over, and do to others what was done to us, over and over and over, and it has to stop. We are smothering in our own filth, we are capable of destroying every living thing on the planet a thousand times over, and it has to stop. We may be the last generation with any choice at all, and my hope is we will choose to stop it.

There will be critics who say this story is incomplete; our lives are incomplete. Others will say there are huge gaps; all our lives have huge gaps. Some will say it is, at times, disjointed; please do not insult me by believing that is an accident. I worked damn hard to get those jarring disjoints! Some will say I am bitter, others will say I am too sentimental. To all of them I say Stop nit-picking and bitching, get off my back and out of my face, if you know so fuckin' much why aren't you writing fiction instead of reviews and critiques?

"Critics are like eunuchs; they know how, when, where, why, with what and to whom – but they can't . . ."

There are no simple answers. But could someone explain to me why it is we can always afford guns and bullets and never afford love? Why we can always find the money for a war against our cousins and never find the money for a war against the harm we do ourselves? Why we can always screw more money out of the working class taxpayer so we can drop bombs and destroy things but never find the money to undo the pollution? Why are we so willing to pay more money to break up a family than to help that family heal? And why does there always have to be "fault" found and "blame" assigned, and why is the victim always the one to be blamed?

Why do we call them victims? Why can't we call them survivors?

For my children
Alex
Erin
Pierre
Marianne
For my grandchildren
Sarah
David
Terry
Daniel
Sheldon
Jen
Andrew
for Stanley and Nancy Colbert who know I love them
for Jim Erickson: hofta!
for my sister Judy who shows every sign of having more guts
than you'd find on the floor of a slaughterhouse
for my cousins whose love and support has always been there
for my mom, Annie, and my aunt, Elsie, for more reasons than I
will ever be able to express
and especially for Eleanor, who has, in her own way, repeatedly
boosted more than one person over the tailgate of a pickup truck.
Anything your little heart desires, kiddo!

Fran Williams was ten and a half years old before she found out her father wasn't her father at all. The news was both a heartache and a relief. It got dropped on her at three-fifteen of a Sunday morning by her ever-lovin' mother, who was draped over the big chair in the living room trying hard to pretend she wasn't shit-faced. On Saturday Jo-Beth had been dressed to the nines, her hair crimped and done just so, her still-elegant legs rising like a promise from her brand new black patent leather high-heeled shoes, but that was when she left the house at six-thirty with Scotty. Seven or eight hours of dedicated drinking had changed things a bit. The hair was still blonde and still crimped but it was as messy as a rat's nest, the dress was still the best in Eaton's cat-alogue but it needed some work, the shoes were mud-smeared. Jo-Beth looked like she'd been dragged through a hedge back-wards. She was holding a mickey of rye, from which she stu-diously took dainty ladylike sips. God forbid Jo-Beth should guz-zle, she just had a lot of sips, one after the other, without ice or chaser.

Scotty wasn't with her, which meant life was about to take on the quality of an air assault on a jungle village.

"Just see if I care," Jo-Beth maundered. "If a person can't hold their liquor, I say that person shouldn't drink. No excuse for it, none at all."

"Come to bed, Momma," Fran tried.

"When I'm ready. Not a minute sooner."

"Please, Momma . . ."

If Jo-Beth was in bed and asleep when Scotty finally caught up with her, sometimes he would just laugh and say the old girl was getting too wore out to cut 'er any more, then, with any kind of luck except bad, he'd flop down on the bed with all his clothes still on, sip at a beer and fall asleep, and it was easy to get the beer before it tipped over and soaked the bed or the floor.

"It's cold and I'm sleepy."

"You wanna go to sleep, go to sleep. Stop naggin' me, Fran, I'm warnin' ya."

So Fran told her right out. "Daddy'll be mad," she whispered.

Sometimes that worked. Sometimes you had to tiptoe around a thing and manipulate Jo-Beth into it, but sometimes if you just dared to put it in words she'd stop in her tracks and get on with it. Jo-Beth looked at her, squinty-eyed, poured herself another little sip and tossed it back like a movie cowboy.

"And who is *he* that we tiptoe around like mice in the presence of the resident house cat?" It was funny when Jo-Beth talked as if she was someone other than who she was, but it could be scary, too. Especially when Scotty was around, because he would get owly and ask her what in hell it was she was tryin' to prove, and she musta picked up that fancy talk from shackin' up with a lawyer or something.

"Momma," Fran tried again, "Momma, you know Daddy –"

"Well, he isn't." Jo-Beth sounded stone cold sober all of a sudden. "He's not your daddy at all. *your* daddy didn't work in any sawmill. *your* daddy didn't come home smellin'a diesel with sawdust on his clothes. *your* daddy grew up in a big house in town, with a piano in the parlour. And," she added, as if it proved everything, "he could play it, too. Scotty, he never even set eyes on you until you were almost a year old. *your* dad probably never got 'mad' in his life." She tossed off her little sip and poured another. "We'd'a been better off, maybe, if he had. Oh well," she shrugged and sighed, the alcoholic philosopher, "learn a lesson kid, that's the screwin' you get for the screwin' you got."

Fran would have found out more but the cab arrived, and within seconds of the headlights sweeping along the side of the house, Scotty was in the door. "You hoo-er!" he roared. "Take off and leave *me*, will you?"

"Ah, don't get your shirt in a knot," Jo-Beth answered, pouring a sip and handing it to Scotty. "I told you I had to leave, didn't I? Just came home, that's all. You know I can't stand it when those bunkhouse bozos get goin'." She grinned, cheeky and flirting. "If I'm going to listen to anyone sing, Scotty, I'm going to come home and wait for you to get here, then there'll be singing."

It worked. Instead of busting up the house and sending chairs through windows, Scotty Williams laughed. He put down the case of beer he was carrying and tossed back the little sip. "G'wan to bed, Fran," he said easily. "Nothin's comin' down on you."

"Yes, Daddy," said Fran, her knees suddenly weak with relief. She left the kitchen half running and climbed into bed with Buttercup and little Scotty, curling her shivering body around their sleepy warmth.

"Scotty's not my real dad, you know," she said quietly to her cousin Liz. Liz's dad was Jo-Beth's brother, so no matter who Fran's dad was or was not, Gowan was still her uncle – not that anyone would ever bother bragging about that.

"You're kidding."

"I'm not. My mother told me."

"So who was?"

"She didn't say."

They sat on the side-by-side swings hanging from the bottom bough of the huge cedar tree, scuffing their feet in the dirt and not really swinging.

"Want me to find out?"

"Want to?"

"You want me to?"

"Why not?"

And that was just about all there was to it, that and wait for Liz to fish around.

Liz waited until her mother Wilma was pouring rinse water over her head. "Fran says Auntie Jo-Beth said Uncle Scotty isn't really Fran's dad."

"When did Jo-Beth say that?" Wilma sounded surprised.

"The other night. She was drunk."

"Oh, I'd already figured out that part. You want another pot of water?"

"What do you think?"

"I think you need another pot of water. Your hair's getting long, maybe you should get Auntie Jo-Beth to cut it for you."

"I don't want it cut. So is he?"

"No, he's not. But if you want to know more about it than that, Miss Big Ears, you can ask your daddy."

So Liz asked Gowan. They were sitting on the back steps watching the broody hen with her chicks, Gowan smoking yet another hand-rolled cigarette. "If Uncle Scotty isn't Fran's dad, who is?" Liz asked.

"Who told you that?" Gowan blew smoke rings one inside the other, four of them.

"Fran did. She said Auntie Jo-Beth said it, so I asked Mom and Mom said I was to ask you."

"Well, he's not."

"So who is?"

"What do you care?"

"I don't. But Fran does. And she's scared to ask in case Uncle Scotty gets mad, so I said I'd ask for her."

"Thunder, lightning and dynamite," Gowan sighed. "She said he said they said we said. Anybody else have anything to say about it?"

"Who's her dad?"

"Not for me to say."

"Why not?"

"Because it'll kick off a whole big hoo-rah is why. You'll tell Fran and then sooner or later Scotty'll get to yelling and roaring and Fran'll holler You're not my dad and the sky will just about go green, let me tell you."

"She said he had a piano and could play it."

"Well, that narrows 'er down some, don't it."

"Sometimes, when Uncle Scotty's mean, he yells about Aunt Jo-Beth learning big words from shacking up with a lawyer. Is that who it was?"

"What is this, you in training to join the Secret Service? Just shut up or you'll get a kick in the ass, okay?"

"Okay."

There were only half a dozen lawyers in town, and two of them were too old and doddery to be possibilities. Of the other four, two of them had only just scraped their way through law school before coming back home. That left two. One was married and the other wasn't and, people whispered, not equipped. Too limp in the wrist.

"So maybe it's –"

"Maybe. But he's got kids older'n you and other kids younger'n you so . . ."

"Right." Fran kicked her foot, scuffing dust over the ragged toe of her running shoe. "Well, Scotty said it was a shack-up."

"Yeah, but he was mad, right?"

"When isn't he?"

Scotty wasn't always mad. But when he was, the whole town knew about it. When he was really owly he'd bring home a case of beer and a great big jug of Berrycup and sit at the table drinking them both, with his special tobacco can on the table in front of him. For the first couple of hours he would just look at the can. Then, sooner or later, he would take the lid off and dump the contents onto the table. The clatter was like a warning, like the rattle of a snake. As soon as Fran heard it, she'd freeze.

But you couldn't stay frozen. Something about what was in that can would pull you like a magnet pulling nails, and the next thing you knew you'd be sitting in a chair at the end of the table, with Scotty on the long side of it, sifting and sorting his souvenirs.

"Know what this is?" He always held it up. "This is the Iron Cross. It's about as good a medal as anybody in this town ever got!" He'd look at it a while, then get the jeweller's rouge and the soft cloth and do a job on it. "What it was, see," and his voice was soft, as if he was telling Buttercup a bedtime story, "they gave us all these tests, first day of boot camp. Push-ups, sit-ups, chin-ups, you name it. Well, I done okay at that. So when they saw I could outdo the yahoo they'd put in charge, they hauled me aside and handed me a Lee-Enfield three-oh-three. See if you can hit that target, they said. The target was like a big black shadow of a person, from the waist up. So I put one in the middle of his head. So down goes the target and another one comes up a few yards farther away, so I put one in the middle of his head. Well, after a dozen or so shots I went to lunch, and after lunch I'm doing the lefty-righty bullshit and this snotnose comes up and says Sergeant wants to see you. So I go see the sergeant. I don't even have my damn uniform issued to me, the whole bunch is still wearin' our own clothes, with one or two bits of Queen's issue, so I'm standin' at attention in a shirt and my own jeans."

About then he'd stop talking for a while and sit with his beer bottle pressed against his bottom lip, not drinking, not talking, just staring. And if you sat there long enough, and Fran always sat there long enough because the magnet wouldn't let her go, Scotty would start again.

"So the long and short of it was the sergeant says How would you like to go to England right away? Well, I knew we weren't fightin' the damn English, although we ought to. Kill the fuckers, too, every one of 'em, down to the ones haven't cut their teeth yet. Yes Sergeant, I says. Why not? When's the last time the government offered *you* a trip to Trafalgar bloody Square?" He drank deeply, put the Iron Cross on the table, played with it a bit. "So I get a brown uniform and new boots and a towel, and the next thing I know I'm on this goddamn boat, and every day from dawn to dark it's lefty-righty on deck and all this get-fit crap. When I get to England it's no Trafalgar Square, it's off to some fog-infested bog. Might's well have been at home when it came to rain! Give me a red cowpie hat, dropped me outta airplanes, Jesus, it just went on without end amen. And then I get a leave, and finally I see the pigeons and Nelson's damn monument and before the hangover has worn off I'm in a truck being driven across half of goddamn France. No Eiffel Tower for me, by gods! Not yet. It's a funny feeling, me and a driver in a jeep, same as if I was someone important. And the gun they gave me! Hey, that wasn't no damn army issue Lee-Enfield three-oh-three. That wasn't no standard issue. Coulda took the eyeball outta a mosquito with that baby!"

He picked up the Iron Cross, wiped it clean and put it back in the tobacco can. "First man I ever shot, I was up a tree like a monkey, with binoculars and the whole shiterooni. And there's this Citroen coming down the road, a driver, a guy next to him and three officers in the back seat. So I took the officer in the middle. Then the driver. And then," he drained his beer, "I got the other bastards, too. Took their ID tags, took their medals, took the goddamn pips off their uniform shoulders! Let *them* figure out who'n'hell they are!"

Then he'd start sorting the stuff. Medals of all kinds, buttons off uniforms, the things he called pips, hat badges. "Look at this bloody thing," he'd say, picking up the big gold ring. "The Masons had *this* guy in their club! Goddamn Nazi officer's good enough for them but not the likes of me. Well, who's got the ring now, I ask you?"

If Fran looked at Scotty's face then, she'd see somebody she didn't ever want to meet, not in a dark alley, not in the bright light of day. "And the officer, he says to me he says Williams, he says, don't you think it's a bit much to collect souvenirs like that? No sir, I says. At home, do you shoot a deer, you put his antlers on the wall of the garage because it's how you give him some respect. You don't just leave 'em on the floor of the bush for the rats, I says. Barbarians, he says. So I says Well, sir, maybe so, but you notice it ain't us barbarians givin' the orders. Damn English twerps! It's like givin' the reins of government to Elmer Fudd. Fuckin' English," he sighed deeply, "sent us all out and we went, told us to kill and we killed. Shoulda killed off more than the krauts, shoulda killed off the officers, too. Barbarians, he says. Maybe so, I says, but you notice it ain't the barbarians givin' the orders."

Hours of it. Medal by medal, button by button, pip by pip, and he polished them all with the jeweller's rouge and the soft cloth.

One time, and only one time, he looked up at Fran and smiled the craziest smile she ever saw in all her life. "When you think about it, Frannie," he said calmly, "it was learning to shoot for food and learning to work hard for money equipped me for what they sent me off to do. So you better be careful what it is you learn around here or you'll wind up doing it whether you want to or not."

The phone rang, jarring her awake, sending her running down the hallway to answer it before it woke the little kids.

"Fran?" It was Jo-Beth, and her voice was trembling. "Fran, get the little kids up, get something on their feet and get them *out*. Now!" and the line went dead.

Fran was sobbing before she replaced the phone. Oh God, oh Jesus, not again.

"Come on." She jerked little Scotty out of bed and he started crying. "Shut up, Scotty, I mean it," she warned. She stuffed his feet into woollen socks, then hauled on his pants and a heavy sweater. "Go get your gumboots," she yelled, grabbing Buttercup and pushing her arms into her winter coat.

She took them out of the house and through the back yard,

along the alley and up the dirt road to where the bush started. They were too out of breath to cry, too frightened to protest. "Here, sit on this," Fran said, putting one of the blankets on the ground. The three of them sat with the quilt draped over their shoulders, but they shivered anyway.

In the light from the cab's headlights, they could see Scott lurch for the front steps. Then the cab left, the house disappeared into darkness and all they could hear was the sounds of the night – frogs croaking, wind soughing in the bush, a dog yapping thinly somewhere.

"We have to find a place to go," Fran decided. "Someplace close, someplace where it doesn't get wet."

After a while the little ones fell asleep, but Fran couldn't even doze. She sat watching as the sky lightened and other people came awake. You knew they were awake because smoke started to come out of the chimneys as the normal ones put on water for coffee, or started to cook bacon and eggs or something.

By the time the little kids wakened, the worst of the chill was gone. They folded up the blanket and quilt, then walked back down the dirt road and along the alley, past their own house, to the corner, where they turned left and went the back way past three houses to where their cousin Liz and their Uncle Gowan and Aunt Wilma lived.

"Oh, Christ," Gowan said when he opened the door and saw them standing there.

"I'm sorry," Fran mumbled, feeling so ashamed, so guilty, so awful, and wishing she could have thought of something else to do.

"Come on in, sweetheart," Aunt Wilma said, lifting Buttercup and giving her a big smooch. "I bet I know somebody who could eat sixty dozen silver dollar pancakes. Am I right?"

Fran didn't feel hungry, she felt sick to her stomach, but she did a fair job on the breakfast and didn't hurt Aunt Wilma's feelings.

Uncle Gowan went over to their house and was gone almost an hour. When he came back, Jo-Beth was with him and she looked like holy old hell.

"Oh, my dear!" Aunt Wilma sighed. "Oh, my poor dear."

"I'm okay," said Jo-Beth. But she wasn't. It had been one helluva go-round. She had fingermarks on her throat and welts on her face, and there was a big sore-looking bruise on her arm and one side of her lower lip was swollen. She winced when she drank her coffee.

"It could be worse." She forced a grin. "You got anything to put in this coffee?"

"No," said Gowan.

"Cream," said Wilma.

"Jesus aitch," said Jo-Beth.

Scott came over an hour or so later looking as if he was bleeding to death from the eyeballs. He didn't knock, he just walked in, went to the stove, poured himself a coffee in somebody else's cup and stood sipping it and staring. Nobody said anything.

"You comin' home?" he asked quietly.

"You calmed down?" Jo-Beth replied.

"I'm fine."

"You sure?"

"I said so, didn't I!"

"See, you're still proddy. Maybe I'll stay here a while longer."

"Suit yourself." He had another coffee, and still nobody said anything. "So where did *you* go?" he demanded, glaring at Fran.

"Me?" She felt the blood drain from her face.

"Yeah, you."

"Leave her be, Scott," Aunt Wilma said quietly.

Scott whirled and looked at her. He shook his head, little short sharp jerks. "Butt out, Wilma."

"No." She stood up and faced him across the kitchen. "You leave those kids alone or I'm going to call the cops."

"I never hurt those kids!" he roared.

"Look at them. They're terrified."

"Bull," he snorted, but he was ashamed and everyone knew Wilma was right. Nobody said anything more, and after a while Scott reached up and took a leftover pancake from the warming rack. "You make a good pancake, Wilma," he said, chewing. He took another.

"What did you do to set him off this time?" Gowan asked.

"Oh yeah, Gowan, sure, what did I do," Jo-Beth snapped. "Of course the man can't be expected to act like a civilized human being. Of course it must be something I did wrong! You want to know what I did, Gowan? I sucked air in, and then I blew it out, that's what I did wrong."

"Were you drinking?" her brother asked.

"What does that have to do with it? If I stay home he gets mad. If I go with him he gets mad about that. If I don't say anything he gets mad. If I talk he gets mad. If I drink or don't drink, he gets mad. If I stood on my head in a corner and spit five-dollar bills the man would get mad. Because the man *is* mad. Mad as a goddamn hatter!"

"See?" Gowan said. "See what you're doing?"

"Oh shit, Gowan!" Jo-Beth lowered her voice. "You got such a good line, a body would think you knew what you were talking about."

"She was switchin' her tail all over the damn beer parlour," Scott implored Gowan, as though he wanted something only Gowan could give. "I'm having a drink in there with those guys and there she is, table-hoppin', givin' them all the glad-eye and —"

"Here we go," Jo-Beth laughed. "Here it comes. Jo-Beth got up and went to the biffy and the town nutcase lost his mind. I'm goin' home!"

Fran waited but Jo-Beth didn't say Come on, kid, or You kids come home now, so that meant it wasn't over yet. She looked at Uncle Gowan and he jerked his head down, telling her to keep her backside pressed tight against the chair. Scott finished the pancakes, drained the coffee in the mug, then walked to the door without saying one word.

"You be careful, Scotty, okay?" Gowan said quietly.

"Yeah. No problem."

They slept at Uncle Gowan and Auntie Wilma's place that night. Buttercup and little Scotty slept on the couch and Fran shared with Liz.

"You okay?" Liz asked.

"Yes," Fran lied.

"Where did you go?"

"Bush."

"Wow."

"I have to find a place." Fran was suddenly shaking from head to foot. "Someplace warm and dry. Then we wouldn't just be running around in the dark. And in wintertime it rains and what if Buttercup gets sick?"

They found it together. It took most of the summer to find it, but they found it. Not five minutes away, and perfect because nobody knew about it.

Where they lived wasn't really a neighbourhood. There were no real houses. It had been the army camp, with barracks for the soldiers and an administration office and a mess hall. But after all the soldiers came back from the war there was what everyone called the Housing Shortage. Lots said it was because all those guys from Saskabush and Ontari-Hairy-Asshole who had been stationed on the Island knew a good thing when they saw it and didn't want to go back where they came from, so stayed. And that meant those from the Island who had been shipped somewhere else and sure as hell weren't going to stay there had no place to live when they came back home. It was so bad that for a while some people had to live in tents or move into someone's basement or garage.

And then someone took a look at all those empty barracks up in the army camp and asked the obvious question. The barracks got divided into apartments, two or three to a building, and people could move in and pretend it was home.

Not all the barracks got made into apartments. Someone said the school was already so overcrowded the teachers would quit if they got stuck with any more kids, so the last couple of barracks stood empty. And under one of them was this place. You wouldn't even know it was there if you didn't know it was there.

When the kids in the neighbourhood found it, nobody broke any windows, but they got in and ran screaming down the long empty hallways, their voices echoing. They found the trap doors leading up into the attic, and they even found a way into the crawl space underneath. At first they just sat under the barracks and grinned at how hidden they were. You could hear people talking outside, you could peek through knotholes and see people moving about their business. After a while, without anyone saying anything, one of the empty barracks became the boys' one and the other the girls' one.

It was cool under there. The dirt was dusty dry and secretive. Some sacks were piled up, one on top of the other, and when you poked them you could feel sand inside. The sacks stuck out from the wall into the crawl space, and you could lean against them and just let all the stuff going on outside stay outside, with you under here, where they couldn't see you.

Fran liked it under the hut. Especially when she was under there all by herself. It was okay to be there with Liz, and with the others, but it was best when there was only her. And one day, without even knowing how it happened, she thought about how big the hut was, how long it was, how wide it was, and she realized the hut was bigger than the crawl space under it. A *lot* bigger than the crawl space. The difference had to do with the sand-stuffed sacks.

The first chance she got she swiped the flashlight and took it under the hut. She crawled on hands and knees from the outside wall, along the sacks to the corner, then along the sacks to the next corner, then left and along the sacks, back to the outside wall. She knew that there were more sacks against that wall, even if she couldn't see them.

She got inside the hut and saw that it was easy to find where the sack place ought to be, right under the floor, but there was no sign of any trap door or anything like that, the floor just kept on going. So she went back outside and skinned under the siding and took another look at that wall of sandbags.

On the front corner, where one row of sacks met up with the other row and made a corner, there was something just a bit different about the way the sacks were piled. The top ones were stacked up okay, but the bottom sack was upright, not tucked under or over anything. So she gave it a good tug. It toppled. And in front of her was a little creephole tunnel. She took a good look before she crawled in. Double rows of sandbags with a space between them. Gripping the flashlight, Fran crept down that little tunnel. A kid could skin along here without any problem but an adult would probably have to lie on his side and slither.

At the far corner the tunnel turned, so Fran did too. Halfway down the back wall one of the sacks was missing from the inside pile of them. Fran went through the hole and dropped down and sat on the floorboards, shining her flashlight all around, hardly believing what she saw – an entire house thing made of sandbags. Even a ceiling, for Pete's sake! Now how would they do that? How do you get a ceiling made of sandbags?

You put angle iron across. And you hold it up with other pieces of angle iron stuck in the ground just this side of the sandbags. Then you've got a thing almost like a bed frame and you can put your sandbags on that.

A table, the legs cut off halfway up so it would fit. And on the table piles and heaps of paper. Maps, all kinds of neat stuff. Some empty khaki-coloured boxes with rope handles on the end. And best of all, some kind of radio. When Fran turned it on the lights glowed, but she couldn't find any stations so she figured something in it must be broken. Or it was tuned to special stations they'd turned off when they all got what the dads called The Discharge. And a couple of metal tripods. Machine gun tripods. In case the Japs came.

Fran knew. Just across the road, over by the lake, there was a zigzag of a ditch thing, the walls all shored up with cedar posts and poles, and the dads said it was a barricade trench in case the Japs landed on the west coast and hiked their way through miles and miles of nothing but miles and miles. Uncle Gowan thought it was all just too silly for words.

"Jesus aitch," he laughed, "can't you just see 'em? There's not one of 'em over four feet tall, so how'n hell they're gonna make 'er through the rain forest, over fallen logs and blowdown and deadfall and what-all, I'm sure I don't know. And the buck-toothed little hissers all wear glasses thick as coke bottles, and you know how glasses steam up in the rain!"

"Gowan, that's *awful* " Wilma said, but she was laughing. "That's just awful!"

"Now, now, Willy." Gowan shook his finger at her, still joking. "Don't give me any of that We're all brothers and children of God stuff, because I'm never going to be a brother to any Jap and you, my darlin', are never going to be a brother to anybody!" and they all laughed. But there was something under the laughter that made Wilma uneasy, you could tell.

So not just the zigzag trench, and not just the thing up on the bluff looking off toward the mountains, that big concrete jobby with the frame where something big and heavy had sat. They used it for a fire lookout station sometimes now, but that wasn't what it had been for to start with. And now this.

It was easy enough to do the rest. Fran went around picking up other people's empties and carting them down to the bottle depot for money. She went to the big dump just the other side of the road and loaded little Scotty's wagon with old batteries and whatever those things were in old motors that had all the copper wire wrapped around some kind of flat thing. The junk man looked at them and asked if she could bring in the motors she took them out of. She nodded, and waited. "Two dollars each," he said. She nodded again.

With the money she got for the junk and the motors, she bought stuff. Candles and a coal oil lamp from the secondhand store. A gallon of coal oil. Cans of sardines and some other food. You could get an old army overcoat for twenty-five cents at the secondhand store, and red army blankets with a big wide black stripe on them for fifty cents.

And the next time the phone rang and she had to get the kids out of the house, she was ready. She got them into their boots and coats and they ran in the direction the cab would come from, not away from it, and she shoved the rock aside, pushed the little kids through, then went through herself and pulled the rock back in front. It was so easy. Just move the sack and send them in with the flashlight. "I'm right behind you," she said. "Keep going or I'll pinch your bum!" and she even got the sack more or less over the hole before she went after them. She had to slap Buttercup, who whined about being scared of the dark, but only the first couple of times. After that they knew as well as she did how to get where it was safe, and they knew it was a secret, and they knew what would happen if a hint of their secret got breathed.

They could just get comfortable in there before the cab arrived. Fran would give them a bottle of pop or open up a can of peaches, or they'd have crackers and peanut butter, something to make it all seem special, almost a party except for being scared stiff. Then they could lie down on the overcoats and pull the blankets over top of them and be warm and dry no matter what was happening outside.

One morning when they woke up and crawled out there was snow everywhere. That was scary because they would have to leave marks by the place where the rock covered the hole, and through the wet white to the roadway. But it was on the back side of the hut so nobody noticed. Later, just to be sure, Fran took the little ones out to play in the snow and got them to run around behind the hut and all around it, until there was such a mess of footprints nobody could have guessed anyway.

It was okay if you only had some warning, which Fran usually did. The sawmill paid off every two weeks, the middle and the end of the month. The other two weekends were all right because by the time the rent was paid and the groceries bought and the money went for the big go-round on payday weekend, well, the next weekend had to be pretty dry and quiet. And of the two dangerous weekends you could be pretty sure, although not always, that Friday night wouldn't be too bad. First there was supper, so Scotty had food in his belly before he started, and then a bath and all, so they didn't take off to paint the town red until half past six or seven. But Saturday, the one after pay Friday, was almost guaranteed to be a toot.

Not all the toots were bad. Time and again they'd come home still laughing, dancing to the music from the radio, maybe even kissing and hugging in the kitchen, by the table with the oilcloth cover. Lots of times they'd come in with a huge armload of take-out Chinese food, Hey you little buggers, you get yourselves up out of bed and dig in, we're joining up with the Joneses here! Sometimes they even came home early, with big newspaper-wrapped packages of fish'n'chips. "Get me the vinegar, get me the ketchup, where's the salt and pepper, smell that, will you!"

Just every now and again, and no rhyme or reason to it, there'd be wigs on the green for sure. Liz, the know-it-all who spent so much time with her nose in a book, said that was a saying came down from some big revolution where one side wore these fancy long powdered wigs and the other side, Cromwell's round-heads, shaved their hair, and when they killed the other side they threw the wigs on the village green to let people know and to warn them just who was winning it all.

Given even five minutes' warning, Fran could get the kids out of the house, even if they had to go out the back window while the yelling and smashing went down in the kitchen. But sometimes there wasn't any warning. She'd be asleep one minute and the next minute all she could do was throw open the window to make it look like they'd managed to get out, then get the kids under the bed, against the far wall, and make sure Buttercup didn't start crying.

The worst was when the neighbours had a gutful and came over to put a stop to it, four or five or six of them hanging onto Scotty and him throwing them around as if they were nothing at all, and everyone knowing about it. That was the worst, everyone knowing about it. Looking at you and feeling sorry for you, making you want to curl up in a ball and hide, making you want to turn yourself into a dust bugger so their eyes wouldn't look at you like you weren't a person at all, just some poor thing. Poor thing.

Sometimes it looked as if it was getting better, looked it so convincingly you got yourself sucked in.

Jo-Beth went to the bingo and won the jackpot, the one that had been building for almost two months. She couldn't believe it. "I thought the only kind of luck I had was bad luck," she said over and over again. "Isn't this just a whole lot better than a poke in the eye with a sharp stick!"

The first thing she did was pay off all the bills. Then she got Scotty a new shirt, a new tie, a pair of almost-dress pants and a nice jacket. And each of the kids got a bike. "Merry Christmas," she said, even though it wasn't December. They had steak for supper, one each. Big ones for Jo-Beth, Scotty and Fran, smaller ones for little Scotty and Buttercup, who of course whined that she liked hamburger better.

"Oh, shut up," Jo-Beth laughed. "If it was hamburger you'd want fish, if it was fish you'd cry for something else. Just shut the hell up and eat!"

"There's somethin' wrong with that kid," Scotty decided. "If you gave her the moon on a string she'd complain she wanted ribbon."

"No pleasing her," Jo-Beth agreed.

"Eat your goddamn supper!" Scotty slammed his hand on the table. "Or get yourself to your bedroom and let other people enjoy theirs!"

So of course Buttercup wailed and Scotty got off his chair, scooped her up, took her to her room and tanned her backside, and about time somebody did, too. Buttercup wailed, but she'd been set to do that anyway and at least you could close the door on her noise.

Steak and French fried potatoes and then, for dessert, vanilla ice cream. Buttercup decided she'd be good, but Scotty made her eat everything on her plate before she could have her ice cream. "And take a telling from it, too," he ordered. "Had enough of your goddamn bullshit, Lady Toots."

They went out to celebrate and came home laughing like loons. Jo-Beth had on different clothes than she'd been wearing when they'd left, and carried her old ones in a fancy shopping bag. "Look at that!" Scotty shouted, laughing loudly. "Doesn't she look just like Mrs. R.B.! God*damn* but you're a good-lookin' woman!" and things were great for a couple of weeks.

Then it started. "Don't give me any of that crap about how you're gonna phone the cops," Scotty roared. "It's the goddamn cops are what we're discussing here! One of 'em anyway."

"No, Scotty," Jo-Beth insisted. "No, it's not like that at all. You've just got some idea in your head."

"Don't you tell *me* what ideas I've got in my goddamn head! Goddamn pleece think that because they've got guns and bullets the rest of us are gonna just fall down in the dirt and say Yessir, nosir, three bags full sir. I *shot* better men than them! I *killed* better men than them!" and out came the tobacco can.

"Oh sweet Jesus," Jo-Beth sighed, "here we go. He'll be singing the goddamn funeral march next. Dum dum de dum dum de dum de dum de dum, put the boots in the stirrups backwards, the weekend warriors are gonna tell us all how much they sacrificed for the flag. Want to know somethin', Scotty? I could have a tobacco can full of junk, too. Every goddamn pawnshop in the country has *bins* of it!"

Even the little kids knew she was going out of her way to make this one happen. They went around white-faced for days, little Scotty as quiet as if he'd been born with an empty throat, and Buttercup snivelling just for the sake of snivelling, until Fran thought she'd up and bust her one to give her something to snivel about for a change.

Saturday morning Jo-Beth left the house before nine and walked the two miles down to the bus stop. She was back again by three and you could already smell the little sips she'd packed away. By the time Scotty got home a little after five, everyone was walking on eggshells, but even Buttercup had enough survival instinct to eat her hamburger patties and gravy, mashed potatoes and canned peas without complaining.

They got dressed as if they were two different people in two different hotel rooms with a wall between, and they left together, still not speaking. Fran was ready. She had already set up the hidey-hole and she put the kids to bed in their clothes. Then she lay in bed stiff as a board, waiting. But there was no phone call.

She heard Jo-Beth come home and move around in the

kitchen, heard the *scaaaart* of a match, heard Jo-Beth inhale deeply. "Smart ass bastard," Jo-Beth muttered, probably to her glass. "Just as tough as hell when it's women and kids. Him and his goddamn medals and pips. Like the woman said, Mardon me pister, you're not so muckin' fuch!" She prowled around the kitchen some more, and there was the sound of another little sip being poured. "*My* fault, I suppose. I have control over what other people do with their eyeballs, whether people look at other people or not? Then the big war heeeeeero gets proddy, and it's *my* fault, I suppose? Makes my ass ache, I'll tell the world."

It went on and on and got so boring Fran shut her eyes, just to blink, but not to sleep . . .

And then it was coming down and Scotty was crazier than he'd ever been, throwing chairs and yelling, and this time Jo-Beth was yelling, too.

"See? See, you crazy bastard? I *told* you! I *told* you every pawnshop in the country was drownin' in that junk! Five dollars. Five rotten lousy stinking dollars outta my bingo money is all it took and I got *three* tobacco cans of stuff! You got an Iron Cross? Hell, I got the *Victoria Cross*, see!"

God knows what else she had in the tobacco can. Fran had the kids out the window and racing through the rain, and already the lights were going on in other barracks, and people racing out of their doors, in their pyjamas or pulling their jeans up over their bare asses, racing down to where Scotty was screaming and screaming and screaming as if someone was pulling his eyes out with a violin wire.

When Fran took the kids home, Scotty wasn't there. Jo-Beth's face looked as if someone had backed a tractor over it, but she was as defiant as an alley cat.

"Last damn time, too!" she vowed. "He can just stay gone, too."

"Where is he?" Fran asked.

"In the goddamn loony bin, where else would they put him? More nuts than an Oh Henry, I'll tell the world."

It was quiet for a few months, and that was good. But the bikes went to the pawnshop and that wasn't so good. And then Fran started to put two and two together and understand what it was Scotty had been ranting and raving about from the start. The cop started showing up at very odd times. Fran would come home from school and there he'd be, in uniform, at the table, his jacket over the back of a chair, and him drinking tea and eating lemon pound cake.

"What's it mean to see the inside of a uniform?" Liz asked.

"How would I know?"

"My mom said to my dad if your mom wasn't careful she'd see more than the outside of that police uniform, she'd see the inside of it, too."

"Take it off, stupid, that's what it means. How can you spend all your life reading your brain into train oil and still be so stupid?"

"You think you're smart but you're not. Someone oughta tell you you're suffering from a delusion."

"Oh har har, Liz. You don't understand all those books anyway, you read them because nobody'll have anything to do with you."

"Look who's talkin'! Old bust-up-the-house's daughter!"

"Am not. He's not my dad. *My* dad was a lawyer with a piano and everything."

"Oh yeah? You're a bastard is what you are. An illegitimate bastard."

"Dumb shit. All bastards are illegitimate. Go drown in a puddle."

So there they were, starting out as if it was going to get better, with new clothes and new bikes, and then there they were with the bikes gone, the cop eating cake, and Jo-Beth seeing the inside of his uniform just like Aunt Wilma said.

But the inside of the uniform vanished as quickly as the outside of it when Scotty walked back into the kitchen and put his little brown paper bag of toothpaste, toothbrush and shaving stuff on the table.

"Get out," Jo-Beth said coldly.

"Oh, I'm going," he smiled, as if his smile was hours away from the rest of his face. "But not one minute before I'm damn good and ready to go."

He had a minor fit when he couldn't find his tobacco can. "Maybe the cops took it," Jo-Beth shrugged. "Or the guys who came after you went to the rubber room."

"Eat it, bitch."

But she didn't eat it, she drank it. Bit by bit, sip by sip, for two or three days Jo-Beth drank and Scotty waited. He slept on the floor in the kitchen, with a blanket and a pillow. He hardly spoke. And then on Saturday afternoon he put on his best clothes, his very best, and left the house. He didn't come back for supper, he wasn't there when Jo-Beth got herself dressed to the nines, and there was still no sign of him when Fran took the little kids through the gathering darkness to the hidey-hole.

"Why we comin' here now?" Scotty worried. "There's no trouble."

"Might as well be here before it starts as have to jump out the window."

"Can we read comics?"

"Sure."

They set themselves up with the little coal oil lamp and a few stale Digestive cookies. It was so nice, so quiet, so safe, so much their place and theirs only, they all got sleepy very early and turned out the lamp.

"Night night," Fran said softly.

"Night night," they answered, Buttercup yawning.

They slept until after ten in the morning, then crawled out of the sandbag bomb shelter gun bunker and went home.

"Oh God, where have you *been?*" Jo-Beth was on the verge of total collapse. At least a dozen other people were in the kitchen with her, all of them looking as if they'd had their eyes cleaned with a chimney brush. "I've been worried *sick!*" Jo-Beth started to cry. She scooped up Buttercup and hugged her until Buttercup started to cry too, then Jo-Beth put her down and grabbed for little Scotty. "Oh, God, I thought he'd come home and taken you all off somewhere."

"Who? Dad?"

And they all started talking at the same time. Fran sat at the table trying to make sense of it, watching as everyone ran around packing up everything in the house. Someone came in with another load of cardboard boxes from the grocery store, while someone else carried an armload of packed boxes out the front door to a big rented truck.

"What's going on?" Fran asked, but nobody seemed to hear her. "What is going on?" Finally she had to scream and scream and scream, "*What is going on?*"

Liz jerked her head toward the front door. Fran got off her

chair, still yelling about how nobody ever told her anything at all, and stomped out of the house. She and Liz went back to the hidey-hole and sat there looking through the tobacco can, poking through the medals and pips.

"Why'd you hide it?"

"Because in case he came back he wouldn't sit and poke through it and get himself all worked into a big stink is why, dumbbell. He'd be halfways okay until he started looking through this stuff and then holy wow, he'd be off again."

"Nice watch." Liz wound it, then held it to her ear. "Works, too."

"They all work. That one's gold. You can have it. Just don't let anyone *see* it, promise?"

"Sure. Thanks."

"So what's going on, anyway?"

"Well, nobody can find that cop who's been hanging around your mom, and they can't find his cop car, either. And they can't find your old man."

"So they think —"

"Yeah. So you and your mom and the little kids, you're all moving. The rate they're going I think you'll be gone tonight."

"Moving? But I don't *want* to move."

"You know what they say. Nobody wants to know what you want."

So Fran took the tobacco can back to the house and made sure it was packed in the box with her own things. Then she wrote her name all over the box so nobody else on the other end would open it before she did. And that, as they say, was that.

Liz wasn't having any easier a time of it. In fact sometimes she thought she'd rather have a family like Fran's, where things were all out in the open, with lots of noise and yelling and the neighbours coming in and putting a stop to the worst of it. At her place, nobody even knew about the worst of it.

She was eleven the first time Gowan picked her up as if she weighed nothing at all and carried her into her bedroom, folded up a towel on top of the blankets, laid her down on her very own bed and fucked her. Wilma was at work and knew nothing about it. And Liz sure wasn't going to tell. She didn't tell about any of the other times, either. Wilma would just come apart like a cheap watch. Liz knew because Wilma had said so, when their friend's sister was up a stump and everyone knew it. Uncle Scott said he expected to see three Chinamen on camels the way everyone was going on about it, as if nobody else had ever had a baby, and if Jesus was born in this day and age wouldn't everyone carry on just like this about Mary, who had found herself in the same damn position?

"Not the same at all," said Wilma. "Mary conceived without sex."

"Yeah, sure," Uncle Scott laughed. "I wonder how many times she had to tell *that* story before someone believed her!"

Everyone knew whose baby it was, too, and that he'd have probably made an honest woman of her, but she had said no, she wasn't interested in marrying someone at gunpoint, thank you. And Wilma had said that if it was her daughter, praise God it wasn't, she'd be so broken-hearted she'd just come apart like a cheap watch.

Besides, Wilma would blame herself. Why not, she was busy blaming herself for everything else. Every time another magazine came into the house it had another article on how bad it was for the family if the mother worked outside the home. All kinds of problems, the articles said. Kids stole cars and smoked cigarettes and developed mental problems if their mothers worked. And Wilma worked. Not because she was a money-hungry person, not because she wanted chesterfields and drapes and piles of other stuff, but because if she didn't work there was never enough money for things like rent and food.

It wasn't that Wilma wasn't a good manager. She could make a meal out of two rocks and a handful of grass if she had the rocks and the grass. But Gowan wasn't what anyone would call a good provider, even though he'd been working since he quit school at age fourteen, and given half a chance Gowan always let everyone know that he'd never once collected unemployment. Even when he had to get his back teeth taken out he hadn't missed any work or any pay, he had this thing called accumulated sick time so the couple of days he spent rinsing his mouth with salty water and spitting blood down the toilet were paid just the same as if he'd been on the job.

But he never brought home his full paycheque. He might or might not show up for supper on pay Friday night, but even when he showed up he didn't hand his cheque to Wilma. He had supper, changed his clothes and headed downtown himself to cash it. And then you could just sit and wonder when he'd be back, and how much of it he'd bring home.

Gowan loved to play cards. There were people who said watching Gowan with a deck was like watching a musician with his instrument. Liz thought that was a bit thick. There wasn't anything to shuffling a deck of cards. She could do it and she didn't even play cards! Sometimes when a pack of relatives wound up at the house and sat around the table playing for pennies or matchsticks, someone handed her the cards and said, "Take my turn, Lizzie," and she'd shuffle, and Gowan would grin and shake his head. "If ever I had any doubts," he'd say, "there'd be the proof. If she was a boy I could fleece the whole town," and then there'd be the stories about this woman or that who was a dealer in this place or that, and maybe they could still make a fortune in spite of the bad luck of Liz being a girl.

Liz hated playing cards. It was so boring. Sitting waiting for other people to make up their minds about what would they keep, what would they throw away, as if it mattered one little bit. When she said so, Wilma laughed and said, "You get that from me, dear. I'd rather watch two flies climbing up the wall than play cards. Total waste of time, by me. Your father, now, he'd bet on which fly would get to the top of the wall first."

Sometimes that's where the money went. Other times it was something else. Gowan had as much sense with money as some people had with dogs, pick the wrong one every time. There was never a full paycheque and sometimes no paycheque at all, with the rent and electricity still needing to be paid. So Wilma worked.

At first there were uproars over it, Gowan blowing his top because Wilma was on afternoon shift and for supper there was lukewarm macaroni and cheese or something, but Wilma, who usually wouldn't say boo to a goose, just hung in, and somehow each time Gowan just about had her talked into quitting, he'd pull some stunt and she'd say, "See, Gowan? And where would we be if I didn't have my job?" and he'd grit his teeth and shake his head angrily, but keep it quiet. After a while he stopped snarking about it and just let her have her own way. But you always have to pay when you have your own way, and after a while he seemed to have decided they could live on her pay and he'd call his pay his own.

Wilma felt bad about it. Read all those articles and then waited for one of the kids to show signs of mental disturbance. So no way in the world could Liz go to her and tell her what was going on when Wilma was on afternoon shift and the other kids were asleep. No way. Wilma would come apart like a cheap watch. No need for two of them to do that – Liz was just about ready to come apart herself. Sometimes she was afraid if she opened her mouth without first thinking about what she was going to say, it would all pop out and then the whole thing would burst. And if it burst, the entire world might just split open, and all of it her fault for opening her big trap.

So mostly when she heard her doorknob turning she shut her

eyes and tried to imagine herself somewhere else. She got so that sometimes she could start going somewhere else even before she went to bed, and there were nights when the whole world was pretty much gone just about the time her sister Louise was getting out of the bathtub, climbing into her pyjamas and going to her bed, a fold-out couch at the far end of the kitchen-dining-whatever room.

Sometimes Liz would finish reading a book and realize she had no idea what it was about, so she would start again at page one and move toward the end, only to find when she got there that she couldn't remember the middle of the story. People laughed and said, "My heavens, look at that kid, nose in a book all the time!" But even though she couldn't always remember, it must be locked away somewhere, because sometimes in school the teacher would ask a question and Liz would have the answer without knowing where it came from. The teacher would smile and nod, and Liz would sit there astonished.

It was the same with music lessons. If anyone asked, she'd say she practised a half hour every day as soon as she got home from school. Yet other people practised the same lesson at the same time and come Saturday they were still sawing away while Liz tucked her violin under her chin and let rip. "Just let her hear it once," Gowan bragged, "and she'll play it for you." Liz thought the difference might be all the time she spent practising in her head. When Gowan came into her room and she couldn't imagine herself somewhere else, she'd go over the music in her head and look at her fingers, watching them move as she heard each note in her mind. Maybe what you did in your head was almost as good as what you actually did.

Grandpa Harris would come over sometimes and sit with his cup of tea and his mickey of rye and visit. Or what passed for a visit with Grandpa Harris. Other people would talk and laugh and tell stories about what had happened since the last time you saw them, but Grandpa Harris was, as Wilma said more than once, a man of the moment. Never any talk about the past, never any plans for the future. And Gowan was still afraid of him. Gowan could tell anybody in the world to take a hike. He had a quick tongue on him and the fists to back it up – even Uncle Scott wasn't going to get into it with Gowan because, as everyone knew, they'd wind up hammering each other into the ground with nobody the winner and the both of them turned to pulp. But Grandpa Harris would speak and Gowan would be like a little boy again. Yes, Da. Thank you, Da. And when Grandpa Harris said, "Would the girl play a bit, then?" Gowan would say "Yes, Da. She'd be happy to," and he'd look at Liz and she'd go for the violin.

Grandpa Harris just sat and listened when she played. Sometimes his head bobbed a bit, and you could only hope it was approval and not the old man nodding off to sleep. She'd play everything she knew, starting with the easy ones to loosen up her fingers and wrists, then going through all the lessons and then, if the old man was still listening and still interested, she'd play the other stuff, the tunes and songs she never got at lessons but seemed to know anyway, and when the old man gave a big nod she'd stop. Even if she was in the middle of a phrase, she'd stop at the nod. And without fail he'd pull out his wallet and bring out money, usually a twenty at least, and he'd hand it to Wilma, not to Gowan, and say quietly, "I want that girl to keep on with the music."

And yet Gowan was afraid of him and so was everyone else in the family, and Auntie Jo-Beth was terrified. They knew he had little or no use for any of them or anyone else, and everyone said the old man had some screws loose.

"Every time I go to the bathroom and take a pee I'm amazed," Auntie Jo-Beth said once when she was just about four-fifths packed. "I'd'a swore on a stack of Bibles the old man had pounded all the piss out of all of us years ago."

"Oh now Jo-Beth," Gowan said mildly, "he didn't hammer on us all that much. Why, even he said we were getting off lucky compared to what he could have done and we deserved. We were," and he lifted his bottle of beer and sipped quietly, "a very badly behaved bunch of hellions."

"Bullshit, too, Gowan."

And yet the old man never raised his voice that Liz heard – except once.

Every Saturday night there were two big public dances, one at the Speedway Hall and the other at the opposite end of town at the Quarterway Hall. Gowan went every Saturday, first to one then to the other, turn about, week by week. Wilma went with him when she had Saturday night and Sunday off, and this weekend she had both days off. By two-thirty in the afternoon it was starting to feel like a party. She had washed her hair first thing in the morning and Auntie Jo-Beth had helped her set it, then she sat in the sun so it would dry for sure, and even had a glass of beer with Auntie Jo-Beth, Uncle Scotty and Gowan.

Fran and little Scott and Buttercup came over after everyone was gone and the little kids played with Louise and the twins, who everybody called Pete and Repeat but whose names were really William, after Wilma's father, and Gavin, after Gowan's father. "Oh, hell," Auntie Jo-Beth said, "it's always been that way, back to the year dot, Gavin followed by Gowan followed by Gavin followed by Gowan, like the books of begets in the damn Bible. No more imagination than a salamander." Liz wondered who it was had decided salamanders had no imagination. So they lived under woodpiles. So what? Maybe they lay there in the cool, wet-wood-smelling darkness, listening for bugs they could catch and eat, and maybe while they waited they dreamed wonderful things, entire movielike things, played on the inside of their eyelids. Maybe they imagined wonderful music, maybe they painted their own invisible pictures. Who knew?

Fran and the little kids left about eleven-thirty, and Liz knew they were going to the hidey-hole because Scotty and Jo-Beth were sniping at each other even before supper, just little bits of digs, the kind you knew would build and build.

Maybe two-thirty, maybe three in the morning it broke out all over hell's half acre. Only it wasn't Scotty and Jo-Beth, it was Gowan roaring bloody murder and Wilma sobbing with terror. Liz had been all set for one rip-snorter and here it was a different one. Slap slap and crying, slap slap and sobbing, slap slap and him bellowing, "Damn well learn to take a telling, you bitch!" and Wilma wailing, "No, Gowan, for God's sake you're *wrong!*" and he hit her again. The sound of her body hitting the wall, then the floor, was too much. Liz was out of bed and moving, her feet pounding while her brain yelled Stupid, stupid, get back to bed.

"Stop it!" she yelled, grabbing at Gowan's arm.

He turned, his pale face like a blur of the moon, and raised his other arm and Wilma shrieked and the next thing Liz knew it was past breakfast time and there was the smell of bacon, but not from their kitchen or their stove. She was lying on her bed – on top of it, not in it – and she could hear the old man holding forth in the Gaelic, enraged, his words punctuated with strange whapping sounds.

Liz got up from the bed and winced when her head tried to split down the middle. Her face felt stiff. It hurt when she blinked her eyes and she couldn't see very well. It took her a long time to get downstairs.

In the kitchen the old man had Gowan backed against the wall. Uncle Scotty was sitting at the table, looking as if he was going to puke, and Auntie Jo-Beth stood looking out the window, pretending nothing at all was going on in this room or in the whole world. Wilma was standing near Gavin, not daring to touch him but pleading with him to stop, Oh please stop, Gavin, you've gone too far already. And Gowan was nearly unconscious, not even trying to defend himself, sagging against the wall while the old man, who was still tougher than most of the twenty-five-year-olds in any given logging camp, pounded him on the ribs, rhythmically, *thump*, then some shouted words, *thump* and more words.

And it happened again. The feet moved while the brain was yelling Stop, you fool, stop.

"Grandpa!" Liz saw her own hand reach out and grab the old man by the wrist. "Grandpa, please. Stop, please."

Old Gavin turned, his face tight with fury. Little spots of red stood out on his cheeks like the face of some insane clown turned into a nightmare. His eyes were as yellow as a cat's, and his skin was stretched tight, as if all his muscles were coiled.

"And what did ye say?" he demanded.

"Please, Grandpa!" They stared at each other. "I'm frightened."

"Och, aye," he growled. Then he did something he had never done before, as far as she could remember. He reached out and gently, as gently as Wilma ever had, touched Liz on the face. "I'll no hae it," he said, forcing English out of his mouth as if the very taste of it turned his stomach bilious, "I'll nae allow it," and he turned to his son. "Gowan Harris." He was used to being obeyed. "This will stop. Ye'll nae beat on yer wife, and that my fine laddybuck is that. Ye've nae reason and nae excuse."

Gowan didn't say anything. He just leaned against the wall gasping for breath, looking about as rotten as Liz felt. "And, my laddybuck," the old man gritted, "ye'll remember for aye your life this wa'in is your ain mother's granddaughter. If ye do this tae her again I'll brek both arms at the elbow for ye. I mean it, now." He turned to Liz again, and shocking her even more than the first time, he touched her face gently. "This is my ain," he said clearly, "and I'll no hae this happen tae her. She doesnae desairve it."

"No," Auntie Jo-Beth said, "but somehow *we* always did."

"Shut yer gob, bitch," the old man laughed. "Shut your bloody gob," and then he said something in the Gaelic that made Jo-Beth go pale with fury and a kind of defeated fear.

Of course the goddamn neighbours loved it. You didn't have to pay a quarter to go to the movies if you lived anywhere near any of the crazy Harrises. And a good job there were so many Harrises, otherwise none of them would have had anybody at all to talk to or play with because nobody would let their kids anywhere near them. You never know, it might be contagious.

And then everything in the kitchen froze. Liz felt as if she was watching it all through Alice's tunnel. Eat me. Drink me. Her feet were ten miles away from her head and her legs didn't know whether to carry her forward or backward, but she made it to a chair and sat on it. Everything went somewhere else for a while. Then Jo-Beth was nudging her and telling her to drink her tea, and old Gavin was pouring a dribble of rye from his mickey into her cup.

"Thank you, Grandpa," she said.

"Welcome, lass," he answered. He gave Wilma a bit in her tea, too. Then gurgled a good slurp into his own.

Jo-Beth shook her head no thanks but the old man hadn't offered her any, nor Scotty either. And he acted as if Gowan didn't even exist. "Fix her bloody face," he growled.

Aunt Jo-Beth hurried to get the enamel basin and put water and salt in it. She got a clean cloth from the ragbag and came back to the table. It hurt when Aunt Jo-Beth wiped her face, but what was more amazing, when Jo-Beth put the cloth back in the water to rinse it, the water turned pink. And by the time Jo-Beth was through, the water was almost as red as ink.

"What . . . ?" Liz couldn't put it into words.

"Aye, well." The old man patted her hand. "What it is, lass, is ye can thank God ye were nae beauty before, and this way ye've lost nothing. It is nae a pretty sight but I've seen worse. Ye'll no snivel about it, ye hear."

"Yes, Grandpa."

All the top teeth on the right side were loose for months. Uncle Scott told her to make sure she bit down and pushed them into the holes where they belonged. "They'll heal," he said, "just like a broken bone." The broken nose healed too, but it didn't look much like a nose, it was sort of not there any more. In a mirror it looked pretty well normal from the front, but as soon as Liz turned her head the nose just kind of vanished. She decided to make a joke out of it. "Hey," she learned to laugh, "how many people do you know can play hide'n'seek by just turning sideways?" With her nose flattened, her cheekbones were ten times more noticeable, and they had always been prominent. Whenever Liz looked in a mirror or looked at pictures, she knew she was seeing a face that had been changed by that lunatic punch and she wondered what she, Liz Harris, really looked like. What would she look like if he had missed? And who was this flat-faced person anyway?

Her teacher looked at her and sighed. Didn't say a word, just sighed. And a fat lot of good was done with that sigh. At recess time she came up to Liz and asked, "Whatever did you do to deserve that?"

"I did nothing," Liz answered, but who would believe that? And if nobody would believe it, why bother opening your mouth about something even worse? If they did believe it, Wilma would come apart and then old Gavin would up and kill Gowan. He'd probably been waiting all his life for a good excuse to finish him off anyway. So keep your damn mouth shut, Liz Harris.

Except she didn't keep her damn mouth shut. She wanted to, but it was the same thing as with her feet.

"Good God," the school nurse gasped, "what happened to you? Were you in a car accident?"

"My dad nailed me a good one," Liz answered, as if it was easy to say it.

"He *what?*"

"He punched me out."

"What did you do to make him that angry?"

"I was breathing. Sometimes that's all it takes."

Well, at least that time someone did more than sigh. The school nurse took her down to the nurse's room and put Mercurochrome on the big scabbed-over cut in her eyebrow.

"There," she said, as if she had done something. "There, that's better."

Wilma's parents might have done something about it if they had known, but they were out fishing at the time and when they got home it was all healed up, the marks all gone. The face was still pretty well flat, but Liz wondered if maybe it had always been kind of dished, because they didn't say anything about it, not in front of her, anyway. They were gone more than half of the year. They started in April, out after the herring, and when that was done there was time for one good drunk, then change the nets and off for salmon. Grandma Larson went, too. She was Grandpa's deckhand.

"Best ever," he would laugh. "I'd'a been a rich man if I'd'a had her working with me all those years. Damn kids cost me a fortune!"

"And me my teeth," she'd add. "A woman loses one tooth minimum for every baby she has."

"You'd think she grew up on a boat," Grandpa would tease.

"I did, you fool!" And it was true, Grandma had never really lived in town until after she was married. Pregnancy had moved her into a house, with a yard she had no idea how to look after and neighbours she didn't need. "I can't stand this nonsense of just dropping in for coffee and a chat," she would grumble. "My God, if you sit for two hours on Monday talking about everything under the sun, what have you got to say for two hours on Tuesday? As if life was one round of frenzied activity after the other!"

She raised eight kids, and when the youngest said he'd had all of school he could stomach she said Fine then, boy, you're on your own now, and she gave each of them a key to the house. Then she went down to the dock, hitched a ride on someone else's boat and deck-hopped from one boat to another until she tracked Grandpa down, just off Alert Bay where he was fishing, and waited. When he tied up to get groceries and sit out the three days' compulsory closure, she walked down the planking with no hint of a smile, just her duffel bag. And that was that. She was finished with everything that had anything at all to do with fences, gates, sidewalks and sweeping maple leaves off the grass. And after that, except for what she called High Days and Holy Days, you hardly ever saw her. "Oh, they've got their own lives to ruin," she shrugged, "and every one of them bound, bent and determined to ruin 'em, too."

Probably because she didn't care who knew Gowan had punched her face flat, Liz started catching the belt for next to nothing at all. He'd just whip it off, fast as a fish heading for deep water, all you'd see was the blur of his hand, then you'd hear the *swiisshh* as the leather went through his belt loops and came down any old where at all. No sooner would the two-inch welts start to fade than there'd be a whole new crop. On her butt, her back, her arms, her legs, he didn't care where it landed. Liz learned to half turn away from him, covering her face with her hands and her breasts with her forearms, the way boxers protect themselves in the ring. And that made Gowan mad, so he swung harder. Liz refused to cry, which made him livid. He knew she knew if she cried he'd stop. She knew he knew, so she refused to cry where he could see it.

Liz learned something else, too. She learned that she could win whatever this war was. She could win if she could just make herself get up off the floor one time more than Gowan dropped her to it. She could never have explained what she was winning, she just knew she could win if she could get up again.

And in between beatings, any chance he got, he came into her bedroom and fucked her. And who do you tell about that?

One night Liz wakened and it was as bright in her room as if it was ten in the morning, but she knew from the smell of the air coming in the window that it was still nighttime. She felt excited, as if something wonderful was happening, better than a birthday party, better than Christmas, better than anything. She got out of bed and opened her bedroom door.

Their family's part of the old barracks, like all the other parts, was divided right down the middle by a narrow hallway. On one side of the hallway was the big kitchen-dining-whatever room, on this side were three bedrooms side by each, and at the end was the door into the place.

The light was on in the kitchen. Liz could hear Auntie Jo-Beth and Uncle Scotty, she could hear Wilma, hear Gowan, hear the slip slap of cards being dealt onto the table. So even though it was as bright as morning in her room, it must have been about midnight. She crept down the hallway and zipped real fast past the doorway to the kitchen area so they wouldn't see her. It was very important, she didn't know why, that nobody know she was going outside.

She slid down the banister so there wasn't even the sound of her bare feet on the stairs. At the bottom she ran toward the road, past the hut with the hidey-hole, to the big cedars flanking the side of the road. There she sat on the grass, her back against the smoothish bole of the huge tree, and looked around at how pretty everything was in the soft, bright light. Not the moon. Not the moon at all, you could hardly see the moon for the long nighttime clouds stretched across it.

Something was happening. The fingers of her left hand were twitching, trembling, and she wondered if it was because she felt so excited. And why should she feel like this, all tingly and on edge, wanting to yell and shout but unable to summon the energy?

The twitching and trembling became shaking, and moved from just her fingers to her entire hand, then her arm, and finally even her leg – only not twitching by now, but flopping. The left side of her face was grimacing, and something warm trickled down her face. The sound in her ears was like the rush of water, sometimes as though waves were crashing, other times as if she was trying hard to wake up from a deep sleep, and her arm and leg flopped so hard her body was moving, her head hitting the trunk of the tree.

She lived and relived the sound of her mother's body hitting the wall, then the floor, a sound so like the sound of her own shoulders convulsing against the cedar that she could have mixed them up. She saw Gowan's face again, round as the moon, white as the moon, featureless and flat with insane rage, and she saw the fist coming at her, his hand and fingers so like her own, only bigger, and she saw the punch landing and something – *some thing* – in her head, a vein maybe, swelling, like a bicycle tube when it's time to put a shoe in the tire, only no shoe, no patch for that bit of blood vessel, and a scab or something – something, she didn't know – was loosened now, leaking, lifting at the edges, and she was suddenly calm in spite of all the flopping and the dizziness, calm with the knowledge she was dying.

They came then, as silent as voles, and she wasn't the least little bit afraid. It had something to do with her nose. They had things that measured, things she had never seen, like bits of shiny pipe. She wasn't sleepy, not like that at all, more like it had been after Gowan decked her and she felt as if she was walking around with Alice in Wonderland, all the distances stretched. Measured arms and legs and how long were her fingers and how did her thumbs fit her hand and when they put the pipe thing on her face it sort of *bip bip bipped* and something flashed pinkish, some kind of light.

They got very interested then. She knew if she ever saw them again she would recognize them, but she couldn't have drawn a picture of them. She remembered slanty eyes, not like Chinese or Japanese, not the skin folded at the corner, the whole eye socket long and thin, rising at about a forty-degree angle from the inside corner to a higher outside one. And little mouths, with smiles.

For a minute or two her whole face hurt like bloody bleeding fury. My sweet Jesus aitch but it hurt! And then the hurt was gone and it was almost like that first chew of spearmint gum, before the sweetness, when there is just the taste of the mint stuff, only in her whole face. The coolness spread, up from her nose up into her head, like something moving, maybe a kind of a little wire-jigger, and then there was only the light, inside her head and outside, the light, and the hurting and a surge of fear. Then, quicker than it had started, the mad jerking of her arm and leg subsided, became mere flexing, then eased again until there was only the faintest of twitching, something she could feel rather than see. She wondered how anyone could weld or solder something like meat, or vein, or whatever a person had in their head.

And then, quite simply, they put a little screw in her nose. Just a little bit of a screw-seeming thingamajig. Right up in that part of the nose between the inner corners of your eye, about where the nose bone meets the forehead bone, if there are even any bones there. *Ping*, it was like a hot needle, and then it didn't hurt at all.

Something about where her teeth went into her jawbone, too. But she was dizzy when that happened and not all there for most of it. Hummm, and her teeth vibrated. Hummm.

So nice under the cedar tree. So calm and peaceful and everything gentle, the stars bright in the sky and the moon out from behind the clouds, and Wilma yelling "Liz! *Liiiiizzzz!*" and other people with flashlights, so nothing to do but stand up and wave and yell, "Over here."

Such a fuss. Wilma crying and Gowan angry and Aunt Jo-Beth looking at her as if she had rocks in her head.

"It was just such a nice night," she said. "And I wanted to watch the stars and listen to the wind in the trees."

"Sleepwalking," they decided.

"No. I just wanted to see the stars."

"You want to see stars, I'll show you stars, loony tune," Gowan threatened. "You scared your mother out of ten years of her life."

"I didn't mean to, I was just —"

"Shut up." He raised his hand threateningly so she shrugged. That made him madder, but he lowered his hand because she hadn't *said* anything.

And then Wilma noticed all the blood on the front of Liz's pyjamas, and started yowling and crying, sobbing and accusing him of having hit Liz again, but he hadn't and everyone there knew it, even Wilma.

"I had a nosebleed, is all," Liz said.

Sometimes after that, when Gowan was in one of his moods and Liz was scared stiff day and night, she'd wake up and she could sort of hear music, not exactly harp music, not exactly anything except if you could play intricate sounds with wind chimes, or crystal handbells. Not tinkling, but something gentle and sweet and magical which made you think of icicles sparkling in pale moonlight. No matter how she tried, Liz couldn't find those sounds anywhere in her violin. Sometimes she'd catch the melody, sometimes she could even begin to catch the counterpoint, but she couldn't catch anything that made the same kind of clear silver-crystal sound.

One night, a night when Wilma was home so Liz could relax and not have to send her brains off to Brazil just to keep herself from screaming, she was sitting up in bed with some paper and pencil crayons, amusing herself. Louise came into the bedroom to change into her pyjamas before crawling into her bed in the other room. "What you doing?" Louise asked.

"Just playing around pretending to draw pictures." Liz looked up, smiling, and saw her little sister looking at her as if she had never really seen her before. "What?"

"I'm sorry," Louise said.

"Sorry? About what?" But Louise just shook her head, then

hurried from the room and closed the door quietly behind her. Liz sat there trying to figure out what mood was on Louise. In the other bedroom the boys were arguing over whose turn it was to sleep next to the wall. And over their nattering she heard Gowan laughing, then Wilma's voice. And it was like a bucket of cold water, a bucket of dirty cold water. If the boys could share a room, why was Liz alone in the bedroom and Louise sleeping out on the couch? If you could get two boys in a double bed, why not two girls?

She couldn't look at that one. To look at that one would mean having to look at what Wilma knew and didn't know, what she suspected and wouldn't suspect, and Liz knew if she did that she would lose it all, lose everything, lose the last little hint she was hanging onto that someone else in the world gave half a shit what happened to her. In some book, she had read about Catherine the Great going out for a ride in her big three-horse sled with three peasants sitting across the tailgate and two soldiers between her and the peasants. If the big Siberian wolves started to chase the sled, one of the soldiers shoved off a peasant as wolf bait, so that the rest of them could get back to the palace or castle or whatever heap of rocks they lived in. Was Liz the wolf bait for the rest of the family? Was that why she had a bedroom all to herself and Louise got to keep her clothes in the drawer and her stuff in the closet but slept on the fold-out couch?

Liz folded up this thought as neat as a lace hanky and put it in the same dark hole she put the other stuff she couldn't think about. Without Wilma there was no sanity, no world, no life. She couldn't lose Wilma. Not even for a minute. She fell asleep thinking of the music, and just before she made it to safety and that dark no-place place, she saw a spiral made out of thin silver, and a sort of hammer thing, padded at one end, striking the spiral like a xylophone only not stretched into a straight line, and she knew that was the instrument she had been hearing making those sounds. Someone was playing a spiral.

/ / /

It wasn't just Gowan and Scotty and Gavin were nuts. The whole lot of them were short enough two-by-fours to build a woodshed. Even Aunt Phoebe was just about as haywire as any of them. Liz hardly ever saw her, though, because Aunt Phoebe lived in Victoria. She'd been married, or married so-to-speak, for a few years to a navy guy stationed at Esquimalt, but nobody talked about him, and as near as Liz knew Phoebe had off-loaded him the first time someone better came along. Then off-loaded the second one too. One time she showed up for a visit with her kids, Doris and Fred, and got to drinking with the rest of them. She didn't look like the rest of them, she had her blonde hair touched up so it looked as white as dandelion fluff, and she had eyebrows pencilled in just so, and clothes like in the magazines and long bright red fingernails. Even Aunt Jo-Beth looked small-town alongside Aunt Phoebe. Who, it turned out, could drink her brothers under the table any day of the week. And who, it also turned out, made a point of never losing her temper no matter what.

"Well hell, Phoebe," Scotty slurred, "you're doin' okay for yourself even if it's true that if you had as many pokin' out as had poked in you'd pass for a porcupine."

"You'll never know for sure," Phoebe answered easily. "Drool all over your chin if you want, you won't even get a taste."

"It is manners to wait until you're asked, Phoeb," Scotty gritted.

"Ah, but I don't have to ask, Scotty. I've never had to ask in my life."

Of course old Gavin wouldn't come near the place when Phoebe was there. "Maybe I should rent myself out," Phoebe laughed. "You could take turns hiring me to stay with you so the old fart would lay his poison on the others. Whenever someone else was about ready to die from it they could pay me and I'd go to their place and they'd get a break for a while. Or maybe I'll just open the family rest home and you can check in one or two or three at a time. You'd get a good rest, he won't come within five miles of me."

"Don't it bother you?" Scotty asked.

"If you had a nail in your shoe and someone finally came along and pulled it out, would you feel bothered because your foot quit hurting?"

Nobody would talk about it to Liz. "Mind your own business," was the best answer she ever got. And then Phoebe up and married herself a dentist. The old man nearly died of festering fury over that one. There she was with a big new car and a brand-new enormous house and all she had to do for the whole thing was look as gorgeous as she had always looked and laugh as easy as she had always laughed. And her two kids suddenly all over with new clothes, and the dentist's own kid laughing and calling Phoebe "Mom." She even piled them all in the car and drove up to introduce the dentist to the family, and stayed for supper before they headed back down-island.

But before they left, Aunt Phoebe came into Liz's room and sat on the bed talking about nothing at all, while she looked at the paintings thumbtacked to the wall, mostly pencil crayons but some watercolours, too.

"Could I buy that one off you?" She pointed to the one with the blue heron sort of standing in the middle of a going-away sky, with the ocean below and the moon to one side, only the moon looked as if it might be an egg with another heron curled inside it, and maybe another moon, maybe not, where the curled-heron's head might have been. Mostly blues and greys, some darker, some lighter, and the moon a weird silver-grey with a touch of a hint of blue.

"You don't have to buy it," Liz laughed. She stood on the bed and pulled out the tacks and handed the watercolour to Phoebe. "Here, it's yours."

"Okay. But you got to sign it for me," and she took a gold pen from her purse and handed it over as if it was any cheap one. Liz signed the bottom right-hand corner, then handed the pen back. "You keep it," Aunt Phoebe said. "Use it to write me some letters, okay?"

She wouldn't fold the picture, either. Nothing would do but she take the waxed paper off the roll and then carefully make a skinny tube of the heron picture and slide it in the cardboard. "I'll send you a picture of it," she promised, and to Liz's total amazement, she did. Sent a thank-you card and a photograph of the heron picture in a plain silver frame stuck up on the wall of her fancy living room, on a plain white wall.

"Looks very different with a frame and all, doesn't it?" Wilma marvelled. "You'd hardly think it was the same one at all."

"Cryin' out loud," was all Gowan said about it.

The letter and photograph gave Liz another place to go to when Gowan was pushing into her. She would think about Aunt

Phoebe's living room and the big chesterfield under the heron picture, and she'd go there and sit herself down on the chesterfield, staring across the room at the big red brick fireplace.

She'd been feeling sort of puny for a week or more, just all the time sleepy and not quite up to snuff, like before you get the flu, before you find out that's what you've got. She was so tired on Tuesday she didn't bother going to school. "I don't feel well," she said, and it was true, she was starting to feel like she would puke.

"Better stay home, then," Wilma agreed. "You look kind of washed out."

Liz went back to bed with a hot water bottle for her feet, and she went to sleep with no trouble at all. Slept from seven until noon without so much as waking up for a pee. Then woke up, went down the hall to the bathroom and thought she'd figured out why she'd been so sleepy. It was her period, a few days early but there it was, and she was starting to flow heavy, too. Well, better early than late, they said.

She went back to bed and slept some more, then woke up feeling fine. Went to the kitchen thinking about maybe a sandwich or something. Wilma and her friend were having tea and knitting sweaters for the coming winter.

"How are you feeling?" Wilma asked, smiling.

"Fine. Lots better," Liz said.

And then the friend's face was showing shock and fear, she was pointing and starting to get out of her chair, and Wilma was dropping her knitting.

And just like that Liz was waking up in a hospital bed and it was the middle of the night. She tried to sit up but they had something on her, a pyjama top or something, only it was tied somewhere on the bed frame and she couldn't get herself sitting. She couldn't move her arm either, because something was stuck in it. So she just yelled, then went back to sleep.

Next time she woke up it was after supper on Wednesday and Wilma was standing by her bed looking as if she'd aged twenty years. Surprisingly, Gowan was with her, smiling and being his charming self, the one he could pull out at a moment's notice and use so convincingly on those who didn't know him better.

"What am I doing here?" Liz asked. "What happened?"

"You fainted," Wilma said.

And that was all Wilma ever said about it. Liz asked several times what was wrong with her and Wilma just said, "Growing pains," and that was that. The nurses wouldn't tell either. They just shook their heads and said things like, "You'll have to ask your doctor about that, dear." And she never even saw the doctor!

She still wasn't allowed out of bed. So when she had to pee so bad she thought she'd burst, she pushed the buzzer and they brought her a bedpan. The nurse pulled the curtains around the bed, Liz lifted herself up, the bedpan got slid under her, and no sooner was she sitting on it than she gushed like anything, big dark jellylike clots of blood falling into the bedpan. It made her dizzy, but the nurse put her arm around Liz's shoulders and held her steady.

"What's happening?" Liz asked, certain she was about to die.

"Relax, dear, it's all better out than in. You'll be fine."

They let her go home five days later. By then her period was finished, although she did dribble and spot for most of the next month. Wilma looked as if she'd spent the whole week on her feet, not eating and not sleeping. And Gowan had been on a real toot, obviously one of the ones where he wound up talking when he should have been listening, because he'd been fighting – you could see it written all over his face. But Liz was too tired and too weak with the last of the flu or whatever it had been to think twice about any of it. She went to bed and slept until suppertime.

Wilma told her to stay home from school for another week, and then she was over it and could go back again, and things went back to being pretty well what they had been. Except Gowan didn't come into her bedroom any more. Not ever. And it was announced that Louise was big enough and responsible enough to share with Liz.

"After all," Wilma said clearly, "we can be sure you won't wet the bed."

"I never have!" Louise protested, insulted to her very bones. "Not since I was a baby! I never did, not one single time."

"Then you won't do it now, will you?" Wilma smiled, her face ghost-white, her eyes swollen and dark-shadowed. "You get the outside, Liz gets to sleep by the wall," she said firmly. Gowan got up from the kitchen table, grabbed his jacket and cap and walked out of the house without a word.

Liz didn't want to think about that, either. Everyone was safer with this whole puzzle locked off with the rest of the mess.

/ / /

It seemed so strange to load everything into the back of a pick-up truck borrowed from the shirttail relatives who had the gas station over on Tenth Street. Everything put in boxes, the dishes wrapped in several layers of newspaper so they wouldn't clatter against each other and break, the glasses stuffed with tea towels, then wrapped in papers.

"Christ, you'd think you were packing up the Queen's crystal," Gowan growled.

"It may not be the Queen's crystal but it's all we have in the way of dishes," Wilma answered, and Gowan glared.

Wilma had changed a lot in the past year. The one who wouldn't have defended herself against an angry duck was suddenly standing up straight and answering back. Gowan blustered and warned her she was farting against thunder, but something had changed and he knew it.

Wilma had the move all planned. The beds had been knocked apart and moved first, set up in the new place with the mattresses on the springs, waiting for the bedding to arrive. The bedding came with the chests of drawers and the bundles of clothes, and after the beds were made, everyone took their bundles and put their clothes away lickety-split, get it done and get it done right the first time.

The kitchen table and chairs arrived, then some of the pots and pans, and finally the dishes, which were put away in cupboards that had been scrubbed with hot soapy water and bleach.

Wilma gave Liz some money to get on her bike and go to the fish'n'chips shop so they could feed everyone, especially those who had taken time from their own weekend to help with the move. When she got home with the food the worst of the job was done and people were sitting around on the new back steps sipping beers and saying My God, it never gets any easier, does it.

There was no stepping out to the Speedway or Quarterway that Saturday. Gowan stayed home willingly enough, putting groceries away and helping move this a foot or two to the left, shift that away from the window sill a bit so nobody bangs her head if she leans back. That's better, don't you think? Looks fine by me.

Sunday was more of the same and in the afternoon they went back to the old place to scrub it all out and leave it clean for the next people, even if there weren't going to be any next people. The housing shortage was over, it seemed, and the whole camp was being phased out, whatever that meant. For the Harrises it meant find a place now, before everyone else is looking too.

The new place was way lots bigger. Way lots bigger. A kitchen twice the size of the other one and three bedrooms plus a living room – a real one, not just one end of the kitchen. And a downstairs basement Wilma said could be fixed up to be another bedroom or two, for the boys, when they were older and needed more privacy from each other.

Louise and Liz got a room at the front of the house, and they put their bed against the side wall so they could lie there and look out at the streetlight and the traffic at the corner. The boys got the biggest bedroom, which Louise said wasn't fair, but Liz said Who cares, for crying out loud, they need more room for all that mess they make.

The entire backyard had been laid out for a garden, so Wilma decided it would be a waste not to have one. That meant it had to be dug all over again, because winter had flattened everything out and made the ground hard. Liz spent every night after school for a week digging it up, breaking the lumps into smaller ones, over and over until it was good enough to suit Wilma. Then there was the thing with the seed packages and Louise decided they needed a scarecrow, although the robins just used it as a place to perch between raids.

The new place was lots closer to work for Wilma and close enough to town Liz could get a weekend job too. It was funny how it worked out. They'd been moved a month or two when Wilma sent Liz off for fish'n'chips again, and as she jumped off her bike outside the place, the man who cooked the fish was standing on the front steps in his white pants, white shirt, white cap and big white apron, getting ready to put a sign on the door. *Help Wanted*, it said in big letters, and *Weekends* in smaller letters underneath.

"You really want someone on the weekends?" Liz asked, not even daring to hope.

"Friday night from five to midnight, Saturday from three to midnight. Dollar an hour and you keep your tips."

"Could I apply for the job?" she asked.

He looked at her, sizing her up. "You ever have a job before?"

"No, sir," she admitted. "But I help my mom at home all the time and I've done lots of babysitting and stuff."

"You bring me a note from your mother saying it's all right with her and it's all right with me," and he didn't put the sign on the door.

She took the fish'n'chips home, ran off at the mouth a mile a minute until Wilma nodded yes, and before seven o'clock she was back at the shop in clean clothes, with her permission note.

"Harris, huh," he grunted. "Which ones?"

"Gowan is my father," she answered. He gave her a long, hard look, then nodded and showed her where the big aprons were. "And a hairnet," he said, digging in his pocket for change. "You can get one at the corner store across the street. Health regulations."

It felt strange, wearing a hairnet like a little old lady, but if it meant the difference between keeping the job and losing it, she'd wear it.

The potato peeler was a huge barrel thing with slanted ridges on the inside, the whole thing smeared with a layer of rough concrete. It fit into a riggin's against the wall. You grabbed a big handle and pulled it down, the lid opened as it descended, then you put in the rinsed potatoes and gave the big handle a push. The barrel went back up, the lid closed, and you pushed the big red button. The barrel started to turn just like a cement mixer and the potatoes tumbled against the rough concrete so that the skins were rubbed off in a minute or two.

Then you pushed the tub of water in place on its little flat-wheeled table, and you pushed the big red button again, reached up, grabbed the handle and pulled. The barrel tipped, the door opened, the peeled potatoes fell into the tub of water, and you let go of the handle so the door could close. Pull the tub of water out of the way, open the machine and put in another five pounds of potatoes.

Then sit with a sharp knife taking out all the eyes, removing any bits of skin still brown against the white of the spuds. And when they were all done you went to the thing on the wall.

Another handle. You lifted it, the top came up, you put in a potato and pulled the handle down. The lid went down, down, down
and out the bottom came the cut strips, ready for deep frying.

Liz loved it. Especially the chip slicer. It was so easy, so obvious, so exactly right. If nobody had ever invented one and someone asked her to think about it, she'd have come up with exactly that thing. In at the top, pull the handle and out the bottom
come the chips.

She also had to clean off the tables and set them, and fill the
salt, pepper, vinegar and ketchup. Wipe off the counters. Take
orders. Give the orders to the cook. Answer the phone and write
down the takeout orders. Deliver in-house orders to the booths.
Refill coffee cups. Get Cokes from the cooler. Make sure there
was lots of butter for the bread. It was go go go the whole
evening, and not even time for a drink of water until after nine
o'clock.

"Time for supper," the cook said loudly. Liz was surprised. He
grinned. "Guess what you get for supper in a fish'n'chips shop."

"Soup!" she laughed. He and his wife chuckled. "What kind
of soup?" she dared.

"Tomato. Cream of tomato with cheese grated on top." And
they all sat down to fill up on fish'n'chips.

The movie up the block ran from seven to nine and from nine
to eleven. They got a break of maybe fifteen minutes, and then
the people who had been to the first show came in for their meal.
And it was up and go go go again until finally, blessedly, just
about the time Liz thought she was going to go nuts with all the
Hey girlie, and Could you get me more, it was time to check and
make sure everything was washed clean and put away, time to
turn out the lights, time to smile determinedly and head home,
feet burning.

The next day there she was again, and fifteen minutes early.
Time for a Coke with Mr. and Mrs. Devlin before the phone started to ring and the first people began to arrive. Friday was mostly couples going to or coming from the show. Saturday it was
people on their way home from a day of shopping, usually moms
and dads with kids, and later it was people heading out to paint
the town.

"How come you don't stay open longer on Saturday than
Friday?" she asked.

"Because if we stayed open until one, we'd wind up still try-ing to close the place down at two-thirty," Mrs. Devlin said. "We used to do it but it's just too much. It's not worth it for the money you make. They come in drunk and there's things spilled and glasses knocked over and broken on the floor and one time there was a fight and it cost sixteen dollars for a new front window. You have to sell a lot of fish to get back that sixteen dollars. So we decided we'd close before the pubs did. If they want some-thing to eat they can go home or go to Chinatown. My feet are weary enough," she added, leaning sideways to check the fat heating in the big cookers.

By eleven Liz was glad Mrs. Devlin's feet were weary. She wasn't sure she could have gone on until after the pubs closed. And it was true, the later it was the more they'd had to drink, and the more they'd had to drink the harder it was to do the job.

She got paid at the end of Saturday night. She looked at that first money and felt just fine, thank you. Just fine. Five hours for that first Friday and nine hours for Saturday, at a dollar an hour, was fourteen dollars. Plus the three dollars and change she had from her tips.

"See you next weekend," Mr. Devlin smiled. "You tell your mother I said you do a good job."

"Thank you." She wanted to bust out laughing, that's how good she felt.

But when she handed the money to her mother, Wilma looked as if she had come face to face with something she didn't want to see.

"Oh my," she said. "Oh my, you're not a little girl any more."

"I haven't been little for a long long time, Mom."

"No, but . . . My, you've done well!" She looked up, her eyes bright with tears. "How much of this is tips?"

"Three dollars and change."

"Then you should keep it for yourself. They're *your* tips," and it was just like the feeling when Mr. Devlin said she did good work, the kind of feeling that makes a grin spread across your face.

Sunday afternoon she took Louise and the twins to the ice cream parlour beside Palm Dairy and bought them big sundaes. They sat at the little round metal table with the funny twisted black metal legs and made soft noises of appreciation as they mixed the chocolate or butterscotch topping into the softening vanilla ice cream.

"Boy, Liz, this is sure good," Pete and Repeat kept saying. "Sure is good. Best I ever had."

"*First* you ever had, dum-dum," Louise laughed. "First I ever had, too."

One Saturday evening when she was almost run off her feet at the shop, a couple of little ragamuffins showed up at the door, sticking in their big-eared summer haircut heads, grinning hopefully. "Got any scraps for my dog?" the littlest one asked.

"What kind of dog you got?" Mr. Devlin grinned.

"Cocker spaniel, sir," the boy lied.

"And I bet it's show quality, too." He scooped up a piece of newspaper and cleaned up all the little tiny bits of fish, the chunks of broken-off batter, the stuff that usually wound up in the waste barrel. Then he added a handful of perfectly good chips. "There you go, boys," and he handed the parcel to Liz, who folded it shut but didn't bother putting on any sticky brown paper to hold it together because everyone knew they'd have the package open and be eating it themselves not two steps from the doorway.

"They've got no dog," she said quietly.

"No, but they might get one someday," he winked.

"Anyway," said Mrs. Devlin, "they're a right pair of cheeky-faces and this man is a softie for cheekyfaces."

"Married you, didn't I?" he grinned.

"Must mean I'm a softie for cheekyfaces too, because you've got a right cheekyface yourself."

You'd have thought they were young people out on a date, not a couple with grey hair and grown children. Funny how some people are with each other. Easy. Friendly, even.

And one night in the woodshed, Gowan made a grab for Liz. She hadn't heard him coming and there was no reason in the world for him to be there, but all of a sudden his hand was on her arm and he was turning her toward him, roughly. Liz didn't have time to decide what to do about it. Her right hand reached out and closed around a good-sized piece of dry alder, and she lifted it up and he stepped back, his face suddenly tight with rage.

"Back off," she said. "You just back off and leave me alone."

No bluster, no threat, not a word. He spun on his heel and

left, as quietly as he had come. Liz was so scared she thought she'd pee herself – it almost felt as if she already had. She leaned against the woodpile, still holding the piece of alder, her knees too weak to hold her up. Words raced through her head, like those little comics in the upper corners of magazines, where the faster you flip the pages the more it looks like the figures are moving. But the words wouldn't connect into sentences, so she couldn't tell what she was thinking.

She put the alder back on the pile and turned to go back to the house, and before she knew it her hand had moved again, picked up the piece of alder and put it on the little ledge above the window-hole. Not so much to have it handy if she ever needed it again, as to have it where she could see it, to remind herself. And to remind Gowan too, if he ever came into the woodshed again.

But she paid for it. Paid for it the hard way, because halfway through supper he decided he didn't like the way William was sitting at the table. "All slouched over as if it was just too much damn trouble to sit properly. If you're that bloody tired, boy, maybe you should just lie down on your bed and stay there."

"Sorry, Dad." William sat up stiff and straight.

"Not half so sorry as you'll be if you ever do it again."

"Yes, Dad."

"And you!" He slammed his fist on the table right in front of Gavin's plate, and Gavin started shaking like a leaf, his face white. "What'n hell's the matter with *you*? I wasn't even talking to you and you're sitting there with tears in your eyes like some kind of goddamn girl."

Gavin couldn't say anything. He never could say anything. As soon as Gowan started up, Gavin froze. Sometimes he had a bellyache so bad he had to go to bed with it, and the doctor Wilma took him to said he had a stomach ulcer but Gowan said that was bullshit, nobody had stomach ulcers at age ten and a half, it was all just more of Gavin's mealymouthing, getting people to feel bloody sorry for him.

"Turn off the water faucet, you damn sissy! Jesus, maybe I should go get one of your sister's dresses for you to wear, then you could swish around like Tinkerbell."

So Gavin vomited. Suddenly and without warning, right across the table and some of it even overboard onto the floor.

"Jesus suffering Christ!" Gowan was up off his chair and back-handing. Gavin fell to the floor, and the entire front of his striped tee shirt was suddenly wet not only with vomit but with blood from his nose.

Wilma would have started screaming then but Wilma wasn't home, she was at work, and it was Louise started the high-pitched wailing. "Shut up, for God's sake," Liz hissed, "you'll make him worse!" and Louise managed to put a sock in it.

Liz moved to help Gavin up. "Leave him lie in his own bloody mess!" Gowan raged. "It's all goddamn bullshit anyway."

"Leave him alone," and she was screaming, but not the way Wilma screamed, with fear and terror, she was screaming with fury. "Look at him!" Blood came from Gavin's mouth now, every time he retched there was more of it, some of it bright red, some of it dark. "Look what you've gone and done! Nobody can pretend to bleed to death, you goddamn fool!"

She picked up Gavin and ran from the house carrying him, blood on both of them. The neighbour saw her coming, saw the blood, and met her halfway. He took Gavin and tossed him up over his shoulder, the car keys already glittering in his hand. "Get in, Lizzie," he gritted, "and hold onto your hat."

He backed out of the driveway, twisted the wheel and floored the pedal. If it hadn't been so scary, Liz thought, it would have been fun. The neighbour leaned on the horn all the way and people pulled to the side, out of his way.

At the hospital they didn't ask any questions, they just grabbed Gavin and raced down the corridor with him curled on his side, still spewing blood. The woman at the front desk came over and got his name, date of birth, names of his parents, and who was going to sign for his admission.

"I will," Liz said.

"You can't," the woman told her, "you're too young."

"I'll sign," said the neighbour.

"Are you a relative?"

"Yeah. I'm his uncle."

Liz only got a minute to see Gavin before they took him into the operating room. He was so scared she could have cried with him, but she made herself smile. "Hey, you're going to be all right," she told him. "They're going to turn off the tap and you'll be fine."

"I'm scared, Lizzie."

"Yeah. Me too," and telling him that did him more good than anything else she could have done. "But I know you'll be okay."

"Why does he always pick on me? Yelling and slapping and nothing I do is ever right!"

"Because he's a lunatic," she said quietly, and smiled at him. "You can't make sense out of things a lunatic does and you'll go lunatic yourself if you try. Just stop crying, Gavin. Every time you cry the blood gets worse, okay? We'll have a real good cry when this is all over, I promise."

When they took him away he was still crying, and the nurses looked at her as if she had two heads. Small wonder. Her clothes were soaked in blood and her hair was wild from the car trip. The neighbour took her home right away, everybody looking at her and all, just awful, almost as awful as how sick Gavin was.

Gowan wasn't at the house when she got home. Louise and Bill were trying to clean up the mess but they were both crying and shaking so bad they were useless. Both of them had finger-marks on their cheeks and if Bill didn't get some ice on his lip pretty soon, it was going to make him look like he was part bull-dog.

"What's wrong with him anyway?" Louise sobbed to Liz. "Why does he act that way?"

"Because he can," Liz yelled. "Because nobody stops him! Because we're not strong enough! Because the cops are too busy playing tiddlywinks! How in hell would I know why he does it? I don't understand anything. So just shut up, Louise!"

They all yelled at each other for a few minutes, and then they felt better and they could clean up the mess from supper spilling and Gavin puking and bleeding and Gowan tipping things over and stomping around cursing the mess and blaming it on every-one else.

When Wilma came home from work at midnight, the kitchen was clean, the broken dishes were in the garbage and the unbro-ken ones were clean and dry and back in the cupboard. The counters were scrubbed, the floor was scrubbed, the table was standing up again and washed clean, the wall where all the stuff had splashed was shiny clean. And three Casper-the-ghost faces were turned toward her, belonging to three kids sitting on chairs not talking or fighting or playing the radio, just sitting waiting.

"What?" she whispered.

"Gav's in hospital," Liz said. "He started puking and then he started bringing up blood."

"Dad was yelling at him," Louise offered.

"Is he going to die?" Bill blurted.

"Why didn't someone come and get me!" Wilma screamed. "Why didn't you come and tell me? What's the matter with you all?"

"Oh, sure!" Liz was yelling, too. "Blame *us!* Everything is *our* fault, right? Not his! We didn't come and get you because we were cleaning up the goddamn mess around here is why we didn't come and get you!" And in livid, enraged detail she told Wilma about the mashed potatoes on the front of the stove and about all the food and vomit and blood and slime on the linoleum and the table and the wall. "I'm sure you'd have really been happy if we'd left all that and gone down to tell you all about it. And then what would you have done," she added cruelly, "*cried?*"

Louise stood up, her arms hanging at her sides, looking straight ahead, mouth open in a round *O*, and she screamed. Not a high thin one, not a broken wailing one, just a medium-range almost-moan, and when she was winded she took a deep breath and started again, *Aaaaaaaaaaaaaaaaaaagggggghhhhhhhhhhhh*, breathe, *Aaaaaaaaaaaaaaagggggggggggggggghhhhhhhhhhhhhhh*, breathe, until Wilma got out of her paralysis and grabbed her and held her, rocking and saying There there, baby, there there, it will be all right.

But of course nobody believed that. It never had been all right, why would it suddenly start now?

Wilma went up to see Gavin in the morning, but they wouldn't let Liz or the other kids go up. Gowan wasn't home yet, and a good thing too, or there might be a few others in the family in hospital as well.

Four or five days later, Wilma said Gavin could sit up in bed and it might cheer him up if the other kids stood on the lawn and waved to him. So up they went and stood waving like dipsticks. Maybe Gav waved back or maybe he didn't, you couldn't really tell the way the light reflected off the windows, but Liz went to the parking lot after school every day and waved, and sometimes she did bike tricks, showing off to make Gav laugh. Other times she just sat there where he might see her – or he might not, who would ever know, but you can only ride no-hands so long before it gets dumb.

One day she was sitting waiting and Wilma was inside visiting when who came over and sat next to her but the old man.

"Hi, Grandpa," she said.

"How's the lad?"

"He'll be okay."

"Ye didnae come tae tell me."

"No. Dad said he'd scalp me if I did."

"Aye? And ye obeyed him."

"I have to, Grandpa. He might kill me if I don't."

"What I was told was the boy has a bad digestion. Born with it, I was told. By Gowan himself."

"He lies." Liz didn't care if the old man got mad at her or not. "Bill doesn't have bad digestion, and he's Gavin's twin. Dad picks on Gavin all the time."

"Aye?"

"Yes," and Liz knew she hated her father. She wasn't just frightened, she wasn't just angry, she wasn't just feeling mean. She hated him. "If Gavin tells a joke he's called a fool. If he doesn't tell a joke he's called a dunce. If he sings he's an idiot and off-key in the bargain, if he doesn't it's because he's got no music in him. He couldn't win, Grandpa. If he eats his supper he's a pig. If he doesn't eat his supper he's being a baby." She couldn't believe how calm her voice was. "Dad is trying to drive Gavin crazy. He wants Gavin to put a rope around his neck, tie the other end to the bridge and jump over the side toward the river."

"That's a dreadful accusation, girl."

"He hates him." She looked at old Gavin and smiled, and the old man's face paled when he saw that smile. "But not as much as I hate *him*," she added gently.

Old Gavin looked away, and for long seconds there was only the sound of their breathing, only the sound of the wind swishing dry bamboo stalks in the little grove near the entrance to the hospital.

"What do you want me to do?" he asked finally.

"You can't do anything," she said. "All you do is shout at him or punch him. How can you teach him not to beat people up by beating him up when he beats people up? How can you teach him not to be mean by being mean? Gavin will just have to get tougher."

The old man got up and walked away, looking even smaller and thinner than she remembered him. Why was Gowan so afraid of such a gnarled, withered gnome? Maybe one day Gavin would be grown up and Gowan would be a scrawny old fart and Gavin would still be afraid of him. Even now Gowan wasn't all that much bigger than Liz, hardly any bigger than Wilma, and Liz wasn't afraid of Wilma so why was she afraid of Gowan? Why was anybody ever afraid of anybody?

Gavin came home with a big red healing scar on his belly, and smaller, pinker marks like railroad ties across it, where the stitches had been. In a few weeks the smaller marks were gone and Gavin looked as if he had a zipper holding his guts together, but finally that faded too, and by the next summer you could hardly see it when he was wearing his bathing suit.

And even though it was Gavin they'd cut open, something had been taken from Gowan, too. He quit picking on Gav. Hardly even bothered talking to him. Gavin was just as quiet as ever, still spoke softly, still made sure he was as polite to his father as he was to the school principal, still went stiff as a rod if Gowan yelled at someone else. But he was different too. He no longer made himself choke down cooked onions or cooked cabbage, he just pretended it wasn't on his plate, and there was a new sound in his voice, almost like triumph, when he said matter-of-factly, "I'm afraid I can't eat that. The doctor says it isn't good for me." When Liz asked him later, he grinned and said that wasn't exactly true. "What he said was I was to be careful about eating stuff like that because it can give you gas. What it is for me is that I don't mind the taste of it, it's just when it gets to the back of my throat, about to that place where that little jigger hangs down the back, it feels so slimy that I choke on it and start to gag."

"Slimy?"

"Sure. Don't you think it's slimy? I can't stand Jell-O, either, because it's slimy. Or oysters."

"Jesus, Gav. He nearly kills you because you get the idea in your head that stuff feels funny?"

"It wasn't an idea, Lizzie. And it wasn't in my head. It was my throat. It would just –" and he pulled a face, grabbed his throat and pretended to puke. They both started to laugh.

"At least he leaves you alone," Liz said.

"He couldn't leave me alone enough to suit me!" Gavin declared.

The new place wasn't bad, it was just so far from everyone Fran knew. Not just miles away, days away by bus. They lived within sight and sound of the rail line, and the little kids loved to run up the hill and stand waving like fury as the train thundered past, clickety-clack clickety-clack. The engineer always blew his whistle and the kids thought it was for them.

"He blows when you aren't there, too," Fran told them.

"That's to say hello, anyway," little Scotty insisted. He was so convinced Fran didn't have the heart to make him believe the truth.

There were two bedrooms, a small living room and a kitchen about big enough for you to sit at the table while frying bacon on the oil-burning stove. The bathroom was a partitioned-off section of what had been a big porch before it got closed in and called a spare room. "You can have that for your own," Jo-Beth said apologetically, but Fran shook her head. It was blistering hot in the summer and as cold as the Arctic in winter. Besides, who wants to have a washing machine and a dirty clothes basket in what's supposed to be your bedroom, and a back door without any kind of lock, where people can just saunter in if they want to and there's your bed, and no privacy at all? Might as well sleep in the middle of the highway, with the white line for a pillow.

She shared the bedroom with the little kids – probably a good decision, all things considered. There was a slide bolt on the inside, and even though Jo-Beth rambled on about What if there was a fire, how would I get in there to get you out, Fran slid that bolt shut at night. There were just too many yahoos she didn't know who wound up at the place after hours with a case of beer or two.

Jo-Beth was working as a dispatcher at the taxi office, and the best shift was the one where she left the house after supper and worked from eight at night until eight in the morning. After that shift she would come home, make breakfast for everyone, maybe even help Fran with the laundry or something, then go to bed and saw logs until suppertime. She'd get up, have a meal with them and be a mother until it was time to go to work. She supervised the bath, washed hair, laughed, smooched and let them watch while she put on her face and got ready for work. She was sober the whole time. But after the other shift, from eight in the morning to eight at night, she'd stop off at the pub for a couple of cold ones on her way home. And Jo-Beth was no more capable of having just a couple than she was capable of joining the Olympic snowshoe team. Fran knew it wasn't going to change, no matter how many promises Jo-Beth made. She just couldn't walk past a pub unless the door was locked.

And it seemed as if the rest of the world didn't want her to leave alone at closing time either. If Jo-Beth came home with just one guy things weren't bad, and if that guy stayed two or three days things were all right, sometimes almost nice. It was when the whole damn troop arrived, and your life got invaded by people you didn't know from Adam's off-ox and didn't want to know either. Sometimes the mad hatter's beer party would go on for days. Fran hated Jo-Beth's days off. Either you didn't see her at all because she was at the pub or at someone else's place, or you saw too much of her and her noisy friends.

"Ah, don't be that way," Jo-Beth pleaded, "they just want to be friendly, that's all. God, Fran, the world isn't halfways near as bad as you seem to want to think it is."

"Wake up, Momma. Take a look at what it really is."

But not Jo-Beth, she wasn't going to look at anything ever again. "Put on his best clothes," she wept, "went off lookin' like some kind of movie star or something, and for all I know he stepped off the edge of the earth and fell up to the moon. Just gone."

Fran knew it was nothing of the sort. Fran knew what had happened. It was like watching a movie, a private movie in her head. There were only two possible versions, neither of them with a happy ending. Either big Scotty had lived or he had died. In either version, the cop was bear meat. The cop car hidden in a gully or a ravine or off the Malahat and down three hundred feet to the chuck, maybe with the cop and big Scott both still inside. She didn't know if Scotty had taken one of the handguns he'd lifted off a German he'd killed or if he'd used a violin string or a rolled-up magazine or any of the other things they'd taught him to use, but he'd done it, as sure as God made little green apples. Probably just waited in an alley until the cop came along the sidewalk playing his part, being the lawman, walking the beat. Then grab him by the elbow, swing him into the alley, the sharp outer edge of the hand on the end of the nose driving the nosebone up into the skull, then back into his own car, on the floor probably, and drive away as calm as calm could be. Or maybe wait in the parking lot outside the police station, the last place they'd think anyone would dare try it. For big Scotty it would be easy, he'd been trained by the best in the world. *Thump*, then drive away, obeying all the traffic laws. Maybe up Green Mountain, maybe along a logging road up Copper Canyon way, or maybe down the highway and off through Cowichan into Paldi or Youbou or any of two thousand places where a crumpled wreck would be raided by bears, ravens, wolves, mink and rats until only bones were left, then the salal, blackberry and you-name-it would cover the car completely, the alders would grow up and punch through the glass, and before long the thing would rot down so that even if someone did find it they would think it was just another ancient hunk of junk.

And either big Scotty was dead inside it with a bullet from his own gun lodged in what was left of his skull, or he'd just as calm as anything caught the ferry to Vancouver and then a bus to Seattle or to Tampa, Florida. That one Fran didn't mind at all, Scotty working a charter fish boat out of Tampa, his hair bleached snow white by the same hot sun that had tanned his skin to the colour of arbutus bark. Barefoot, bare chested, in shorts or cut-off jeans, he ran his charter boat, catching bluefin and swordfish, drinking beer from bottles kept cool in the fish hold where the crushed ice was loaded in by the half ton. Fran could almost smell him, see him standing at the wheel, his body layered in muscle, singing and ignoring the admiring looks of all those women. Scotty would never get married ever again, and he'd never have another family of kids, he wouldn't do that, he wouldn't betray or abandon them that way. He'd live on his boat, alone except for the people he took out on charters, and everyone would wonder what a good-lookin' man like him was doing on his ownsome.

If he wasn't dead he was on the run, and one way or the other they'd never see him again. Even if he wasn't her real dad, even if she'd been nearly a year old before he set eyes on her, she had thought he was her dad before she found out different. And maybe what you believe somehow becomes real. Maybe what seems to be, is. He'd have made three of any of these idiots, that's for sure. Even when she was drunk, Jo-Beth knew it. And cried, lots of times. "Oh, Fran, what am I going to do? I'm so scared."

Fran hated school. Nobody there said anything to her about Jo-Beth's parties, but she knew they knew, and she knew they talked about it to each other. They pretended to be friendly, but it was only pretend. Fran hated knowing the teachers sat in their coffee room and talked to each other about how sad it was, how awful, how difficult for the poor children. Poor, poor things. But she couldn't tell Jo-Beth how she felt because Jo-Beth would go into a fury and start slapping and hitting, with a kindling stick or a leather belt or the cord on the iron. Then not only did nothing change, but she had to go to school with welts on her arms and legs and even in wintertime with a long-sleeved sweater it was impossible to cover all of them. Then they had even more reason to say poor thing. Poor, poor little thing.

It was bad enough and scary enough when the men fought, but when the women started fighting it was horrible. Men – well, they do that, and you walk around always half expecting a fight to break out, especially if there's the smell of booze in the room. But when the women fight, you know things have gone as far as they can go before people go insane and start doing things like setting themselves on fire or carving their initials on their cheeks. The first time Fran saw women fighting all she could do was stand in the open doorway gaping. It wasn't like in some silly movie, with a lot of rolling around and hair-pulling and nobody's makeup getting smeared and the women looking as if they were practising to make love to the men. In real life, women fought just as mean and as hard and as awful as men, with grunts and punches and terrible scratching, like tigers, with long bleeding claw marks. You slimy cunt, I'll tear your fuckin' eyes out. You scabby twat, you'll be sorry.

And Jo-Beth watching, shaking her head and saying Good God, girls, try to be ladies, will you, and then laughing, as if some point had been proved. I mean, my God, girls, if you can't be ladies you're in trouble. Because whatever else she was, Jo-Beth was a lady. In her own mind, at least. She didn't roll on the floor grunting and cursing, nor stand there swinging away like a fool.

Even worse than that, the really awful one, the one Fran knew she would never get used to, was when some guy started hitting on his woman. And all the women would run to huddle together, calling out things like Oh, God, stop him, and Jesus, some of you guys *do* something, and Call the police, he'll kill her. The men sat there looking as if they wished they could put a stop to it, looking uneasy in the same way as if someone had suddenly decided to pee on a parking meter downtown. But they didn't interfere. So someone would get well and truly beaten to shit by someone who was bigger, heavier and way lots stronger, someone who would be ashamed to beat up a man half his size but thought it okay to teach the old lady a goddamn lesson, by God.

All through the good weather, all through the fall and into the start of the cold season, one party after another and nothing but noise going on so much of the time.

The weather was another shock to the system. This wasn't the Island, with lots of rain and fog but no real bitter cold. This was the Interior, and Jo-Beth was right when she said Don't let your nose drip or it'll freeze and you'll have an icicle going from your top lip right up into your sinuses. It was so cold that your nose would bleed from it. You couldn't put enough blankets on the bed. Not even Christmas time and you had to have hot water bottles in the bed before you could bear to crawl in between the sheets.

"Momma please, don't go to the bar," Fran begged. "We can't afford it. Not if we're going to have Christmas too."

"Don't you worry about Christmas, Frannie, we're going to

have a good one. You just trust me, you hear?" and Jo-Beth smiled as if nobody had ever had any reason to worry about dollars and cents.

Fran never knew where the money came from or how Jo-Beth got her hands on it, but there was money for a new coat for each of them, and warm fleece-lined rubber boots for the snow that just fell and fell and fell as if it would go on for the rest of everyone's life. And a great big roasting chicken, twelve pounds if it was an ounce. A capon, Jo-Beth called it. With stuffing and sweet potatoes and everything, just like when big Scotty was at home and working steady at the sawmill. Candy and oranges from Japan, oranges that came in a little wooden box you could use afterward for a stool or a bedside table, with the label end turned out so the pagoda and the foreign writing showed. Or the other kind of label, the one with Mount Fujiyama with the top covered with snow. It was just like Mount Shasta, where they said there was a whole underground civilization if you could just find the hidden entrance. And wouldn't that be something, get together an expedition and go to the mountain, explore it methodically, walk all the way around it until you got back to where you started, then move up, say, a hundred feet and do it again, like a spiral, up and around and up and around and then the entrance, probably hidden behind a big boulder and . . .

better yet, no expedition, go by yourself. Yes. Then the entrance, and nobody but you goes in, and you are faced with all these possible choices, tunnels that go nowhere, so you have to turn back, and others with booby traps, and when you're just about at the end of your rope you pass this test, the tunnels are a test, of endurance, of dedication, of rightness, and you pass and you are allowed to visit these people who turned their backs on the outside world for reasons we understand only too well.

And a Christmas tree, with brand new decorations.

"See, I told you," Jo-Beth laughed. "I told you just trust me. I'm not as bad as you think I am, Fran. I might not be the best, but I'm not as bad as you think I am."

"I don't think you're bad."

"You remember this the next time you start to get down on me. I do my best. I always do my best, no matter what it is I'm doing."

It was a double shock when the police walked into the house on Boxing Day, uniforms and all.

"Excuse me, sir," Jo-Beth said coldly. "Did your mother not teach you to knock?"

"Search warrant," he said, holding out a paper.

Jo-Beth took the paper and read it, then shrugged. "Oh, be my guest." She took out a cigarette, lit it and sat at the kitchen table while every cop in town toured the house, looking in drawers, checking the cupboards, even looking in the tank of the toilet and the tub of the washing machine.

"And what, might I ask, prompts this little investigatory foray?" Jo-Beth drawled. "Have we lost our handcuffs or something?"

"*We* haven't lost anything, sister," the cop smiled coldly. "We're looking for something someone else had taken from them."

"Really. Might one inquire what?"

"Read the paper."

There it was, the next day. Someone had gone in the back window of Quinlan's Jewels, bypassing the alarm system, and had managed to get into the safe. No details were given other than the cryptic "a quantity of explosives was used." And Fran couldn't help but remember the man with nothing much left of his hand except part of his thumb and his little finger, the man who had sat in their kitchen drinking hot rum and muttering about how they'd turn themselves inside out to make sure that you didn't get the kind of pension would make you anything other than pathetically grateful for the next piddly installment. "Kid," he had said to Fran, "I probably brought out enough gold for them to buy half of Europe with, and when I had my accident what did they say? Said I was forty percent at fault my own self, and put me on a handicapped dole. Well, the joke is going to be on them, I tell you."

Whatever it was had been taken, the police didn't find any sign of it at Jo-Beth's house. "Don't relax, sister," the cop said easily, "We'll be back."

"By all means." Jo-Beth walked to the door with them, smiling as if they were a convention of Fuller Brush salesmen. "Should you care to let me know in advance I would be more than happy to bake a cake and put on the coffee pot for your arrival."

Fran was terrified. "Momma —"

"Shut up," Jo-Beth said coldly. "Just shut the hell up, Fran."

It was all over the paper for days. No leads. No clues. No progress. Continuing investigation. The same few facts hashed and rehashed and the police did come back, but only two of them, and Jo-Beth wasn't there.

"Where is she?" one of them asked.

"My mother is at work," Fran answered clearly. She could hardly believe her ears. She sounded like Jo-Beth, cold, definite, and very very ladylike, no sign at all of the terror gripping her guts.

"What time will she be home?"

"I think I'm under no obligation to answer questions without a lawyer of my own choosing," she managed. "Besides which, I think you aren't allowed to question anyone who is under age."

"Don't get smart, sister."

"I am not your sister, sir," she said, and they left.

They came back again, but she didn't let them in the house. She stepped out onto the frost-whitened porch.

"We'd like to ask you a few more questions," one of them said.

"No, sir," she answered.

"Come on, now, don't be that way. We'll go inside, we'll just ask a few —"

"Do you have a search warrant?" she asked. They stared at her, both of them suddenly very angry. "Good day, sir," and she stepped inside, closed the door and locked it. Then went to her room, sat on the edge of the bed and shook until she thought she'd fall off. She'd just wait until Jo-Beth came home from work, that's all. She'd just wait.

But it wasn't Jo-Beth who arrived. It was two police and two others, a man in a suit and a woman in a fur coat. They didn't have a search warrant, they had another paper. Apprehension, they called it.

"What? Why?"

It didn't make the front page, but it was there on page two: "Woman Found Dead." The woman was Jo-Beth, which was hard enough to accept, but they said she had been so drunk she had fallen into a ditch and been unable to get out. Exposure, they said, hypothermia. Half a day later they were saying it was alcohol poisoning, then they changed that too because the doctor's report said she hadn't had enough alcohol to even make her unsteady on her feet. She must have slipped on the ice, fallen head first and broken her neck when she hit the frozen ditch. Except her knees weren't skinned, her palms weren't skinned, and her face was only slightly bruised. It was just unbelievable.

Or maybe you believed that a sober person had managed to slip on sand-and-salt-seeded ice and snow and broken her neck after falling two feet. Or that the police had decided to hell with the search warrant, you asked for it, sister. Or maybe you wondered whether big Scotty hadn't gone so far away after all and was cleaning up some loose ends. Or the man with half a hand decided he wasn't sharing. Or someone else had a fit of temper. Fran couldn't stop remembering that all her dad needed was the edge of his hand and he could break the neck of anyone in the world. She wanted to believe all of it and none of it, so one day she believed one thing, another day something else.

Three kids, three different foster homes. What was that about? How come not all of them at one place? But no. Three kids, three different houses in three different parts of town. Well, two in town. The one Fran got sent to was nine miles out of town, and wouldn't you know she'd be the one to wind up on the farm, she who was afraid of large animals and not comfortable with small ones. little Scott, who would have loved the farm, wound up with people who ran a tourist court on the banks of a large lake. And Buttercup, now called Jo-Beth all the time, wound up where Fran ought to have been. In town, in a nice house in a nice neighbourhood, with a nice fence with roses on it and a nice ornamental evergreen tree by the front gate.

Stupid. The whole thing was just too stupid. But at least Fran got to change schools, and nobody knew enough of the real story to put two and two together. "If they're so impolite as to ask questions," said Elsa, the foster mother, "tell them you're our niece and you moved here because you want to go to agricultural college when you finish school and you want the experience on the farm."

It was a lie. A lie so far from anything true that Fran grabbed at it eagerly. "Oh, yes," she said, sitting at the long table in the school cafeteria and eating her lunch with the others, "we all talked it over, the whole family, because we're close-knit, you know, and everyone agreed it made such good sense. I write almost every night, and they write to me and send pictures and stuff, and I'll go visit as often as I can. Of course it's all a puzzle to them," she chuckled easily. "You don't expect any of your children to become veterinarians if you yourself are in love with fishing and the sea, but in our family it's Follow Your Dream, so . . ." and she shrugged and smiled.

Fran took everything she knew about Aunt Wilma's family – the fish boat, the months and months nowhere near town, all of it, whether it was true or not – and stole what she needed, just the way other people steal money or food. Scotty out on the charter boat off Tampa and the rest of them on a gillnetter in Growler's Cove. When they needed supplies they'd put in at Alert Bay and the cash buyer would come to the boat, tie up alongside and send the bucket on a winch cable from one craft to the other. Once the salmon were off-loaded and the pay slip was made out, checked carefully and signed, they'd get a cheque. They'd take it to the bank and deposit it in the family account, except for what they needed right away for food and clothes. After all those days out on the fishing grounds they'd be hungry for real meat, so maybe they'd get a chicken and . . .

Sometimes she almost believed it. Except the part about being a vet, she could never believe that. Everything about animals was enough to make you sick to your stomach. If it wasn't shit it was blood, and that was the whole story. If you weren't shovelling up after them, you were burying some part of them. A lamb may be cute when it's first born, but after a month or so it starts to get little willnots stuck to the wool around its bum, and there you are, as if you had nothing better to do than take your scissors and snip away lumps of dried poop from the busy end of a smelly ramling. Next thing you know the fleece is draped over the fence and the old washtub is almost to the rim with steaming loops of who'd-care-to-put-a-name-to-it. Then someone expected you to sit down and yum yum munch munch.

Fran phoned little Jo-Beth and little Scotty whenever she could. Jo-Beth always cried, and little Scotty never wanted to talk about anything but boats and fish and fish and boats. In winter Scotty's foster family cut holes in the ice with chain saws and people from the city drove a very long way to sit around on boxes freezing their backsides and drowning worms in the frigid water, while little Scott ran back and forth to the house with thermoses of hot coffee and convinced himself he was helping. When the ice thawed he was full of how he was learning to row, learning to steer the motor boat, learning and laughing and having a good time. And Jo-Beth finally quit crying, right around the time she started forgetting who her mother had been and started calling the foster mother "Mommy."

"She's *not* your mommy," Fran yelled. "We had our own mother!"

"Don't you yell at me. I don't even like you," and Jo-Beth hung up the phone, leaving Fran fuming and frustrated.

Part of Fran kept expecting that they would all be put on a bus and sent back to the Island. After all, hadn't Auntie Wilma phoned and said not to worry, dear, we'll have you home before you even know it?

"There isn't one of us who can take all three of you," Wilma said, "but your Uncle Hamish wants little Scotty to live with him, and Uncle Gordon and Auntie Sal will take little Jo-Beth, and you'll come to live with us. You can share with Liz and Louise until we get the addition built onto the house. So don't you worry, dear, we're going to get it all arranged."

Except that the next thing you know the worker is at the farm and Fran has to get into the car with her and drive in to the office and sit there until her Grandfather Harris comes in, wearing a suit complete with vest and gold chain going from buttonhole to small watch pocket.

"Grandpa Harris." Like a fool, she smiled at him.

"Frances Mary," he said, nodding slowly.

"Your grandfather," the worker said with a phoney smile, "thinks you'd be much better off if you stayed here."

"*What?*" Fran yelled. "But Auntie Wilma said –"

"The town is nae place for ye," the old man said firmly and loudly. "There's nae soul in it doesnae know about yer mither and feyther. Stained and painted is what they've got ye. Stained and painted. And I'll nae hae it."

"But Grandpa – !"

"It's for yer ain guid, lass," he said stubbornly. "And what would ye do livin' wi' Gowan, anyway? He's half daft at the best a' times. And Hamish, well, he's nae sober a' that often, and

Gordon and Sal half in and half out a' divorce court any day of the week. Nae, it would be but upset and uproar."

She argued. She tried to reason. But when your grandfather gets dressed up and travels all that distance to tell the Welfare he doesn't want you back in town, nobody is going to listen to you or anyone else.

So there she was, living on a farm, shovelling out cow shit, washing udders and putting little rubber cups on teats so machines could pull out the milk so someone in town could open their door and get a bottle off the porch before breakfast. And each cow eating endless bales of hay and dropping endless pats of soft shit. And all that shit to be cleaned up and the floor to be disinfected and Fran having to pretend everything was just exactly the way she had longed for it to be all her life.

"No, you will *not!*" she screamed. "I won't *let* you!"

"But Fran, there isn't much you can do about it except make it all very unpleasant. Your grandfather agrees, your aunts and uncles agree –"

"She's my *sister*. She's *got* a mother and father!"

"No, she doesn't. Not any more," and who cares what they're taking away from you, if the law says your very own sister is adoptable and if the foster parents want to adopt her, you can make all the bloody fuss you want and she's still gone to another town, she's got another family and another name. It's enough to make you wonder who *you* are. Because there's your little brother and he's in the same town as your sister, who isn't your sister any more, and he sees her two or three times a week and is quite comfortable with the situation, and the family he lives with is talking of adoption, too.

So Jo-Beth Williams became Jo-Beth Carpenter and Scott Edward Williams became Scott Edward Branston, and Frances Mary whose-father-was-a-lawyer-or-something stayed Frances Mary Williams and that had never been her real name anyway.

Sometimes she wakened at night and lay in bed staring into the dark and wondered about names and what they meant, what was really going on with them. Why was she Frances Mary and Jo-Beth the one named after their mother? Maybe they hadn't been joking when they said they found her under a big lump of seaweed at the beach. You wouldn't call a foundling after your own self. Maybe she wasn't anybody she thought she was. Maybe she was altogether someone else.

In which case it didn't matter who got drunk and who stayed sober, who disappeared and who got found dead, it didn't matter who was trash in the old home town and who was acceptable, and it didn't matter what anyone thought of her and her brawling, noisy, lowlife family, because they weren't hers anyway. She came from somewhere else, from other people, from anyplace or anyone she chose. And one day everyone would know it.

Oh, they'd say, that's Frances Mary Williams, the lawyer. And that other lawyer, the one with the piano, would come to her office and ask the receptionist for an appointment. Fran would sit behind her desk, cool as can be, and he'd sit in the second-best chair, the one the clients used, and he'd hesitate and stammer a bit and then he'd tell her about how she came by her lawyering skills naturally enough, because he was a lawyer and his father and grandfather had been, and the family wanted her to know she was one of a long line of lawyers. Fran would just yawn, and say Excuse me, sir, is there a purpose to this visit? He'd start to say who he was and she'd smile, cool and distant, and say Oh really, *that* old story. Your time is up. If you need another appointment I'm sure the receptionist can accommodate you.

/ / /

Grade ten was hard because there was all the uproar and fuss about being transferred to a new school, moving to another farm and a foster family she pretended weren't fostering her at all, and she had to spend her summers working on the farm she was supposed to call home or on other farms, picking strawberries, picking raspberries, picking tree fruit, picking potatoes. Grey dust on everything, and you were afraid to lick your dry lips in case you ate some of the fertilizer or bug killer, but when you mentioned it everyone laughed and said, Oh, come on, that stuff is safe, haven't the gentlemen in the suits and lab coats told us so?

Then grade eleven and things calmed down a bit, but there was still the feeling of having been erased, first by Grandfather Harris and you'll be sorry for that one day, old man, then by the adoption procedures. But Fran wanted to let them all know what they had taken the big Pink Pearl eraser to, and one of the ways she could do that was to crack the books, fill in the blanks and get the answers right.

Grade twelve vanished somewhere. Fran was too busy to brood or feel abandoned, what with a full slate of school subjects, plus band, Junior Achievers, her work on the farm, her babysitting and her trips to visit Elsa and help her out with the work that just piled up no matter how hard a body tried. Then there was her weekend job mucking out the stables at a farm two miles down the road, where a few Arabian horses stood around eating and shitting while some Americans pretended to raise them for a tax exemption. And Fran wasn't at all fond of horses, thank you. Long-legged cranky spoiled things with yellow teeth and the dispositions of junkyard dogs. But the Americans paid well and Fran couldn't stand not to organize and fill every hour of her waking day. Just keep working and you won't have to worry.

And then school was winding down, and everyone expected her to zip off to veterinary school or agricultural college. After telling that story for a few years she couldn't just up and say Oh, I changed my mind, so she invented the perfect way out. "I'm going to do a year or so of Fine Arts at the university," she lied, smiling widely, "before I settle in and decide exactly which course I'm going to zero in on," and people nodded, smiled back at her, swallowed the whole thing. Even Elsa, who you would expect to know better.

No sooner did Fran have her graduation certificate in her hand than she was packing her things and heading to the coast, ostensibly to find room and board and get herself squared away over the summer so she'd be ready to set the university on its ear come the start of classes in September. With her high school certificate she got a double handful of job applications. With her high school certificate and a handful of change she could also have got a cup of coffee, and a doughnut too.

With the job applications and only a bit of trouble she managed to get hired at Grainger's Floral Nursery. It was almost like being back on the farm, only under plastic and glass, planting seeds and cuttings in little green plastic pots and trays, tending the sprouts, thinning them, transplanting them, checking the humidity, watching for the first dreaded sign of damping off, making sure there were no aphids or mites or root-eating grubs, hands never quite clean, back always just a bit stiff and tired from bending over potting tables.

But it was only eight and a half hours a day, and what do you do with the rest of your time? A half hour or so each way on the bus to and from work, and there are still at least fourteen hours left, and precious little money to do anything interesting. So Fran took a second job, a part-time one, to fill up some of that scary dark what-to-do-now time.

Then she thought she might take some courses, and right there in the paper was a notice about a class that taught clog dancing. So Fran paid her five dollars and once a week went to the basement of the United Church and learned to pound her feet on the floor more or less in time to the music, most of which came from scratchy old records with songs like "The Glory of Eirenn" and "Scotia My Heart" and "Jim McFinney's Inspiration."

When she could clog away to almost anything except maybe the Blue Danube waltz, she learned to play canasta. And she lucked out. She met Ted.

He wasn't very tall and he wasn't muscular or athletic. He was wiry, medium tall and not the least bit graceful. He had straight dark hair combed back from his forehead and held in place with some kind of hair stuff that smelled more or less like violets, and his front teeth were chipped in a small *V*.

"Want to go for a milkshake or something?" he asked.

"Thank you," she answered, smiling her I-know-something-you-don't-know smile.

On Saturday, after she got off work at Grainger's, he was waiting in his sedate-looking car, which he had doctored up so it would pass anything on the road, and they went out to watch other cars racing around an oval track.

"That's funny," she said, "they call this the Speedway, that's what they called the dance hall at home. One of them, anyway."

"Yeah?" he grinned. "Well, you won't dance on *this* Speedway!"

The noise was incredible and the stink made you wonder why people would pay money to sit on hard benches and watch other people drive around in circles, but Ted was so knowledge-able about it. He knew how much gas each car sucked, how many races each driver had won – more than you'd think there was to know. And then he was on his feet, smiling down at her.

"I'll be back soon," he promised. "Our car is in the race after next. I'll be back."

She sat through three races, not knowing which of the red, blue, red and blue, black, white, black and white, yellow or pick-your-colour car was the one Ted called "ours." And then he was back, grinning and laughing, eating up congratulations from the more knowing members of the audience.

"I didn't know . . ." Fran trailed off because she wasn't sure what it was she didn't know. Did he drive, was he the inventor, did he own the thing?

"I'm a good mechanic," he said smugly. "I've got a feel for it."

She tried to look wise and appreciative, and she waited. And by the time they finally left she had pieced it together. His car had come in third. Well, that was better than coming in last.

But there was more to piece together, a lot more. Ted's life came to her in bits, like a jigsaw puzzle.

"Separated?" She was astounded.

"Yeah. When it doesn't work, it doesn't work," he shrugged. "And this didn't work."

It had, however, worked well enough for long enough that there were three kids, one running, one walking, one crawling. And another one waiting to come forth. The almost-ex-wife had her baby just about the time Fran and Ted rented a basement suite and started calling themselves Mister and Missus. Then the almost-ex-wife announced she was moving in with her boyfriend and he worked shifts and couldn't stand the way the baby howled, it kept him from sleeping. "Anyway these kids are half yours," she said, as crisp and businesslike as any banker, "so you get two and I keep two. And since I've done all the work so far, I get first pick." She kept the two oldest – both girls, who could walk, pee in the toilet and feed themselves. And anyway, Ted wanted his son, of course he did.

"But Ted, I –"

"Oh come *on*, Fran! How much money do you make a week? And how much can I make? So *I* should stay home to look after these kids while *you* work? We wouldn't even make the rent."

"What about daycare?"

"You're kidding me. It'd cost your whole paycheque to have Robbie in daycare, and they won't even take Nancy so we'd have to get a sitter. That's all of your pay and a big hunk of mine and we still couldn't make the damn rent!" So Fran stayed home and looked after Robbie and Nancy.

But talking to Elsa on the phone, she presented it differently. "They're just the most adorable little things! Ted idolizes them. He'd have liked to take all four of them, but how fair would that be? I mean his wife did nothing to deserve losing all her children. When people are incompatible, they're incompatible, I say."

When Ted went on the circuit with the car, she packed up the kids and some things in a shopping bag and caught the ferry back to the old home town to show everyone how well she'd done with no help from them, thank you for nothing. "Oh yes, it's really quite wonderful," she told Aunt Wilma, sitting with Nancy on her lap and Robbie playing on the floor with a truck. "Ted's doing very well with his professional racing career and we'd have bought a house except, well, you know how it is, he's on the move a lot . . . he has a few other options, like California, or even Toronto-London-and-Montreal . . . we don't want to tie ourselves down, so . . ." and she smiled as if there had been long husband-and-wife discussions about it instead of instant invention within the confines of her own skull. "We'll just wait and see."

If what she said wasn't exactly true, that didn't make it a lie. Ted could easily do very well with his mechanic's work. Sooner or later he might even decide it was just a bit boring to work on the same car at different tracks, doing the same things over and over, getting paid very little money for all his time, effort, energy and undeniable skill. He might decide to take his toolbox into the bush and make real money keeping heavy machinery running, or work for a big repair shop in town, or move the whole bunch of them out of the city and into some nice small town and open his own shop, and for excitement find a few others like himself and start racing cars there. You never knew, so why be negative?

It was getting crowded in the two-bedroom dungeon. Even bomb shelters are better designed. Sometimes, especially at night with the kids asleep and the radio turned low, Fran would sit on the half-empty double bed with a book she wasn't really reading and she would wonder how the first wife had hung in as long as she had. Two bedrooms, neither of them much bigger than a closet, a kitchen-cum-living room, with table and chairs at one end and sofa at the other, the inadequate television near the sofa, the heat and cooking provided by an oil burner that smelled and leaked. Each time Ted came home from one of his trips he would take the thingamajig apart, clean the carburetor, stop the oozing and dripping so Fran wouldn't have to catch the mess in a soup can, then ride herd on the kids to make sure they didn't drink it.

Sometimes, not always, but often enough to spook her, she wakened somewhere between midnight and dawn, and for a befuddled moment or two she would think she was in the hidey-hole under the army hut, with Buttercup and little Scotty sound asleep nearby.

Her twentieth birthday came and went, and her twenty-first, and she and Ted and the kids were still in the basement suite and still broke. And Ted was still off following the circuit as much as he was at home. All the same, things were looking up.

"Oh, I don't think it would be a good idea," he laughed, "after all, I've already got a kid called Teddy."

Fran stared. "No. You have two daughters, Ted."

"Yeah, of course," he laughed again, "Melissa and Melanie. But Teddy is mine, too. He's seven and a half now." He reached for his beer on the bedside table. Fran looked at him, bare chested, his hair curling softly, his skin pale in the light from the lamp. "Teddy," he explained belatedly, "lives with his mother in Aldergrove. Carol."

"You never mentioned any Carol or any Teddy, either."

"What's to mention?"

She'd have argued with him, but by now she knew that Ted never shouted or yelled or stayed around if someone else was shouting or yelling. There was none of the kind of thing Jo-Beth and Scotty had got themselves into, thank God. Ted just put on his jacket and left. If you were still angry when he finally came back and you picked up where he had aborted it, he'd leave again. If you wanted something done a certain way you asked him if he'd mind. And he'd tell you. So you always knew where you were with him.

Except right now she didn't know where she was at all. "Are there any other little surprises I might be interested in knowing about?"

"That depends what you'd be interested in, Fran. Some of it I figure is none of your business, if you know what I mean."

"Tell me what you mean."

"When I'm home, I'm home, okay? And we got us a good life.

You, me, the kids, and that punkin you're carrying behind your soup and sandwiches." He patted her belly and laughed softly. "And you get my paycheque and you know when I'm here I'll take the kids with me if I can. I'll go do the daddy thing with them at the park, teach 'em to throw a ball and all that. And when I'm not here, when I'm on the road, well, I'm not here, am I?"

"I always expected you'd be . . . faithful," she said quietly.

"I am." He laughed again.

"So who else is there besides this Teddy?"

"His brother Eric."

"And how old is Eric?"

"Five." Ted's voice had changed. There was no joking in it, no teasing, no warmth. He lit a cigarette.

"And how does their mother feel about our arrangement?"

"She doesn't care. Why should she care?"

"Correct me if my arithmetic is wrong, but she may have expected something when you separated from your ex-wife. I mean if Teddy is seven and a half he's right in between Melissa and Melanie, and if Eric is five, he's just a bit older than Robbie."

"That's right." Now his voice was cold.

"So didn't she feel . . . something . . . when you and I –"

"If she did she didn't say anything," said Ted, who suddenly didn't look like anyone Fran knew. He didn't even look like anyone she had known in the past.

"What does she do? In Aldergrove, I mean."

"She's married."

"She's what?"

"Married. You don't understand 'married'?"

"I guess it's just a bit complicated, is all."

"Nothing complicated about it. I had a kid, okay, and things weren't going very well, and I was away from home at the track a lot, and she was there with her husband, and things weren't going well for them, either, and one thing led to another and he quit racing and went off on a fish boat, and she got pregnant. After he'd left," he added, as if that explained it all, and in a way it did. "So then he comes back and he wants to try again and by then things weren't so bad with me'n the ex, and he came back with a pocketload of cash from fishing, and she and I talked about it a lot and it seemed like maybe we should just let things continue on and see how it all worked out, with us, you know.

Except it didn't, really. I mean we got along just fine but not much more. And he figured Teddy was his kid – dumb bugger can't count so good. Anyway, what was done was done. We didn't see each other for a long time because we were both busy patching up our lives. But," he sighed, stubbing out his cigarette, "the patches didn't hold good, I guess."

"And you started seeing each other again."

"Seeing." He snorted, and sipped his beer.

"And you were right back where you had been."

"Right."

"So why, when you separated – ?"

"Because she'd patched it up with him. Besides, I was out of town at the time."

"Oh. And seeing someone?"

"Well, of course," he laughed. "I'm not a man to brood over water that's gone under the bridge, Fran, you know that."

"Are there any other children I should know about?"

"No," he said. Too quickly.

"Well," and she pulled the hair on his chest, pretending to be playful, "are there other children whether I should know about them or not?"

"Yes."

"You ever find out what it was caused them?" She pulled his hair again, but not hard, and he laughed.

"I figure it's the tap water." He gave her a little hug and Fran wondered if that was her reward for not getting angry, her reward for teasing and making a joke out of what was a big mess, so tacky and low-rent it could have been made by the Harrises themselves.

She tried to figure it out. Four with the ex, two in Aldergrove, the one under her own apron, and how many others? Probably enough for a couple of basketball teams. Except they would all be too close to the floor for basketball.

Fran didn't push it. She already knew more than she was comfortable knowing. She had to make some plans of her own, but first she had to have this baby. "We had ducks on the farm." She rolled on her side, tweaking his little hard button of a nipple, "and this Rouen drake. Rouens look a lot like mallards, except they are much, much bigger because they've been crossed with domestic meat ducks. And that drake spent all his time either eating,

shitting or chasing the ducks. There seemed no limit to the number of ducks he could keep fertile. All we had to do was pick up
the eggs, and when we had enough of them, put them in the
incubators. He bobbed his head, bob-bob-bob, because that's
how they flirt. And duck after duck after duck after duck gave egg
after egg after egg that hatched into duckling after duckling after
duckling," and Ted was laughing almost helplessly, looking at her
with approval, as if she cared whether he approved or not. "And
we hatched ducklings, sold ducklings, fattened ducklings and
slaughtered ducklings. At the end of the season, out of the very
last hatching of eggs, we kept one – repeat, *one* – duckling
drake." She wriggled down in bed, getting comfortable, and pretending to yawn. "Guess why," she suggested. And he just kept
laughing.

She was so relieved when her daughter was born. No need
to worry about calling it Teddy or Edward instead of Theodore
so you could say Eddie rather than Teddy. No worry that Ted
would get all strange about another son.

"*Brandy?*" Ted gaped. "Why in hell would anybody fill out
the registration papers with a name like Brandy? It sounds like a
goddamn St. Bernard dog!"

"It does not," she laughed.

"I never heard of a kid called Brandy!"

"I know." Fran reached over and tweaked his nose. "But
you've got so many kids scattered over so many places I didn't
want to double up on a name, like I might have done if it had
been a boy and I had called him Teddy." She leaned back against
her pillows and grinned at him. "So I picked a name that wouldn't
be a duplicate."

"What a nut," he said fondly. But did she care if he felt a bit
of fondness right now? How long would it last, anyway? Probably
until he got to the exit door, and by the time he got down the
three steps to the parking lot she'd be lucky if he remembered
her name, let alone the kid's name.

The basement suite was like a sardine can. But that wasn't
going to be the case forever. He was due to go off in a few days
and fiddle with car engines, then see how long she stayed in a
sardine can. If he wanted to have a few secrets, fine, but he
wasn't the only musician playing a tune in this orchestra.

"You sure you'll be okay?"

"Oh, pooh," she said easily. "It's not as if I've never changed a diaper. You might think this is my first baby but I've been around babies all my life."

Except it *was* her first baby, and she ought to have been allowed to be as excited and dizzy and feet-off-the-ground as any first-time mother, but instead it was somehow old hat. The glow didn't even begin, let alone shine on everything, and *why* was she always being cheated like this?

At nine o'clock the morning after Ted left whistling, Fran was standing at the counter asking to see someone and getting an appointment for the following week. Why had Jo-Beth never gone on welfare? Why had she always got some rotten job that kept her away from her family? Why go to all that bother when all you had to do was what Fran had done for several years in high school and was more than prepared to do now. Go drop it in the lap of those who got paid, and paid extremely well, thank you, to take care of such things.

After all, the kids weren't hers, only Brandy. Maybe Mister Smarty Pants Rouen Drake Ted would learn a thing or two if he came back and his bomb shelter was empty except for the official notice on the table saying Robbie and Nancy were in foster homes and he could phone such and such a number and talk to such and such a worker about visitation rights.

It might have worked, too. He might have looked at that notice and known in his heart what he had done to everyone. He would have sat heavily in a chair and put his head in his hands and seen himself for what he really was, then pulled himself together, phoned the welfare, and changed his life. Got a job – in town, where he could make amends with all of them. Then he would say My God, Fran, I don't know what I was thinking about, it was all so stupid. But listen, Fran, there's this little town without any engine repair shop at all, I mean people get their cars towed fifteen miles just to get the simplest thing fixed. And what I thought was this, I'll go on ahead and get something set up, then you and the kids can join me, and so help me, you will never, never ever again have to even lose one minute's sleep because I know now what's real and what's just a fantasy, I learned my lesson when I saw that notice and Jesus, Fran, I'll do anything to make it up to you.

Except he was driving the tow car, with the racing car on a

special trailer behind, and coming down the highway through the Fraser Canyon the whole thing went for a shit. Witnesses said the car hit black ice and skidded, the trailer fishtailed then jackknifed, and the whole rig flipped. No out-of-control drunk coming over the centre line, no mechanical failure, no nothing except some overgrown kid laughing and outracing his own ability to drive.

In the Fraser Canyon there are parts of the highway where the pavement ends and then it's three hundred feet straight down to the river.

They found one shoe. A boot, actually. And about a pickup load of crumpled metal. World without end, amen.

/ / /

"Are you sure?" the worker asked.

"I'm all the mother they've ever known," Fran said firmly. "It would have been different if their father had lived, but he didn't. And they don't know their biological mother at all. Nancy hasn't even seen her since she was a week old. Sure, I'm sure."

"Why, Auntie Wilma!" she cried, face crumpling with hurt, "they're as dear to me as Brandy is! They're like my very own, maybe even more because I've known them longer and become just that much more attached to them. It would be like having a part of my body amputated!"

It was funny how the welfare worked their money. If she had applied by herself, there would barely have been enough to pay rent on a dumpster, but because of Brandy it was more than doubled. If Robbie and Nancy had been hers, she'd have had just a meagre increase over that first allotment for herself and Brandy. But because they weren't hers, because she had filled out the forms properly, she got foster payment for them, and that was a lot more. The foster payment for one of them was more than she got for herself and Brandy. And with two of them, plus her own mother-and-dependent-child allocation, she was doing just fine. Far better than she had ever done with Ted and his little bit of paycheque.

"But don't you want a job?" dumb Liz asked.

"I have a job," Fran answered primly. "And it's probably the most important job in the world – mothering the next generation."

"Oh, yeah?"

"Yes," she nodded as if there could be no question at all. "Why is it that people think nothing of paying five hundred dollars to get a six-week-old poodle puppy but consider newborn humans to be disposable? Why don't we even question why a person gets good money to cut down trees all day, and then a psychiatrist gets sixty or seventy dollars an hour to try to clean up the messes walking around because nobody got proper parenting? Why shouldn't we take care of the people who raise kids so they don't need the psychiatrist?"

"Maybe, but if you ask me it must be as boring as hell."

"Boring? Watching little minds develop?"

What's more, she wasn't in a basement suite any more. She had a really nice rented house on a quiet street, with a big fenced yard for the kids to play in safely. She got a metal swing set out of the catalogue and paid for it with the foster money for Robbie. It even had a slide and a whirligig, the biggest and best in Eaton's Wish Book. She made the sandbox herself and every night, after dark, when the kids were all asleep, she walked down to the neighbourhood playground and filled two plastic pails with sand from the municipal sandbox, took it home and put it in her own until there was more than enough for the kids to have a whale of a time. She even filled two garbage cans with sand and stored them in the basement, for refills when needed.

She knew they would phone. They'd phoned Elsa often enough, and Fran could remember many extras who stayed for a week or two, a month or two. There are never enough people willing to take in the shocked and traumatized, to put up with the chronic bed-wetting and temper tantrums. But it didn't bother Fran. It was no worse than life with the Harris clan and at least she got paid for it. The more disturbed the kid, the more the welfare paid.

"Fran, I hate to ask because I know you've got as much on your plate as any one person should have, but this is really and truly an emergency."

"Oh it's no bother, really," Fran would say. "Bring your little emergency over right away. Is it a boy or a girl? Will it need a crib or can it have a bed?"

And over they came, the Georgies and Brendas, the Brandons and Shawns, the Rickys and Tommys and Alices and Susans. Fran stopped trying to keep track of who was called what and just addressed them all by what she called love-names. Button. Muffin. Wee one. "Come on, sweetie pie, you let Auntie Fran fix that shoelace. Oh, it's a *bad* shoelace to come untied and make a little heart break, isn't it."

If you take the real emergencies, the welfare even pays for a babysitter so you can get a break and have an hour or two to yourself. "Oh, the poor wee thing," she crooned, "oh, and she can smile for her Auntie Fran. That's a good girl. That's my good little one. Here, we'll just prop your head on the pillow and you can watch the others as they play. That's the way. Easy, now, easy, that's it, don't choke on me, dumpling, here, put it more under your shoulder, that's it. There, isn't that better."

"How can you?" Liz whispered, "I mean . . . look at it."

"Is it her fault? We weren't all lucky, you know."

"Lucky is one thing, unlucky is another, and that kid is something else altogether. I mean, my God, you have to shove a rubber tube down her nose to her stomach and then pour liquid glop down because she can't even *eat!*"

"She's a dear loving little soul."

"Yeah? Well, they couldn't pay me enough to have it around."

"I do hope you don't think it's the pay! They couldn't pay *me* enough, either, if money was all we were talking about," Fran lied, believing it herself. "She's entitled to some love. We're all entitled to some love."

Anyway, what would Liz know or care about looking after the helpless? Liz didn't seem to give two hoots in hell for anybody but Liz.

F O U R

Liz went to high school, worked at the fish'n'chips shop on weekends, helped Wilma with the house and yard, and waited, as patient as a snake, for her chance to hit the road and get as far away from all of this anger and hatred as she could get.

It was as if a boil had been festering for years and then, instead of bursting open and spewing itself clean, dozens of little pressure points opened around the base of it and oozed constantly while the carbuncle just sat there, never changing, inflamed and ugly, dripping and sliming into everyone's lives.

The first pressure point to open and drool had been whatever in hell had gone down with Uncle Scotty. Sometimes Liz wondered if the guy had just spread his cape like Superman and headed back to Krypton. Then there was Auntie Jo-Beth. After that there were whispers about Phoebe and her dentist, but the subject got changed as soon as Liz walked into the room. One of the uncles got in a fight in a bar and broke a guy's jaw and had to go appear in court. Another uncle took a poke at a police constable and that hit the papers. Gowan no longer made any attempt to cover up his bullshit. He had been seen more than once sashaying down the main street of town with a woman on his arm, smiling down at her as if he was someone else. Wilma did the best she could at home and took herself off to work at the laundry and dry cleaner's, bringing home groceries and paying hydro bills.

"Why don't we just leave?" Liz raged.

Wilma shook her head calmly. "We'd be worse off than we are now," she said, "because he likes to eat, so now at least we get a little bit of his paycheque. With him it's out of sight, out of mind, so it's better we're here."

Maybe so. But ever since the Harris Kiss of Death on the idea of Fran and the kids coming back to live with family, the whole thing had started to unwind and get nasty. It was one thing when the neighbours tsk-tsked and thought some people were less than acceptable, but the old man himself? Getting on a bus and travelling all the way to the back of beyond itself just to tell the authorities that nobody in his entire family was fit to take care of their own?

Privately Liz agreed with him. Where were they supposed to stuff another person? With barely enough groceries coming in already, where were they supposed to find more? Weren't there enough people in hand-me-downs, made-overs and patched-ups, and wouldn't the occasional sober breath be a welcome relief?

But Liz knew almost nothing about what was going on. Nobody told the kids anything, they just argued and quarrelled, drank and yelled and fought. What you learned, you got by osmosis, and all of it crap. Rather than absorb the crap, Liz chose to stay ignorant. She got her schoolwork done with passing grades, and when the uproar got to her she went off with her violin and played herself calm again.

"She's good enough for the symphonic," one of them said.

"Yes, she is," Wilma agreed, "but the symphonic has these rules about dress. You have to have a fancy outfit, so that's that."

"We ought to all chip in for it."

"Nobody has," said Wilma, knowing nobody would, either.

And then grade twelve was winding down and Liz had her acceptance from the nursing school. Not that she particularly wanted to be a nurse, but everyone had been telling her for years that she ought to Go On And Do Something, and you weren't going to Do Something on this big floating rock covered with rotting seaweed and arguing relatives.

She could have gone to the city and stayed with Fran until she found a place of her own, but no thanks. Fran and Ted had this little basement suite with windows up near the ceilings, long, thin windows just above the dirt line outside. Sitting in what they called the living room, which was really the other end of the kitchen, with this awe-inspiring vista of other people's ankles as they walked by on the sidewalk. If they stayed there much longer they'd start to go blind and grow sleek grey fur and enormous hands for digging, and sprout a little flower on the end of their noses for smelling out what they could no longer see.

So she went off to nursing school. And wasn't that fun, my dear. Living like Protestant nuns, in residences where the house mouse has the key to all the rooms and can check on you at any hour of the day or night. In by ten, in your room and bed by ten-thirty. You, my dear, please go to room nine-six-six and save old Mrs. Tindall's life, then go to your cubicle like a good girl and stay there, because you can't be trusted to find your own mouth to feed yourself, let alone go out on the streets alone.

But she kept herself busy learning about muscles and bones, blood vessels and digestive systems. Couldn't they call something by a name you could say without strangling yourself? And from what zoo, Jesus aitch, had these other student nurses escaped? Until she went to nursing school Liz had no idea how many pris-sy-issy Christians there were on the face of the earth. Some of them actually sat at the table in the dining room in front of every-one else and bowed their heads over their clasped hands and prayed before they put food in their mouths. Gentle Jesus meek and mild, keep this food from poisoning me.

Sometimes, oh whoopy-ding, there were social events at the nurses' residence and you could invite your friends. Sure, and when and where would you meet any friends to make unless you'd grown up a half mile down the road from the place? Did they expect friends and family to leap into cars and drive four hundred miles for a chance to stand in an echo chamber and eat cucumber sandwiches?

On her days off she went to see Fran and Ted. And wasn't that just a barrel of laughs, Ted and his grease, Fran and his kids, everything so upbeat all the time, just as soon as this or that we'll buy a house, just as soon as this or the other we'll get a car that isn't falling apart, just as soon as something or other we'll fart wonders and shit miracles.

It was better when The Big I-Yam was off fine-tuning the fritz-diddle or whatever it was he did to motors. Then Liz and Fran could talk. Maybe it wasn't any more real or grounded but at least it wasn't dominated by this smirking fart with the grease in his hair and tight black jeans that outlined his knackers and that little bit of a root he seemed so proud of.

"I had the marks and was all set to go and then I met Ted," Fran smiled placidly. Jesus, if she tells that one again she'll believe it herself. "It's hard to get in, you know, they've got a waiting list so nobody gets to go right out of grade twelve, and I knew that, but anything worth having is worth waiting for, right?"

"Right." Might as well agree with her.

"But it's funny to think of, in a way. If I *had* gone right from high school I would never have met Ted. And who knows, maybe it would be me instead of you with a book full of colour diagrams of muscles and veins."

"Yeah. Funny, huh?"

There was nothing funny about it. Fran was like a zombie, smiling, smiling, smiling, kids crawling all over the ratty furniture and her behaving as if her life were just the way she wanted it to be. You'd think a person who had grown up looking after her brother and sister and never having enough time alone to so much as go swimming would want a life of her own. But no, instead of keeping herself safe from the world even for a few hours on the weekend, she was stuck on the machine gun emplacement twenty-four hours a day, seven days a week, for as many weeks as it would take her to go all the way crazy and get lugged off to the bin.

Liz would have loved to grab Fran by the hand and say Come on, get a sitter for the kids, you and I will go out for supper. But student nurses don't get enough money for bus fare, let alone for supper, so she didn't.

Until the day she got sick and tired of it. Until the day she saw herself not in a nurse's uniform but in thong sandals and a coolie hat, doing work people ought to do for good money instead of a passing grade. How many beds do you have to make, how many bedpans full of diseased shit and puke basins brimming with bile do you have to empty before you know how to do it?

So she spent her days off going around the hospitals and nursing homes, applying for work.

"But you're a student nurse, dear," the supervisor said, shocked. "Why would you want to downgrade yourself this way?"

"I have to," Liz lied, taking a page from Fran's book. "My father isn't well, he's had an accident at work and we need the money." She knew she had the job right then and there.

Now all she had to do was pack her stuff in cardboard boxes and find a place to set them down again. The paper was full of furnished room-for-rent ads, and she managed the rent, barely, by dipping into the tips she'd managed to save from the fish'n'chips job. It was tight, and by the time payday rolled around she was so hungry she could eat a horse starting at the arsehole, but she did it.

The first six months or so she worked all the time, sometimes double shifts for the extra money. But you can only do that for so long before you get sick and tired of the sound of your own breathing. Sometimes she went to movies, sometimes she walked for hours watching the outside of other people's lives, and sometimes she went to see Fran, mostly because when she left she felt so much more positive about her own life.

"You need diversions," Fran lectured, sounding more and more like a grade two teacher. "There are lots of things you can do, lots of groups you can join."

"What about you?" Liz said. "You don't get out as often as I do!"

"Ah, but this is the life I want," Fran laughed easily, and damned if she didn't believe it. "You're still looking around and making your choices." And then she was talking about how much fun clog dancing was.

Well, my dear, aren't we just about ready to burst with the excitement of it all. Clippity hippity cloppety hoppety, have you ever gone into an Irishman's shanty and walked through the kitchen and into the pantry and all of the children are sitting around and they don't know their ass from a hole in the ground.

But Liz went, mostly to shut Fran up, to say I tried but it wasn't for me. The dancing part wasn't hard. Fran had already demonstrated the moves and they'd practised a bit, laughing together almost as if it was the good old days instead of now. But the music. My God in heaven, every record scratched as if the dancers had practised on top of the turntable, and even the two pennies scotch-taped to the needle arm couldn't stop it bouncing and jabbing more scratches and holes into the vinyl. Finally Liz couldn't stand it any longer. She took her violin along and played some half-decent sounds.

"That was *fun!*" one of the women laughed, her face red, sweat beaded along her hairline. "Oh, that was wonderful!"

"You're good," the guy in the ugly pants said.

"Why don't we each chip in fifty cents a night and hire her?" another suggested.

I have to tell you, my dear, thirty of them bouncing around clicking and clacking may not seem like an art form but it *is* fifteen dollars. And the one in the ugly pants turns out to be a real culture vulture, he belongs to the Buttons'n'Bows Square Dancing Club as well, and wouldn't you know they too would like the chance to dance to some real music.

Off she went, and by a quarter after seven it was do-si-do and allemande round the town and twenty bucks in the kitty when the night was over.

"You busy on Saturday night?" The guy was middle-aged and had lines in his face, most of them from too much smiling.

"Busy? Me? Saturday night?" she laughed.

"Yeah. Well, tough luck for us, I guess," and he turned away.

"Hey, what do you have in mind?"

"We've got a bit of a band going," he blurted, "but we could sure use a good fiddle."

And there she was of a Saturday night, not sitting in the movie house with a box of popcorn but up on stage with the Fraser Valley Pioneers. Even more unbelievable, on the other side of the stage were almost three hundred people sliding, gliding and God-knows-whatting across a waxed board floor. Liz had sore spots on the tips of the fingers of her left hand when she finally packed away her violin, and the muscle running from her shoulder to her elbow was tight and sore. But she had thirty dollars in her pocket. Add that to the twenty and the fifteen and she was way ahead of the hourly she got for emptying kidney basins of swill.

"We have Maple Ridge on Friday night and Langley on Saturday night," Dave Walker said. "Can you make it?"

"Me? Uh, sure, except for the getting there part of it. I don't drive," she told him.

"I can pick you up." He looked as happy as a pig in mire. "Hey, Sid," he called to the guitar picker, "she said yes!"

"Great! Hey, great!" said Sid, looking as if someone had just handed him a cake with candles on top.

"Can I give you a ride home?" Dave offered.

So there she was with money every week from the clog dancing, and money every week from the square dancing, and money
every weekend from the Fraser Valley Pioneers. That was four
nights of hard work every week and no time for afternoon shift, so
she quit the nurse's aide job and settled herself in for the long haul.

"Isn't it kind of hard to know you're prostituting your art?"
Fran looked even prissier than usual, her pregnancy filling her lap
so much Ted's kid had to perch on the edges of her knee bones.

"You know how it is," Liz played along with it, "even Mozart
had to play what his patrons wanted to hear. It's no worse than
practising, and my fingers get a good workout."

"I'm not sure I could do it." Fran had something up her nose,
that was for sure. "But I'm glad you aren't, you know, stuck all
alone in a morbid little room any more."

"Yeah," Liz nodded, as the light bulb finally went on over her
head. "Listen, Fran, I guess I owe this chance to you. If you hadn't
practically dragged me by the hair down to the clog dancing,
well, I'd still be bouncing off the walls in the hospital holding
people's heads while they barfed all over my uniform." That was
it, by God. The prissy disapproving pout was gone and Fran was
smiling and nodding, as if she'd only been waiting for Liz to get
her head out and co-operate.

The morbid little room was no more. Liz had a room on the
second floor of an old yellowish brick building with sliced-off
corners and big white bricks set into patterns around the windows outside. Inside, the place was three walls of big windows,
with a board floor, high ceilings and patterns in the plaster. She
had what they called cooking privileges, bathroom down the hall,
and for furniture she only needed a single mattress on the floor
with brand new sheets and a down-filled sleeping bag zipped
open for a quilt. Her little wood table fit under a window, and
her three chairs looked okay once she had taken sandpaper to
the ugly paint some fool had slathered on. The two chests of
drawers were old too, and took forever to sand back down to the
wood, but it was worth the trouble and anyway, what else was
she doing with her time?

Well, seeing Sid for one thing. They went to Chinatown for
supper, they took long walks in Stanley Park, they went to the
movies, and a couple of times they went down to have a cup of
tea and a brief visit with Fran.

"Is this serious?" Fran asked hopefully.

"No." Liz shot that one from the sky before it picked up any speed. "No, he's a nice guy and I really like him but . . ." She was going to say it was more by way of recreational sex than anything else, but Fran might get her tail in a tangle over that one so she fit the news to fit the audience. "It's not like what you have. It's not . . . you know, the real thing."

That made Fran nod, but not so much with satisfaction as with a kind of quiet regret. Liz didn't get it at the time, but it was all explained when Ted wound up smeared over the rocks in the Fraser Canyon. Fran carried on something awful. "Oh, my God," she moaned over and over, "I feel as if I caused it!"

"Jesus Christ, woman, you weren't even in the tow car!"

"I know. Maybe if I had been he wouldn't have been driving so fast!"

"Then it would have been both of you over the cliff. Come on now, you had nothing to do with it."

"Oh, but I did. I *did!*" and she sobbed and sobbed until Liz thought it really had gone too far. There is a difference between scratching your bum and ripping out huge bleeding hunks.

Funny, though, how things happen. If Ted had taken even a few days off to help the family move from the cubbyhole to the rented house he might not have been on the highway when the one-in-charge-of-such-things decided it was time the police and paramedics earned their keep. But no, he leaves all that for Fran, the way he left everything, off he goes and it's Liz helps pack things up and it's Sid who comes around with his car to load the stuff. By eight at night they're moved in and sitting on what you might be inclined to call furniture in this new semi-furnished place, eating fish'n'chips off newspapers, and Fran is going on about how maybe for the next little while Robbie and Nancy will be staying with friends, just until she gets settled in, you know, and has had time to establish a relationship with Brandy, whatever that means.

And no time later, it seems, a week at most, she's sobbing into the phone and blaming herself and working herself into such a state of helpless hysteria that there's nothing for Liz to do but go over and see what she can do. There's nothing, of course. What could you do? What if all you could feel was a large dose of puzzlement that a woman could be so torn to shreds by the eradication of one more cipher?

"Listen, Fran, I have to get a wiggle on here, go play for a few hours. You just hang on, okay? I'll be back as soon as I'm finished with the do-si-do'ers."

"I know," Fran nodded, "the show must go on."

And it went on. Not just while the Buttons'n'Bows twirled and stomped, it went on after she got back to Fran's place. The shuddering and wailing had subsided, replaced by the water torture. Sniff. Sigh. Sniff. Sigh. Sniff sniff sniff. Until Liz began to wonder just what in hell Fran was crying about, really.

"Come on," she said firmly. "Get a grip, old girl." Fran looked up at her, wide-eyed and wondering. Ida Lupino couldn't do a better job of it. "Come on," Liz repeated, reaching for some Jane Wyman herself. "Nothing you say or do is going to change what has happened. And you have those children to think of. I know it's going to be the hardest thing you've ever done but you're going to do it, Fran, because of the kids. You're going to get into the bathtub and have a really good howl, and when you get out of that tub, that's it. For them. You put on a brave face, you convince them their world hasn't come to an end, and you just . . . you *go on*, okay?"

"The best part of my life has ended," and the eyes brimmed.

"Yes, it has," rah rah Jane Wyman, "but your *life* isn't ended. You have those children to think of. Now come on, stiff upper lip and all that stuff. You can do it, Fran. I know you can."

Bravely, Fran rose from the tatty sofa, back stiff, head up, chin firm, and went to the door of the bathroom. She's going to stop at the door, a voice inside Liz's head told her, and turn and say something, something she thinks I will never forget. Fran stopped, turned, and in a voice hovering somewhere near the outer fringes of a whisper, she said, "Of course you're right. After all, those children are his immortality. And my future."

Sid wasn't easy at Fran's place, and Liz could understand that. She wasn't always easy at Fran's place, either. Especially after the fosters started arriving, and for sure after the gibbles showed up.

"She can talk all she wants about caring for the ones not as blessed as the rest of us," she told Sid, "but by me they're just wrecks, and most of them smell funny."

He stared at her.

"I mean you lift them out of the bath and they dangle like rag dolls, and you dry them off, put clean clothes on them, and they still smell like something you'd find at the bottom of the potato bin."

"Yeah?"

"I've got all I can do, I tell you, to put up with ordinary type kids. I don't see why Fran puts herself to all that bother for kids who probably wouldn't know if she ignored them most of the time."

"You don't like kids?"

"I just feel like I've had my fill, thank you."

"Well, at least we don't have to worry about that," he laughed. "One more area of agreement between two people who so far see eye to eye on most things."

They didn't, but why bother mentioning it? Sid had already talked of finding a place together, and Liz had told him no, but he seemed to think she meant not this week, maybe next week would be a better time. Sid had plans to buy acreage out past Maple Ridge and raise quarter horses.

"I wouldn't think there'd be much money in raising a fraction of a horse," she said, straight-faced. "Wouldn't you make more money if you raised the other three-quarters as well?"

"You mean you'd rather raise thoroughbreds?"

The man had some faults, there was no denying it. You can't explain what's funny. If he doesn't get the joke, he isn't going to get the joke.

Dave had no ambitions to raise quarter horses or any other kind of horses, he wanted to sink his money into an old school bus, convert it to a tour bus and go on the road in a serious way. "There's all those small towns all over the place," he said. "They've gotta be going out of their skulls for the chance to hear some good music."

"Yeah," Liz agreed, "but do they want to hear ours?"

"Come on, we're good."

"Not as good as you think we are," she said firmly. "We're barely mediocre. Sometimes we're down and out bad."

"Well, what can you expect when people come and go as if they had no loyalty to the band?"

"Why should they? What has the band done for them?"

"They get paid!"

"Hell, Dave, people get paid for sweeping the streets, that doesn't mean they owe their heart and soul to the broom. People have to work to get shoes for the baby, okay? And the bossy don't look kindly on someone saying I need every Friday and every Saturday off because I'm loyal to the band. You say something like that and it's the pink ticket."

"You can be a real bummer, you know."

"Okay, I'll say what you want to hear, it's no skin off my nose. We're great, Dave, and we're playing timeless music for a world that so far has not yet wakened up to appreciate us the way they should. That better? Because if it is, you're in trouble, fella, I just waved my arm and slung bullshit."

He started to laugh. "Sometimes I think you do that on purpose! You sit there and come out with exactly the opposite of what I'm saying, just to make sure I've thought 'er all through."

"Believe what you want, the rest of the world does. What do you think, Dave, the Big Break is just around the next turn in the road?"

"Yeah!" Dave shouted. "You're damn right! Otherwise, what do I do? Go home and look at my kids sleeping in their beds and think This is as good as it is ever going to get for them? I might just as well smother them! This isn't good enough, not for me and not for them either. Christ almighty, Lizzie, there's people sleeping in wrecked cars at the junkyard, standing in line for breakfast at the Mission, begging from people whose goddamn shoes cost more than the other poor buggers'll see in a year."

"So?" Liz yelled back. "What am I supposed to do about it? Did I cause it? Is it going to change if I work myself into a lather over it? Cut me some slack, Dave. It's one thing to have dreams and ambitions and it's another thing to refuse to face up to reality!"

"Ah, Lizzie, you're old before you're twenty-five!"

They kept on playing the same tunes to the same crowds. The faces changed, the bodies changed, the dance continued, in one legion hall or another, in one veterans-of-the-wars club or another, in one army, navy, air force vets' lounge or another. They did wedding receptions, they did family reunions, they did whatever the booking agent called to tell them about. Now that they had a booking agent, Dave didn't have to do all that stuff himself, which left him more time for his playing and more time for his family. And more time to work himself into a frenzy over the percentage the booking agent took, and what piss-poor service they got in return for their money.

"I had a phone call the other day," said Sid, who lay naked on the bed, a cigarette drooping from his mouth, ashes sprinkling onto Liz's sleeping bag. "From Andy Adler."

"Yeah?"

"You don't recognize the name?"

"Of course I recognize the name. I know the face, too. Andy Adler and the Westernaires. So?"

"So he's reorganizing his band. He's got a year and a half's work lined up, six days a week, all the way east to Newfoundland, then down the eastern seaboard of the good ol' Hew Hess Hay, across the bottom and back up the west coast through Cali-la-la-land."

"Nice work if you can get it," she laughed.

"We can get it."

"We? Who's we?"

"If you'd break down and answer your phone once in a while he'd'a talked to you directly, but you were never here so he phoned me. And what he wanted to know was, would we be willing to sign on the old dotted line."

"A year and a half? Jesus! That's a long time to be gone."

"It's good money. It's steady work. It's more than enough to get the acreage and a start on the quarter horses."

"I told you how I feel about that. Six dances a week? Who goes dancing on Tuesday night?"

"Not just dances. Performances, concerts, like that."

"God. I need time to think about this. I'd have to put my stuff in storage or give it to Fran or something. And I like this apartment."

"You live like a nun! You could put all your stuff in a beer box and still have room for enough beer to get drunk. And the city is full of apartments."

"Don't rush me, Sid. You've had some time to think about this and get excited, I've only just had it dumped on me," but already they knew she would say hell, yes, eh? Why not. "Where do we sleep? In the damn bus?"

"Probably there, and in motel rooms. Don't you worry, babe, I'll see to it you sleep the sleep of the pleasantly exhausted."

"You be careful, you might dislocate your elbow tryin' that hard to pat yourself on the back."

Liz walked to the window and looked out at the street below.

You'd think it was the Empire bloody State Building the way they carry on about it instead of what it really was, something you could stuff in your sock and still walk around comfortably. "I guess," she said softly, "it's better than a poke in the eye with a sharp stick. And it's work. And it's money."

When she told Dave, he looked at her as if she had just slit his throat. "Well my God, what can I say? I mean, it's going to be one helluva setback for us, but of course, if you've got a chance like that, we aren't going to stand in your way." He looked over at Sid, who was telling the rest of the band. "He's riding on your coattails, kiddo," he said flatly. "I know Andy Adler. I'll bet a dollar against the hole in my hat that he only phoned Sid to get a message to you. And I'll bet another dollar Sid made it sound like you two was a unit, take one you have to take the other."

"Aw, he wouldn't do that," Liz protested. "Anyway, it's not as if I'm *that* good."

"Go ahead," Dave sighed, "shit on your own head, why don't you. Listen, kid, didn't anyone ever tell you if you don't blow your own horn nobody else will blow it for you? Find out from Andy himself."

So she did. Without saying a word about it to Sid she phoned Andy Adler and asked if she could meet him to talk about the proposed tour.

"I'm glad you're going to be joining up with us," said Andy, signalling the waitress for a menu. "I've got a so-so fiddle player but he already knows he's gonna be playin' second and back-up for you. What I want, see, are some real fiddle pieces, a change of pace, a featured spot. People go nuts for 'Orange Blossom Special'," he grinned, "and you can't get a good freight train sound out of any other instrument, not even an electric guitar. And you do one hell of a freight train sound!"

"Maybe they'll put it on my tombstone," Liz laughed easily. "She did a great freight train."

"I'm going to lay it on the line with you, Lizzie. I'd'a gone direct to you if I'd'a been able to catch hold of you, but only because at the time I didn't know Sid was your manager. I won't make that mistake again, it was just I didn't know how things were."

"I think maybe neither of us is working with a full deck here," she answered. "Sid isn't my manager." Andy looked down at the tabletop and gnawed his bottom lip. "About all I have by way of anyone putting my collar on my neck and a chain on my collar is the business agent we all had with Dave's band. Sid and I are . . . well, more than friends but not much more, if you understand what I mean."

"Well, I'm not sure I do." The waitress brought the menus and they both took time out from what was starting to get a bit sticky to decide on hamburgers with the works and milk shakes rather than coffees.

"Maybe you could just sort of go back to where you were when you were dialling my phone but I didn't answer," she suggested. "So far any agreement you have is with Sid, not with me. I'd like to know for myself what it is I'm signing on for."

"Sid negotiated a package," Andy said, his eyes again on the tabletop.

"I didn't negotiate anything and Sid doesn't negotiate for me."

"Oh. Well. Okay," and he took a deep breath but didn't say anything.

"Listen, if what you want is Sid and not me, that's fine," she blurted.

And Andy laughed. "Turn that one on itself, Liz. Just turn it inside out and you'd be a lot closer to the truth. I want a first fiddle. I want a showpiece. I need a second-rate picker like I need an impacted wisdom tooth, okay? I called Sid to find out were you at his place or did he know where I could get hold of you. I'd'a called Dave but I didn't want to have him gnaw my ear off about stealing his fiddle player. And Sid, he said you were over to your cousin's place, and that he was your personal manager and it'd all have to go through him, anyway. He said him'n'you went as a package and nobody got one without the other."

"Fuck." Liz suddenly wished she was almost anywhere else in the world hearing almost anybody else say almost anything else. "Fuck," and her eyes started to well with tears.

"Listen, I'm sorry, Lizzie, I mean . . . well, I just put my foot in it here . . ."

"No." She shook her head and blinked rapidly. "No you didn't. Nothing of the sort. But I need a minute or two, so maybe we'll just talk about the weather until our burgers come, and then we'll eat the burgers and then maybe we'll get back to this and talk about you and your band and me and my fiddle and eye-to-eye, face-to-face we'll find out how much I can rip out of you. Seeing as how," she laughed softly, "you're in dire need of a showpiece who can do a great freight train."

"If I don't have to pay for a picker I don't need, I can offer my fiddler more than the last offer she heard."

The hamburger was amazingly good. Liz had thought it would taste like a shit sandwich, but she enjoyed it so much she ordered a second. By the time she and Andy shook hands across the red-with-silver-streaks arborite, her belly was pleasantly full, the lump was gone and she was feeling so good about everything she was starting to get excited.

"I'll phone Sid," Andy said gently.

"Yeah. I think I'll make myself scarce for a few hours until the dust has settled. Thanks, Andy."

"It's between him'n'me anyway. He's the one did the misrepresenting and I'm the one was sucked into believing it. I'm glad you phoned and set up this meeting. Now you go on home and pack your clothes."

To do that she was going to need a decent suitcase or two. You couldn't just pile into a tour bus with a bunch of shopping bags, sleeves and collars sticking out every which-a-way. But it doesn't have to be a brand new suitcase either, so go check the secondhand stores and pawnshops first.

And there it was, not in a pawnshop but in a little music shop that looked as if it used to be an alley between two buildings until someone put in a back and front wall and a door in the middle. There was nothing special about it at all. In fact, it was almost dowdy. The scrollwork was hand done, the finish on the wood was nothing like you'd get on a made-in-Japan new one. It hung quietly on the wall behind the counter making no claims for itself at all. But Liz went into the store to see it, not to see the shiny new ones or the special-reduced-price ones.

The storekeeper gave her a long, cool look, then reached out and took her left hand as if it belonged to him instead of her. He looked at her flattened fingertips, even dared to touch them, then brought the instrument down from the wall. Liz plucked the strings. Out of tune, and anyway they needed replacing, they were a million years old. She turned it upside down and tapped gently. Turned it right side up and looked through the scrollwork to see the post. On a yellowed piece of paper, in spidery handwriting, the faded brown ink proclaimed, "Recherche 1923 made by Orlando Scott, Victoria Canada."

"You got a set of new strings?" she asked quietly. "Extra fine, concert quality?"

"Sure," he nodded.

She took off the old strings and started putting on the new ones. "My uncle was a repairman," the storekeeper said. "One time he got asked if he could repair a Strad. So he got calipers and he made notes, everything, every damn sliver, even compared the propolis for stickiness and how it reacted to warmth. And then he started trying to duplicate. The thing was, you see, he wanted to do it with the wood available here on the coast. And most of what he built wasn't what he wanted. Oh, they were good enough fiddles as fiddles go, but they weren't what he wanted. Then, both at the same time, from the same wood, he made Recherche One and Recherche Two. This one," he smiled, "is Recherche One. The other one, Recherche Two, well, Rubinoff's got it."

"So why are you selling this one?"

"Because," he shrugged, "I've got probably two or three hundred others he made. I've got a bloody bank vault of them. And it's costing me vault rental every month! Anyway, I can't play 'em, I've got no kids to leave 'em to, and what's a fiddle if nobody makes music with it?"

"Yeah, but this isn't a fiddle," she corrected gently, "this is a violin," and they both laughed.

"We could have a long discussion about music, and snobbery, and who is and who is not the expert and what is and is not kulturni and all that stuff most people don't want to hear about, let alone talk about," he said hopefully.

"We could," Liz grinned, "or we could just nod like hell and agree with each other. Could I borrow a bow, sir?"

He went into a back room and came out with an old bow she knew immediately was rosewood and Russian horsehair. "Try this old thing," he winked.

"Hey, how'd you like to write me into your will? You bet I'll try this old thing!"

She did some finger stuff, nothing fancy, just getting the feel of the balance, just introducing herself to Recherche. Then she just sat holding her, smoking a cigarette, letting her feel the warmth of human flesh and blood. And then she stubbed out her cigarette, looked the old man in the eye and lifted Recherche into position. She snuggled in to her, rubbed her cheek briefly across the wood, lifted the bow and, without knowing what she was going to play, she went into "Hungarian Dance Number Five."

The old guy put his elbows on the counter, put his chin in his hands and closed his eyes. It was then Liz noticed the twisted fingers of both hands, what the arthritis had done to his knuckle joints, his wrists, even his fingernails. It made her feel so goddamn sad she wanted to cry, but there was a better way to howl at the moon, and a better thing to do for him than hand over some cheap pity, and Liz did it. When the last notes of Number Five had faded she went into "Humoresque," and then, to add some schmaltz and make him grin, she did "Golden Earrings," and practically brought out the gypsies, gold earrings, head scarves, stolen chickens and all.

"How do you do," he asked softly, "with jazz violin?"

"Oh, not too tacky." Liz did some probing to find out who he thought did what with jazz. "How are you on Appalachian fiddle music?" and his grin was the answer. "Yeah," she breathed, nodding.

"Do you drink tea?" he asked. She nodded. He went to the door and pulled down the blind, locked the door, then went into the back room for cups, kettle and teapot, and the whole time Liz played bits and snatches of whatever came into her fingers. When the tea was made she put Recherche aside and enjoyed her social visit with the old guy. They talked of this and that and nothing at all, and smiled at each other a lot.

"How much?" she asked.

"Three hundred fifty," he answered easily.

She nodded, then looked longingly at the bow. "And is that for sale, or do you know a good thing when you see it and figure to keep it for yourself?"

"Hmmph! That old thing," he said fondly. "Why I bet it isn't worth more than oh, six or seven thousand dollars."

"You know a good thing and you've decided to keep it for yourself," she shrugged. "If I had the six or seven thousand, I'd say wrap 'er and I'll take 'er with me, but . . . oh well."

They smiled at each other and finished their tea, then Liz brought out her chequebook.

He threw in the case. It wasn't the one Recherche deserved, and it probably wasn't the one Orlando Scott had originally set her in, but it was a good enough case as old battered ones go. "Will you be playing her often?" he asked hopefully. So Liz told him about Andy Adler and the Westernaires and about the year and a half rattling around in a converted bus. He grinned and nodded happily. "Maybe by the time you've finished you'll be able to play 'Orange Blossom Special'," he teased.

Sometimes a hint is as good as a kick up the arse. Liz picked up Recherche, then put her down, pretended to spit on the palms of her hands, wiggled the fingers of her right hand, picked up the fiddle and the bow and stood up. "Can't do this one sitting down," she admitted.

Well, the old guy might never play the fiddle again, but he did a fine job with the palms of his hands and the pads of his fingers against the polished surface of his counter. It was fun. It was the most fun she'd had in a long, long time and when she finally let the wail of the damn train drag on and on and on they both started laughing as if they'd known each other for all the time the earth had been developing. "You have a good tour," he said, picking up the cheque and reading the name printed on it. "You have a really good tour, Miss Elizabeth J. Harris."

"Liz," she corrected.

"Max Gibson," he said. "If you ever get around to making a tape of your practices or rehearsals, don't forget there's some of us might like to hear them."

She went back to a blessedly empty apartment, had a long soak in the tub down the hall, then got dressed and took her old fiddle off to play for the Buttons'n'Bows square dance club. Dave and his wife grinned and waved from the floor where they were having a great time dancing their feet off and working up a good sweat. They came over at the break to drink ice-cold lemonade and talk with her, and none of them broached the touchy subject. They all pretended everything was as fine as silk.

Sid didn't show up for several days, and when he did he left volumes and truckloads of stuff unsaid. Whatever he had or had not said to Andy, whatever promises had or had not been made, he was still part of the Westernaires, but as a backup strummer, not a picker. He didn't bring it up and Liz left it alone too.

She wondered why it was so easy to be totally honest with

people you barely knew, people with whom you did business of one kind or another, and so impossible to be honest with people you were supposed to know personally.

F I V E

Clancey had his plastic building blocks five rows up and Fran could see the tilt already. She supposed she could go over and point it out to him, but he had to learn something for himself, otherwise he would never learn to build his own castles, only hers. You wondered how old they had to be before they could see for themselves that a big gap or a misfit block in the second row would make the whole thing topple when they got to the eighth or ninth row. If no one ever pointed it out to them, would they go years and years trying to stack things on space?

Melinda brought her a roll of toilet paper and Fran ripped off a piece, gently wiped the sore little beak and top lip, then applied a soothing layer of ointment from the tube she kept in her apron pocket. She gave the crumpled wad to the little girl, who dropped it in the wastebasket carefully before going back to flop on the floor and stare at the TV with fever-heavy eyes.

Robbie would be back from school soon. Pray to the god who made oranges and apples he'd remember to pick up Nancy at kindergarten, otherwise there would be snivelling and accusations all through supper. Sometimes Fran wondered if Robbie did it on purpose, to prove he was needed, or to prove that Nancy was eminently forgettable. Anyway the frequency of "I forgot" had slowed noticeably since Fran started fining him a penny each time he forgot. She made him watch, too, while she unscrewed the cover of the hole in the pig's belly and took out the shiniest penny she could see. "Maybe next time you'll remember."

"Not *fair!*" Robbie thought everything was unfair unless it was done his way, to his benefit and satisfaction. "I hate you!"

"Well, I don't hate you," she said each time. "It's okay to be angry as long as you don't let your anger hurt someone else."

"I hate you, I said!"

"I know you said that. I heard you," and his shoulders would slump, his eyes fill with tears. It hurt him to find out his anger was so puny it didn't bother her one little bit. Might as well not bother yelling as have someone just smile. That would teach him to control his emotions himself, not depend on someone else.

Clancey's crazy-cat construct toppled. He stared, uncomprehending. Then he started all over again. He'd been stacking bricks and having them topple on him for two hours, and Fran wasn't sure if it was patience or idiocy. Either way it kept him quiet, and Clancey quiet was like a gift from God. Poor little Barney still had the marks on his forearm where Clancey had chomped him, each tooth clearly outlined. But there wasn't much to be done about it. Clancey didn't know enough to connect the pressure in his belly to the wetness in his pants, even though he didn't look different in any way. Oh well, takes all kinds, they say.

Fran went back to Liz's letter. Two pages in that straight-up-and-down loopy mess Liz called handwriting. And for all the real news in it, the so-called letter might as well be a tourist bureau handout.

Some people had luck, other people had to make their own. It hardly seemed fair. Liz would still be sitting in that dreary little rabbit hole reading *True Detective* and going to work at that smelly place to clean up after other people's sick and dying forgotten relatives if it hadn't been for Fran. You'd think a person would give some acknowledgement for that, but all Fran ever saw was the occasional scrawled letter from someplace where you could tell by its name there was nothing to fill the time but sit at the artificial-wood desk in the crummy motel and push the pen across the cheap paper.

One thing for sure, if Fran had been given the breaks and chances Liz had been given, Fran wouldn't be rattling around in some silver and blue bullet of a bus playing caterwauling old hayburner ditties. There was no excuse for it – Liz could play real music. If a person could play "Billy Fogarty's Jig," couldn't she play with a symphony? And who in hell was this Billy Fogarty, that someone named a jig after him? You'd think a person would rather put on a pale blue evening gown and travel by cab to the symphonic, than pull on jeans and a plain blue shirt and ride in a bus to a barn.

Well, Liz never did have much in the way of imagination. And it wasn't fair at all that the old man had given Liz the family fiddle because Liz wasn't the oldest grandchild, Fran was, and it wasn't Fran's fault if the old man hated Jo-Beth so badly, for whatever unfounded reason. One thing for sure, if Fran had been the one to get that little fiddle, she would have made sure she took more than half a dozen lessons on it! All Liz ever did was what she was told to do anyway, and when Aunt Wilma quit sending Liz off down the street to her music class, that was it, Liz quit going. And never mind the BS and heifer dust about how Liz had taken that thing off where she could play it without having people eavesdropping, because she never had, so there! Just luck. Just blind luck and her too thick to appreciate it.

Anyway, wherever Markham, Ontario was, it was snowing there, and that was the biggest piece of news in Liz's letter. Tucked in with it was her schedule for the next two months and the address you could send stuff to and it would get to the band. Some blatant hint that was. Once the kids were in bed and settled, maybe Fran would sit down and write a long, long letter, a real one, with some real news, set an example.

Robbie came home with Nancy in tow, and they changed from school clothes to play clothes, then went down to the basement where Fran had hung some small swings from big screw-eyes set into the beams. You couldn't send them out to play in the backyard in rainy weather, they just came in with hands blue, noses running and clothes so wet you got choked by the smell of drying wool.

Their noise and clatter disturbed Jerry, and Fran could hear him moving around in the bedroom. She heaved herself off the sofa and went to the kitchen to start the kettle for his coffee. Then she went to the freezer, brought out two huge foil-covered glass casseroles and put them on the countertop. The advertising said you could whip them right from the freezer to the hot oven but

Fran couldn't bring herself to trust that, they'd tell you anything to get you to buy something. She turned on the oven, checked the timer, then went and got the mugs and the Yuban instant. It was Jerry's favourite kind, and the man was certainly entitled to have his favourite kind. He worked hard for his pay and never complained about the noise the kids made or anything.

There'd been some upset, of course. The welfare regulations were pretty strict and pretty clear, and the way they had it set up a person had little choice but to stretch the truth or evade it all together. Why should a man be expected to feed another man's kids just because that man is in love? But if Jerry moved in, the welfare allowance for Brandy was cut off. Fran could see why they'd cut hers off, but why cut off Brandy's? At least they hadn't dared take away the money for Robbie and Nancy, that would have been stretching it just a bit too far and they knew it. If they did that, they could just pack up the other kids and find some other place for them, and how many other places could you find for kids so dim they couldn't stack building blocks?

"Hi, darling," she smiled.

"Hello, babe," he yawned. "Jesus, that kid's got one helluva cold, eh?"

"She always gets like that. Even when she's well, she isn't. And just let one of the others bring a germ into the house and guess who's half packed in with it. How are you feeling?"

"Oh, you know, sleepy. A couple of cups of coffee'll fix that. Any mail?"

"My cousin, you know, the one I told you was on tour? The letter's on the sofa if you want to read it."

"No, thanks." He sat down and reached for a mug of coffee.

"Your wife phoned."

"Oh, God. Not yet. Jesus," and he closed his eyes, yawned again, and shook his head. "That fuckin' woman!"

"Easy on the language," she said automatically, "little pitchers have big ears."

"Sorry. What does she want this time? Let me guess. Money."

"Clever boy!" Fran put the casseroles in the oven, sat down with her own coffee and smiled across the table at him.

"What did she say?"

"She said you haven't signed the papers for the house. She said if you don't sign it over to her, her father's lawyer won't release the money. Then she said if the money doesn't get released so she can pay off the mortgage and have the house in her name, she's going to go to court for permission to sell the house and confiscate your share of it and buy another one, in her name only. And she said if she has to go to all that carry-on to get things straightened out, she'll go back to court and ask for spousal allowance as well as child support."

"What did you say?"

Fran sipped her coffee. "I said I'd tell you what she said."

"What else?"

"She said your child maintenance cheque was NSF."

"Oh, God." But he didn't sound upset. "I'll go down tomorrow and fix it up."

"You can't go down tomorrow," she laughed softly. "You won't even be here tomorrow, remember?"

"Oh, right. Well, I'll figure something out. Anything else?"

"Just her usual kind regards and gentle messages."

"Burn your ear?"

"No, I just pretend I'm watching a very bad movie. Anyway, sticks and stones will break my bones but names will never hurt me."

"Like to slit her goddamn throat."

"It's not worth it. You might ruin a perfectly good knife."

"I forgot about the trip starting tonight. Must be going as dotty as hell. How could a person forget a thing like that?"

"Because you'd rather not go. Because you'd rather stay home. Because you know I'm going to miss you terribly."

"Yeah," he nodded. "And probably because I just woke up and my brain isn't in gear yet," and he nudged his mug suggestively. Fran got up, plugged in the kettle and took the jar of coffee from the shelf. She heard the building blocks hit the floor again. Clancey whimpered.

"What's wrong with him?" Jerry asked.

"It's his hand-eye co-ordination. He can't get them piled up right, so a few bad rows and the whole thing topples."

"Poor little retard."

"If he's a retard . . . who's a tard?" she teased.

"I guess the tards are only half as witless as Clancey is, and he got tarded twice, re-tarded, and that's why he's so fuckin' dumb."

"Uh uh, no f-word in the house. Next thing you know one of the kids will be saying it and we'll have the school on our backs."

"You sound like my mother."

"Sometimes," she winked, "I feel like your mother. You have got to get this mess straightened out with your wife, dear. She can make things very nasty for you."

"Up her nose."

"No, it will be up *your* nose if she gets nasty. She can fix it so your paycheque doesn't even get to you until after she's got her money – not just the child maintenance, but all the rest of what she's claiming, too. And if you look at that paper there by the sugar bowl you'll see just how much that would leave you every month. Not even cigarette money."

"What do you think I should do?"

"I think you should have your paycheque signed into the bank, into my account, and I'll see to the budgeting, that's what I think."

"Okay," he nodded.

"I'll make sure she gets her payments." She put his coffee in front of him, then scratched gently at the mop of curls on his head. "And I think it's only fair that your overtime money be yours, no questions asked, no answers expected."

"Yeah?" He sipped, and nodded. "Whatever. It bores me numb. I still wish she'd trip on her lip and break her f-word neck."

"Now, now, you can't blame her. She's worried about her kids. Even an alley cat fights for her kittens. She's just doing what comes naturally."

"She's a bitch."

"She's the mother of your children."

"How would I know for sure?"

"Jerry!" Fran laughed. "What an awful thing to say."

She fed Clancey and Melinda while Jerry had his bath and shaved. Then, with those two fed, full and content, she set the children's table and put out supper for Robbie, Nancy, Brandy, Suzette and Lyle. "No fighting, no arguing and no snitching other people's juices, okay?" she said. They laughed, and started eating. She could probably sell tickets to the event. You'd think they hadn't had a bite in days!

While the Fear-Inspiring Five were eating she set the table for herself and Jerry and put the kettle on for tea. He came out of the bathroom with his face tight and shiny from the safety razor. "Smells good," he grinned widely, and Fran felt her face flush warm. He was so appreciative! His ex-wife must have been the world's worst cook the way Jerry praised Fran's cooking. It did her heart good to hear the approval in his voice.

"Finished, Mom!" Lyle piped. "Is there more?"

"There's always more, Lyle," she answered, and went to get his plate. Made you wonder where this kid packed it all away, he could eat and eat and eat until you were sure the next bite would split him down the midline and then he'd still have room for dessert. They had said he needed it, he burned it all up with his hyperactivity and nervous energy. Just keep giving it to him, sooner or later he'll begin to trust that there will always be more.

She filled Lyle's plate, checked to see if anyone else wanted anything, then hurried back to serve Jerry his dinner. It was nice, the kids all loved lasagna and they were so busy with their own suppers she actually had time to sit down and eat her own.

"Mmmm," Jerry said. "Real good, hon. Real good."

"I'm glad you like it." She didn't tell him her little trick with the sauce, making it up ahead of time and letting it sit for three days. Fran never made one of anything. If she was going to make something, well, you might as well make ten as one, it doesn't take much more time. Spaghetti sauce has to cook for three hours, that's all there is to it, so you might just as well make two gallons as two quarts. And if you're going to get out the great big pot to cook the lasagna, why cook up one package when you can do five or six? The same with chicken or stew or anything else, if you're going to do it, do lots and freeze it up in trays. Then, if anything should happen, touch wood God forbid, you're not caught short.

When Jerry was full she cleared away the plates and got out the dessert. She didn't eat it herself, as she was once again fighting the old battle of the bulge. It happened in her seventh month, set the clock on it, go to bed at night at the end of your sixth month and the next morning you get up twice the size you were when you went to bed. Oh well, time enough for dessert once this one is here and the weight has gone.

Jerry was such a dear. How many other men would roll up their sleeves and lift little ones out of the bathtub like that! She was getting too thick around the middle to bend over easily, and some of them still couldn't get in and out by themselves. You never knew when a little foot was going to slither on the wet porcelain and my heavens it wouldn't take much of a bump against the toilet to do some serious damage. Head injuries were awful, make your stomach knot up just to think of what all could go wrong.

Then they were in bed, settled down, prayers all recited and the lights out, except for Mickey Mouse in the hallway to help them on their way to the bathroom if they needed to go. And there was even time for some adult conversation before Jerry had to get his little blue plastic satchel with the clean clothes she'd packed for him, kiss her cheek and pat her bum, then drive off down to the yard and check out his International Harvester Load-Star – the Cornbinder, he called it. All she had to do for the next four days was keep the show on the road until he got back home again.

Funny, when he was home she was in bed by ten, fell asleep immediately and stayed that way until at least eight in the morning. Some mornings Robbie had to come in and wake her up. They could dress themselves and get their own cereal, and their lunches were already packed and set out for them on the counter, but they did like to see her before they headed off to conquer their little worlds, and she always got up and made sure everything was as it ought to be, with hair brushed and tidy and socks matching. She knew all too well what it felt like to go off to school without seeing an adult soul. Made you wonder if the world was still stuck in its orbit or if you were all flying off on a tangent on the way to the sun, where you'd be burned to ash.

But let Jerry go out of the house for a night and do you think she could relax and get to sleep? Not on your life! It made Fran so impatient with herself. She hadn't been like that before Jerry came into her life, why be like that now? Even after the horrible twist of fate that took Ted from her, when she was on her own and determined to keep the family together as a memorial to him, she'd been able to sleep with no problem. Then Jerry came, and who knew what happened. All of a sudden, the minute she knew he was gone for the entire night, she couldn't get to sleep, and if she did she couldn't stay asleep. All it took was one kid to get out of bed and head down the hallway and she was wide awake, sitting up in bed, eyes open, heart pounding, asking "Who's that?" as if Jack the Ripper would answer, "It is I, Jack, come to cut you into little cubes." If Jack had half the sense he must have had, never being caught and all, he'd answer, "Just me, Mom. Gotta pee," and there'd be no worries at all.

So she filled her nights with all the things she didn't want to do on those precious days when Jerry was home. Made mountains of food and froze it so she wouldn't disturb him with the clatter of pots and pans or the rattle of spatulas, baked cake after cake, pie after pie, turned out several dozen cupcakes or muffins each night and froze them in big plastic bags, for later. She had no trouble keeping herself occupied. Here it was almost time to start getting the garden started again, and they still had some vegetables frozen or canned from the last one. Enough pickles here to put Heinz out of business. You'd be amazed how much money a person can save with a bit of ground and a package of zucchini seeds. And if all else failed and she couldn't jam another thing into the freezer, she could spend her nights doing what that ingrate Liz couldn't quite manage: keep the family informed.

Family is all you have in the world, after all. If you don't have family you don't have anything.

Fran got out the big pad of lined paper and the good ballpoint, black with the silver cap. She set it on the table, made herself a pot of tea, tuned the radio to the all-night soft rock station and settled herself on the most comfortable chair.

Dear Jo-Beth:
Hello, my sweet little sisterling. How is everything with you? I hope your life is as full and as happy as mine is, and that you're feeling more yourself now that the exams are behind you and the pressure has lessened. I'm sure you did well, you have a fine mind and the added benefit of knowing you have a loving family – two loving families, actually – which must give you a strong sense of security. I'm sure your other family feels as we do, that we know you are capable of great things but we do not have our expectations of what those things ought to be. If you don't want to go to nursing school, don't go. If you don't want to go to college and get a diploma, then by all means don't do that. Your happiness is most important. Mind you, there are times, I have to be honest and

admit it, when I almost regret my own decision *not* to go to vet school. After all, it would have given me what I needed to, for example, open a small pet clinic right here, although I have to be reasonable about that, when would I find the time? Maybe instead of vet school I should have taken psychology or something, certainly with all these poor little underprivileged who live here now I could use some training there. Whatever else, we can thank God in Heaven that our dear mother never abandoned us! Yes, we wound up fosters but you can't blame a woman for dying, how was she to know about pneumonia or whatever it was, they were never very clear on that.

My dear brother:

You must be so excited about having your own car! Of course I worry, who wouldn't, there are so many idiots out there on the road, just ask someone who knows firsthand the kind of heartache which can be caused by someone else's lack of attention, but I'm sure you won't be one of those people who do things like the fool who nearly went into the side of Ted's car and who was, when all is said and done, responsible for the sudden braking which caused the skid that ended the happiest time of my life. But enough of *that!* I tell myself no more grief, I have a new life, and a wonderful husband who can't do enough for us all. And a brother who has not only finished his Young Drivers course but has a second family that loves him so much they gave him a car. You are so lucky. Many others would envy you. I might envy you myself if life hadn't been so kind to me. We have been blessed, you know.

The news around here is very quiet, the way I like it. Jerry is working his usual long hard hours and when he's not driving he's busy here at home. He's been making flower boxes for the windows and planning a real show of colour out front. We moved the children's swings, etc. to the side yard so I can get the planned beds all spaded and ready for this absolute mountain of bulbs the postman is going to deliver soon. He'll probably have to rent a truck to get them all here!

Are you still busy with your little boats and things? It must be nice to have a hobby which pays for itself. I guess tourists really need something to do once they've driven all those miles to get somewhere and it's nice that you recognized that and decided to capitalize on it.

Dear Aunt Wilma:

Hello, it's your loyal niece here, burning the midnight oil to make sure you're kept up to date on the doings and goings-on of that peripatetic cousin of mine! Yes, I got a letter from Lizzie today. Well, not so much what you or I would call a letter, it's another of those scribbled hasti-notes which Lizzie seems determined to specialize in, but it's the thought that counts, isn't it? She's in Ontario, sounds as if they are practically snowed in, and I do worry about the driving conditions and that ugly old bus they insist on keeping, and I'm not sure anything good can be said of the roads or highways (if they even have them) in any place called Markham. Would you buy a used car from someone in "Markham"? No, nor me, either.

Anyway, Lizzie enclosed the schedule again, and I've copied it for you so you can write to her, just in case she didn't think to send you one.

I'm feeling well, a bit tired, but that's only to be expected, isn't it. My husband Jerry is doing everything he can to take most of the load off me and the children seem to understand that Mommy can't always be right there for them for everything. They help out, too, it's really heartwarming to see them being such brave little soldiers. The doctor says everything is just fine, and I'm taking my vitamins so don't give me that lecture, please, I know you worry and I know you're concerned, and I know it's only because you love me. And I love you which is why I try not to cause you any worry of any kind. You don't see me rattling around in a rustbucket ha ha that's a joke, dear, I'm so big now I'd never fit in the bus. In fact they might want to fasten the licence plate to my backside, it's that old water retention problem again, but I've cut out salt and what more can you do? I told the doctor not to scare me with those toxemia stories. Told him that since I'm not sure I can spell it, I'm not going to get it! Another joke, just to keep us all from getting grey hair, right?

My dear Liz:

So nice to get a letter from you. Finally. Lecture number one right here, and it will be followed by lectures two and three, you know the ones, I work my fingers to the bone and what thanks do I get . . . don't you have any real consideration for anyone else . . . it only takes a minute or two to keep in touch . . . and the one What about your poor mother she was in labour for hours just to give life to you . . .

Duty done. I can write Aunt Wilma and honestly tell her that I sounded off at you for not doing a better job of keeping her informed. You know how she worries and you know life with your dearly beloved and much respected father is not exactly easy.

Have you heard from or written to your brother Bill? Well, in case you haven't, and in case Aunt Wilma hasn't wanted to say anything, the news is that he's doing much better. His eye has healed and the medical board gave him permission to start boxing again, turns out it was only the eyebrow and eyelid and not the retina or lens or whatever it was they first thought. So he's at it again, punching things in preparation for punching people. His girlfriend had another baby, a girl this time, they're calling her Felicia, which I personally think sounds like something you'd hear on afternoon TV but it takes all kinds, as they say. Little Billy is almost three, growing like a weed and as hyper as ever. Young Gavin is still not married, of course, why should he buy a cow when he gets all his milk, cheese and yogurt for free? Your dad is still chewing nails and spitting tacks because Gavin's son is called Neal, not Gowan. Billy told your dad right out that if Gavin is ever going to follow the old family tradition of Gavin-Gowan-Gavin-Gowan ad nauseam ad infinitum he'll get a dog, call it Gowan and then shoot it in the head. Your dad had another fit about that but you know Billy, he only does it to get a rise out of him.

I don't know how you can stand the life you've been stuck with, really I don't. Nothing but motels and restaurants and all those people smoking cigarettes and drinking beer, on and on and on. Listen, any time you get to the point where you can't stomach it any more you just tell them to go out in the garden and eat worms, and come stay with me, there's always a bed here for you.

Everything here is as wonderful as it can be. We're hoping to get Jerry's kids for the spring break, it's none too soon
if you ask me, they deserve the chance to get to know their
father, who adores them, and they certainly deserve to see
some kind of normal family life. What they have to put up
with is enough to break your heart into little pieces. I don't
care what anyone says, it isn't natural for a mother to work
all the time and leave the children with paid help, especially
when sooner or later the kids will find out it wasn't even the
mother who paid the help! Her family has too much money
and she's spoiled rotten but there I go, I get so upset about
those poor little rich kids of his. We both feel it will do them
a lot of good to see a normal family and to learn that the
world is full of those who need just a little bit of a boost up
out of the mess into which they were born.

And I'm waiting for this next little precious miracle, I can
hardly wait to see him-or-her. We haven't decided on a name,
I would like to call "him" Jerry Junior but there already is one,
so that's out. But Geraldine is so old-fashioned and clunky!
"Gerri" doesn't offend either of us if it's a girl. And I guess we
could always fall back on good old "Scott" if it's a boy
although he never was my real father, but still he did very
well by us for the time God loaned him to us. And if something intervened and we no longer had him, well, I'm sure it
wasn't because he wanted it that way.

Fran managed to arrange things so she could get over to visit
Wilma and Gowan for a few days before her due date. Jerry rented a station wagon and helped pile all the kids in the back –
tards, re-tards and all – then he drove them to the ferry and even
helped with the looking after.

Wilma had the downstairs bedrooms ready, and Jerry stayed
long enough for a cup of tea and a sandwich, then headed back
on the afternoon sailing to return the car and go collect his own
kids in the sports car. That silly sardine tin was a pain, not a con-
venience, but he loved it and heaven knew he worked hard
enough he was entitled to some pleasures.

It was nice for Fran to sit with her feet up for a change. Wilma
fussed over the kids as if they were her grandchildren, although
she did have some trouble with the fact that Clancey still needed

diapers and you had to keep remembering to put lots of vaseline on his chin so his constant drooling didn't lift the skin off. Gowan, well, you'd hardly know this was the one who had been so stern and strict with his own children. He just played and played away as if he'd been waiting all his life for a chance to get down on his knees with marbles and matchbox cars.

"Too bad Jerry couldn't have spent more time with us," Aunt Wilma said. "It would be nice to get to know him."

"I know. It's a shame. It's just he has so many demands on his time, you wouldn't believe how busy they keep him, and it just about sends him into fits when he has to miss even a few hours of the time he's got with his own children! We wanted them for the holidays but . . ." Fran sighed, "oh well, given time any fire will eventually burn itself out, but the waiting is hard, I tell you."

"Messy, was it?"

"Well, the wife's father had to get into it, too. Really, you'd think people would learn to leave well enough alone. But no, Mister Moneybags had his own ideas! I just decided listen, this is *not* my business, I am *not* going to do what her parents are doing, I have no reason to get into any fights with anyone about anything," and she folded her hands over her belly and smiled.

Wilma nodded and watched the little spastic one trying to roll over and sit up. "Should I help him?"

"No." Fran shook her head firmly. "The only way he can learn is by trying, trying, trying. Anyway, he doesn't really mind. Oh, he gets frustrated sometimes, but I go to him as soon as he starts to yell."

"I don't know how you do it, I'm sure."

"Sometimes I don't either, but . . . we can't just throw them away, can we?"

"And Jo-Beth?"

"Well, I suppose she's fine. I hope she's fine. It's hard to tell when they don't write, isn't it? But if the space between notes gets too long I just up and phone and never mind the long distance charges! She's still in school, and I think she'll make it this year, although grade eight was hard as I remember it. And Scotty, well, he's in grade eleven this year and they've let him get his driver's licence, which I think was a big mistake, made worse by the fact, can you believe it, they bought him his own car? I mean my God, haven't they heard about teenagers and cars!"

"I hope he's more level-headed than most, that's all I can say. And you, dear?"

"Oh, Aunt Wilma, life is wonderful. I am so lucky! My life is just so full and so rich and so jam-packed with love, I can hardly believe my luck sometimes."

The living room looked like a holy shrine or something. One entire wall was covered with pictures. Old Gavin looking like some religious leader, a patriarch of the old school, gazing into the camera as if daring it to take anything but the world's best portrait. Billy in his jeans and tee shirt leaning on the fence laughing, Billy in his boxing trunks and gloves posing as if ready to fight even though you could tell he was in a photo studio miles from the ring, Billy in the ring, actually fighting, all sweaty and with a big lump on his nose, Billy in his bathrobe or whatever they call it, hands up in victory sign with some official declaring him the winner, Gavin in his graduation suit with a white carnation in his buttonhole, Gavin and some girl on their way to the grad dance, Gavin with his suitcases going off to radio announcer school, Gavin laughing like a fool with a microphone hanging in front of his face. And then Louise. My heavens, Louise! In her cheerleader outfit, in her grad gown, in her student nurse's outfit but with no cap, then in uniform with the cap, another in uniform with a cap that had a stripe on it, then another with two stripes and a pin on her lapel, and still another of her at someone's bedside fussing with a drip going into their arm. And Lizzie, good old Lizzie, you'd think she was the Child of the Holy Virgin herself, with violins and without them, on stage and off, so many photographs it was a relief to the eyes to look at the next wall where there was nothing at all, just space, probably waiting for more photographs. And the third wall already started, only this rogues' gallery was for grandchildren. You'd think people wouldn't be bragging about the fact their sons were barely out of training pants before they were acting like tomcats! And neither of them married. Just no responsibility at all, not the least bit interested in commitment of any kind. Always checking a room before they went in it to make sure there were plenty of ways out again.

"What do you hear from Auntie Phoebe?" she asked. Wilma talked about Phoebe and her kids and the new car and the travel agency and how well Phoebe looked, why you'd hardly know she was in her mid-fifties, except the hair was starting to seem a bit dry, probably all that bleaching, it couldn't be good for your scalp, just think what it can do to a pair of jeans if it spills on them!

But you had to take it with a grain of salt. Aunt Wilma sometimes was inclined to find fault no matter what, as long as it wasn't her own precious children were the subject of conversation. *They* could do no wrong! Not even Billy and what the sports announcers called his highly developed killer instinct. Hurricane Harris, they called him. Anyone could batter someone else senseless. And wasn't it perfectly obvious that every punch Billy threw was actually aimed at Gowan's head? Couldn't they all see that? There's no trick to being too vicious and no great bravery in not knowing when you've been hurt. So there to that.

Liz Harris amazed everyone when she showed up with her three suitcases and two violins and announced she was off the road for a while. Nobody expected her to really settle down, nobody expected her to do anything other than take a month or two holiday.

And there she was, snugged in like a flea in a shag rug. Oh, she still played her fiddle, but not for money and seldom when anyone else was around, although with a bit of persuasion she'd bring it out for someone's birthday.

And after all that travel, meeting people from all over the continent who were out doing things, to think she'd come home, get herself a little three-room apartment the same as anyone else she'd gone to school with, and the next thing you know she's seen around town with a big hunk of a pulp worker who probably spent his days poking a long stick through a hole to keep the glup sliding down the chute. And did he play the guitar or the fiddle or even the tablespoons, for that matter? He did not. In fact, if you got any closer to tone deaf than he was, you'd never hear a thing but noise.

But there was Liz, burrowed right in. Her and Wotzisname there. Willard? William? Wilburt? No, by God, Bert, that's his name. Big good-lookin' sucker with broad shoulders and a smile that was free advertising for every dentist in town. Part something from the looks of him, hard to tell what, though, maybe just black

Irish but you never know with them Harrises, as apt as not to be any damn thing you could put name to and none of them caring a bit.

Liz could almost hear it. Well, let them talk. If they were gossiping about her, they were leaving her friends alone, and she had nothing to hide or to be ashamed of anyway.

She and Bert lived together six months or so before she would agree to get married. "I don't want to sound mean," she said over and over again, "but you don't know a person until you've lived with them through the rainy season. If you aren't at each other's throats after the monsoons, you'll make it through anything."

Bert was easy enough to live with. Didn't expect to be waited on hand and foot, anyway, and my God in heaven rent space on a billboard, the man knew how to put his own clothes in the hamper. Sid had never figured that one out, nor Andy either.

"I'll do your washing when I do mine," she told him, "but if you want something ironed you might wind up doing it yourself. And if I'm the only one in the house smart enough to figure out how to clean the toilet, I'd just as soon be the only one in the house, okay?"

"I don't know where you got all these ideas, Liz," he said. "I only want to marry you, I don't want to sell you into bondage."

So they got married. She told Wilma they wanted a small wedding, just the close and immediate family, no big deal. "And I mean it, Momma," she warned. "No white dress, no veil, no Aztec sacrifice-of-the-virgin community blow-out. We're having a civil ceremony and that is *all*, no preacher, no prayers, no church. And if we had our way there'd be no reception either, but I know you're going to kick up sand about that."

"Well, you have to have your grandparents."

"Okay."

"And your brothers and sister have got to be there."

"Okay."

"And Fran and her family."

"Oh shit. Okay."

"And Auntie Phoebe, and –"

"That's it, Momma, really."

"You can't ask your cousin Fran and not ask your cousin –"

"Momma! Let's scratch Fran if it means the whole clanjamfrie has to come! We don't need five hundred people!"

"Now Liz, you stop that. I don't know why you go out of your way to be so bloody-minded about things. Of course your aunts and uncles are coming. And your cousins. Why be rude about it?"

"Because if I'm not rude you'll go hog wild. All you need for a wedding is the bride and groom and two witnesses! Does anybody *care* that I don't want –"

"No," Wilma snapped, "nobody cares one little bit. Left on your own you'd probably forgo the whole thing and sneak off in the middle of the night, I know you!"

It took three enormous temper tantrums for Liz to keep the thing reduced to eighty people in the Arbutus Room in the basement of the Colony Motor Inn. Or, as the drip in the suit kept calling it, the ray-de-show-say.

Eighty people. Forty little thank-you-so-much cards to be signed, put in envelopes and mailed out. Five coffee pots. More goddamn crystal jugs and glasses than you could shake a stick at. Vases, my Christ you could open a flower shop with the vases. And big plates. Platters, whatever they called them. Cake dishes. All carefully wrapped back up in the blue boxes they'd come in, then stacked in bigger boxes with lots of crumpled-up newspaper and stored in the basement, out of the way, and if the house ever caught fire just see who risked their life to take the buggers outside, too!

And all of them looking around trying to catch a glimpse of Bert's family. Bert, who didn't have a family, ha ha, not within a thousand miles, so there.

"Maybe I should send invitations to the Manitoba Children's Aid Society," he teased.

"Sure," she agreed, "and the Westernaires and every audience we ever had. Why not just invite the whole damn world?"

"We can sneak off in the middle of the night, you know. Get the jump on them."

"Yeah, and come back to find them all sitting here in our living room, waiting to have the party anyway."

Gowan and young Gavin got into it, predictably enough. After all, there was enough alcohol there to float the HMCS *Magnificent*. But at least it happened after she and Bert had left and they only had to hear about it later, after they came back from their trip to Portland.

"If it wasn't in the States," she told Wilma, "I'd move there tomorrow. It's gorgeous, really, you should go down and take a look for yourself. But no way I'm living down *there*, not with that government, doesn't matter which party they elect, they get the same industrial-military strange bedfellows imperialist expansionism."

"Whatever are you talking about?"

"War war war, all the time war, if they aren't blowing one little country to shit they're invading another and setting up a puppet dictator."

"Why work yourself into a sweat about things you can't change? Anyway, someone has to do something to stop the communists, otherwise who knows what will happen."

"What difference will it make to you whose flag flutters in front of the courthouse? You'll still pay too much taxes for the little bit they hand out, you'll still have to obey the law, and the police will still be the ones with guns."

"If they take over, those ideas of yours won't be safe to hold and how will you feel then without the freedom of speech?"

"What good is freedom of speech if nothing you do or say can change things? Is it freedom when nobody is paying any attention? Look at her, see, over there in ring number two, the one who's saying what awful bloodsuckers we are, that's democracy folks, she has the right to say any silly thing she wants because we're benevolent. And the show goes on!"

"Whatever *are* you talking about, Liz?"

"Nothing, Momma."

"Why don't you use all that energy to find out who Bert's family is?"

"I've told you time and again, he doesn't have one."

"Oh pooh, Liz, everybody – *everybody* – has family. Might not know who they are but they're there all the same."

"Not when you've been left in a garbage can, Momma. You don't have family when the only reason you're alive is that the guy who collected the trash got there early and heard you crying. An hour later Bert would have been too cold to cry and he'd have wound up on the dump with a ton of garbage on top to smother him."

"Oh, Liz, stop telling that tall tale."

"It's true."

"How could you marry him, knowing nothing about his family?" Wilma blurted.

Liz stared a long, long time, then started to laugh. "You knew Dad's family. You knew about them back two or three generations, even back in the old country, for heaven's sake. And you married him."

"It's not the same thing at all!"

"No. It never is the same thing, is it?"

Wilma didn't believe the story about the garbage can. Nobody did, it was too much like the story of the cabbage leaf, or the pile of seaweed on the beach. After a while they stopped trying to find out the "truth," which was funny because Bert really *had* been left in a dumpster behind a Chinese restaurant, and he *had* been crying when the crew came to empty it. The swamper thought he heard a litter of kittens, looked in and saw a newborn boy, yelled with shock and rescued him. But Liz's family said that didn't happen in real life, that Bert must have needed to separate himself from his own people. In any event, whatever was in his past, he was nice enough to Liz and that had to count for something.

It seemed like no time at all before there were three little kids in the picture. Martine, the firstborn, was so much like Bert it made you laugh to see them together, and Reba, born a year later, was almost like a twin, just shorter and slighter. The youngest, Ronnie, was a good mix of the two, not as dark as Bert but much darker than Liz, showing every sign of being as tall as she was but heavier, more like his dad.

"I think your father is disappointed," Wilma told Liz when Ronnie was born. "He would have liked it if you'd called the baby Gowan."

"Tell him to fall on his lip."

"Liz! That's awful!"

"Momma, that name is awful, that's what's awful," and then, so fast and so slick you hardly knew it had been done to you, "have you seen him? Isn't he just about the funniest looking little face you ever saw? Like a monkey, without hair."

"He's beautiful! He's just beautiful!"

And he was. They all were. Healthy, happy, no snivelling or grizzling or whining, they just puttered through each day as if all they would ever have to do was eat, sleep, grow and laugh.

When Louise got married she didn't drag her heels through it, she let them throw exactly the wingding Liz had flat-out refused.

But then she and her husband moved to Saanich, and you didn't just hop the bus and drive down there whenever the idea took hold. Once in a while they came up of a Friday night and stayed over until Sunday morning, but like as not Liz would refuse to change her own plans. Sometimes Fran would come over with her family but you needed a fair bit of warning to arrange that, her family being what it was. One afternoon the poor little spastic-y one choked on something, and by the time Fran got him to hospital he had been oxygen-deprived for so long he never did recover and had to be moved to Woodlands. Fran cried and cried as if some big part of her was being taken out there, too. And the kid who always seemed to have a cold or something was diagnosed with some rare allergy and she was in hospital as much as she was out. Then there was the one played with matches and nearly burned the house down so often the fire insurance got cancelled so the Welfare itself had to take out a new policy. And several others who wouldn't eat or wouldn't stop eating or got sent home from playschool for playing sex games with other five-year-olds. How Fran could just keep smiling smiling smiling was a marvel and a mystery.

"You might think these little things are nothing but hard work and trouble," she said, looking past several concerned people to the far wall and focussing her gaze there, "but they are no different from any child. Yes, some of them look unpleasant or have bits and snippets missing, but don't we always say beauty is only skin deep? Under that we're all as ugly as the floor of a slaughterhouse! And yes, some of them do some very strange things, but nothing stranger than what goes on in every house in this country. Every house."

Which was ridiculous, but the poor girl was so overworked and so worried you had to just give her the benefit of the doubt.

They gave Liz the benefit of the doubt, too. Whatever had happened to send her back to the Island couldn't have been too awful, because the police weren't involved and it never hit the scandal sheets. Then again, you don't walk away from a career in show business for no reason at all. But the answers you got if you asked about it were just too silly to be believed.

"I got tired of being tired."

"After a while the inside of a bus starts to look like a jail cell."

"When you work until three in the morning and don't get to

sleep until six, you wind up snoring through the best part of the day and by the time you open your eyes it's getting dark again. So for all we travelled everywhere I didn't get to see much."

"I wanted to come home."

"It's not what it's cracked up to be."

"Try it for a while and you'll find out what I mean."

"Of course I understand." Fran broke her cupcake and put a tiny sliver of it in her mouth. "My heavens, you don't have to explain to *me!* If anyone knows the joys and satisfactions of raising a family, it's me!"

But privately she wondered what had happened. Liz hadn't changed at all, she was still as self-centred as ever, kids or no kids. Imagine being so stuck up and snobby as to brush aside a good suggestion as if it was the second stupidest thing she'd ever heard.

"Me?" she laughed. "Give music lessons? It seems an awful lot like digging a hole, climbing in and pulling the hole in after me."

"There are several children in the family have some talent and all they need is –"

"But not from me, Fran. I'm not a teacher. You have to be a special kind of person to be a teacher."

"You'd make really good money at it."

"If I'm after really good money I'll get a job pulling lumber on the greenchain. I'd be a dreadful music teacher! The only thing I ever wanted out of school was me!"

No sense trying to talk to Miss Know-It-All, queen of the entertainment industry, she who would still be slinging bedpans and barf basins if she had been left on her own.

Liz didn't bother telling any of them about her big mistake, which had been so dumb, so predictable and so unnecessary she knew she was making it even while she was making it.

"Well thanks, Liz. Thanks a heap!"

"Sid, stop it, will you?"

"One-way Corrigan, aren't you?"

"We sit in that bus with everyone and we're so ticked off with each other we don't talk to anyone else, either! Then we get to the motel room and all I want to do is soak in a tub, have a real honest-to-Jesus rest, and instead here we are and you're pouting."

"Pouting? *Pouting?*"

"What would you call it? I'm not the one decides what we'll

play, you know. It is not my band. All I do is play what's been decided. Period. Pee-ree-uhd! If you think you're being slid off stage, go talk to Andy about it, not me."

"*If I think?* I'm down to five chords and no imagination. How would you read it, Liz?"

"I don't know, Sid. But I wasn't consulted, it has nothing to do with me."

"All you have to do is make a point of paying some attention on stage. Look over and smile. We could get a thing going where you make sure I'm doing some special backup for you. It's not as if you had to really *do* anything. Is a smile going to break your goddamn face? We could practise some stuff together and when it was ready we could show it to Andy and –"

"Go talk to Andy about it. You want to practise, fine, I'll practise. What have you got in mind?"

"Well, I don't know! Gimme some time to think about it!"

But it wasn't the time, it wasn't the thinking, it was something else. Andy grinned, said Great idea, and started making room in the show for what Sid wanted. The trouble was, Sid wasn't as good as he needed to be to carry it off, and Andy was quick to point out the flaws.

"You want *Liz* to take that part? Well, what the fuck am I doing while she's getting fancy, Andy? Standing with my thumb up my bum?"

"If she doesn't cut loose here we're going to have to listen one more time to that sound you don't ask people to pay money for: fuck all, dead air, silence. There is a hole there, man! Don't believe me, ask the rest of the guys."

Sid burned with resentment. And took it out on everyone, not just Liz. He got so touchy and snarly nobody wanted to sit near him, which made him touchier and snarlier.

"I'd expect more loyalty from a wire-haired terrier than I get from you!"

"Maybe because I'm not a goddamn wire-haired terrier, okay?" and Liz left the room, slamming the door behind her. She went down to the desk and asked if they had another unit.

Then she had her bath, she had her rest, and the desk clerk phoned in her wake-up call. She had time to go back to Sid's room to get her luggage and her violins, then get changed and grab a hamburger in the coffee shop.

But before the first of the crowd arrived she was the old Liz, laughing and teasing, joking and cracking the puns and insults that pass for humour and a show of affection. "Ah, come on, dickhead," she teased, "we give you the benefit of the doubt all the time, it's why you're here instead of in the rubber room."

If Sid knew she had moved out he didn't say anything, he just went ahead and did his job, straight-faced as ever. If anyone had asked Andy, which so far nobody had, he'd say Sid could play as well as most but no better. Sid didn't practise enough and he didn't put enough of himself into his work, because Sid didn't want to be a good guitar player or even a good band member. Sid wanted to be a fuckin' star, and he thought magic dust would fall on him and that would be all it took.

Liz, now, was something else. The world was full of better fiddle players, but she worked at it. Even when she didn't have her little box of strings in her hand her fingers were moving, index to thumb, middle to thumb, ring to thumb, pinkie to thumb, thumb to index and middle, the hand moving all the time.

After the show they went back to the motel and headed to their rooms. Liz walked to the left, down the hallway to her new room, and Sid stood watching her back before turning to the right. Nothing said. Nobody knew whether they'd agreed on this or anything else, and nobody asked. They just waited.

It didn't take long. Sid got into one hell of an argument with Andy. Nobody knew what kicked it off and it didn't matter. One night they got to the hall to go to work and the two men were standing practically nose hole to nose hole, hissing and slit-eyed.

"Well, fuck you, Andy Adler. Fuck you *and* the Westernaires!"

"Fine by me, sausage fingers."

"You just fuckin' remember you said that. You'll look like some kind of goddamn fool out there tonight!"

"Shit, I could replace you in two seconds. Find a kid with a cold in his nose, give him Kleenex and tell him to blow any old time."

Sid went pale, picked up his not-very-expensive guitar, and left. The awful part was Andy was right. Everyone just worked a tiny bit harder on stage and the sound was no thinner than it ever had been. And it was more money, too, because they split Sid's portion among the rest of them.

It took five or six months but the time came when Andy was

staying in the same motel room as Liz. They got along well, and the weight was off her coattails. Almost. Everything seemed comfortable and easy and the fatigue she had been starting to worry about lifted. Well, to be fair, it had started to lift about a week after Sid caught the plane back to Vancouver. But even with Andy in the picture she could have some space and time to herself, go for a walk, go for a swim, sprawl across the bed and sleep as sound as she wanted. Andy could entertain himself, he didn't need her ear to hear his every word or her eye to see his every move.

Liz got a camera and took pictures. Every town they visited had a few sights-to-see and every town had old buildings which looked as if the cobwebs and spiderwebs were the only thing holding the boards together. Some of her pictures won second or third prizes in photo magazine contests, and one of them, a shot she took at night out behind some nameless joint where they'd been playing, won a fifty-dollar first prize. It was a picture of a drunk, taken from behind, as he leaned on an open garbage can, retching. The light from the neon bar sign was stark at the mouth of the alley, but the alley itself was dark, the shapes darker blurs.

She and Andy shared a room, shared a bed, shared the stage, but they didn't share their lives. Sex was occasional and even comfortable, a bit lazy, like two people who have been dance partners for thirty years and can move gracefully to the music while sound asleep.

But something was wrong. She thought it was maybe nerves or something. You never can tell about nerves. The back of her neck started to itch, a bit at first, then more, up into her hair until it was all she could do to not drop her fiddle on the floor in the middle of the show, bury both hands in her hair and claw at her scalp until it bled. She got coal tar shampoo, thinking it might be dandruff or something, but it didn't help. By this time it was her armpits, too, and her muff, and even the skin on her forearms. Well, if this was nerves it was one hell of a way for it to manifest itself.

"What?" she asked.

"Most people call it crabs," the doctor replied.

"And how in hell do you wind up with them?"

"Oh," he said, "you can get them from bedding, from a mattress, from the seat of a car, from a toilet seat, from someone else who has them."

"You're kidding. I never heard of them."

"They're not uncommon and they're easy enough to get rid of once you know what you're dealing with."

She bought the stuff he told her to buy, went back to the motel room and told Andy the bad news.

"Hell's bells and peanut shells," he sighed. "If it's not one thing it's another, eh? Oh, the joy of the open road!"

They showered together, checking to be sure each of them had the glup smeared in the right places. Then, still covered with it and feeling more than a bit conspicuous, they went down to the laundry room in the motel and fed all their clothes into the washers and dryers. All except their on-stage stuff, which had to be sent to the cleaners.

"Thank God we've got some stuff hasn't been touched since it came back from the last time."

But it had gone in the garment bag with the other ones and they had to do it all over again. They had warning, though, and scheduled the cleanup for after the show Saturday night. Friday afternoon they went to the dry cleaners, and by the time they left town they were free of bugs. The itching stopped. The scratching stopped. They made little private jokes about it and bit by bit the whole thing faded from memory.

"It's what? How would a person get *that?*"

The doctor told her and Liz just stared. She got her prescription and went to the pharmacy, and the pharmacist gave her two small brown paper envelopes.

"Name of the partner, please."

"What?"

"Your sexual contact. I have to have the name of the other person."

"What in hell for?"

"Regulations. It's a requirement."

So she told him. He wrote down Andy Adler's name, then handed both brown envelopes across the counter. "One for you, one for your partner, the instructions are on the envelope."

"Are there any side effects from this?"

"No," he said.

"Christ," she muttered, "and I pay for *his* bloody pill, too."

Andy looked at the envelope, then looked at Liz and that was all she needed. "Swallow like a good boy," she said quietly, and went to the closet to start packing.

"Liz."

"Shut up."

"Liz, honey, listen."

"Swallow your pill, peckerhead. Swallow your pill, pussy bandit."

"What am I, married to you or something?"

"No fuckin' way, man," she smiled.

She moved down the hall. A month later she moved back to the Island.

The first time she went back she stayed six months, then got a phone call from her agent. The offer was good, better than anything she had earned in her life, and a person would be a fool to say no to the chance to hit the mid-level circuit and still save money.

She made good and sure nobody shared her room, let alone her bed. She re-established her on-the-road routines, she practised two hours minimum every day, she took up jogging because she was spending so much of her life sprawled in a bus or in a train compartment or standing on stage. She got a bullworker for the muscles in her forearms to protect herself from carpal tunnel syndrome. She started reading books of a kind she had never bothered with before, not exactly how-to books, but who-am-I books, although she didn't share them with anyone in the band. You'd tell too much about yourself if you shared your incest survivor's handbook.

But a bar is a bar is a bar is a bar and a dance hall is a dance hall no matter where it is. Public performances are like bars without booze, except at intermission when the audience swills it back at great rate, and even "Wildwood Flower" starts to seem repetitious and mind-numbing.

Liz wrote duty letters to her family, sent postcards to Max Gibson at the store where she'd found Recherche, and a couple of times a year sent him tapes of the music the band was playing with increasing skill. When she wound up in the city she dropped by for tea, taking Recherche with her to play music for Max. She enjoyed those visits more than any other in her life, and the day he brought out the cherished bow and handed it to her, then kissed her on the cheek, was one of the highlights of her memory box.

And then Max was in a nursing home, and she wasn't

surprised when he got out of it the way the smart ones do. But the letter from the lawyer flabbergasted her. Max had said often enough he had no relatives, but people aren't hatched on hot rocks. Still, there it was, Liz had inherited a bank vault full of handmade violins. It was a magnificent gift, but she never forgot that he had given her the cherished bow while he was still alive.

And somehow, with Max gone, her link to something else was gone, too. It just wasn't fun any more. It was, in fact, a very large and growing pain in the bush.

People stopped, watched and smiled when Fran took her crowd to the park. She walked behind them, a long, soft white rope tied to little Lee's stroller handle, and the others walked in front of her, side by side in twos, each child holding the rope. When the front pair got near a corner, Fran called, "Wait for us!" and tugged gently on the rope. The kids, as well trained as any team of Belgian draft mares, stopped and waited patiently.

"Oh, isn't that cute."

"Surely they aren't all hers!"

"She's too young to have a tribe like that, it must be a day-care centre."

"Wouldn't catch me with that many!"

"God, haven't they heard about birth control?"

"Probably Cath'lic."

At the bus stop she lifted Lee from the umbrella stroller and folded it down to carry-size. "Easy, now," she warned, "you wait with me until the nice man has the door open. Okay, no push-ing and no shoving, by twos, up we go." They moved down the aisle to the long seat at the back, then settled like birds on a branch while Fran paid the fare.

The welfare now paid not only foster fee for five, two of whom went to school all day, but mother's relief for three others, one of whom was only there in the afternoons. Mother's relief was a subsidy for kids whose parent or parents were about to fold under the weight of crisis, responsibility or their own kids. Maybe one of these days Fran would schedule herself a nervous breakdown and get some mother's relief, too. Farm out the whole army to homes all across the city and go sit on the beach with only seagulls and sand fleas for company.

When they got off the bus it was the same thing in reverse. "Wait for me now, just go to the bus stop booth and hang tight to each other's hands." And off they'd go to Stanley Park, to fight the damn stroller through the gravel and salt-and-pepper blast rock on the cunning little paths. Usually she wound up folding it up and lugging Lee on her hip. It must have been men, and childless men at that, who designed what were supposed to be walking paths. Someone ought to tell the parks board that stroller wheels don't work in gravel.

She had a bag of grain for the ducks and swans in the streams and another bag for the pigeons. People stopped, stared, then smiled as the kids came forward one by one to get handfuls of grain for the birds.

"Oh, isn't that cute!"

"Got them as well trained as can be, hasn't she."

Well, she had some of them as well trained as they'd ever be, but don't expect much more than hang onto the rope and fling birdseed. Still, they weren't much trouble and the welfare did pay almost double for them. Not that she was doing it for the money, of course – someone has to look after the poor little things. It's a shame and a pity that people will go to a pet store and pay unbelievable sums of money for some exotic species that may well have been captured and imported illegally, then glory in paying more money for special food and medicine to keep alive something which ought to have been left in its own jungle or cave, but those same people cringe at the mere thought of looking after a disabled child. They enjoy having some form of monkey swing from their drapes and smear the apartment with shit, but shrink from a child who will never be toilet-trained. Oh well, takes all kinds.

When little legs got tired they found a place to sit and Fran slipped off her backpack, opened it and brought out sandwiches and a big thermo-jug of juice. It was nice to just sit and enjoy the sunshine, listen to the birds and keep half an eye on the kids. Lee lay on the blanket with his bottle, sucking noisily and waving his legs. He was getting awfully heavy and Fran could only pray to the great god of chubby legs that soon he would tuck his under him and start walking on his own. Ritchie and Garnet had both been walking long before they were this big or this old. And Brandy! Well, they said girls walked sooner and were toilet-trained sooner, but not one of the boys had come anywhere near Brandy. Fran had thought Nancy was fast, but she didn't even try to talk until she was ready for entire paragraphs, whereas Brandy was jabbering away almost as soon as she had front teeth.

/ / /

Jerry was long gone, and so was Nick, and she'd had a month or two with a weekend daddy named Kurt, who she'd met at the park and who hadn't been the least bit put off by her little flock. Which was a relief, because sometimes she felt as if she was walking alone in a crowd. It might be her own crowd, and it might be the way she wanted it, but it was lonely. But Kurt didn't last either. Funny how things just didn't have much glue any more. Well, no reason for two people to hang on if what they were hanging onto was each other's throats. She did miss seeing their kids, but she had her own and she had her memories and what more can you expect, in a world where things go faster and faster and faster?

Little Jo-Beth was Buttercup no more and hadn't been for so long Fran was the only one who still remembered the nickname. Jo-Beth hadn't gone to nursing school, in fact she hadn't even graduated high school. She got married halfway through grade eleven, and those people who had adopted her thought it was just wonderful, even signed the papers and everything.

Then again, Jo-Beth had made a good marriage. Some kind of minister or preacher or something. Fran had managed a sitter for the three days and showed up by herself. And just as well – the hosts were unprepared for much of anything. People Fran had never heard of got the spare bedroom, with the carpet and closet and everything, and sleeping accommodations for the bride's very own flesh and blood were a fold-out couch in a semi-finished room in what you had to admit was the basement.

But you can't hold Jo-Beth responsible for other people's ignorance. After the wedding Fran made good and sure any time

Jo-Beth and Frank came to the city they had a bedroom all to themselves. That would show those others who it was put store by family and who didn't.

Frank seemed nice enough, a bit short and too soft to be called stocky or chunky, but not enough to be called fat. Plumpish, maybe. And if Jo-Beth didn't mind that he bossed her around as if he was her daddy and she was still in grade school, why should Fran get a rash about it? Maybe there was some kind of feeling of security went along with being permanently cast in the mould of Child Bride, and he *was* fifteen years older than Jo-Beth. Fran couldn't help wondering what kind of mentality would send someone after a kid in high school, someone from a totally different generation, someone who thought the Gaza Strip was a dance and the Bay of Pigs was a sausage factory. Oh well, to each her own, and Jo-Beth seemed happy.

It was hard to think of little Scotty in uniform, though. Even harder each time she heard a plane overhead because she had to wonder if that was him, standing on guard like the song said.

"Unca? Unca?" Ritchie would yell, pointing.

"Yes, dear," she always told him, "that's Uncle Scotty. Wave to him. Wave to your uncle who loves you."

All they knew of Scott was the photo on the china cabinet, of him in his dress uniform, taken at graduation. And didn't he look just like his father! His real one, not the guy who had signed the papers all those years later. It could almost give a person a chill down the spine how much alike they were, even though there weren't that many photos. People didn't all have cameras – you'd be lucky if someone else in the family had one, or a neighbour.

Fran had this image of a revolving door, like the one in the Hudson's Bay, like a windmill or a fan or something, half a dozen little barriers set on a centrepost, turning around and letting you in and out one at a time. Oh, the doors swing in and the doors swing out, some pass in and the drunkards pass out. Just like Momma used to sing when she was feeling no pain. That was Fran's life, somehow.

She dreamed once she was in an airport, but she knew *she* wasn't going anywhere. All these faces, and she recognized them even if she couldn't always put a name to them, all of them rushing toward her, smiling widely, so happy to see . . . whoever was standing behind her, because the smiling people she knew went past her and when she turned to see what lucky person was being greeted by all these people, nobody was there. She tried to grab people by the arm, "It's me, it's me, I'm here waiting for you," but their arms vanished, she grabbed at thin air and they raced past her to the person who wasn't there for them at all. A terrible dream. And when she made herself wake up she decided she'd never have it again, thank you.

And the next thing she knew she was in hospital. The welfare was good about it. They found a couple of Friendly Aunts who were willing to move right in, one on day shift, one on night shift, and take care of the whole show, not just while she was in hospital but after she came back out again and was recuperating at home, feeling very sad and very very upset.

"Now, now," the doctor said, "you've got a fine family already. Just think of all the women who can't have any at all, then think of how lucky you've been."

Easy for him to say! But there you had it, and there you didn't. All it took was some pain you thought was appendicitis and a monthly that just dripped and dribbled into another one, then another one, and the next thing you knew they were saying ovarian cyst, but when they got in there it wasn't a cyst at all.

"The report came back from the lab and it was benign," the doctor told her, "but we can't be too careful in these cases. I want you to have a Pap every couple of months for the next while, to keep a jump ahead of it. Just in case."

Well, that's a great thing to walk around with, like little Joe Gloom in the funny papers, with the black cloud that never goes away. Two black clouds, really – she might have wanted another child or two. People seemed to think children were just accidents, or the price you had to pay for the affection you sometimes found.

And then that other nonsense, the cutting out of all that living tissue, without so much as waiting for the biopsy results to come back. Hmm, what have we here my dear, why, a lump, dear me we'll have to excavate, and out goes the rubber-gloved hand, chain saw, please, nurse, and roarsy roarsy, no need for this or that, no need for these or those. If that lump was growing inside someone's scrotum you can be sure there would be no unseemly haste, but when it comes to the ovaries, fallopian tubes, uterus, cervix and part of the vaginal wall, well, my dear, we are doing you a favour. No more monthlies, aren't you lucky, just take this estrogen, better than Mother Nature. Of course we have to watch you for liver cancer and whatnot, but think how lucky you are, why, you're a walking example of the miracle of modern science.

It was the doctor asking her what the family history was. Had anyone in the family ever had this disease or that disease or the next disease? What about this one or that? The list just went on and on, you wouldn't think there were so many things a person could be born having or lacking or developing later. "No," she said, "no, no, no," and then she said, "Listen, we've always been very healthy. There's nothing wrong with any of us."

But it got her thinking, and when she was recuperating and Aunt Wilma came over to help the Friendly Aunt, Fran asked. Bit by bit, a snippet from here, a snippet from there, things she knew had happened got left out, things she knew nothing about got exposed, and things she had suspected or overheard got denied. "Oh, no, dear, nothing like that."

She sat in bed with a big school binder on her upraised knees, one of Robbie's he didn't need any more because he'd quit and gone to work in a logging camp, and didn't that make your hair stand straight up. The broken backs, broken necks, smashed pelvis, arm ripped off, leg chopped, chain wrapped around the face – every time you picked up a paper another one had been hit by a rolling log or a falling tree or a snapped-off top or gone off a cliff in a runaway truck. But they made good money until it happened and Robbie was convinced he was made of stainless steel. "Don't you worry about me, Princess," and he was gone. Sending money every month, too, but she put it in an account for him because sooner or later he'd need it.

And in the meantime she just started writing it down. All of it. The things Auntie Wilma told her, the things she remembered herself, the things Auntie Wilma said had never happened, most of which Fran was sure had so happened.

When she had it written down it was maybe thirty or forty pages of close-lined neat handwriting. She read it over and over and over and over again every chance she got. But it didn't fill the blanks. It didn't even start to fill the blanks.

Then she cried, for almost a week. Just cried and cried. The doctor said it was only to be expected and he upped the dosage of the Premarin, take one a day every day for three weeks, then not take them the fourth week, then one a day every day for three weeks, just like a menstrual cycle, only no menstrual cycle, and that was why she was crying but no sense trying to tell them. No sense trying to explain she didn't know who she was supposed to be if she couldn't be a mother any more.

"Oh, silly girl," Aunt Wilma said softly, smoothing Fran's hair, "you'll *always* be their mother!"

"That's not what I mean."

"I know, dear, I know," but she didn't. There was that hole. That big black hole.

She started rewriting, then. She had seen a program on the education network where an Adlerian head shrinker said that you just had to make up a story, even if you had big holes in your memory, make up a story because what you made up would tell you as much as if you thought you remembered every detail. Nobody remembers every detail, the head shrinker said. That's why three people, telling about the same thing, tell three different stories.

And wouldn't it be nice if you could just start at the beginning and rewrite the story of your life? But you had to try to be honest, and nobody likes a sugary story even if Harlequins do outsell the Bible, which Fran didn't think was true even though some people said so.

She changed some names to protect the guilty, altered some events because otherwise it would be too complicated, and combined several characters into just a couple because you can't bring the entire world on stage and still have room for the audience. And you had to change some details or everyone in the family would get their shirt in a knot, and then there'd be trouble and who needed that? Not that any of them would ever see it, but still . . . well, you just never know.

The Island moves a little closer to the mainland all the time. Once, before the arrival of the ones who claimed to have found what had never been lost, it took a day, sometimes two, for people to get from the mainland to the floating rock. A thirty-puller Glwa, complete with sail and a sort of outrigger (which the latecomers claimed had never existed, or had existed only in fantasy, story, song and the fevered imaginations of the unschooled), was loaded with baskets of food and piles of trade goods secured in a sturdy twisted cedar bark webbing extending from the struts of the outrigger to the cross frame of the outer pontoon, or whatever that hunk of supposedly nonexistent gear was called. This vessel might leave the territory of the people whose chief for fourteen thousand years had been called Khahtsahlano, and surge paddle stroke by paddle stroke across the gulf, which eventually got named after a syphilitic king but which at that time was called the Home of Foam Woman. It would follow the path the sun laid down across the water just before he ducked behind the blue rim of mountains, and complete the trip in a day. Smaller craft might take longer, or might instead be invited by the Under the Sea People to take up residence with them.

When the sons of the stalwart followed the sons of heroes and discovered that which had been unwittingly lost, the island was only an overnight sail from the mess which they called a city and which they named after an exiled Dutchman, who for years was identified as an Englishman by the history book writers – a mistake that is easily made, since those people all look alike anyway.

Navigational regulations direct steam to give way to sail, but history demanded sail move over and make way for real progress. By then the Island was on the move for sure, it only took four hours to go from the Hub City to the growing metropolitan sprawl. Bit by bit by bit the distance was cut and gnawed until it took only an hour and a half to make the trip. Today you can climb into a hunka junk, take your life in your hands and go from one harbour to the other in a half hour, dry and unscathed if you're lucky, and with your luggage if you're luckier.

There's something done to the minds of those who live on an island which doesn't have the good sense to stay put. How can anyone grow up with any certainty about anything if the very rock on which they set their feet is always moving closer and closer to the mainland? And how can anyone know what to believe when those deemed to be experts deny their own experience and insist that the island is actually moving away from the mainland a centimetre every million years?

So there you are, standing on a rock which may be speeding east at great rate or drifting west at virtually no rate at all, and to add to the disorientation the bloody water won't stay put. Just when you get used to tide pools and mud flats here it comes, splish splash, quart after quart, gallon after gallon, and if you don't shift yourself you could be ass deep in it half an hour later. In it comes, up it creeps, wave after wave of it, and the experts say every seventh wave is bigger than the others but generations of kids with sunburn-peeling noses say it's the fifth wave is bigger, but what in hell would they know? Scabs on their knees and elbows and barnacle cuts on their feet, and no good sense or appreciation of manifest destiny.

The sons of the heroes discovered what had been misplaced and they claimed it for their own. The sons of the stalwart followed and were immediately put to work stripping the bones of the discoveries. They continued to think of themselves as the sons of the stalwart and didn't know or care what it meant when the sons of the heroes referred to them as workies. As for the dipshit dispossessed who had managed to misplace thousands of square miles of wealth and treasure, it hardly bears remembering what they got called by all who arrived grasping. They were pushed onto the worst hunks of land, denied rights and recognition as human beings, and left to make do or do without, to live or die, but somehow to vanish.

And all the while the island was moving closer and closer to that other place. The sons of the heroes sent their sons off to be educated so they could come back and oversee the workies and ignore the Siwash and shovel fortune after fortune into banks that would never put a head office on that drifting boulder. The daughters of anybody at all were cajoled, coaxed, flattered, flarched and bedazzled into believing stories of a new life in a new land with freedom and justice for all, and if that didn't work they were just banged on the head, knocked up and moved, like it or lump it.

Their children were supposed to be exactly like them. But the patchass, scabby-kneed, slit-eyed illegitimate spawn of the workies did not turn out the way they were supposed to. Perhaps they went feral. Perhaps, in spite of Christianity, child abuse and genocide, it was true that the placenta is the connection between the spirit of the child and the spirit of the land in which it is buried. Well then, burn the placentas. Put the midwives in jail, get those women into hospitals, slap 'em in stirrups, make everything as messy and painful and medical as possible, then chuck that goddamn placenta in the incinerator and throw the ashes away.

But what the silly fuckers forgot was that there is no away. The ashes got offloaded in landfill and junk piles and garbage pits. They got tossed in the back of dump trucks and driven off to any old where at all, and the wind blew the ashes over the sides of the trucks, scattered them along the roadsides, dumped them into creeks and streams, blew them over stick fences into flower gardens, into pea patches, lettuce beds, hay fields and orchards, spread them all over the place. Then the rains fell, and fell and fell. The ash leached into the soil, then leached out of it again and was taken over hill and dale by rivers and creeks, until from one end of the long suffering chunk, clear to the other end, placental essence was scattered and sown.

And the kids of the workies benefited. When they learned the fate of

Khahtsahlano, something inside their hearts flared. Nobody deserves to be put on a barge with all his people and towed out and turned loose, left to the mercies of wind and tide without food or water or any means of sailing or paddling, just because the hunk of land onto which they had been jammed has suddenly become worth money. Yes, even the women, the children, the babies and the grannies. If anyone mentions it later on, we can say it's all a damn lie, it never happened, with the full complicity of all the governments, that Chief Khahtsahlano and his people were set adrift in the Gulf of Georgia so the approach and the supports of one end of the Lions Gate Bridge could get put down on that land. Worse things have been done for worse reasons, and they named a section of the city after him, after all, even if they did spell his name wrong.

And the sons of the heroes accumulated wealth. Generation by generation they lied, cheated, stole and snatched with both hands. Coal, wood, fish, transportation, you name it. Gimme gimme gimme, take take take, it's mind over matter – we don't mind taking everything and the rest of you don't matter.

Gregory Bowen was a fourth-generation son of the heroes, and he figured that made him a west coaster. Hadn't his father, his grandfather and his great-grandfather all lived their lives and ended them here? Well, then. Of course the pure bald fact was he had only managed to become a fourth-generation arseltart. Arseltarts may visit the west coast, they may move to the west coast, they may live on the west coast, they may even have been born on the west coast, but an arseltart is always an arseltart. And Gregory Bowen came from a long, thin, pallid line of arseltarts. He went off to school, he went off to university, and then he duly married the daughter of one of the sons of the heroes and set about impregnating her. Somehow he hit the mark three times, but in heroic circles the three marks were more like near misses – all three children were female.

Gregory Bowen's three daughters, Faith, Hope and Grace, were brought up in the traditions of the heroic. Sadly for them, in spite of their placental ash being spread on the rock with everyone else's, their education ensured that nothing said or written by the suffragettes would get near them. One after the other, from oldest to youngest, they fell into a sea of booze and damn near drowned in it. They lost their individuality and became not Faith Bowen, Hope Bowen and Grace Bowen, but "those Bowen girls."

Gregory Bowen managed in half a lifetime to squander, misplace or have taken from him most of his mind-bogglingly enormous inherited fortune, which had been accumulated by generations of pirates, privateers, barons and crooks. And nobody to inherit it but those Bowen girls, any of whom might be found at any hour of the day or night shitfaced, sozzled, pissed and playing doctor with any number of fishermen down at what everyone called Chinaman's Wharf. Those Bowen girls loved it down at Chinaman's Wharf. All they had to do was show up with a bottle of whiskey and they were as welcome as the flowers in May. That one bottle of whiskey miraculously became glasses of rum, bottles of beer, jugs of wine, quarts of moonshine, you name it and they drank it. And they fucked fishermen. Tall or short, fat or lean, young or old, clean or dirty, what did that matter? It was fun, or at least something to do, and the best part of it was it was driving the old son-of-a-bitch insane.

Faith's first wharf catch was a seven-pound boy who, with a sizable sum of money, was handed over to a family of Ukrainians who used the money to buy a twenty-acre farm. They called him Jarislov, Jars for short, and accepted the boy as one of their own. That was the end of it. If he looked different from their other kids, so what? Anyone who wanted to cast aspersions could step out into the alley and be hammered flat.

Jars grew up knowing the value of honest labour. His family worked, worked and worked. They were up at dawn and seated at the breakfast table minutes later, holding hands, saying a prayer, then eating. They ate quickly, no polite conversation, no lallygagging or time-wasting, get that fuel into yourself, turn it into energy and get outside and start working. They could pack away in ten minutes what would take anyone else an hour. Fifty minutes at lunch and fifty minutes at supper and fifty minutes at breakfast, so almost two hours a day was saved, seven days a week is fourteen hours, fifty two weeks a year is seven hundred twenty-eight, the average work week is forty hours, that's sixteen-point-two extra working weeks, times however many people were in the family, and years, even decades of work got done while other people were sipping tea, discussing news headlines and musing on what they might do to pass the evening.

By the time Jars was three he was feeding hens, gathering eggs and opening the gate to let the dairy cows into the meadow to graze. By the time he was six he was milking the cows, and by the time he was twelve there wasn't a thing on the farm he couldn't do. He could speak, read and write English and Ukrainian as well as Polish, Czech and several Slav dialects. Nothing unusual in any of that, every other member of the family could do as much, or more.

The twenty acres became twenty-five, then thirty-five, then fifty. Then it became thirty because the oldest daughter got married and needed land for a house and a small farm. The family worked extra hard to make up the difference, and when the farm was up to sixty acres, someone else got married. The Island moved either east or west, the water came in or went out, time swelled in direct proportion to the amount of effort put into things, the farm got bigger then smaller then bigger then smaller, food was put on plates and vanished, and in, around, between, with and in spite of all the flux and change the kids grew up, married, had kids of their own, worked and laughed. When Jars was old enough, the people he thought of as his parents sat him down and told him the bald truth. He listened and he drank coffee. He remembered all he had heard of the rumour, gossip and gospel of the town, and then he devoured four large, delicious poppy seed buns, smiled at his adoptive father, patted the hand of his adoptive mother, and shrugged. "That whole bunch are nothing to me," he said, "I know who my family is." Just to be sure nobody had doubts or wondered if they had misheard, he said it again in every language he knew, and added "I love you."

Gregory managed, with another fistful of prunes, to get Faith married off to the son of a stonecutter with social aspirations. Giovanni d'Onofrio sent his son Lorenzo to school, then to university, and then told him face to face he was going to marry Faith Bowen.

"No," Lorenzo gasped.

"Yes," Giovanni told him. "And go to work saving some of that money. For us."

Lorenzo wept, but Lorenzo knew his old man's fists were harder than the granite he cut into tombstones, so he went on a four-day drunk and then married Faith.

Faith had two other children, both of whom may or may not have been Lorenzo's. He didn't ask, she didn't say and neither of them knew. Fortunately both of them were girls – after all, if a man's son is his immortality, why feed someone else's?

When they weren't down at Chinaman's Wharf, the Bowen Girls could be found up in Chinatown, exploring all the mysteries of which the locals could, for the most part, only whisper and speculate, which gave rise to suppositions and fevered imaginings that would make your eyes pop. A Scots exile who lived up there had been seen and heard jabbering away with the Celestials in their own language. He had worked in the mines, married, raised a family, socked his money in the bank and seemed just as real and as normal as anybody, right up until the day he retired, then he signed everything over to his wife, lock, stock, barrel and bung, packed his clothes and walked up the hill to Chinatown. Moved into one of those little cedar-sided shacks, started a garden on the side of the slope, took his meals in the chop suey house and sat on the bench with the old men, smoking that foul stuff, and no matter how many times someone went up to try to talk sense

to him, he just smiled, shook his head and said Awa' wi' ye, laddy, awa' awa'.
He supported himself by translating newspapers, tax notices, contracts,
summonses and other English-only documents and by writing letters, usually of a business nature, for those who had become his neighbours, and by
bootlegging the whiskey he made himself in the cool darkness of a shaft of
an abandoned coal mine. The police knew he was selling liquor and they concentrated on trying to find his still. The tunnel in which it was situated ran
all the way to Cassidy, more than nine miles, with ventilation holes irregularly spaced all the way along. The smell of the enterprise, though it lingered
in the air in some places, never helped the police pinpoint the still, but at
least it gave them something to do instead of interfering with honest folk.
Oh, and there was that other one, the blond skinny one, they said he was the
only white man in North America with permission to deal pan gini and
how'n hell had he learned that, damn foreign gambling game, six decks of
cards or whatever, sat up there from suppertime Friday until past midnight
Sunday, then walked down the hill, kicked the shit out of his wife, scared the
poop out of his kids, went to sleep, got up Monday morning and went off to
work as if the weekend had never happened. Crazier than a goddamn coot,
that one.

Hope Bowen's first wharf catch was a girl who wound up with a family
of Irish coal miners. The second was also a girl, and she wound up with a
different family of Irish coal miners. Both families used the money to buy
fish boats, which caused hilarity in some circles, what with the girls starting out on the docks and then because of them a bunch of others winding
up there, as well.

Grace Bowen's first two pregnancies were aborted. She tried to abort
the third, as well, but failed. The child was born the same night Lorenzo
d'Onofrio slit Faith's throat, then hanged himself with several pure silk ties
knotted together and tied to the overhead pipes in the basement. The spawn
of the heroic were, predictably enough, shocked to shit at such a display of
emotion and poor taste. Workies and losers snickered and made very bad
jokes about Faithless Faith.

In all the kerfuffle over that, somebody forgot to send the newborn
packing with a sack of prunes to lead the way, and somehow she wound up
being raised by the same hired help who got stuck with Faith and Lorenzo's
two kids, the ones who may not have had anything to do with Lorenzo at all.

It was all more than old Gregory's heart could stand, and they held off
burying Faith and Lorenzo so they could plant them with the old man and
have one big do instead of two.

Grace Bowen sent someone down to Chinaman's Wharf to find Hope and bring her home to be sobered up. "Here we are," she said grimly, "Grace and Hope and Faith's kids, and the old man's money is ours!" Hope didn't bother to point out not all of the kids were the children of Faith and somehow, more by good luck than good management, everyone else forgot too.

Those who are dead always wind up more respectable than those still alive, and more respectable than they would have been had they lived. Faith Bowen became, posthumously, the only respectable one of those Bowen girls, which was nice for all three kids, especially the one who wasn't hers and who otherwise would have wound up as a permanent foster or, worse, as the child of Grace, who was often referred to as The Worst'a the Bunch.

Nobody knew bugger nothing about fetal alcohol syndrome. Maybe that's why there was so little sign of it in that kid of Grace's, the one who thought she was the daughter of poor dead Faith, the only good one of those Bowen girls, the one killed by a lunatic husband, cut down in the prime of life by a crazy Wop bastard who had married her for her money.

The old man's will provided the fuel for a two-day scandal. He left his money to his surviving daughters, but he left the whole thing in trust until such time as the daughters proved themselves sober, fit and capable to care for the money. Until then all decisions would be made by a group of trustees chosen from the ranks of the sons of the heroic. The lawyers, doctors, dentists, judges and bankers of the town.

Neither of the surviving Bowen girls managed to stay sober enough long enough to get her nicotine-stained fingers on the diminished heap of prunes. They both died early, Grace of liver disease and Hope from drowning in her own stomach contents, when she puked while lying on her back drunk. The lawyers, doctors, dentists, judges and bankers continued to serve as trustees for the dependent children. The oldest two went off to boarding school and from boarding school to university, and in spite of skeletons in the closet married reasonably well. The sisters married brothers from a fine old heroic family, a family which had wisely used their vast transportation holdings to ensure that the illegal stills on Texada, Lasqueti, Nelson and a hundred other islands could ship their rocket fuel south across the forty-ninth to a very dry United States of America whose citizens were trying desperately to survive Prohibition. The profit from the rocket fuel kept the transportation company looking so profitable its stocks sold for thousands of dollars more than they were worth. Before Prohibition was repealed the girls' father-in-law off-loaded the stock, selling the tugs and barges and getting the hell out while the getting out was good.

They all lived happily on the windfalls. But what of the bag of prunes? And what of the child of Grace who thought she was the child of Hope, or was it Faith? She came of age. Her sisters, who were really her cousins – now safe, secure and respectable in the lap of a family no better than their own but perhaps smarter – decided they wanted to cut all ties with the scandalous Bowen girls. They did not want this cousin who thought she was a sister showing up later and cadging a handout. There weren't that many prunes left, really. Might as well give them to her in return for her quit-claim on any plums they might acquire themselves.

So Lorraine Bowen inherited the little handful of prunes, and that's all she got from her mother's family. Nobody knew who her father was. He may well have been nobody at all. He was surely the son of a woman, and since Lorraine Bowen neither looked, thought nor acted like any of those Bowen girls, and since she didn't look, think or act like the cousins she thought were sisters, there is every chance in the world she looked, thought and acted like the woman who was mother of the nobody-at-all who had been Lorraine's father. Whether she took after that woman, or she had in her veins the spark of whatever sent the sons of the heroic out to steal everything they could, or her placental ashes had landed in the right place, whether it was by accident or design, Lorraine Bowen grew up very differently than any of her family.

Instead of going off to boarding school and learning how to talk through her nose, keep her upper lip so stiff as to seem paralyzed and walk as if someone had rammed a coat hanger up her twat, she went to the local public school and sat at a desk with all the other barely-to-be-noticed workie kids. She read the same history books they did, but she also heard their stories, and the stories told by the children of those who had been there were very different from the stories put in history books by people who had never set eyes on the rock.

Instead of learning to ride to hounds she learned to prowl the beaches and pick oysters and dig clams, and cook them on rocks set around a small driftwood fire, and eat them and wash them down with creek water. Instead of paying through the nose for fish eggs in a jar she ate herring spawn on kelp with the kids on the reserve. Instead of jarred venison she ate mow-itch, and she had nothing but contempt for the idea of hanging ducks by their legs until they fell off their own bones, then lift them from the litter and cook them.

Where other girls learned decent things, like embroidery and water-colour painting, Lorraine Bowen learned to roll her own cigarettes, swim naked in the chuck and call a shovel a shovel. Her vocabulary alone guaranteed that no matter what else she might do, she would never be well thought of in genteel circles. But mostly Lorraine Bowen listened. Listened to the stories told by people who had charitably forgotten or overlooked or were ignorant of or disinterested in her origins. Stories of real estate coups, transfers of funds, alterations in municipal zoning rules, stories of the kind everyone has always heard.

She was eighteen years old when she headed down to the capital and signed on at the university. She was almost thirty when she came home again, and the wild scandal with the deep suntan and the hair that grew every which-a-way had changed into something to make your blood run cold.

A bitch. A bitch of the first order. A right total perambulating bitch. A right total perambulating educated bitch who looked at the withered little prunes in the teeny weeny sack, then looked at the names of the trustees, examined their assets and shook her head.

"Where's the fuckin' money?" she asked.

"Beg pardon?" The judges, lawyers, doctors, dentists and bankers gaped.

"How come you fuckers have just been getting richer'n'richer'n'richer all these years and there's diddly-piss-all left in the trust account?"

"Ahem," they said. "Harrumph," they said, looking at each other.

"The money," she said quietly.

Ah, yes, the money, indeed. The sons of the heroic were running into that bit of truth about fooling some assholes all of the time and all assholes some of the time but not fooling the slit-eyed bitches at all at all at all. There are some who just refuse to be fooled.

But even the hardest-nosed bitch isn't going to win when pitted against the sons of the heroic. Generation after generation of them have honed their slimy skills. They weren't going to dig into their own pockets to replace what had been slowly siphoned off the trust account to their interests. When one needs to pay, one does not pay with one's own money. There is always another pocket into which we can dip.

Right smack dab in the middle of town was as fine a sports field as you'd find anywhere. The workies had hacked it from forest, hewn it from bush, backfilled a swamp and filled a ravine with the discarded ash of the coking company. Bing-bang, surrounded by hills, hills and more hills, a flat playing surface, perfect for soccer, lacrosse, softball, baseball, you name it.

"Or a shopping mall," one of the trustees whispered. And before you knew it the old shell game was on, here we are here we are look and see look and see, three shells and one dried pea and now you see it now you don't. By the time the populace had slowly begun to come awake and smell the bullshit, the paperwork was done. Zip zap, is it here is it there, well what do you know you picked the wrong shell. And the sports field which had been given by the workies' union to the children of the town in perpetuity was gone, in its place half a dozen ticky-tacky stores under one roof, the first real honest-to-God shopping mall in town, and as the scream of outrage grew and the workies began to yell *And where in hell do we have our soccer games now?* the answer appeared like the three wise men on camels.

Why, the old Bowen place, of course. And the taxpayers bought the old homestead for six thousand times what it was worth, and Lorraine Bowen wound up with more than a small sack of dried prunes.

She knew she should have had a bag of plums *and* the old place, she knew she had been halfways had, she knew very well just exactly what had been done, and she knew there wasn't much she could do about it except maybe keep tilting at the windmill until it fell on her head and she wound up with nothing, not even raisins, and maybe get her throat slit some dark night. But she'd learned how to cut bait. And there's no sense continuing to fish if you know there's nothing left in the pool but sharks and bloodsuckers.

Lorraine Bowen appeared to have cut bait and caved in. And that just shows to go you what appearances are worth. The last thing in the world she was about to do was let the Philistines get away with it. She just hadn't yet figured out how and when.

It's hard to get your feet under you and do when so much has been unstable in your life. It wasn't the confusion over which of those Bowen girls was her mother. Lorraine didn't care, you don't miss what you never had anyway. It wasn't the not being sure if her sisters were her cousins, if their children were her nieces and nephews or barely shirttail relations. It was this great hunk of granite either speeding eastward or slowly drifting westward and that alone is a huge puzzle. Which way is it going and how fast? Will we bang into North Vancouver or slowly ease over to Hawaii? It wasn't the bloody water inning and outing, upping and downing, sometimes three times in twenty-four hours and figuring out high tide low tide neap tide, it wasn't the thing that happens to your sense of timing when perpetuity comes early and within your own lifetime. It wasn't any one of those things or even any two, it was a combination of all of them. Lorraine Bowen had to sit down and think.

She could have used some of her plums to pay the tab at one of the many hotels in town, she could have moved into an apartment, she could have done anything she wanted. What she did was buy a boat. Not a yacht, not even a houseboat, just a good solid clinker-built which had been used as a fish boat after a lucrative life as a rumrunner.

And didn't the whole town have a good hoorah about that! Apples don't fall far from the tree, they said, or from the horse's ass. Another of those damn Bowen girls, and back down at Chinaman's Wharf, did you notice? Up to her bloody eyebrows in Chinamen, too, if you please. Well, that bunch always was tight and Scotch with their own money, it's only with ours they're open-handed, and the Celestials will work for next to nothing. It might even explain where Lorraine Bowen got those weird slanty greenish eyes, and how come she's always been so bloody smart. Not everyone is smart enough to get blood from a stone or money back from the grasping. Maybe she wasn't got on a fish boat at all, and maybe that ain't all suntan, either. You just never know with those Bowen girls.

But Lorraine paid the Celestials the same wage she'd have paid anybody. It was the way they worked convinced her, that and the fact that they seemed to know by instinct what would float and what wouldn't. They ripped out everything under the deck, bust out the ballast, the whole thing, then scrubbed and sanded, scraped and scratched until all stink of cod and salmon was gone. They mixed concrete, they poured it, and then, while it was still wet, they laid on smooth slabs of gorgeous black slate they had hand-cut from the cliffs of Guano Island. It shouldn't have worked. The boat ought to have been top-heavy, ought to have flipped and gone under, Jesus, everybody knows you can't have more out of the water than in it. But it didn't flip, it didn't even tip, it just rode as proud as hell.

Smiling widely, bobbing their heads politely, the Celestials carried boards sanded to a fine fare-thee-well and disappeared with them. The whole thing was refinished, the old paint scraped off down to the boards, then the boards were worked and sanded, worked and resanded, then layer after layer after layer after layer of varnish was applied. The old engine was hauled out and carried off, God knows where, and the very latest and absolutely best Easthope a body could get was stuffed in. And that wasn't all. Everybody knows those engines can work like an expensive Swiss watch but was that good enough for that bunch down there? No by God it wasn't, and the tinkering and fine-tuning was enough to make you pull out handfuls of hair. Fuss fuss fuss, as if what we were working on here was the Queen goddamn Mary, and didn't everyone know that you can't make a silk purse out of a sow's ear no matter what you do with it, up down or sideways? It's a damn fish boat!

But it hadn't been a fish boat to start with and pretty soon wasn't one again, it was something else. Something so bloody pretty all you could do was smile. Across the back of her, same as almost any other boat you could think of, in nice neat black letters, *Osprey*, and beneath that her registration number. But on either side of the front, enough to make you shake your head and worry, a great big googly eye and some kind of weird symbol they said was Chinese writing. Nobody had the sass to ask, but word got round all the same, so it was almost a disappointment when it turned out there wasn't any exotic or magical meaning, just *Osprey* written in Celestial. You'd'a thought if she was going to all that trouble she'd'a come up with something, you know, different, not just the Chinese word for fish hawk.

Lorraine paid off the workers and had a huge party at the chow mein palace, but of all the various and delicious food served and eaten, there wasn't one plate of chow mein. No chicken chow mein, no chef's special chow mein, no beef-broccoli-and-peanut-sauce chow mein. You'd have thought they'd never heard of chow mein. But they did have half a dozen cod cooked in black bean sauce, eyeballs and all. They had squid, they had baby octopus, they had sea cucumber, they had sea urchin, but no chow mein. They ate until they could eat no more and the mess they left behind would have fed six working men. And isn't it weird, with our good manners we pick at our food as if we barely wanted to eat it, itty-bitty bits and pieces, wipe your mouth with your napkin, chew slowly with your mouth closed, don't talk, don't laugh. But they act as if the food is so good, the chef so skilled, the feast so incredible you can't control yourself, you dive in, hands and faces, maybe even your feet, chewing and laughing, chewing and talking, dropping bones any old where at all, dribbling sauce, my God it's all just too good, look out I might swim in it next, where did the cooks learn how to do this, have you ever, no I haven't, well I'll just have to have some more, and when you can't possibly hold another bite, belch like hell and make room for one more chicken foot. The mess they left behind meant more to the cooks than the substantial tip Lorraine pushed under her plate.

After which she took her work of art in the opposite direction of the yacht club and tied up to a log secured by logging cable to a tall cedar snag in which a pair of eagles had made their nest. It was almost dead centre of the reserve where the losers had been penned. Hell, some said, a thing'a beauty like that, plunked down with the Siwash, what's the world comin' to, anyway.

What indeed? The movers and shakers had pulled off double-you double-you one, and enough workies got sent off and got killed, maimed, crippled, made crazy and/or disappeared in action to ensure a good turnout for poppy day. And when those old warriors began to pack it in, the same movers moved and the shakers shaked and double-you double-you two was choreographed with much the same result. The survivors limped home and no sooner had they turned around three times than the deal with the sports field, the shopping centre and the return of a fraction of the money swiped from those Bowen girls, and then by God it was time to ship more warm healthy bodies off to Korea, wherever that was, which distracted attention from what was going on just around the point from the reserve.

Oh, the Salish, now, they complained, said it was their land, never ceded or handed over and they didn't want any such thing done there. But nobody asked them, sir, and nobody listened to their protests. It was jobs, and God knows jobs were needed, and it was progress, and you can't stand in the way of progress, and it was development, which will run over top of anything or anyone as gets in its way. The construction crews were brought in from somewhere else and the project went ahead, infusing vast sums into the local economy because all those out-of-town carpenters, finishers and labourers needed a place to stay, food to eat and plenty of beer to drink as they sweated and toiled on the new version of the pyramids. Then more out-of-towners were brought in to run it and to train a few locals in the mysteries of turning living green to toilet paper. The stink was incredible. Ah, they said, not to worry, that's sulphur you smell, it's the smell of money.

Gasping and blue in the face, the workies swallowed that the way they'd swallowed everything else. Bullshit baffles brains, and fancy footwork prevails. Just about the time the pulp mill was ready to start production, the coal mines closed down, so there were plenty of warm, unemployed bodies to choose from, who were just desperate enough not to make any trouble, not to object to putting in shift after shift at the stink factory, not to object when the ones to benefit were the owners who never came near the place.

Liz hadn't expected to be so happy just because Fran decided to move back to town. It wasn't as if a great horde of rellies wasn't already available if a person got so mentally ill that being with kin seemed a wonderful idea. So why feel so excited, so eager just because a cousin a year or two older than her had decided to move in from the fringes and set herself up closer to the middle?

Liz hadn't expected Fran to bring the whole clanjamfrie, either. Well, she didn't exactly bring them, some were certainly big enough and old enough to bring themselves. Robbie working in the bush, Nancy in nursing school, they didn't need to be shepherded. She didn't bring the sad ones either, the little ones who couldn't hold up their heads without a brace or the ones whose legs folded up like spaghetti, she only brought her own. But my God, that made a tribe in itself.

Still, it was nice. It was very nice. When Fran asked Liz to look for a house, Liz got right to it.

"Not right in town, I've had enough of that," the voice said from the phone. "But not stuck out in the toolies, either."

"Okay. Sort of half'n'half. Maybe on the bus line?"

"That sounds great. Five bedrooms. If you can find more, that's great, too, but five for sure."

"Not many five-bedroom places available any more. There used to be tons of them but the Realty bought them up a few years ago. Then, when they had three or four of them side by each, they ripped them down and put up apartment blocks. And I mean *blocks*. My God! You'd think people were born with square bodies the way they build these places. But I'll see what I can do. The kids and I go bike riding just about every day so we'll see whatever is available and I'll check the paper and phone the multiple listing people. How high are you willing to go?"

"What I figure," said Fran, "is houses over here cost an arm and a leg more than over there because cities always charge more than towns, right? Even if what they have to offer is quantity not quality. So I'm getting a very good price for my place here. And if I put pretty well all of that into someplace over there, I'll actually move up the scale. What do you think I could get with a hundred and ninety-six thousand?"

"A hundred and . . . ninety-six *thou* . . . Jesus Christ in heaven, you could probably buy City Hall! What bank did you hold up? Hey, this is going to be easier than I thought!"

Just shows to go you! Onehundredninetysixthousand. Not bad for someone who might once, at some point maybe a dozen years ago, have had a job for a few days. In a town where even the mayor would stand in pigshit to her knees and eat garbage with a dirty spoon for six dollars an hour, no fringes or benefits, Fran wasn't going to have a lot of trouble finding a house.

"How much?" Bert laughed softly.

"One hundred ninety-six thousand."

"There you go, another chapter in the story of my life." He pulled her down so she was sitting on the couch beside him, her head on his lap. "I picked the wrong cousin!"

"You're crinking my back, you big dummy." She twisted around and got herself half comfortable. "You might shift over to the end of the sofa and make some room here if this is how you think I ought to watch TV."

"Shift over? Hey, there's a *lump* down there."

"Yeah, there's another one under my head!" She squirmed, then sat up and sat against him, her head on his shoulder. "Anyway, you're not her type."

"Seems like if you're breathing you're her type."

"No, she likes them short-term with itchy feet. At least that's the only kind she ever picks. She ought to choose a name she really likes, one that's easy to remember, and just give it to each of them as they come through the door so she wouldn't have to remember the new names."

"A hundred ninety-six thousand? I could remember a name or two for that much!"

"Yeah? How come you can't remember to put your underwear in the laundry hamper any more?"

"Give me ninety-six thousand and I will."

"So where's the hundred ninety-six thousand for *us?*"

But Bert wasn't good with money. Somewhere between the getting it and the keeping it, something went wrong. No use getting bent out of shape about it because Bert wouldn't argue, he just nodded, listened, nodded some more and then went right on as if nothing had been said. You might as well go to the beach and pry oysters off the rocks as try to change Bert's way of doing things.

"What don't you have that you need?" he asked.

"Nothing," she agreed. "But Bert, you're making better money than most guys in town and we don't have enough saved up to carry us for three months."

"Why do we need carried for three months? What's so great about stashing money away in a sock?"

"I'm saying we should be saving something on a regular basis."

"Is a regular basis better than a sock?"

"I'm not joking, Bert. Please."

"Lizzie, baby, we've got this house three-quarters paid off, we've got furniture paid for, we've got the car, we've got three kids with just about everything they need, what in hell do you want?"

"We've got the house three-quarters paid off because I had a hunk of cash in the bank when we met, so we had a big down payment and we went into this with no second mortgage. The car isn't paid off. The furniture was bottom-of-the-line when we got it because we knew we were going to have kids and they'd just trash it anyway. And they have. We're doing okay, but we could do a lot better."

"Yeah? You really think so?" He tilted his head, thinking about it, then sighed deeply. "Is it really that bad, Lizzie?"

And somehow there she was again, saying No, it's not bad, Bert, it's not the least bit *bad*, it's just . . . and after a while she began to suspect it was a merry-go-round. Hand in your ticket you get a ride, but only around and around in circles in the middle of a cow field.

Bert picked up his paycheque, took it to the bank and deposited it. So much in the grocery-and-house-expenses account, so much in Lizzie's allowance account, and the rest in the account for everything else. Bert made the payment on the car. Bert handled the real money. Liz made the mortgage payment, Liz did the grocery shopping and Liz let Bert know if the kids needed anything. The Family Allowance came to her, so much per kid, and she had her own allowance, for things she needed.

"God, Liz, if you need something, just say so and you've got it, babe."

"I want my own account, Bert. I don't want to ask you for tampons."

"Whatever you want, sweetheart. Your own allowance, sure. You should have said so before, that it meant this much to you."

But it stuck in her craw. Allowance. Who allows who to have an allowance, who decided who it was would do the allowing?

How many dance halls, how many concerts, how many hour after hour on that damn bus with the smell of exhaust fumes because even if more mechanics than you could shake a stick at said there was nothing wrong with the tailpipe system there was always this smell in the air, and sometimes it was enough to give you one helluva headache. How many motel units, how many meals so forgettable you had to compare notes to remind each other you'd put food in your belly at some point that month. And Fran, who hadn't held any job long enough to have to pay income tax had onehundredninetysixthousand to put into a house. You couldn't squirrel money away if you were on welfare, they were determined not to let a person get ahead, so it must have been that small insurance policy on the first one, what was his name, Fred, Ned, Ed, something like that. And now the place had increased in value.

Well, maybe one day their own place would increase in value too. Certainly ought to. Bert had done wonders. Sometimes, when she was feeling grumpy, Liz would remind herself of just how much Bert managed to accomplish. He was laid back and you could never get his shirt in a knot, but if you just shut up and waited, things happened. Things that would amaze you, things other people had to phone someone to do for them, Bert just got up one morning and did.

"Have you ever jacked up a house before?" she asked worriedly.

"Saw it done," he replied. "Can't be a whole helluva lot to it if those dim bulbs could do it. I expect all you have to do is take it slow and make sure you keep 'er all level."

"Maybe we ought to phone –"

"And spend six or seven thousand dollars? Stuff that crap. Up their nose," he winked, "with a rubber hose. Up your bush with a wire brush. Up your gee-gee with –"

"Oh, shut up, fool!" and she gave him a little shove. So he gave her a shove back and she gave him another and there they were on the living room carpet, rolling around like five-year-olds while their kids howled with laughter and then got in on the rasslin' match, too.

"I got 'im, Momma, I got 'im," Reba yelled, holding tight to Bert's hair.

"You hold him and I'll hit him."

"I give! I surrender! White flag!"

"Gimme a kiss and I'll let you go."

As leery as she felt, Liz went along with it.

"Are you sure he knows what he's doing?" Wilma worried.

"What makes you think he doesn't?"

"Well, people get paid to do this, Liz! For some people this is their job of work, their trade. But it isn't his. What if something goes wrong?"

"What can go wrong?"

"The house might fall off the thingamajigs!" Wilma snapped.

Liz neither knew nor cared what Wilma was angry about, whether it was that Liz hadn't leaped up and screeched Momma's worried, stop what you're doing! or that she knew that even if he'd never done it before, Bert would do it and do it well. Sometimes it seemed as if everything Bert did well was like a reminder of how inept Gowan had always been, a reminder that Wilma hadn't chosen someone for herself who was handy. Or maybe she just resented the fact Liz didn't have to live with someone who was a total asshole.

The thingamajigs looked like railway ties and were shoved

like hollow squares under each corner of the house. Bit by bit by bit the jacks were raised and when there was enough clearance, another layer of railway tie things were rammed in place. Up went the house, balanced on what looked like a log cabin with wide chinks between the layers. And when it was as far up as they wanted it, the rest of the work started.

Bert did hire some people to help with that. "I could do it," he told her, "but it would take time, and time is like money. We have to rent the jacks, rent the ties, rent the forms, rent . . . so the quicker it's done the better. Would you mind making up some chili and stuff?"

Gallons of it. And spaghetti and sauce and then the pot roasts and the chickens and on top of that Bert paid them. It took no time at all. It took far less time and money than the estimate had said, and there they were with a house with a basement. And a first floor, and a second floor, which had been the house. Actually there were two and a half floors, because the basement wasn't dug down too far. Bert said nobody wanted to live with slit windows like peepholes in machine gun emplacements.

"Looks a bit tall and small, doesn't it?" Wilma criticized it. "Odd shape, that house."

"It is now, but it won't be when the addition is done."

"Addition? My God, Liz, how much room do you need?"

"Wilma," Bert said mildly, even kindly, "shut the hell up until you know what you're jawin' on about, will you? Conversation is like a car. Before you put the mouth in gear you have to turn the ignition key to the brain, okay? This won't happen tomorrow. Or next week, either. And it isn't just 'room,' okay? It's investment. We just doubled the value of the house and it isn't even finished, okay? But Liz needs a place for her stuff, not just crammed in the far corner of the utility room between the washer and the ironing board. And I need a place to leave my tools without the kids deciding they're going to give me a hand. Like the bookcase," and he started laughing.

The laugh took the Boy-you're-gonna-catch-it look off Wilma's face. She laughed, too. What the kids had done to help Daddy with the bookcases would go down in family legend.

"Oh my, what a mess they made with all that paint," she agreed.

"Right. And since you value their lives, I'm going to get me a workshop with a deadbolt lock. Here, gimme a paper, I'll show you what I got in mind."

Only Bert could make Wilma stop nagging. Nobody else could. The world was full of people who had given up in exhaustion. Wilma was the shitpicker of all time. Tell her you were going to Vancouver on the ten a.m. ferry and she'd find fault because then you'd get there in time for the noon rush hour. Leave at noon and you'd miss the worst of the crush. Tell her you'd decided all on your own to leave at noon and she'd be the first to point out that by the time you got there you'd also have missed more than half a day's shopping time. Always something wrong with any idea anyone else had and she'd just harp away until Liz wanted to ram something – anything – in her mother's mouth.

So even if Bert couldn't keep track of money, how could you complain too much? The guy worked like three men and he was fun. You could forgive just about anything if someone was fun.

"One thing about it," he promised, kissing her cheek with soft little nibbles, "life will never be boring. I promise you that. If it gets boring you just say so."

And it was never boring. Except for the go-round with the cars, which did get boring after a while.

"Jesus, Bert, I never know when I step out that door what kind of car will be sitting in the driveway! Trade up, trade down, trade sideways; two-door, four-door, station wagon; red, blue, black, grey, two-tone – are the ashtrays full? Well, just drive 'er down and bring home one with clean ones, and service charges every time, refinancing charges . . . can't we just get a bloody car and *have* it?"

"What do you care? You don't even drive!"

And she didn't. She had her bike. She got it brand new before Martine was born, and had a baby seat put on the crossbar. She didn't like the idea of the kid riding behind her where she couldn't see her. When Martine was big enough she got a trike, then a small two-wheeler with training frame. That's when Reba went in the baby seat. About the time the baby seat was needed for Ronnie, Reba was ready for the two-wheeler with the training frame and Martine went up to a small-size regular bike.

"A new one," Bert said stubbornly. "I went through my whole fuckin' life on secondhand rust buckets. I thought fenders had to rattle or the bike wouldn't move. I'm workin' hard and makin' good money and my kids are havin' good bikes."

It was stupid to get a seven-year-old child a hundred-and-fifty-dollar bike, but that's what Bert came home with. Liz could have argued, but didn't. If making sure his kid had a new bike took some of the sting of the rust buckets out of his system, get the new bike. Get three if that's what it takes!

"Okay, Marti, I'll hold 'er while you check the angle . . . can you see there?"

"A bit."

He moved the rearview. "Then how about there?"

"How's this?"

"Too far, Daddy."

"There?"

"Yah. That's good."

"Good girl. So now you promise me, okay, you keep checking this thing. Before you make any kind of move at all, whether it's left turn, right turn or stop, you check this thing. Make sure you know who's behind you. Promise?"

"I promise."

"That's my sugar lump. Because Marti," and he lifted her off the bike and held her close, one strong arm under her bum, the other across her back, his huge hand, tanned and brown, curled around the curve of her skull, "if anything happened to you I'd come to pieces."

"Oh Daddy, you wouldn't."

"Marti, you don't know how much I love you. You don't know what a miracle you are to me and you won't know until you're grown up and have kids of your own. You're my family, Marti. I never had a family until I met your mommy and we got you. No mom, no dad, no gramma, no cousins, no nobody at all. So you're my world. Something happens to you," and he blinked, then worked overtime to lighten it up, "hey, I'd be rollin' around on the ground, and I'd be screamin' and yellin' and howlin' and roarin' and belly-achin' and everyone would point at me and laugh."

"Oh, *Daddy!*" She squeezed him tight around the neck, peppered his face with kisses. "I'll be fine, you'll see."

The sun rose and set in the crack of Marti's ass as far as Bert was concerned. And Reba's, too.

"You scared, Rebe?"

"A bit."

"Yeah. That's okay. Being scared means you're smart enough to realize something could go wrong. If you think about it, though . . . what you feel when you're scared is just about pretty near the same as what you feel when you're all excited, right? Little flutterbyes in the tummy? Little dry place in the throat? Maybe kind of a hard egg thing in your belly? Almost the same. And it's funny, because being excited is fun and being scared, even though it's almost the same, isn't any fun at all. But it's okay being scared. And if you don't want to do it, you say so because I don't *ever* want you doing something you don't want to do. You're my darling. I love you as big as the whole wide world."

"Well, I can ride with training wheels, but . . . without them the bike wobbles."

"I'll give you wobbles." He tickled her. "I'll wobble your ribs and I'll wobble your neck and if you aren't careful I'll pull off your shoes and wobble the soles of your feet!"

You could put up with endless car payments when you saw your kid safe in the arms of a man who would cut his own throat before he'd grab her and throw her to the floor and teach her what scared really means. You would mortgage your life to Detroit if the hands that picked her up were sane and gentle and protective.

With the bikes they went wherever they wanted, up streets and along alleys, to the playground, up to the lake. For birthdays Liz got them bike gear or sports equipment. They had rat-trap carriers on the back fender and frame, they had saddlebags, they had wire carrier baskets on the handlebars, they had red reflector lights and orange berries on their spokes. They had softballs and basketballs and a hoop set up on the garage door. All they had to do was put sandwiches here, plastic jug of juice there, bathing suit and towel here, and off we go, hi-ho hi-ho. No need for aerobics class, no need to worry if they were getting enough phys-ed at school, put some fruit in a bag and head off, especially on weekends if Bert was working.

"Well, isn't this a fine fare-thee-well," he'd say, pretending to be fed up. "I work like a dog all day and then come home and start supper so's a buncha vacationing upper-crusters can come in all suntanned and their hair still damp from swimmin' and sit down at the table and gorp away like Berkshire hogs," but he was handing out and receiving hugs and smooches, and he patted Liz on the butt when she went to hang the wet sandy towels on the line.

"I like having my days off in the middle of the week," he told her. "It means I get you to myself for a change."

"You lecherous old man."

"Lecherous, maybe. Old? Hey, didn't they tell you the older the bull the stiffer the horn?"

"Brag brag brag," and she moved against him, deliberately tantalizing him with tongue and finger, with hand and leg, "Promises, promises, all I get around here are more promises."

So why did it stick in her craw that it was called "Liz's allowance"? Why did it make her feel like a ten-year-old getting a few bucks' handout each week to cover the movies and some popcorn, in return for good behaviour and the chores done on time?

"Job? What the hell for?" He stared, his brow furrowed with total puzzlement.

"Why does anybody get a job, Bert?"

"I've got one to keep this show on the road. To buy food and clothes. If I didn't need to do that I'd be at home all the time, bet your bottom dollar on that."

"The only dollar I have is the bottom dollar." She tried to tease him, tried to get him grinning. He wasn't buying it, though.

"You want money? Fuck, say so I'll give it to you."

"And what does that make me? A charity case?"

"Liz, what in hell is it?"

"Ronnie's in school every morning until noon. The girls are there until three. I could get a job. I could actually get out of this house and talk to adult people for a change. I'm sure there's conversation alive and well out there in the middle of the day, Bert. I'm sure of it."

She didn't know at the time that you wind up doing what you've done before, over and over again. That whatever you fall into doing is something you fell into at some other time.

"Listen, I have to tell you, if I could fiddle like you I wouldn't be filling out an application form to work here."

"Nobody pays you for fiddling around," she grinned.

"Oh yeah? I bet you're wrong about that!"

"Nights? Jesus aitch Christ, Liz! Eight at night to one in the morning isn't exactly the same as a few hours while the kids are in school!"

"No, it's better. They're ready to go to bed, practically, anyway."

"Right. Fine. They can go to bed and I can sit by myself watching TV while I babysit."

"Babysit? Babysitting is what you do with someone else's kids. You don't babysit your own kids. You just *be* with. The way I've been with them ten hours a day every day since they were born!"

"Easy, easy, easy. Jesus you're proddy!"

"Why do I have to justify every idea I have or every move I want to make? Why can you just announce 'I bought a new car' and that's great, but I want to do something and I have to go Perry Mason and defend the idea?"

"Oh for fuck's sake, I'm not arguing with you. You want to do it, do it, never mind about me or what I think about it, Liz, just off you go and do whatever the hell it is you want. Honest to God, my life is controlled so much by your premenstrual tension it's a wonder my fuckin' nose doesn't bleed every twenty-eight days!"

"Off I go and do whatever I want? Why is that so horrible, but when *you* do it, hell's bells, it's just the way of the world? Don't you ever get tired of being omnipotent? God*damn*, it can't be easy being a godlike creature!"

"Don't I just wish. I'd arrange it that when you had these bloody fits of secondhand feminism, you'd go mute as a post! Fuck *me*, but this is boring!"

When the kids heard about it they decided to act as if they had been left naked on a rock in the middle of absolutely nowhere without so much as a peanut butter sandwich to sustain them until the rescuers arrived.

"But I want you to be *here!*"

"You'll be so sound asleep you won't know who's here and who isn't. Daddy'll be here."

"I want *you*."

"Well, you'll have me from the time you get home from school until you're ready for bed. And then you'll have me from the time I get home until you get up to go to school."

"What if I *need* you for something?"

"You just stop this right now. Halt. Cease. Desist. Give over. No more! You don't need me to do your breathing for you! If you *need* me so badly how come you get home from school, whip off your clothes and rip back out of the house again, full-tilt boogie off to your friends? If I was so vital to your existence you wouldn't want to leave the house! I'm going to work. Period. I'll leave here at about half-past seven and I'll be home just about the time the late show is winding down on TV. And *you* will be in bed, asleep, and won't even know. And that, my friend, is that."

Bert watched and listened and said nothing. He just sat, as patient as that same old snake, taking it all in and letting none of it back out again.

"Well, I don't like it," said Reba.

"Oh Reba, for God's sake go clean your room and when you get to the part where you're hauling your old socks out from under the bed, ram a couple of them in your mouth, will you?"

Bert turned away, and Liz was sure he was angry.

"Yes?" she moved to stand near him.

"Do they do that very often?" he asked mildly.

"Do what?"

"Whatever in hell it was Reba just tried to do."

"Oh, that," she sighed. "Reba does it sometimes. As soon as there's the least little change. Remember when we switched from those little plastic sandwich bags to waxed paper because of that report about how the bags were going to pile up until they buried the world? Well, Reba pitched a fit for weeks about that!"

"Slap her ass a few times," he suggested. "Christ, I can see *me* yammering on about wah wah wah I don't wanna switch foster homes again, natter natter," he shook his head in amazement. "Do you think we spoiled the shit out of them?"

"Yeah." Liz laughed suddenly, surprising herself. "I think we spoiled the supreme shit out of all three of them." She dropped onto his lap and sat sideways with her legs on the arm of the tired old chair. "They aren't tough, Bertie. I bet you were a tough little guy." She rested her cheek against his, feeling the bristles, inhaling the scent of his hair. "I bet you were one of those little farts of the kind we call 'going concerns' around here. Go to a new neighbourhood and check it out, where's the playground, where's the candy store, where's the dog pound so I can stand at the wire and look at the animals. These kids? They'd sit on the steps and let tears slick down their faces for a week before they even thought to find the gate."

"I didn't want my kids to *have* to be tough." He put his arms around her and hugged gently. "But maybe we leaned too far the other way? Anything happens and this lot'll be helpless."

"Given the two alternatives, I'll stick to this one. You think there might be someplace in between, someplace we could maybe aim for?"

"Hope so. Otherwise," and he pretended to be shocked, pulled a face of horror, "we might have turned out . . . *middle-class soft-underbellied small-l liberals!*"

"Tell me we wouldn't do a thing like that! Please, Bert, tell me we wouldn't betray our origins that way!" And their laughter mingled, warm and companionable.

Wilma was angry Liz was going back to work. She clipped articles from magazines and made a point of leaving them where Liz and Bert couldn't help but find them: the back of the toilet tank, on the counter near the coffee canister, held to the fridge by a magnet. Bert closed the fridge door then stood there, cream jug in his hand, reading the article while Liz and Wilma sat at the table with their mugs of coffee, waiting for the cream. Then Bert took the article from under the magnet, folded it in half carefully, then again, and again until it was about the size of a quarter and so thick he couldn't bend it again. He took it to the table with him, put the cream on the table and dropped the article in Wilma's coffee. She stared, as close to flabbergasted as Liz had ever seen her get.

"Stop it," Bert said quietly, "or the next one goes up your left nostril."

"Bert!" Liz gasped.

He smiled at her, then rumpled her hair. "I cannot stand nagging," he said quietly, sitting at the table. "It makes me so goddamn unreasonable I say things I didn't even know I knew how to say." He looked at Wilma and something passed between them. "Liz is going to work," he said coldly. "I want you to know I don't like it one damn little bit. I don't think we need the money, but she wants to do it. And that means I don't get to see her as much as I'd want. So when I can, I don't want any goddamn go-round, okay? Some nights I am going to have to get a babysitter in, and if you want to be that babysitter it's going to mean no nagging about how the poor little abandoned angels deserve to have momsiepie and daddypie at home with them. I don't want to tell you to butt the hell out of this, Wilma, but if I have to say that, I will. Real loud, okay?"

"Well, if you don't want Liz working, why don't you just tell her that she can't work?" replied Wilma, who had been working at mean jobs for mean pay for as long as Liz could remember. "I worked, but I had to, to raise my children. You don't have to work, Elizabeth. And if you don't have to work, you should be at home, where you belong. And *you*." She looked at her son-in-law, challenging him. "You should stand up to her and tell her to stay home, the way she's supposed to do. So why don't you do it?"

Bert laughed. "Because she'd tell me to ram it right up my ass," he answered. "I married her, Wilma, I didn't buy her at the auction. She married me, she didn't agree to become a robot for the rest of her life."

What Wilma would never have heard from Liz, she heard clearly from Bert. That only added to the gnawing lump in Liz's belly, a lump accumulating to itself so many other little lumps it promised to grow into a heap.

/ / /

The gentle hissing and glubbing of the coffee maker half-wakened Anna Fleming five minutes before the annoying *neep-neep* of the alarm, and the first siren scents of fresh dripped coffee teased her, relieving some of the pain of awakening.

Some people open their eyes and leap to their feet, full of whatever it takes to march energetically into another day. Anna was not one of those people. She did not fall asleep easily, did not always stay asleep, and wakened grudgingly, her entire body fighting back. One of her most vivid childhood memories was her mother coming to her bedroom door and chirruping heartily, "Rise and shine, rise and shine, a new day has begun!" It was enough to make a child weep, and Anna had wept as she slid from the warm cocoon to the chilly floor. Often she wound up sitting on the table, feet dangling, crying bitterly while her mother dressed her for school, because she simply could not get it together to dress herself. "Wakey wakey, tea and cakey," her mother would say brightly, laughing at Anna as Anna's weeping became sobbing, her sleepiness became anger, but what do you do about that? Show you're angry and you'll just get a couple of good solid whacks on the rump to teach you to control your temper. Anna's hatred of wakening had never gone away, and sometimes she wondered if her inability to go to sleep had something to do with her dread of the horror of waking up again.

But the smell of coffee made it less horrible. She reached out, slapped the off button on the clock, got out of bed and went to the kitchen, stumbling slightly, still groggy from sleep. She poured a mug of steaming coffee, added a spoonful of honey and a splash of cream, and took her coffee back to bed with her.

She knew her blood pressure was in the low range of normal. Maybe it dropped when she was asleep, and maybe that low blood pressure couldn't move the toxins from her body. Maybe she was related to good old Wotzername who fell asleep for a thousand years and a day, then wakened and married the prince. Maybe if Anna could get to sleep and stay asleep for a thousand years and a day she too could waken, although the chances of marrying a prince seemed pretty remote.

She took a second cup of coffee to bed, feeling ready to turn on the radio and hear the early morning litany of grisly horror from around the world. When the news report of yet another famine and drought was about half over, she got out of bed, went to the bathroom and turned on the shower.

By the time she was finally dressed for work she felt almost ready to get up. Maybe she should get a job which allowed her to work steady afternoon shift. Get home from work at midnight, shower, go to bed and stay there until it was time to head off again. And maybe it would be one of those brainless jobs you could do without ever having to think, a job you could quite happily leave behind when you headed home again. Putting labels on dog food cans, checking bottles in a pop factory, something routine.

She left her apartment, locking the door securely behind her, got in the elevator and stood there in a state the next best thing to suspended animation, riding to the basement. It was dark in the underground parking lot, the only light coming in from the wide exit to the street. Anna walked to her car angrily. The idiot got a rent-free apartment in return for caretaking, and couldn't even replace the goddamn light bulbs when they burned out, which they seemed to do with stunning frequency. Maybe she should apply for the job of caretaker. She could sleep in until noon every day, then take one or two hours to check light bulbs and leaky faucets, and have the rest of the day to herself.

There was some kind of advertising flyer stuck under her windshield wiper. She pulled it out without looking at it, crumpled it, dropped it to the concrete floor, then unlocked the car door, got in, locked the door again, put her key in the ignition, started the engine and fastened her seat belt.

"Okay, kiddo," she sighed, "put the brain in gear. Another day, another traffic jam. Onward and upward excelsior."

The car moved slowly toward the bright square that was the exit. Anna checked the traffic, then moved expertly into it.

a long segmented snake of traffic moved toward the city . . .
a blue Pontiac segment, a red Toyota, an orange Datsun,
piece by piece, section by section, the serpent twined . . .

like those plastic toys, red and blue rectangles which click together at either end. A kid can make snakes or lizards or even dragons and sea serpents, clicking the segments together, making the critter as long as they had pieces to click.

/ / /

Liz played Thursday, Friday and Saturday nights from eight until one. She stood on a raised end of the long room looking through a blue pall of cigarette smoke at all the little round tables flanked on two sides by rectangular booths into which people crowded between dances or fistfights and swilled expensive drinks. Up on the platform supposed to be a stage, flanked alongside her, were four other people, all of whom smiled, smiled, smiled, exactly the way she did, while they played, played, played. Friday and Saturday nights the noise was so loud at times Liz couldn't hear the music herself. "I hope we're all playing the same song," she said once. "It would be a shame if I was doing 'Heartbreak Hotel' while the rest of you were singing about how Jeremiah was a bullfrog."

"Nobody would notice," said the bass guitar player.

Occasionally, during the day when she was at home, alone, Liz would put a tape in the player and listen to classical music. As if to remind herself of something it was very very important she learn and never forget, she would play with the great orchestras of the world. She knew, as she had always known, that nothing, not even a sane and supportive family, would have enabled her to actually sit and play with them. She wasn't sure she would ever have wanted to, she didn't feel she needed the reminders, she enjoyed pretending while she played with the best in the world, but still there was a slight tug and it was regretful. She knew she was good, she knew she was very good, and she could easily join the local symphony, but that was different from what she thought of as a "real" orchestra, which probably wouldn't even invite her to audition. You have to be more than very good to join the best in the world. As for those miraculous few people like Itzhak Perlman and Stephane Grappelli, you had to be touched at birth by the kiss of the angels.

And so she accepted what was, and played as well as she could, and those who heard her said things like "Well, she always was good at it," and "Just naturally musical," and "Got the gift, she has." They would never know how much of her life went into practising. What they knew was she played a damn fine breakdown and they enjoyed dancing to her music.

Liz almost broke out laughing the night Gowan wandered in with his latest mattress. He didn't even notice Liz was in the band until after he and whoever-she-was had finished their first drink, ordered their second and got up on the dance floor. For a minute Liz thought Gowan was going to bolt. Instead he pretended he had never seen her before in his life and went on dancing his way around the floor with anybody else in the world but Wilma. Liz realized he knew she wouldn't say a word about it to anyone.

Almost an hour later Gowan was still demonstrating why it was so many people said he was a dancin' fool. And the mattress with him was acting as if the world and all its treasures were being handed to her on a silver platter. Liz imagined over and over again what would happen if she stepped forward, took the mike and made a Personal. "Ladies and gentlemen," she almost heard her own voice, clear and with a little undercurrent of amused enjoyment, "I'd like to do a special number right now. For a special person who is with us tonight. My father, Gowan Harris, the little guy down there in the dark blue jacket, the fancy-footin' twinkletoes who's polishing the floor with that lovely lady with him, the one who happens not to be my mother but what the hell, if we kicked out everybody who was here tonight with someone else's better half the hall would be empty, right? With your indulgence, I'd like to do this one for my dad. One of my favourites."

Gowan would gape, he would cringe, he would feel so small he could sit on a penny match and still swing his legs over the side. He'd get a whap in the face from the woman, he'd turn and flee, he'd be shamed in public. Liz went over it again and again in her mind until she just *had* to actually do it, she *had* to send him scurrying off like a randy rodent.

But all Gowan did was laugh out loud, grab his partner and dance around the floor, singing with her.

/ / /

"You *what?*" Bert sat up in bed and turned on the lamp.

"Sang 'Honky Tonk Angel' and dedicated it to the old fart."

"Liz." Bert leaned over, kissed the tip of her nose and grinned. "You are *bad*. You are so bad you are good! You are the baddest woman I ever met."

"You smell good," she said, kissing his chin. "You smell all clean and after-shavey, and you've got your face so close to mine all I can see is a great big blur with one, count 'em one, eye just above what I think is a nose."

"You need glasses, darling. I've got two eyes."

"I only see one. Great big slanty thing."

"Hey, lady, you're in real trouble," he laughed, "that is not my eye!"

The amazing part was Gowan came back a week or two later, sat at a different table with a different mattress and had a wonderful time. Liz knew he was half expecting her to pull the same stunt again, so she didn't. She just made out as if he was nothing more to her than any other customer destroying his own liver. The old fart.

"Tyler Perkins says he heard his dad and uncle laughing because they said they saw Grandpa dancing with a lady who wasn't Grandma. And," Martine glared, "they said you played him a special song and laughed about it."

"And what, pray tell, was Tyler Perkins' daddy doing in the Pregnant Parrot? Tyler Perkins' mommy is in the hospital having a baby. So who was Tyler Perkins' daddy dancing with that night? I bet it wasn't Tyler Perkins' *uncle!*"

"Did you tell Grandma?"

"No, I did not. I am not your grandfather's babysitter."

"Well, I'm gonna tell!"

Liz wanted to tell her daughter to butt out, but Martine had already had her back rubbed raw by Tyler Perkins' laughter and teasing. And if Liz wasn't Gowan's babysitter, maybe she wasn't Martine's, either.

"I wouldn't if it was me," she said mildly, "but you do what you think you have to do. And if your grandma tells you to mind your own business, don't say I didn't warn you."

Two days later, standing at the kitchen sink helping wash lettuce for a salad, Martine asked, "Know what Grandma said when I told her?"

"Butt out?"

"No," Martine laughed, "she said it doesn't matter what kind of work it is they're doing, whether it's vacuuming the floor, doing the ironing or slopping the pigs, if they're doing your chores, they're your hirelings."

"Good lord."

"Does that mean Grandma doesn't like to dance?"

"You'd have to ask your grandma, darling. I gave up trying to figure it out years and years ago."

"Does my dad go dancing with other ladies?"

"No. Your dad is an honest man. And Martine . . . they aren't 'ladies', okay?"

"Maybe they don't know Grandpa's married."

"Maybe not. But probably they do. If he doesn't care about it why should they?"

"Do you care?"

"About Gowan, you mean? I don't care any more."

They wiped the lettuce with the clean tea towel and broke it carefully into little chunks.

"There's a song like that, isn't there?" said Martine. "About I don't care any more?"

"Hurt. I know one that goes I don't hurt any more. Or something like that."

"Well, why don't you sing it?"

"Right here and now? While we're drying lettuce for the salad?"

So Liz dropped the lettuce, sat on the corner of the table and sang, self-consciously at first, then easily while Marti continued working on the salad, smiling widely and nodding in time to the song.

/ / /

Fran sat on the edge of the blanket watching the kids ripping around on the sand at the edge of the lake. She pulled at the fringe, adjusting it, trying to get a straight line. "Do you think she wonders what kind of work you do?"

"Marti knows what I do, I play the fiddle. And she hates country music, so the fiddle is nothing to her."

"Maybe she wonders what *you* are doing in the bar."

"Playing the goddamn fiddle, Fran! It was Gowan dancing had her upset, not me playing!"

"They get ideas in their little heads and sometimes ask things indirectly."

"Oh, pooh. Marti was never indirect in her life. If she wanted to know what kind of work I do she'd ask if she could come and watch."

"You're sure?"

"Yes."

"Well, I hope you're right."

And Fran sat there staring over at the kids as if anything interesting at all was going on other than her kids and Liz's kids kicking sand in each other's faces. But Fran was different, somehow, since she'd had the operation and moved into the big grey house and all. Even Wilma was wondering just what exactly was going on with Fran. Sometimes she disappeared inside that house for days at a time. You'd phone and there'd be no answer, or one of the kids would answer and say "Mom's in her dungeon right now, Auntie Liz. She can be disturbed for fire, flood, earthquake or invasion by the body snatchers, and nothing else. Are you a body snatcher?"

"Will you remember to leave a message telling her I called?"

"Sure will. I'm writing it on the blackboard right now. Auntie Liz phoned. Call back. Anything else you want to say?"

"Ask her if there's central heating in her dungeon. How are you?"

"Good."

"How's school?"

"Oh, you know, it's school. Oh, I'm s'posed to tell you Robbie's good, he phoned from the airport and he's going into camp for probably three months. And Nancy's got a job on a cruise ship! She's getting paid to take trips, isn't that great? Mom says it's exactly the kind of job any sane person would give their eye teeth to have. And Lee has to have his tonsils out, that's what's giving him the sore throat all the time. Other than that we're all fine except Mom's real mad because the cat isn't a tom, after all."

"Let me guess, it had kittens, right?"

"Four. But Mom says they're all tom kittens so they'll be easy to give away, all we have to do is palm 'em off the way he got palmed off on us. And to be sure to save one for the people who gave us ours."

"I don't want one."

"Yours is grey with white feet."

"I don't want him."

"And a white nose."

That one got run over the first time it poked its white nose out from behind the fence. Liz never even had to buy a dirt box for it. But she did have to get a dirt box for the orange and white one Fran gave to Ronnie.

"But Fran, I don't want that thing."

"Ronnie does."

"Ronnie wants everything."

"He can't have everything, Liz, but he can have Marmalade the cat."

"I'll kill it."

"No you won't. You'll be mad for a while, and the next thing you know Marmalade will be on your lap purring away and you'll think it was all your idea in the first place. I know you."

Fran seemed to know Marti, too. It took a while, because Liz was almost as bullheaded as her daughter, but Fran's words rattled in her head, and finally, one evening when she didn't have to go to the Pregnant Parrot to play for people she didn't know,

Liz sat on the sofa beside her eldest, and put her arm around the tight little shoulders.

"So," she dove in head first, never mind if there were rocks in this pond, "did you ever wonder what it was your old mom did when she went to work?" Marti shrugged. "I'm asking because I used to wonder what my mom did. It seemed as if she sort of stepped out of the door and fell into a big black hole."

"I guess," Marti mumbled.

"I'd take you down but they'd kick us both out because they sell booze there and you're under-age."

"Even if I didn't drink booze?"

"Even so."

"Well, couldn't you pretend?" and Marti's eyes were suddenly damp, and seemed at least twice their usual size.

"Pretend? I probably could. Could you?"

The other kids got into it, too. Even Bert seemed eager. Off went the TV, and while Liz was in the bedroom pulling on her stage duds, the kids got busy with 7-Up and food colouring. Bert jumped into his current car, headed off to the store and came back with a jar of maraschino cherries and some coloured plastic straws. They mixed up their drinks, put them on paper doilies on the coffee table and sat on the carpet. Just before Liz came out with Recherche, Ronnie got up, ran to the kitchen and came back with a package of Nuts'n'Bolts which he put in the middle of the table, where they could all reach in and take some.

Liz wore her highly polished cowpuncher boots, her best jeans, and a shirt that would have stopped traffic if it was draped on a hanger. She put on her big silver bracelet with the turquoise chunks and spent some time getting her Australian-style rider's hat just so on her head. Then, determined to make believe and pretend to the very end, she walked into the living room, her face expressionless. Her kids stared at her. Bert took the shade off the tall lamp and aimed the light at her. Liz put on her stage smile and let her voice slip into the well-practised patter.

"Good evening, ladies and gentlemen, it's a real honour to be with you tonight, and a pleasure to have the opportunity to share some music with you. I'm Liz Harris, and this is my good friend Recherche, handmade by Orlando himself. She's an old girl, and she's in the absolute prime of her life, so let's see if we can get her to do what she does so well."

It was more fun than she'd had in ages. The kids shouted and cheered at the end of each number, they all called out requests for their favourites, and Liz played. Then, when they knew things were going to wind down and end for the night, Liz looked right at Marti, and smiled, but not her stage smile. "I know Martine isn't fond of what she thinks of as hayburner music, so just to prove that Recherche is capable of anything at all, this is for Marti."

It was like playing for old Max in his little store, surrounded by musical treasures; it was easy and comfortable and natural, and she knew she was very *very* good. The look on Martine's face said it all. Whatever she knew, or thought she knew, she hadn't suspected her mom could play this well. She learned something that night, and Liz learned, too: however much you love something, however much you consider it to be personal and private, there are times when opening up and sharing is the most loving thing you can do.

/ / /

Sure enough, Marmalade wound up on her lap. Sure enough, he became a favourite and sure enough, Fran did know her, and know her well. But Liz wasn't sure she knew Fran any more. What did she *do* in that room with the big windows looking out over the roofs to the shore where the plywood mill hammered and banged and pounded and made a mess of the beach? What could anyone do alone in a room for hours and hours on end?

"I'm writing," Fran answered calmly. "I've got a bunch of stuff I want to get down on paper. For the kids, because trying to keep track of the ins and outs and comings and goings of this family is too much strain for my brain, so if I deal with it a piece at a time and get it on paper . . . then if they want to know anything, family history or whatever, well, there it is."

"For hours and hours?"

"How long did it take you to learn to play the fiddle? Hours of practice, right? You think a person just sits down at a typewriter and turns into Margaret Laurence?"

"I never thought about it. I've got all I can do to write a grocery list. Promise me that when you find out you will never be Margaret Laurence, you won't slit your throat."

"Even Margaret Laurence wasn't always *the* Margaret

Laurence, you know. Even she had to start somewhere." And then, out of the blue, Fran was talking about things Liz had often thought, about how a handful of people were blessed, had found their personal voice, could write about things in such a way it was easy to read them and suddenly, hours later, you'd have to pull yourself almost physically out of a created world that seemed more real than this one. "Maybe I'll never be anywhere near that good," Fran said, "but not everyone is, and lots of books are so damn bad you're sorry about the trees that died to make the paper! I think I can learn how to tell a story, and tell it medium well. It's just going to take some practice, is all."

Hours. Sometimes it seemed as if entire days vanished into a hole before Fran got around to looking at her messages on the blackboard and phoning back, or coming over to visit.

"You ever wonder why Auntie Phoebe left town? I mean, out of all of them, why did she leave?"

"She got married, dope."

"Not until long after she'd left."

"Huh?"

"Sure. She'd been down in Victoria for over two years before she met her first husband."

"Really?" Liz couldn't understand why it was so important to Fran. "How many's she had now, anyway? Four? Five?"

"Five at least. But only two kids."

"People are funny, eh? I remember once she came to visit and I was in my visual artiste phase." Liz laughed softly, self-mockingly. "And I had this thing I'd done, of a heron, I think. Anyway, Phoebe takes one look and says she wants to buy it. Framed it and everything!"

"I never understood why you gave up your painting. You were so good at it. If I was that good at it I'd have every wall covered! At least," she sighed, "with painting, people can see what you've done."

"Yeah, and laugh at you, too."

"Nobody ever did any such'n thing! Liz, honest to God, you're so sure everyone is laughing behind their backs all the time. You've got to get yourself past that."

"Oh, listen to who's talking now, Doctor Fraud herself. Want me to go lie down on the couch while you take notes?"

And one night, there was Bert coming into the club, looking

for her, grinning widely and flapping one hand in greeting. Liz almost quit playing. But she got a grip on herself and smiled back, then spent the rest of the night giving herself little lectures about how it didn't mean anything, it wasn't the same, he hadn't come to the bar to hustle someone else's woman, he'd come to see her, he was missing her, he wanted to know what it was she did when she put on her work jeans, work shirt and the fancy cowboy boots she'd hauled out of the little steamer trunk in the basement. He wanted the whole show, not just the ones she put on in the living room, he wanted to see and smell the crowd, hear the laughter and the applause, and now that she was willing to share with the family, he felt welcome to come and watch the real-live Let's Pretend. Let's pretend we're happy, let's pretend we're celebrating, let's pretend life is hunky-dory, let's pretend we don't need point-zero-eight blood alcohol to get up the guts to dance.

Funny how people wanted to know what other people did for a job of work. She'd never once been the least bit interested in going out to the pulp mill and watching people turn perfectly good trees into toilet paper. But half the family was fascinated with the idea she got paid to play, the other half were busy trying to figure out what Fran was doing with her typewriter. Who'd ever given two hoots in hell what the uncles did with chain saws and choker cables?

"God, you work hard," Bert said later that night, when they were back home and curled like spoons in bed.

"Me? Hey, I *play* for a living, remember?"

"Looks like work to me. How do you do it? Stand up there looking as if you're having the time of your life. Or are you?"

"It's a job, darling, that's all."

"But . . . I've seen you at home. Even the shows you do for the kids aren't the same. You don't stand the same way. You don't tilt your head the same way. You play the song the same, I think, but *you* aren't the same. You're relaxed here. Low key. Like you *play* the fiddle, you *play* the song, you . . . I don't know. Then you get up there and it's like sparks or something. Not from the fiddle. From *you*."

"Energy," she yawned. "That's what people are paying for. If all they wanted was the music they could leap and fart around to records. They want our energy so they can get up from the table and move their feet."

"Looks like hard work," he repeated.

"Yeah, it's hard work." She yawned again, the back of her throat stretching so tight it almost hurt. "They pay their cover and come inside so they can swill booze and chew on our souls, as if they didn't have souls of their own. That's what makes me tired. Not the fiddling, I can do that standing on my head. It's that other thing, that energy thing, that give-'em-what-they-want thing. If you don't give it, off they go looking for someone else to consume."

"Then why do you do it?"

"It's what I do. That's all. It's what I do."

Fran liked the house Liz had found for her. At one time, probably back when Uncle Gowan was a boy, the South End had been the second-best area in town. All the mucketymucks lived in Townsite, but the highpockets hadn't felt welcome over there. The lines were drawn. It wasn't enough to be a doctor, you had to be second- or third-generation doctor to fit in. Supervisors didn't live over there, either. Or "people in trade," as if that kind of work was fit only for the degenerate, when it was the Townsite, with all those mucketymucks, where you'd find the real degeneracy.

Someone posh had built this place. The basement was tall enough it could pass for a floor of the house, except for the dragon, the big coal-and-wood-burning furnace. They must have put it there as they built the house, no way would it fit through any of the doors. So it just stood there, unused for years, with the oil furnace tucked in beside it. The kids made jokes about how they should breed the furnaces and sell the litters of Franklin stoves as soon as they were weaned.

Wood floors everywhere except the kitchen and bathrooms, and Fran figured if she ever got around to lifting off the linoleum she'd find wood there, too. But Fran liked the linoleum. They didn't make it like that any more, that's for sure, what Aunt Wilma called "battleship." The colour seemed to go all the way to the bottom, so no worn-out places showed. It must have been down there at least forty years, feet tracking across it constantly, yet all you had to do was scrub it clean, put on a couple of layers of paste wax and get out the polisher and there it was, good as anything you'd buy today.

The first floor had a pantry, a kitchen big enough to hold a convention of the Brethren of the Moose, another room the original use of which nobody could guess but which Brandy chose for her bedroom, an entrance room off the side door, a mammoth living room, a hallway and at the end of it another bedroom with a bathroom behind it. The second floor was bedrooms, bathrooms, more bedrooms and a long thing they decided could be a walk-in closet. "Waltz in and take a hike is more like it," Brandy laughed. Fran laid claim to the top floor, which had several rooms and two bathrooms, one with a shower, one with a tub.

"A boarding house!" Brandy thrilled. "We could open a boarding house!"

"You open it, dear," said Fran. "And you do all the work, too."

"You aren't going to fill it with fosters again, are you?"

"No more than six dozen, don't worry."

She wasn't as keen on all that as she had been. But still, there were considerations, most of them financial. The hundred-ninety-six-thousand she got for her house in the city got her clear title to the big grey box in town. It also got her more than fifty thousand in savings, which would disqualify her for welfare for herself, so she got some decent furniture and a brand-new electric typewriter. She also got a desk and a typing chair that made all the difference to her back.

"Are we going to get a car?" Brandy hoped aloud.

"No, we are not. I don't even drive."

"I can. I'd drive."

"The bus driver already offered."

"Well, gee whiz, Mom! We'll be the only people in town without a car!"

"Good, then we can always get a seat on the bus. You want a car you finish school, get a job, buy your own."

"Grouch."

"Whiner."

"But there's lots of ways a car is really convenient and –"

"Shut up!" Fran yelled. Brandy stopped as if she'd run into a brick wall. "I am not getting a car. You hear that Bran? N, O, no. You hear me?"

"Yes, I hear you! The whole world hears you!"

The truth was, Fran didn't know if she wanted to register as a foster home. They were all starting to get on her nerves. If she'd ever spoken to Jo-Beth the way Brandy spoke to her, it would be suh-*lap!* suh-*whack!* Out would come the old iron. And the boys! Ritchie in grade nine, figuring he could come and go as he pleased with a look on his face to curdle the milk. Garnet spending hours down in the basement with that bench press he'd made, and she didn't even want to know where he got the set of weights. Lee was still a little boy with not much more on his mind than his bike, but even he ticked her off sometimes with his constant need for this or that or the next thing, most of which he was perfectly capable of getting or doing for himself. Well, it was traumatic for them, being packed up and moved from their old neighbourhood, but they were certainly better off. They had more to do now, playgrounds here, sports facilities there, soccer teams and lacrosse teams and something other than traffic and stores to look at.

"Just stop it," she told him. "It's not going to do anything but get you an earful. Four out of five people on earth sleep on sidewalks or in ditches. Millions of people have nothing in the way of a home but a hole scratched into the side of a hill. You won't die a foul death if you're forced to have your own bedroom!"

"Well, it's *lonely!*" and he burst into tears. Fran laughed and turned away, and Lee quit crying immediately. "You don't care!" he screeched.

"Your only problem is you've got nobody else to blame for the mess on the floor," she said casually. "That's why you've got a room to yourself. Nobody wants to share a room with a sloppy pig. And don't bother crying about how lonely you are. If someone was in that room with you, you'd complain about that, too."

"I hate you!"

"I'll live."

She held off on fostering until she had a good start on her family stories, but the thought of pinching pennies forever was a dreary one. Even Liz, who had everything any woman could ever want, was talking about going back to work, and she had never had to wonder how to pay the phone bill, or whether the kids would have new shoes in the fall. What did they do with their shoes, anyway, eat them? And when did sneakers start to cost a year's take-home pay for a third-world labourer? Why did they need a pair of street shoes, a pair of outdoor sports shoes for school, a pair of indoor ones that wouldn't scratch the gym floor and yet another pair if they were on a team?

"I did special services fostering in the city," she said calmly, "but I don't think I want to do that any more. My own children are older now, and the age gap would be hard to bridge."

"Yes," the worker nodded. "On the other hand, they'd be old enough to help."

They really do want someone to take it all off their hands, Fran thought, because otherwise these ones will have to get off their duffs and demand more funding.

"I don't think they want to do that any more," she answered. "They're more than willing to share what needs shared – time, attention, that kind of thing." She smiled, and took all the ammunition out of the worker's little bag of tricks. "But I don't think it does the special care kids any good to live with older kids who resent them."

Then it was the old keep-the-house-clean routine until someone got her finger out of her nose and came around to make sure there really was a house at the address you'd given. Well, let them find something to complain about here!

"It's been nice having time to myself," she told Liz, "but lately I've felt as if I'm slacking off. There are so many of them need what we've got so much of."

"Don't start in on me," Liz said quickly.

"I'd think, what with Bert knowing what it was like, that you'd want to help make things better for even one or two kids."

"I am," Liz laughed. "For my own three."

"Well, I'm sure I can count on you to be extended family and accept the fosters the same as if they were our own."

"Hell, I'm not even sure who our own are! There's been so much adultery, fornication and casual fucking gone on over the years you couldn't prove who was and was not a relative."

"That's an awful thing to say!" But Fran laughed, and so did Liz, as if she had told some huge joke.

"Won't those extra kids make it harder for you to write?"

"I've asked for school-agers."

"So when are you going to show me something you've written?"

"When are you going to play me some music?"

"You want music? What kind?"

"Good music," Fran said, her streak of prissiness rising to the top again.

ANNE ELIZABETH

The sounds of tension hung thick in the air: the clatter of cutlery washed and half-dried, then dumped into the drawer, unsorted jumble of knives, forks and spoons, the egg lifter landing sideways, jamming when she slammed the drawer shut, jamming and bending, and she sighed, a martyr feeling yet another lion's claw. She pulled open the drawer and straightened the egg lifter slowly, doggedly, then replaced it carefully and closed the drawer again with exaggerated patience. The evening stretched thick with silence, only the persistent slip-slip-slip of cards sliding to the table, three at a time, face up, the red ten on the black jack, an endless game of solitaire he called Beat the Chink, even though Momma said *chink* was an awful word and insulted the one who used it as much as the one it was used against. Momma sat on the top step with a cup of tea, watching the neighbourhood, her dark eyes like those of a spaniel hit by a truck: puzzled, wordlessly asking the questions nobody could answer. Why me? what happened? what's going on, anyway? Voices at night, voices coming through the wall between the bedrooms, sounds with no discernible words, his voice insistent and probing, hers dull and lifeless, both of them resentful, both caught in the trap, knowing they had run into it, from different directions, for different reasons, for the same result, to the same end.

And something unspeakable, something spooky and threatening and . . . dirty, loose in the neighbourhood. Something the mothers whispered about and the fathers discussed coldly, something that made them change the subject whenever a child approached. Anne Elizabeth mustn't prowl the bluff alone, mustn't go by herself to sit on the small bridge and throw bits of worm and fly to the sticklebacks and bullheads. It had to do with the police going to the Griersons' house, in which Mabel Grierson was crying, and out of which Mabel seldom came until the day she left with two suitcases to go live with her aunt in Ladysmith, and everyone saying it was bad enough it had happened to her, but to have to suffer such shame on top of the pain and horror . . .

The something meant Anne Elizabeth was never, never *never* to talk to strangers, get into a car alone or open the door for *anybody* unless her father or mother was there. Nobody. Except family.

Cliff was working graveyard shift, midnight to morning, coming home
from work at breakfast time, turning the whole day upside down. On day
shift you could run and yell from the time you got up until suppertime, playing in the side yard or front yard or back yard, climbing trees or pushing
and shoving each other in games of hide-and-seek. Afternoon shift you had
to be quiet in the morning, but around the time the mailman arrived, bringing letters and envelopes with windows in them, he'd get up and come into
the kitchen in his jeans, his feet and chest bare, and pour himself a cup of
tea from the eternal pot and sit at the table staring without seeing until he
came together again and the new day started at the bottom of his second
cup of tea. Then you could run or yell or climb or anything. But on mid-
nights, on graveyard, you had to Be Quiet. You had to go down the road to
the vacant field if you wanted to yell or run or ride in the rattly wagon.
Except you couldn't go alone any more because of ... something. Something
so menacing Momma preferred to have you play – *quietly* – in the house.

He was in bed, sleeping through the sticky heat of the day, and from the
basement came the soft rhythmic *busha-bee busha-bee* of the washing
machine, the round white mystery you mustn't ever go near because you
might get scalded with hot water, or get your hand caught in the wringer, or
get bashed on the side of the head if the overload thing in the wringer
snapped and the spring sent the wotzit flying out the side.

The wooden thread bobbin wheels on the wagon that used to be a
cheese box moved slowly and quietly across the rug that used to be a big
bag of cast-off clothes until Momma and Grandma sat down and ripped
everything into strips, then pushed the strips through shiny metal cones,
knotting ends together and braiding the strips into one long thick strip
which they finally started to wind and roll and stitch into a big round rug
of all the colours and feels in the world. Slippery feels and rough feels, soft
feels and prickly feels and every colour from the faded blue of work pants
to the shiny brown of discarded "good" pants that had travelled downhill
from Saturday night dances to weeknight visits to cutting the grass to fishing, to become, finally, part of the rug. From the still bright red of Uncle
Tamas's hunting shirt to the funny black-and-white patterned jacket found
on the side of the road, one sleeve missing. "The guy musta took it off and
hung it on a rock on his way to the secondhand store," Uncle Andrew said,
his face serious, his eyes dancing. Back and forth, back and forth, the home-
made wooden-wheeled cheese-box wagon on the thread bobbins crossed the
vari-coloured rug. Funny how Grandmother MacDonald so seldom spoke to
Momma, and never spoke to Momma's family, but no sooner had the idea of
the rug been mentioned than she donated a big bag of scraps. Oh well, every-

one would say, Grandmother MacDonald is something else again, and they'd shake their heads and grin. But if one of her sons was around to hear, they didn't say that.

Footsteps on the front stairs and then a knock knock knock at the door. Anne Elizabeth looked up and saw the old man looking at her through the glass oval. Knock knock knock. She got up from the floor, leaving the wooden wagon and its stuffed silk-stocking doll passenger and went down the hallway, through the kitchen, to the steep stairs down to the basement where mother was controlling the *busha-bee busha-bee* of the washing machine. She waited at the top, remembering she mustn't go down those steps alone, she might fall, break her neck and die.

"Mom?"

"Go play, dear."

"But Mom –"

"Go play, I'm busy!"

So she went back to the living room and reached for Lily. Blue-eyed Lily, whose eyes used to close the front of Uncle Hugh's work shirt. The old man outside had quit knocking, waiting patiently for an adult. When none appeared, he began to knock again. Steadily. Stubbornly. Knock knock knock knock.

Twice more she went to the top of the break-your-bloody-neck stairs. Twice more Mother said she was *busy*, for heaven's sake, how many times do you need told!

And then he was coming from the bedroom, hair messy, face pink and hard set, pulling his jeans up over his bare bum. Thumping his heels down the hallway, flinging open the door. A thin, liver-spotted old hand thrust forward a religious pamphlet and almost triumphantly presented The Word.

"Thousands now living shall never die," he said fervently.

"You stupid psalm-singing fanatic old bastard!" he exploded, clenching his huge fists. "Lay off my bloody door and get the hell off this porch or *you'll* die, right here and right now!"

Then Mother was holding his arm, trying not to laugh, trying not to anger him further, pulling gently, reminding him, "He's an old man, honey, don't." The old man scuttled down the steps and skittered off, muttering to himself about the ungodly hardening their hearts, and Anne Elizabeth sat on the rug playing with Lily and muttering, "I tried to tell ya." She looked up at her mother, still holding tight to her father's arm, but laughing now, leaning against his bare, furry chest and laughing with him. "I tried to tell ya but ya was busy!"

She sat on the bottom step, watching as he dug the holes. Stripped to the waist, his pale skin slicked with sweat, his powerful miner's arms and shoulders wielding the shovel expertly, he tossed the earth aside easily. First the thick rich black topsoil, then the rocky brown dirt, then the mainly gravel and rock good-for-nothing fill. Finally he put down the shovel, took his dark blue hanky with the white polka dots from his back pocket, mopped his face, and grinned. "Just about got 'er, my Princess," he promised.

She didn't understand what he was going to do with all that rope, or the pulley screwed into the big beam poking out at the corner of the eaves. But she watched, then tried to help as he dragged the two big posts with the sturdy crossbar, put them in place on the ground, then threaded the rope through the pulley. "You sit on the back steps, now, hinny," he ordered, squinting at that mystery of hemp and wood. "Wouldn't want you catchin' anythin' under the chin and ruinin' all them new teeth."

He pulled on the end of the rope. As his shoulder muscles bulged and stood out like fat snakes under his skin, the crossbar began to lift, the ends of the posts slid into the holes, the whole rig began to rise and even Anne Elizabeth could see the shape being outlined against the sky. He tied the rope securely around the apple tree, mixed cement, gravel and water in a bucket and poured it into the two holes, around the posts. "We might just as well leave 'er for a bit. Go see if them blackberries is ripe."

The blackberries came from the vines easily and the air was ripe with the smell of juice, of summer afternoon dust, of crushed fern and wild mint. The buckets filled quickly. They washed the berries and Mother began making pies, her fingers stained purple, her face soft and pink and calm with pleasure.

"Come on, babe, no rest for the wicked," he said. He shovelled big rocks into the concrete and the holes, then dropped dirt on top, stamping on it and flattening it. "You can get the small shovel and a bucket and lug this stuff back to the compost heap. If you put a screen over the top of the bucket, the rocks won't get mixed in; we can put them in the wet spot at the back gate. Maybe even fill it in before this kid I know steps in it and sinks out of sight."

The next day he untied the rope attached to the apple tree, and the frame stood upright by itself. He shook the posts tentatively, then shook them harder.

"Got that new rope?" He squinted against the sunlight, his unlit cigarette stuck in the corner of his mouth.

She nodded, and ran to him with the new thick brown rope. "You watch your old man," he grinned, "you'll learn how to shinny," and quicker than any of the big boys, he was up the support post and moving across the crossbar with the rope coiled around his shoulder. Before she could think, he had the rope knotted in two places and was coming back down again, the rope hanging in a stiff but recognizable arc. "Got that seat?" he said. "I can't finish this without that seat." She gave him the slab of wood, notched at either end for the ropes, and he shoved it into place, stood back and nodded with satisfaction. "It'll do. Time for the first ride."

The seat was hard under her bum, the rope was stiff and harsh in the palm of her hand, and the apple tree came closer, moved away, came closer, moved away again.

"No more!" she gasped, and he moved aside, watching and smiling.

"How about giving Mom a ride?" he suggested.

Anne Elizabeth held tight to the ropes, but managed to nod her head.

"Hey, Cabbage," he called proudly.

The swing slowed, the creaking of the rope subsided and Anne Elizabeth stepped away from the wooden seat. Her legs felt funny – not exactly weak, but funny.

"Let me push," she demanded. He moved aside and Mother sat on the seat, laughing. When Anne Elizabeth pushed and started her swinging, Mother smiled down at her, then moved away, toward the apple tree and back, slowly. "Not too high, now," she warned, "I'm wearing a dress."

"Oh yes," he teased, "God forfend the dress should flap. Heaven forbid the limbs should show," and then he was swooping Anne Elizabeth in his arms, dancing crazily around the new swing, half singing, half chanting, "Mustn't show the limbs, the limbs, mustn't show the limbs. The polite ones don't have legs, they have limbs, and mustn't show the limbs." He hung Anne Elizabeth upside down, holding her by one ankle, shaking her gently. "Them's nice legs you got, hinny, but where's your limbs?"

Then he took a ride on the swing. He stood up and he pumped until he was so high she was sure he was going to fly right up over the crossbar.

"Careful, Daddy, careful!" she called, frightened, as he laughed and laughed.

A few days later, when she was wearing her bibfronts and an old shirt, he showed her how to shinny. "Just hug it as if you loved it as much as you love me," he said, his hand under her bum, "Now inch up with your hands, and scrunch up with your legs. That's it. Now tighten your knees and push . . . up you go. Just like a monkey. No, you gotta push more with your feet or you'll slip down again . . . that's it."

"How do I get down?"

"Why, you shut your eyes, pray to the good lord, and trust me to catch you!"

She shut her eyes and prayed to the good lord, she let go the pressure in her legs and started down again. The pole slid against her legs, warm against the palms of her hand, and then he had her tight, pulling her away from the pole, cuddling her proudly. "You're a wonder, Anne Elizabeth," he crooned, "You're a bloody wonder. You shinny like someone who's been doin' it for years."

When the fear of coming down subsided, he sent her up the pole again, and this time told her to think about what she had done going up, then do it back-to-front to come down again. That was harder. The first two or three times, she slipped and the pole was hot against her hands, rubbed on the little bone-bumps in her ankles. Then it all clicked into place. She went up the pole, grinned at him, then came down the pole again at her chosen speed, and Cliff grabbed her, swung her in a circle, laughing up at her, his hair loose, hanging over his forehead so he looked like a kid, only grown tall.

"You're just fine," he told her, "just as fine as silk, you are."

Anna Fleming was already too tired to go on when her supervisor came in and asked her to do one of the crap jobs, but then again she was the only worker in the office who wasn't already half hysterical from overwork.

The young mother twisted her hanky nervously and tried to smile, but couldn't. "How can I help you?" Anna asked.

It was like taking the cork out of an overpressurized bottle. Everything bubbled out, punctuated by stifled sobs and self-recriminations.

"I should *never* have trusted . . . but how can you go through life not trusting . . . and anyway . . . I've known him since we moved to the neighbourhood . . . before the girls were born . . . since he was only eight or nine years old . . . a baby himself, really . . ." Anna let her talk, nodding in the right places, making all the right sounds, keeping her professional face firmly fixed in place, as yet one more horror story crept into her mind, one more pile of crud to have to deal with later – or maybe sooner. "And then this morning, when they woke up, they came into bed with me . . . we do that when their dad is away, it kind of makes up for not having him around, although nothing can ever really make it up, they miss him and so do I. I mean, he comes back! He doesn't just go off and not keep in touch! But it's hard on them when his job involves so much travel. So anyway, they got into bed with me and Carol, she's five, she asked me where I'd been and what I'd done, and I told her I'd gone to a baby shower. Ellen, she's just turned three, asked what that was, and I explained to her about how my friend was going to have a baby, and we had a party to celebrate and took presents for the baby. And then Carol said she knew where babies came from, and Ellen said she did, too, and Carol said no, and Ellen said yes, and then Carol said –" The young mother choked and started to sob. Anna passed the woman a handful of tissues and waited, saying only those things everybody says, the things which don't help, don't change anything, the take-your-time and it's-all-right and would-you-like-a-glass-of-water things.

"And then," the young woman said, her sobs quieting, her voice calmer, but her face looking as if she was staring into the open mouth of a huge snake, "she told me what he had done to her. To both of them. I asked her some questions. Not many, I didn't know what to ask or say or do. Asked if he'd . . . if he'd hurt . . . hurt her, and she said it had hurt but he told her it would be okay, and that it was their secret, something special that they shared . . . My God, this kid is fifteen, and he's . . . and so . . . and I called the police, and . . . and now this . . . It's not right! It's just not right! They're only *little girls* and they have to go through all of this, answer these questions –"

"It's good for them," Anna said, with a confidence she wasn't sure she felt. "It gives them the chance to get it out, to break the secret; and that's good because the secret can only fester inside them and cause trouble. It's like cleansing a wound before it becomes infected. We're very careful in the questioning, I promise you. Very careful. Usually the child initiates the exposure. If you think over what happened, how she told you, how she brought it up, how she made sure you knew even before you asked . . . And you knew, or you wouldn't have asked."

"There was something about how she looked at me when she said . . . that she knew where babies came from . . . something in the look on her face . . . something in the way she looked at me, then looked away, again . . ."

"Had you told them where you were going before you left?"

"Yes, I –" The young woman looked at Anna, and blinked rapidly. "You mean . . . you're right . . . we'd already talked about the shower, and about why I was going out . . . they even saw the present . . ."

"You see?" Anna reached out to pat the woman's hand. "Carol knew where you'd been and she asked anyway, so that you'd talk about the baby and she would have a chance, make it possible to tell you." Anna smiled as forcefully as she could. "You must have done a great job with those kids." The woman relaxed slightly. "You can be proud of them. They've experienced an awful thing, but the trust and the bonding you've established will help them through it." She knew it was true, and she also knew it wasn't enough. Not enough to say, not enough to believe, not enough to give this woman as comfort, not enough to protect those kids from the horrors they were sure to encounter.

"They won't have to see him, will they?"

"No. They won't see him."

"Good! Because I'm not sure I could keep my hands off him if I had to see him, or if they have to see him! I could –" She shook her head. "And I don't even believe in violence!"

"That's a very natural reaction," Anna comforted her. "A very beautiful reaction if you think about it. Just let a mother think her child is in any kind of danger and pow, we're back in the caves facing down sabre-toothed tigers. If we hadn't had that instinct, we might never have made it out of the caves in the first place." She stood up and held out her hand, as if inviting the woman to dance. "Come on," she urged, "let's go join the kids. We've got a job to do helping them get past this so they can go on with their lives."

Ellen, the younger girl, didn't have the words for what had happened, but Carol, the five-year-old, did. She knew what she had seen. She had seen a pee-pee. And she knew what he had done. He had touched her private places. Anna had all she could do to stay calm. She had no idea how this young mother, or any of the many others she had met, could sit through it without starting to scream.

"We have to remember," her supervisor reminded her, "he is a child, too. He's only fifteen."

"I know you're right," Anna managed. "I know he's just a child himself, and I know he's very damaged, and *none of that helps*. It's sick!"

"Right." The tone was firm. "He's sick. And sick people need our help."

MARGARET ANNE

The child opens her eyes and sees her ceiling, moves her hands and feels her quilt over her blankets on her bed. Down the hallway the smells of oatmeal porridge and bacon, the smell of toast and coffee. She sits up and sees her wallpaper, her chest of drawers where her clothes are kept. Her window, framed by her curtains, looks out on her backyard, and the sound of the morning train is somehow the sound of her morning train.

Take away that ceiling, that quilt, those blankets, that hallway and those breakfast smells. Take away that wallpaper, the furniture in that room, take away that window, that back yard, the sound of that train, then keep on taking. The worn linoleum. The scatter rugs made of strips of cloth braided and coiled together. Take away the bathroom and the tap that always drips.

Take away the front yard, the gate that squeaks, the ditch along the fence, the ditch that runs full and gurgles in the winter rainy season, the ditch that dries up in the summer but only after the frogs have chorused, been caught and spent a few days in jars and buckets before being released back into the ditch.

Take away the chair with the slight wobble, the mirror with the flaw that makes one part of your face a bit lower and stranger than the other part.

Take it all away and you have taken away a world. What is a little girl without a world? Give her a different world and she has to become a different little girl, she might just as well never have been born as herself in the first place.

Sunlight glinted from the fender of the car, the windshield, the bumper and the grille at the front. She stared at her own reflection in the rounded black fender, her face distorted and somehow flattened by the curve of the metal, her mouth stretched and squashed. Other people had clean cars, some even had polished cars, but Maggy didn't know anybody else who had a car you could see your own reflection in, not even the big scary car at the undertaker's.

They were inside the house, sitting around a table, the huge brown teapot in the middle of the table like the hub of a maypole. She knew if she went in the house there would be a pause in the talk; then someone, probably Grandma, in a changed tone of voice, would ask her about school. As soon as she left the room again the cheerful tone would disappear and they'd go back to the serious discussion they didn't want her to hear. She could go sit under the window behind the lilac bush at the corner of the house and listen. But she didn't want to hear, any more than they wanted her to hear. With any luck they would soon finish all their gloomy talk and everyone could pile into the car and go for a ride. Ten minutes in the car and you'd gone farther from the front gate than you could walk in a whole day. Half an hour in the car and you'd seen more new things, new places and new people than you could see in a week.

Grandpa used to drive the car, but ever since the accident in the mine when the roof came down and a piece of broken timber had clipped him, Uncle Hugh drove. Grandpa walked slower, too, took longer to sit down or get back up again, and his garden was half the size it used to be. Grandma still always sat in the middle of the front seat, but now Grandpa sat over by the passenger's door, where Uncle Hugh used to sit, and Uncle Hugh sat behind the wheel where Grandpa used to sit.

Grandma never changed. She was the only person in Maggy's life gave a good, solid, consistent hug. Momma sometimes let her hug weaken, a sort of absent-minded cuddle, although lately her hugs had been too hard, too squeezy, too fierce. Uncle Hugh picked you up, then swung you around before giving you a squeeze, but sometimes he just did the swinging and forgot the squeeze. Grandpa didn't really hug, he let you hug him while he sort of patted your shoulder and grinned. But Grandma's hug was something you could count on. If I was blind, Maggy thought, I'd know it was Grandma by her hug and her smell. Lavender from the sachet bags in her closet, and soap, and that kind of stomach-twisting smell comes up off clean clothes when they're fresh in off the line and still full of wind-scent.

Daddy used to give a good hug, too. But his smell wasn't always the same. Sometimes it was stink. Coming home from work he smelled of salty sweat and a funny sharp carbony smell from the coal, sometimes a smell of oil from the winch or gas from one of the engines. A touch of tobacco smoke or Copenhagen.

But there were the stink smells, too. Beer mostly, but booze too, and sometimes a smell almost like face powder, but that was silly, men didn't use face powder. It didn't matter, anyway, because now he didn't come home from work, he didn't come home at all. That's what they were all talking about in the kitchen.

Momma sat in the house waiting, sometimes staring at his lunch bucket with the lunch packed inside it yet, waiting and waiting. One day she jumped up, opened the lunch kit, threw the stale sandwiches out in the yard for the chickens and put the lunch kit under the sink, out of the way. At night, sometimes, you could hear her crying. Maggy missed him, too. Especially his jokey things, like when instead of singing "Whispering hope, oh how welcome thy voice," he sang "Lumbering dope, you have stolen my poyse."

"Maggy, would you come into the house now?" Momma's voice was hard and tight, as if she was mad about something, or just trying hard not to cry some more. Maggy ran toward the house, being very careful not to step on any cracks, because you wouldn't want to break your mother's back.

They were all sitting at the table, just as they had been earlier, and there was a fresh pot of tea. Grandpa sat sideways to the table calmly gazing out the front door, Uncle Hugh tried to do some talking but could only ramble around, Auntie Megan, who was younger than Momma and said she was going to university or business school and never getting married, looked as if she had been crying, and Momma just sat, staring at her hands hanging onto her teacup. Grandma finally did the talking, spelled it all out.

You always knew where you stood with Grandma. She never talked at you like you had no brain, and she never said something and took it back later on, or changed it, or said You didn't understand what I meant.

"But what about school?"

"Eh, there's a skyul out our way, lass."

"What about my music lessons?"

"Eeeh, tha's slow today, my precious. We've a piano of our own. Tha'll practise on it every night and not have to gya down'ta't skyul hall after supper like tha does now. We'll bring you in for lessons and if tha needs help, Auntie Megan plays piano like nobody's business."

"But what about Momma?"

"Now tha's not to worry, lass. 'Tis her is the Momma, not thee. Tha's a little girl, and its not tha place in life to worry about tha Mam. She's doin' best for thee she can, and tha has t'trust that. Tha knows we'd none of us do thee harm on purpose. Just go pack tha things, my precious. And leave over worryin', hear?"

They did everything. All she had to do was walk behind them to the car. Aunt Megan and Uncle Hugh carried her clothes and her few toys, Grandpa took the bag of schoolbooks she hadn't even known Momma had picked up from the classroom, and Grandma walked with her arm around Momma's waist, whispering softly while Momma nodded quickly, quickly, quickly.

Maggy got in the back seat with Auntie Megan and stared out the side window, afraid to speak in case she started howling like a baby. Everyone was doing what was best for her, but nobody had asked her about anything. She couldn't even look at Auntie Megan when she reached over and patted her knee. You're only supposed to visit your grandma, not live with her all the time. Couldn't anybody do anything the way it was supposed to be done? Couldn't Daddy stay at home like daddies were supposed to do, instead of going and Carrying On? People staring and asking questions, and

Grandfather MacDonald roaring at Daddy and saying he was a fool, and nobody could clean up one mess by making another, and if Daddy didn't smarten up he'd get a good clip on the side of the head, and Daddy laughing and saying No more, old man, I've taken the last clip on the head from you I'm going to take. And Uncle Tamas, drunk again like always, laughing and laughing until Uncle Cliff told him to shut the hell up and Tamas asked would Cliff like a good bop on the beak and Momma crying and asking why do you always fight with each other and Daddy stomping out, slamming the door behind him, leaving Grandpa MacDonald spluttering with rage while Cliff and Tamas made a lot of noise. Momma said that's why the whole damn town knew everything that went on, the MacDonalds yelled it to the high woods.

The map in the schoolroom showed the highway running the length of the Island from Victoria to Campbell River, leaving the entire top half of the rock to the logging companies. Like an off-centre spine it meandered from town to community, from community to hamlet, with innumerable riblike secondary roads, back roads, side roads and logging roads. Towns and villages were scattered around with no planning, no order, no organization. If there was coal here, why, sink a mine and start a town; over here more coal, another community; here the railhead, scatter some houses on the side of the hill and call it a city. Everything loosely held together by the one informal, incomplete highway.

Off in the distance the slag piles pointed grim fingers at the sky. Maggy would have liked to go there and poke around looking for fossils, but there are rules you don't dare break. The slag is wet when it gets dumped on the pile, and the crushed coal dust, the broken rock and bits of shale settle and dry into a hard crust. Beneath that crust, slowly, every day, things sink under their own weight, and you could fall through the crust into a hole, be buried by black dust and rocks like that boy in Cumberland, and when they finally got to him after two days of digging, he was flat from the weight of everything that had slid down on top of him.

They were driving past the company houses, all of them looking alike, square two- or three-bedroom boxes with wide verandahs but no basements, all of them built with the chimney on the same side. The people who lived in them rented them from the company, and there was a store which everybody called the SkinMe.

Grandma and Grandpa owned their house and the land it stood on – the garden, the fruit trees and everything inside the fence. When Grandpa first bought it, the house was small and all the boys had to sleep in one room, the girls in another, and Grandma and Grandpa slept in the kitchen on a bed they could fold away during the day. "Eh," Grandma said one time, "had I but known! One week in't'place and Will was alterin' it all, and he's not stopped since."

Grandpa was always altering something. He somehow lifted the roof of the house and put another floor on, with four bedrooms and a hallway. Another summer he and the uncles dug and dug and dug until Grandma said she thought the house would fall in the hole, but when they were finished, there was a cellar, and shelves for the canning jars and big bins for vegetables.

Maggy lay in bed that first night feeling cold and prickly all over her body. It wasn't the same as visiting. The bed was the same bed she'd stayed in before, but it was different because now when they said "off to your bed," they meant it. Not a borrowed one. Not one you'd only be in a few nights. She didn't like the new feeling.

The school was painted dark brown with a black-painted shingled roof. Uncle Hugh said you could trust the school trustees, all right, trust them to pay big money for enough paint to cover a huge box of weathered cedar that didn't need paint at all. Trust them to spend tax money on something nobody needed, then say they had to raise taxes because they needed more money for something else, and all the while the kids trying to learn out of books with pages missing, with broken spines, held together with adhesive tape.

In front of the school was a small patch of lawn, rich green and evenly trimmed, surrounded on three sides by round white-painted rocks, and on the fourth side by the fence around the schoolyard. Nobody was allowed to go there. Everywhere else the ground was worn flat and hard by children's feet, with only occasional small clumps of stubborn grass persisting. Behind the school a few swings, but no teety-totters and no hurdy-go-round. A couple of soccer goals and a roughed-in softball diamond with no backstop, and in one corner of the schoolyard a clump of bush, uncleared and untended.

Grandma offered to go with her, but Maggy said she could do it alone, thank you. She didn't need that on top of switching schools! They'd all think she was a sucky-baby, needed her grandma to catch the bus. She walked up the road to the bus stop, lugging a pillowcase-load of books, her transfer papers pinned to her coat. She wanted to put it in with the books but Grandma said No, things have a way of getting lost, so there she was with a big pin holding her transfer paper, like those DP kids in the newsreels.

She stood apart from the others, feeling their eyes on her. At least she knew some of them from weekend and summer holiday visits. Tim with his freckles and grin and a contagious habit of sniffing all the time as if he had a cold. And Mike, leaning against the fence, pretending he didn't know who she was. Carol, who looked like a doll except for her clothes, miner's-kid clothes like everyone else, sturdy material, plain colours, long wearing, long lasting, few frills.

Maggy let everyone else get on the bus first, then she climbed the two steps and sat in the front seat. She felt totally out of place. Not only did she live in an owned house instead of in the company town, she wasn't dressed like they were. Her coat was bright red.

"Reminds me of a stop sign," a voice said.

"How's your belly for spots, new girl?"

"Did jer momma get it at a rummage sale?"

"That's too posh for a rummage sale, you fool. Stole it, most likely."

"Why not? Her dad steals. Steals other men's wives."

"Part jackrabbit, I heard."

They kept it up all the way to school. She waited for her bus to pull away before she walked from the stop to the schoolyard. It was jammed with kids from grade one to grade eight, boys and girls, all sizes, all ages, all body builds.

When the bell rang she went in through the big front doors, and down the hallway to the office. She knew the principal was a right bastard as soon as she saw him. He checked her transfer slip, nodded without saying so much as hello to her, then took her by the arm and led her back down the hall to a classroom.

"New girl," he said, handing over a paper.

She sat in a middle seat by the window, wishing she was anywhere else. Everyone stared at her, whispering to each other, passing on the news they thought they knew. At recess they tormented her, as she'd known they would. And at lunchtime two of the boys knocked her down while the girls watched to see what she would do about it. Maggy did nothing.

By Thursday it had all become, to borrow one of Aunt Megan's phrases, just a little bit chronic. Doing nothing wasn't going to change things. She was going to have to fight.

"All right, you lot, shove off," a voice growled. Sonny MacLean, the toughest boy in school, probably the toughest boy in the district, maybe the toughest boy on the whole Island, standing beside her, not looking at her.

"What's in it for you, Sonny?" one of the bigger boys dared.

"Yap on, garbage-mouth," Sonny smiled easily. "Else I might kick you in the balls and rattle your brains."

They started to drift off, sullen.

"You have to fight back," Sonny said.

"Hit one and the others will jump in," she whispered.

"Nobody will jump you," Sonny said. "Which one do you want to take on?"

"Patch-kneed one."

"He's tough."

"I know."

She took off her coat and laid it on the ground, wishing she didn't feel like running away. You got the strap for fighting. And if you got the strap at school, you caught it when you got home. But if you don't fight back, it won't stop.

Maggy didn't win the fight. She didn't lose it, either. The fight was stopped by a teacher, and both of the fighters taken to the office. The principal glared at them.

"It isn't our policy to give the strap to girls at this school," he said coldly, "and anyway, I'm sure young master MacLean was behind it all, so he will get the strap in your stead. But you'll stand and watch while he gets it, and remember, he's getting strapped because you were fighting."

"He didn't do anything!" Maggy blurted.

"I beg your pardon, Miss." Surprise was written on the principal's face.

"He didn't do anything. It's not fair!"

"Drop it, Mag," Sonny said clearly. "He doesn't care what's fair. You'll just make him madder and then I'll get it harder."

The strap rose and fell ten times on each palm, and Sonny refused to cry. But he couldn't stop the tears welling in his eyes.

"Think on it," the maggot said tightly. "There will be no fighting here! You will behave like civilized people. Now get out of here."

Someone brought Maggy's coat to her and she said Thank you, glad it hadn't been walked all over. Sonny walked away, paying no attention to the other kids, seeming to pay no attention to his red, swollen hands. She wanted to tell him she was sorry, but she had more sense than that.

ANNE ELIZABETH

The steps had been cut into the steep hill by the army engineering corps, the dirt terraced and held in place by strong wooden frames. On either side of the steps the grass, thicket and blackberry tangle had been cleared, and without the choking weeds and sun-defying mess, small wildflowers grew and spread their seeds.

The adults took each step in two paces, but Anne Elizabeth's legs had to stretch to make it in three. Arthur and his little brother were walking behind, Arthur deliberately stepping on her heels.

"He's stepping on me."

"It was an accident. She's walking too slow and pokey."

"Stop squabbling. Arthur, watch your step." Arthur's mother was tall and slender, and sometimes when he'd done something wrong she beat on him with a razor strop. When you went into their kitchen for a drink of water, the strop stared at you from its special hook on the kitchen wall, and you knew it was just waiting.

"Anne Elizabeth, don't poke and he won't step on you."

"He's doing it on purpose."

"No I'm not."

So Arthur was sent on ahead, as he'd wanted, and he stood on the small footbridge over the Cat Stream and spit into the water happily. The stickle-backs didn't know it was just spit, they always hurried to try to get the white bubbly bits of froth before they floated away on the current.

"You're disgusting!" she snapped. "Spitting and stuff."

"Why'n't you shut up!" he hissed, pinching her arm, but she wouldn't give him the satisfaction of crying out, even though she found a bruise on her arm later. Arthur was always pulling pigtails, pinching, stepping on your heels, always shoving and pushing, always tripping you and then laughing his high, dry cackle. He liked to spend his mornings looking under logs in the bush at the end of the valley, finding slugs. He hoarded them carefully in an old cigar box with damp moss on the bottom and sometimes sat staring at them for long periods. When the afternoon train was due, Arthur picked up his cigar box and ran to the place near the lumberyard where the train slowed to unload boxcars at the big malt-smelling feed store. He waited there until the ding-ding-ding of the bell at the crossing started, then he took out the slugs and placed them on the hot train tracks. The heat in the tracks dried their underbellies so they couldn't crawl away. When they were all lined up side by side, their blotchy skins exposed to the sun and their feelers waving frantically, Arthur sat back, well out of the way. Everyone knew the wind-rush under the train could suck you under and you'd get your arms'n'legs sliced off and wind up like a big pink eraser with a head. So he made sure he was safe, but stayed close enough to watch as the train thundered past and the slugs simply vanished. There was never anything left, not even a damp stain. They might as well never have lived at all by the time Arthur and the afternoon train were finished.

"You stink," Anne Elizabeth told him. "You stink and you've got holes in your socks and your mother is always yelling."

He hit her openly, forgetting in his surge of rage that it wasn't safe to let people see what you were doing. She hit him back, and then he pulled her hair while she slapped him. She knew he was going to win the fight because he was nearly two years older, but the others had seen every move. His mother started yelling at him and he quit fighting and looked over his shoulder. His mother pointed, and Arthur nodded. "It's an l-i-c-k-i-n-g for me," he chanted softly. "It's an l-i-c-k-i-n-g, an l-i-c-k-i-n-g."

She was glad. Glad he was going to get the razor strop, glad he'd have red welts on his legs, that's what he got for being so stinky. She was glad right up until the sound of leather on flesh cracked on the hot summer afternoon air, and she held her breath wondering how many slaps like that anybody could take, even tough, wiry Arthur with his pinched-rabbit face and his constantly darting blue eyes. He took ten of them before he started to cry hopelessly.

"You shoulda cried sooner," she told him later, when he was sitting on the bank of the stream spitting for the sticklebacks. "They only hit you until you cry, then they're happy and stop hitting."

"One of these days she's gonna hit me and I'm not gonna cry at all," he said. "She'll hit and hit and I won't cry and she'll hit until she can't hit any more and I still won't cry."

"Then your dad'll hit you. You'll cry then!"

Arthur nodded. He knew she was right.

Arthur's father was older than Arthur's mother. Already he had lines in his face and his hair was fading to a soft white around his ears. There was a streak of white in the front of his hair, and his neck was going wrinkly.

"Why he waited as long as he did and then settled for what he got is one of the mysteries of life," Anne Elizabeth heard her mother tell her aunt one afternoon when they were having tea. "He could have had his pick, a stable, hard-working man like that, already owned his own house, with a big yard and all. But I guess he wanted to laugh, and she loves to laugh. I guess he wanted to dance, and she loves to dance."

"With or without music," her aunt agreed, and both women laughed a secret kind of laugh. "If he ever finds out what kind of dancing she's been doing with that soldier, there'll be wigs on the green before dawn."

Arthur's father seldom slapped the boys, and certainly he never beat them with the razor strop. When she had been especially angry and Arthur was welted and sore, his father would sit beside him on the steps and dry his eyes with his big blue hanky and try to make it all right again. "You have to learn to be good," he would say. "You have to learn to behave properly, Artie."

Behave properly. It was very important they all behave properly. Anne Elizabeth wasn't allowed to climb trees and hang upside down with her skirt dropping around her ears. She mustn't spit, swear, crack her gum or be impudent. She was to ride her wagon only in certain places and never never ever talk back, argue, yell or fight with her aunts, her mother, her father or anybody else older than she was. And Arthur, well the list of don'ts for Arthur just went on and on and on and on. Sometimes it was so confusing you wanted to cry. Sit quietly in the classroom and don't stutter when *she* asked you a question. *She* was seven hundred and ninety-two years old if she was a day and her voice came from somewhere inside with barely any lip movement.

She didn't like Anne Elizabeth which somehow had to do with Daddy's cousin, Frankie and Pete's mother. Something about her coming to school in the middle of the day, coming to the school dressed in her best clothes and smelling of perfume, and the one or two quick gins she'd had to brighten the day. Coming to school in a car driven by a man Anne Elizabeth didn't know and had never seen before. And she went into the school and came out a few minutes later with Frankie and Pete. The next day Blackie, Frankie and Pete's father, came down to the school. He was big and burly, his hair shone like the tail of a rooster, and everyone knew he had a rotten temper.

"Well, what in bloody blue blazes time was it, then, you silly old bitch," he roared, "and for Chrissakes can't you at least remember what kind of car it was? How'n'hell d'ya expect to teach kids anything when you yourself can't tell one kinda damn car from another?"

"It was just before lunchtime ended," Anne Elizabeth offered, "and Frankie and Pete were inside because they had detentions. It was a car with a big Indian head on the hood."

"What colour?"

"Dark green. Real dark, like Einnarr Swenson's green car, but only the colour, because Einnarr's car doesn't got no Indian on it."

"What else?"

"The plate was on both the front and back. Or . . . Or . . . Or somethin'."

"Hear that, you silly old Bezom?" Blackie roared. "Goddamn grade one-er kid knows more'n you do. A dark green Pontiac from Oregon, for Chrissakes!" and he was gone, cursing they would all by Jesus find out nobody pulled this kind of goddamn stunt on Blackie Morgan, by God.

Everyone knew that Frankie and Pete's mother was Anne Elizabeth's daddy's cousin, and soon everyone knew that she had run off with another man and taken her sons with her. And everybody seemed to think that somehow reflected on Anne Elizabeth.

Liz didn't mind taking Fran shopping. It was a much more enjoyable way to stock up on groceries than going alone had ever been. For years Liz had gone shopping on Saturday mornings after breakfast and the kids' sports team practice. They'd all go – Bert driving, of course – and then they'd each take a shopping cart and cruise the aisles, like explorers taking fingers of a river, looking for the treasure of Solomon. Of course, half of humanity was there at the same time doing the same thing. Everybody's kids screeched, wailed and begged for things their parents said they did not need, could not have and would never get, so be quiet or you'll wind up back in the car by yourself.

When their carts were full and their patience exhausted, Liz and Bert stood in line for half a lifetime. Then Bert paid the astounding total, they shoved their buggies to the car to off-load the grub and the kids got in a huge fight over who would take the buggies back to the corral in the parking lot. Finally they drove home, arriving almost too tired to unload the car, carry all those brown paper bags into the house, pile the groceries on the table, then start putting everything in the cupboards.

But that hadn't happened for quite some time. Liz didn't have to wait for Bert any more. She had her own chequing account and her own driver's licence and she could just climb in her own car any time she wanted and bop off to get things done. Still, the car and the driver's licence were a mixed blessing.

"You want me to what?"

"Drive me to soccer practice."

"For crying out loud, Marti, it's only eight blocks."

"So? It's going to rain."

"Next Tuesday, maybe."

"Mom!"

"Listen, Marti, I'm real sorry someone broke into the shed and stole your bike, but I'm even sorrier someone seems to have broken into the house and stolen your feet!"

"Nobody stole my bike, what are you talking about?"

"Good. Nobody stole your bike. So you grab your soccer gear, put it in the carrier, get on the bike and pedal your ass those eight blocks to the place where you're going to run, run, run in the name of fitness and health, okay?"

"You won't drive me?"

"That's right, love. I won't drive you." She tried to turn it into a joke. "Unless you'd like me to drive you on the jaw with my fist?"

"Oh, fun-*nee*, Mom. Fun-*nee*. Boy, what a chintzball you are!"

"And you wanted me to put myself out for you? Maybe I should haul you out of soccer and enroll you in Miss Megadosiah's Mind-Your-Manners classes."

"Well, gee whiz! Everybody else gets a ride there. And back, too!"

"Good, you can catch a ride with someone who lives this way."

"Oh sure, with my bike, I suppose."

"Then stop standing there yammering noise in my ears. Leave now and walk there so you can catch a ride home! Or use your brain since you don't want to use your bike. Make advance arrangements with someone whose parents are more civilized, more understanding and more stupid than yours. Now get going or don't go at all."

The door slammed. Doors slammed a lot. It made you wonder if the kids got a subsidy from the people who made new door frames and hinges. All the things they had been willing to do on their bikes suddenly could no longer be done unless Liz got in the car.

"It's like the vacuum cleaner," Wilma said placidly. "When nobody had them we used brooms and dry mops, and it took maybe five minutes a room. Hardly anybody had carpets and the rugs were the kind you could drag out once a year, hang over the fence, and whap the dust out of. All of a sudden there were vacuum cleaners and big advertising campaigns about dust, asthma, bronchitis and bacteria lurking on your floors. So now it takes twenty minutes to vacuum the room and every couple of months you have to rent the carpet cleaner or get a bunch of young guys in with this steam machine. Labour-saving devices, my eye."

Liz didn't mind driving them to the swimming pool. It was clear across town, and one bus never met another without a long wait, so there they'd be at their transfer point downtown, shivering, hair wet, faces and fingers going blue with cold. Besides, everyone knew kids weren't safe waiting at the bus stop any more. Every time you made the mistake of paying attention to the news you were hit in the heart by yet another story of a kid snatched, then found raped, sodomized, beaten, strangled and mutilated.

But eight blocks? To sit in the car while Marti ripped around out there, working up a sweat and getting covered with mud?

It was nice, though, to just go shopping without having to turn it into a family hunting expedition, like a photo essay in the *National Geographic*, see the happy natives busy gathering their food, attending the market. She and Fran had fun. She parked in front of the big grey house and tooted the horn for Fran. Sometimes Fran was already waiting, leaning on the fence, staring out at apparently nothing at all. Fran did a lot of staring these days. Thinking, she called it, but there were times she seemed surprised, even shocked, to find herself where she was when she came back from wherever she had been while doing this thinking. Other times you got no response at all, and Liz knew the phone often rang, rang, rang unanswered.

Fran shrugged it off as if it didn't matter. "As long as it works when I want to phone out, that's good enough for me."

"Well, what if everyone stopped answering?"

"Everyone isn't going to stop answering. Besides, all I use the phone for is to phone some office where people get paid to answer, or to phone you. And you'd die of a broken back before you'd let your phone ring unanswered."

"Good job the whole world doesn't think like you. What would be the use of a phone?"

"What *is* the use of a phone, Liz? Who really benefits from a phone? Other than the phone company, I mean. How many times have you answered yours and had some voice you've never heard before, and won't hear again with any luck, ask you if you're interested in some kind of food plan where you wind up with a ton of ground mystery meat for only ten cents a pound more than you can get it in the butcher store?"

"Then why do you have a phone?"

"Why are we having this conversation?"

"I tried to phone you and you didn't answer the ring."

"Why were you phoning?"

"To talk, you fool!"

"Then how do you know I was even home?"

"Because I got worried about you and drove over, remember?"

"And did we talk?"

"You know we did! My God, Fran!"

"There. I rest my case, as Merry Pason would say. If I'd answered the phone I wouldn't have seen you."

Liz knew Fran wanted her to drop it and let it lie, but she couldn't stop herself. "Fran, I was worried. What if someone had broken into the house and you couldn't answer the phone?"

"Listen, if it'll make you feel better, I'll get one of those machines with the recorded voice and you can leave messages."

"Just answer the friggin' phone when it rings!"

"No."

"Why not?"

"Okay, Liz. I didn't answer the phone because sometimes I can't stand talking on the phone. And I can't stand talking on the phone because I can't see the person on the other end. And if I can't see the person on the other end I have no way at all of

knowing if what I'm hearing is real. And I have no way of knowing that because there are times I have absolutely clear and vivid
memories of conversations which, it turns out, never happened.
And that can only mean that I'm hearing voices. And that can
only mean I'm cracking up, or I'm Joan of Arc. And the look on
your face tells me I'm not Joan of Arc."

"Have you been to a doctor?"

"What kind," said Fran, looking exactly like someone who
was daring someone else to jump off the bridge into the river,
"head or ear?"

If they were lucky, the store was almost empty and they
could take their time, actually have some choice, get produce that
wasn't wilted or bruised. They could ask each other's opinion
about things, discuss how fresh the chicken seemed, and my
God, don't you wonder about those fish grown in pens, a friend
of mine tried one and said it was just like blotting paper soaked
in sardine oil. Afterwards they could go for lunch together and
actually have a visit, catch up on each other's news if there was
any, then eventually make their way home and put away their
loot before starting supper for the returning horde. It was a great
way to pass most of one day.

Liz pushed her cart down the aisle, past the canned this and
canned that, all the stuff she never bought. Fran's latest temporary was riding in the kiddie seat, looking around as if she had
never seen the inside of a store before, face as grave and sombre
as a kid getting her first look at the false beard on the supermarket Santa. And suddenly the kid was lunging, reaching, making
eager noises.

"Careful, you'll fall."

"Ah," Fran laughed softly, "look at that, Chef Boy-Ar-Dee ravi-
oli, just like Momma used to make."

"You aren't *buying* that crap?"

"Hey, if this kid wants some, this kid gets some. It's called
bribery and coercion. You just put some on the mashed potatoes,
some more on the hamburger patty, the kid eats the whole thing.
Bit by bit you get it eating good food, you just wean it off this
additive sauce."

"But Fran . . . noodly-oodly?"

"Ah, a hundred years from now you won't even remember
you saw me buy any."

The kid sat happily with one can of the garbage clutched in her hands, her next meal secure. Liz blew it off. After all, what could you do with a kid you were only going to have for a couple of weeks? Change the patterns of a lifetime, even a short lifetime?

She wouldn't bother herself. Fran hadn't really wanted to bother, either, but they sure can put pressure on a person. Fran had gone from No, I will not take little ones, I really won't, to Well, just this once and only for the three days it will take you to get into family court with them. And now she'd made it all the way to Okay, but only for a month or so, just till you find a permanent placement. And here they were three months later, with Andrea still riding in the kiddie seat.

Liz didn't mind pushing the cart with Andrea riding in it. That left Fran free to use both hands. My God, what must it be like with a pack like hers. Four of her own and then the fosters. More Kevins, Shawns and Jordans than you could shake a stick at. The names came in waves, one year nine out of ten called Toby, a couple of years later Toby out of style and Abraham in, and all of them winding up at Fran's place.

Andrea was having a great time. Liz had made it to the far end of the aisle and from this end Andy could see the produce section.

"G'ape!" she called, pointing.

"Oh, baby." Liz leaned forward and kissed the tip of Andy's nose. "Don't you know Cesar says no grapes for us? No grapes from California where they're killing people with pesticides, from South Africa where they're killing people with everything they can lay their hands on, from Chile where they fertilize the fields with the blood of the peasants."

"G'ape," Andy insisted hopefully.

That's when Liz heard it. Clear as if it was coming over a telephone, through her ear and into some part of her body that had been asleep for forty years and never wanted to waken.

"Well, yes, she is sweet enough." The speaker was a well-dressed, comfortable, past-middle-aged lady who got her hair done at the best place in town and had them put just a tiny touch of something bluey-grey in the rinse. "And they've got her very well dressed, but still and all, you can tell, can't you, that she's . . . well, got more than a touch of . . . you know . . ."

"Her others are like that, too. They say it comes from her husband, but he looks fine to me. And with those Harrises, well, apples don't fall far from the tree, do they."

They don't know I can hear them, Liz thought. And what's more, they don't care if I can! She looked at Andrea with her can of gluppy sitting between her legs. Someone had been fishing in the genetic pool of all times, and the dominant genes of the world were gathered in one still-too-thin little frame. Andrea smiled at Liz and pointed hopefully.

"Sure, dumpling, what the hell, we'll get 'em," Liz said. "We just won't pay for them."

Instead of turning left and heading on toward the meat section, Liz veered right, toward the grapes. And as she passed the two ladies she smiled from ear to ear, looked one of them in the eye and said clearly, "And fuck you too, you racist twat."

Behind her she heard Fran snicker. That was as surprising as anything that had happened in the past five years. If asked, Liz would have predicted Fran would gasp with horror. "It's contagious," Fran said pleasantly. "A person runs into assholiness a few times and the next thing you know, there she is, she who used to be so nice, and she's tainted with it herself. But as you said, with those Harrises, you just never know."

They got Andy some green ones and some reddish ones, all seedless, then retraced their route and finally made it to the meat counter, still laughing. "You get used to it after a while," Fran said. "You hear little digs from this side, that side and the next side, until you stop giving a damn about the individual nasties because you realize that the whole population is like that. Everybody needs someone to kick around. What was it your sane grandmother used to say? Big fleas have little fleas upon their backs to bite 'em . . ."

"And little fleas have lesser fleas, and so ad infinitum."

But it rankled. Liz told herself that a couple of blue-rinse jobbies like that didn't represent the world, but she didn't quite believe herself.

"You just comin' out of the fog?" Bert laughed sourly. "Hell, Liz, where you been all your life?"

"Did I put salt in your coffee or something?"

"No." But the muscles in his face didn't relax. "It's this nun-in-a-whorehouse 'Oh my, how could they *ever*' that's pissing me off."

"Bert . . . what . . . ?"

"Wake up, Liz. Smell the coffee. You've been living in your own little world for years, having it your own way, keeping it like the way you think you want it to be, but that's not how it is. Everybody knows this is a shit heap, there's just some who pretend it isn't."

"Why are you mad at *me?*"

"Because you've been pretending for so many years that you can't look at how it is without pretending some more! It's not just those two old cunts in the supermarket. What have they said or done that you haven't said and done yourself?"

"I never did!"

He stared at her, his dark eyes so full of anger she was almost afraid of him. "There's more than one way to be a shitass. You can be an obvious shitass and say things about three-year-old kids, or you can be one of the other kinds of shitass and say See me, see how nice I am, why I would *never* . . . because I am not like them . . ." He rose from his chair and stalked toward the door. "Of course you're not like the rest of *us*, either! You're unique as all fuckin' hell! You grew up knowing you were better than my kind. And now you can feel better than their kind, too. Which makes you a very rare bird, doesn't it? Better than the whole pissin' lot of us, dark and light alike. They'll make you a saint next week."

Liz was so full of rage she didn't dare open her mouth, for fear she'd say that one thing that made the world split down the middle and fall into such little pieces that the rest of her life wouldn't be time enough to put it back together again.

"Don't get your shirt in a knot," Fran soothed her, pouring tea from an ugly teapot. The cups were ugly, too. Some kind of local pottery, probably made by some of Fran's kids or something. The tea looked normal, but there was a strong scent of orange rind in the steam coming up from the lumpy blobby mugs.

"He was just about ready to hit me!"

"Well, you've been hit before."

"*What?*"

"He wouldn't have hit you. Maybe taken a swing at the wall or sent a lamp through the window, but nothing you haven't had happen before now."

"He never did! Not one time."

"I wasn't talking about *him*, idiot."

"What, then?"

"You really do have a capacity to pack it in Pandora's box and keep the lid shut, don't you? Gowan, idiot, Gowan."

"Oh, that." Liz waved her hand. "That's over and done with."

"It is not over and done with," Fran said comfortably. She brought a honey tub to the table. It was as squat and ugly as the rest of the stuff. There was a stick in it with a ridged knob on the end, my God, where do people find these strange riggin's and what's wrong with a spoon? "If it was over and done with," Fran continued, "you wouldn't be the mess you are and I wouldn't be the mess I am."

"What are you talking about? Speak for yourself," Liz muttered.

"I am speaking for myself. And of myself. And about myself. And you, too, dear heart. You spend more energy not thinking about things than you ever spent trying to figure out where you were going."

"Who ever knows where they're going? To Long Beach on holiday, with any luck at all."

"And so there we are, in the supermarket, and all of a sudden, after an entire lifetime of not hearing the digs and sly smirks, all of a sudden you hear two old fuddy-duddies making a couple of cracks about a kid who's nothing to you one way or the other. How many other cracks *didn't* you hear? About your own kids, for example. Doesn't it hit you kind of funny that the coach of the soccer team calls Martine 'Gypsy Girl'?"

"That's because she's a roving forward, she gypsies all over the field snagging the ball when it's loose."

"Oh, bullshit. Reba plays goal, she doesn't leave her crease, and what does he call her?"

"Reba? He calls her . . ."

"Right. Corby. And what's a corby, anyway, if it isn't a crow or a blackbird?"

"He calls her that because he says nothing gets past her."

"A corby takes everything back to its nest. When she's goalie the crease is her nest. And nothing gets into Reba's goal! So whatever she is, she isn't a corby! He's just found a fun way to call your kid the next best thing to nigger."

"But she *isn't!*" Liz raged. And when Fran started to laugh Liz felt the fire rush into her cheeks. She was so angry she started to get up and leave the table, leave the big grey house, fuck this shit, who needs this. And instead, there she was, gripping the edge of the table and fighting to keep tears from springing down her cheeks, struggling to keep the sobs locked inside her.

"What you have to do, Lizzie, is find someplace to sit down and start putting it back together. Fill up those big holes where you don't remember anything at all."

Liz sat down and sipped the absolutely terrible tea. Someone was going to catch it for this. Someone was going to eat plates of it for this.

CHRISTIE ANNE

Jenny MacDonald was eighteen and on her own for the first time in her life. She went to the Speedway Hall with two friends and met Alex Fraser during intermission. They danced the schottische and two foxtrots. When the dance ended they rode back to town in the bus and Alex sang the entire eleven miles. Three months later, Jenny was pregnant. Two weeks after she told Alex, they were married. Christie Anne was born seven months after the wedding. Jenny MacDonald Fraser knew what Alex was. She didn't care.

Alex Fraser was not a tall man, not a stocky man, not a handsome man. But he was a strong man with work-corded hands and muscled shoulders. He sang loudly and often, and danced better than anyone else on the Island. He was fourteen the first time he knew a woman in the biblical sense, and what she taught him he liked. Both before and after his marriage he enjoyed fully the company of as many women as possible.

Christie Anne was the first of six legitimate children. Nobody, least of all Alex Fraser, counted the others. "A man'd be a fool to take a bath wearin' gumboots," he laughed.

Her name started a minor furor in the Fraser family. Ever since the year oh-two, the firstborn Fraser had been born to a ready-made name: John for a boy, Elizabeth for a girl. She should have been Elizabeth Fraser, because she was the firstborn. Firstborn legitimate, that is, there was illegitimate blood on the reserve but nobody spoke about that then, and they don't speak about it now. But just before she arrived, there was yet another family get-together and someone called out "Lizzie!" and fully one-quarter of the women present said "Yes?" Not Elizabeth, or Beth, or Bess, or even Eliza. Lizzie.

Jenny MacDonald Fraser stood up on her hind legs for one of the few times in her young life. And the morning her daughter was born, Alex went to tell Grandmother Fraser, who immediately asked, "And how is wee Lizzie?" Alex looked around the room as anxious as a long-tailed cat in a room full of rocking chairs and his frantic gaze fell on a box of crackers on the table. Christie's biscuits, it said. "Well," he managed, his throat tight with something as close to fear as he would ever know, "her mother has named her." Putting all the blame on Jenny was becoming a habit for Alex. "She wants to call her Christie," he continued, "Christie Anne Fraser." Grandmother Fraser stared at him while he looked everywhere else except at her.

Christie Anne didn't so much come into the world as get hauled into it. Jenny had been trying for three days, and everyone, especially Jenny, was tired. The doctor ordered the instruments boiled up, then he fitted the forceps around what he could find of the baby's head, and he yanked. He braced his feet against the foot of the table where Jenny was strapped into stirrups, and yarded until the muscles in his arms were rock hard and the veins stood out in his neck. Jenny screamed twice, then fainted.

When she wakened and saw her daughter, all bruised and with her head stretched out of shape, she screamed again. For years Jenny waited for a sign Christie was afflicted, and for years Jenny was disappointed. Christie didn't stutter or walk sideways or have trouble learning to read or count. But Jenny was a patient woman, and before she died she had all the proof she needed that there had been brain damage from the delivery.

Christie Anne was four years old when her sister Elizabeth Flora was born. Grandma Fraser decided this second child, given the proper name, was the first Fraser child. She wondered when it was Alex had realized Christie wasn't his own, and why it was he accepted it. Jenny MacDonald's wheat-blonde hair and big blue eyes, her soft milk-white skin and large full breasts must have blinded him and kept him tied to her. She often stared at Christie and wondered who this child really was, and she thought she finally understood why Alex had been so uneasy when he told her the name his wife had given her first child.

"Only child I ever knew who didn't like to cuddle," she said disapprovingly. "She'd nurse from arm's length if it were possible."

"She looks like my cousin Jean," Grandpa Fraser said once.

"She looks like nobody we know," his wife contradicted him sharply.

The Lombardy poplars along Wakesiah Avenue had been planted one at a time by a Chinese mine worker. Nobody had known his name so nobody remembered it. He spoke to nobody. He ate only two meals a day, morning and night, and it was on his lunch break he planted the poplars, and other trees. Some of the other Chinese said he had the marks of a Shaolin priest on his arms and that his silence was an atonement for a sin. He planted trees, bushes, flowers and bulbs everywhere he went, and there are still fruit trees gone wild where he stopped and took seedlings from the canvas pouch he carried on his hip. Walk deep into the bush between the college and Westwood Lake and you might even today find jonquils gone wild or roses twining up alder trees or over fallen stumps.

Alex and Jen lived near Wakesiah Avenue and every time they passed the Lombardy poplars, Jen told her children about the nameless man who spent his lunch hours trying to make the world a more beautiful place.

Christie learned that when you walk along Milton or Kennedy Street your footsteps echo hollowly. There are mine shafts and tunnels lying under the sidewalks, empty highways in the bowels of the earth, veins from which the black blood was cut, hauled to the steel mills of Pittsburgh, the fireplaces of San Francisco. From every named and some unnamed corners of the earth, men with thick hands, gnarled fingers and sloped shoulders came to hack coal. And to build houses, plant gardens and conceive children, and to drink, argue, play cards, beat their wives and children, fart, sweat, sing, pray and fight homesickness.

The company controlled their lives and the history of their fighting back was bloody, glorious and ignored. The legendary Joe Hill was afraid to come to the Island, knowing he'd never leave alive. The mineworkers' union tried and the men risked everything to join, but Canadian Collieries (Dunsmuir) Limited did whatever was needed to keep profits high, and when the union finally managed to improve conditions, which narrowed profit margins, the company closed the mines.

It was hot on the beach, the sun baking the mud flats and making heat waves dance above the rocks, shimmer in the air. The bank was thick with white shells: oyster shells, clam shells and a few abalone shells, the bottom layers turned into something else, something almost like chalk, crumbly and dry. When you touched them they lost their shape and became dust. Beneath the roots of huge trees were more shells, whole and broken, some charred by fires dead ten thousand years or more.

. . . and a blast of air coming from an open mouth of a black hole. Christie Anne Fraser climbed four and a half feet up the shell-layered bank, four and a half feet up the side of the tide-and-rain-eroded midden, and crawled inside the cool tunnel.

Seventeen feet inside, the tunnel widened, the roof lifted. Nine feet farther in she could kneel without bumping her head. Fourteen feet farther, she could stand upright. Forty feet from there the tunnel became a room, with other tunnels leading off it. Christie Anne, fascinated, moved along the tunnels, her eyes wide, a sound humming in her head.

. . . nobody ever asked, but if they had, she wouldn't have been able to say where the light came from. She had never heard of a periscope, she knew nothing of the secrets of mirrors and reflected light. But Christie hadn't designed, dug or shored up the walls of the tunnel, and it didn't matter she didn't recognize the mirrors, mirrors set in the wall thousands of years before Captain Cook got lost in the fog and was escorted out of the place of shifting land and changing vision by the Nuu-chah-nulth navy.

The light was faint and soft, but constant. She didn't see the mirrors but she saw the little shelves dug into the walls. When she looked closer, she saw a skeleton in each excavated ledge. Bones, bracelets of gold, decorative shields of copper, labrets of ivory fallen from lips long gone.

and the light becoming a soft blue,
the sound of her breathing become music
strange music like the sound of waves,
the sigh of wind the rush of air
through the feathers of
the wings of ancient birds
rattling gourds and fingertip-stroked hide drumheads
deer hoof rattles and the scent
of cedarbark.

her legs took her to a small freshwater pool
her fingers removed her clothes
she sat in the water
her eyes staring at the gaping sockets in the skull
gaping sockets watching her from a ledge

And when she came from the pool she was chilled and hurried into her clothes. One by one she visited the ledges, examining amulets, running her finger over sacred stones, lifting, touching, looking, but replacing everything, remembering her mother's warning, "Let it not be said and said to your shame that all was beauty until you came."

Then she tried to find her way back out of the strange place.

They had been looking for her for days. They dragged the river. A search party went into the abandoned mine shaft near her home. Her mother was hysterically sure they'd find Christie raped and dead. Her father was afraid to admit it, but he feared the same thing.

"No," Jen's mother repeated often. "No, she's coming back to us."

And then Mary White walked up to the front door carrying a sleeping child. Freshly bathed, smelling of soap, wrapped in a clean flanelette nightgown and a soft blue blanket, her wet clothes in a bundle.

"Should shut up them old mine shafts," was all Mary White would say. "Had no right to make 'em, less right to just leave 'em for kids to get lost," and she refused to answer questions or accept a reward.

Christie Anne never spoke of what she had seen. She never told about the strange light or the graves, she just let them assume she had been lost in a mine shaft. She knew they would neither believe her nor understand, and if they did, and the treasures were taken, the bones disturbed, the entire world would come to an end and it would be her fault, all her fault. Sometimes she dreamed she was again sitting on the floor of a tunnel, resting against the wall, her face grimy and tear-stained, and then all of a sudden Mary White was kneeling, gathering Christie in her arms, and Christie knew this chubby old woman would make it all bearable.

"Laughing Voice," Mary White called her, "I was there and you reached out with that dirty little white hand, and when our fingers touched, you were more mine than some who had come from my body."

"I'm lost," Christie managed.

"Not any more," Mary White said. And she led Christie out of the holy place, back into the sunshine. Christie held tightly to Mary's hand every step of the way. When the old woman realized the child was nearly falling with weariness, she lifted her easily, and Christie clung with her arms and legs. Back at Mary's little house on the reserve, the old woman bathed her and fed her, and while Christie ate, Mary White washed her clothes, removing all evidence of grave dirt and dust that had once been flesh, removing all evidence the child had not been in a coal mine. She took Christie home and waved in the direction of the mine shafts. "Should close 'em all up," she repeated. Christie Anne looked at the old woman, and said nothing to contradict her. Her gold-flecked eyes blinked. She opened her mouth and yawned.

Jen Fraser thought Christie never spoke of it because she had been so afraid. The doctor said it was amnesia. He would have said something else if Christie had told him she had looked into empty eye sockets and heard – and understood – a foreign speech issue from a mouth rotted away when the Druids came down from their sacred oak trees. Christie's silence became the most noticeable thing about her.

Often Mary White would sit on her top step, the child sitting beside her, and the old woman would know that all she knew was not enough. How could she explain to her Laughing Voice child that some things are too sacred for anthropologists? The child was frightened enough, how could she understand that only the most sacred of sacred people are allowed near the place she had found, and that not many years before, an unsanctified person would have died for finding what Christie Anne had found.

Christie Anne said nothing about the bones. When a person who has never told a lie, a person who has just saved your life, when that person tells a lie, you know the lie is important and the truth is dangerous, more dangerous than abandoned coal shafts.

Alex Fraser sat on Christie's bed, his back against the headboard, his legs on the chenille spread, and when she stirred or whimpered in her deep sleep, he stroked her damp curls and said, Easy now, my sweet one, Daddy's here, everything is fine now. He put his huge hand on her small bum and rocked as he had when she was an infant, and she relaxed again. His mother stood at the door and watched, wondering, and when Jen went into the room, Alex stroked her face and told her, "Lie down here with her and hold her and sleep with her, I'll watch the others."

"No," she said, "it's okay. It's enough she's back with us."

"It's none of it your fault," he said. "She's fine, and you're her mother, and she needs you. And you need her. Come on, now."

And Jen did. She lay down beside her sleeping firstborn, and for the first time since Christie hadn't shown up for supper, Jen slept, while Alex stroked her arm and whispered to her.

"I knew someone was there," Mary White told Christie years later. "I was afraid it would be university people. I wasn't sure what I'd do about them. It's hard enough to get rid of one person, but two or three, or four or five . . . what if one of them left maps, or notes or . . . and I put the three-oh-eight deer rifle aside when I heard the voices talking to you and saw you sitting as quiet as a properly initiated person, nodding and listening and hearing. It was the hearing amazed me. I didn't know you people could hear them things."

The first time Christie saw a picture of a conquistador, she knew about the metal breastplate. She began to read everything she could about them and for years her favourite book was a hard-backed green-covered book called *Spanish Gold*. As fascinated as she was by them and the names they left for places on her Island, Christie hated them. She especially hated the priests, long dead and unmourned.

She stayed home from school for a week after Mary White brought her home, then went back, ignoring the curious stares and questions. The school nurse got so anxious she wrote a report that resulted in a special counsellor being sent from Victoria. Christie stared at him and answered his questions with such a convincing air of stupid incomprehension that Mary White would have been proud of her.

"Just leave her the hell alone," Alex said quietly, but with such a force of threat and power they all felt a chill.

Mary White waited, hoping Christie had forgotten everything, hoping the doctor was right with his diagnosis of amnesia, hoping Christie, safe at home with her family, would never remember where she had been, what she had seen. For weeks she waited, worried she had been wrong about Christie, worried the child would tell and those others would come with their notebooks and shovels, afraid the sacred place would be violated and the world would cease to exist, afraid her own weakness had started the destruction of the world. And yet she knew alongside a little girl, with tear streaks on her face and trust in her eyes, reaching out and taking her hand, reaching out and taking her heart, the destruction of the world was nothing, nothing at all compared to murdering that child. Sometimes she would hold the silent, traumatized child on her lap and weep, whispering over and over to herself in her own language, whispering, Forgive me, Laughing Voice, you were never meant to carry the existence of the world upon your head, your spirit has been burdened forever by my weakness, and you can still destroy the world, for I am made weak by my love for you.

In school Christie occupied a chair, sometimes listening, sometimes not. Some days the noise in her head buzzed and nagged, weaving in and out between her teeth, winding in and out of her ears. The teacher gave her detentions for not paying attention, especially in arithmetic. She couldn't bring herself to play softball. She sat by herself listening to the noises. "Christie Anne is having another thinky-thing," the kids chanted. The teacher told them to be quiet and leave Christie alone. "You wouldn't like it if someone did that to you," she warned. "And you all know what a terrible experience Christie had in the old mine shaft."

Christie ran home after school, trying to run away from the sounds in her head. She changed out of her school clothes, told her mother she was going to catch frogs, then raced for the village, unerringly making her way to Mary White's house.

When Mary White turned, the child was there, standing in the doorway, looking into the cool interior of the unpainted board house, looking into the spotlessly clean kitchen where the old woman was bringing fresh bread from the oven. Christie stared with wide, frantic green eyes, waiting to speak, unable to speak. Mary White opened the screen door, picked up the child of strangers, and wept. No, no, my cherished one, she soothed her in Salish, no, there are no answers. Not to worry, not to worry, you are loved and needed.

"My head hurts," Christie sobbed, "it's full of bugs."

"Not bugs," Mary corrected her. "Trust me. Trust me with your life, Christie Anne."

She was home in time for supper and nobody asked where she had been. On Saturday she spent six hours with Mary White, on Sunday, four. By the end of the year she knew how to handle the strange noises and their messages. It was years before she began to understand why the noises came to her, why the messages were sent to her. "You are the first young one in too many years," Grandma White said, staring across the table, holding Christie in the power of her gaze. "My own grandchildren were taken to residential school and when they came back they did not want to know anything of our ways. And their children, now, are in residential school, being taught to be ashamed of us. So the spirits were hungry and you arrived, young and unashamed; now they make demands of you, for they kept you alive while you were lost."

The river flowed from the mountain to the sea as it had from the first day of creation. Two wolves came from the forest. The female went to the water and drank. She waited while the male came to drink. When he lowered his head she kept watch, when he lifted his head to watch, she drank a second time, then watched while he drank again. He turned to go back into the forest, but she moved into the water. He whined. He objected. In the end, he followed. They swam across the river, the female in the lead, and as they emerged on the other side, panting and shaking with fatigue, their fur fell off and they stood erect, the first of The People. His name was Sacqual and he was the first man. The name of the woman he followed is too sacred to be used and only the initiates can know it. The name Sacqual means "blade of grass." Their children were the Sacquadots, many blades of grass, a meadow of grass, an endless expanse of grass. They looked at their wolf pelts lying on the beach and then, for a while, became wolves again, digging a large burrow in the bank. When the burrow was done and done properly, they changed into humans and buried their former selves in the burrow they had dug, and that burrow was the start of the place you found, Christie Anne Fraser, my Laughing Voice child. Since that time, only the special and holy have been buried there, and only the holy are allowed to know about it. You were not holy when you found it, but you are holy now, and the silence with which you protect yourself will go, you will again Laugh.

Sometimes she dreamed of clear cold stars and of falling past them towards a bright glowing light

Sometimes she felt as if she were hungry but nothing she put in her mouth satisfied the hunger

Sometimes she repeated a word to herself until it lost all meaning and became only what it was, itself, itsound

Christie Anne is having a thinky-thing again.

The path along the lake was shady and cool, the deep underlayer soft and resilient. Every morning Christie ran the two miles to school and every afternoon she ran home again. Once she'd changed her clothes she was free until suppertime, unless there were chores or her mother told her to keep an eye on Lizzie and Johnny. After supper was finished and the dishes done, she was free until seven-thirty. Most nights she'd run down the path to the school playground and either get into a game of scrub football or swing on the monkey bars. When her friend got called home at seven, Christie started back down the road, then cut through Thomas's pasture to the path in the bush. As she ran she sang songs in her head, fitting the rhythm of her steps to the music.

And when it was track meet time, Christie Anne stayed by herself, sitting in the shade, talking to nobody, looking as if she was having another thinky-thing. Then she would rise, do her stretches, look around as if she had never seen the track before, and move slowly, easily, to the starting line. She always came home with ribbons fluttering from her chest. She showed the ribbons to her parents, then put the ribbons away in her dresser drawer. Nobody ever saw the ribbons again, except Mary White. Christie gave them to her and the old woman kept them thumbtacked to the wall of her bedroom, where she could look at them before falling asleep, and indulge herself in the sin of pride.

Christie knew little of proud feelings. Mostly she felt numb, but didn't know to recognize numb. She only knew many things frightened her and most things puzzled her. She knew that much, at least.

She was puzzled by the way people behaved, the things they didn't do and didn't say, and the puzzlement often became terror. Uncle Cliff showed up one Friday night with a woman who wasn't his wife. They brought a case of beer with them and sat in the kitchen talking with Momma and Poppa. When Christie went to bed Momma was sitting in a chair with a cup of tea and her crochet, listening but not smiling or nodding, just being polite, which you always had to be if possible, and Poppa and the others were laughing together. Later, the two men and the woman were singing, but not loudly, not enough to disturb anybody. Uncle Cliff and his friend visited several times after that, and Christie knew her mother wished they wouldn't, but didn't know what to do or say about it.

Summer moved quickly into autumn, and Christie spent a Saturday helping Jenny prepare the gardens for their winter rest. She raked and burned leaves, cleaned dry stalks from the flowerbeds and kept the trash fire together, using the rake to pull unburned stuff back into the soft white ash and hot glowing coals. The dried leaves, withered grass and discarded flower heads flared briefly and were gone, poof, just like that, and something in the rake rake rake, tidy tidy tidy soothed Christie.

She had supper and went for a long walk, although most of it she didn't remember later, then had a long hot bath and went to bed. She knew before she put her head on the pillow she was going to plummet into sleep. Sometimes she drifted, and she enjoyed that, not here, not there, just floating slowly, but there was something about the giving over of control, the knowing it was going to be fast fast fast that was almost exciting, and she placed her head carefully on the clean white pillowslip because the times when she leaped into sleep she hardly moved all night, and waking up with a stiff neck is an awful ending to a nice night.

And then she was awake, and someone was holding her, and Christie was too terrified to scream. She flailed her arms wildly, trying to make a sound, any sound. Someone laughed softly, and then Poppa was there, scooping her up, holding her to his shoulder, patting her bum, saying Uh uh baby, uh uh, back to sleep, there's my hen. Christie let herself go and lay as if boneless, her head against the curve of his neck. "No, Cliffie," Alex Fraser said coldly, "not the bairns, and not when you're drinkin'."

"No need to be upset," Uncle Cliffie slurred. "We just wanted to see her, was all."

"No," Poppa repeated. "She scares easy since her gettin' lost, and anyway, not when you're drunk."

"I just wanted to see her," Cliff's friend insisted, her voice blurry and damp. "She's next best thing to my niece."

"No," Momma said firmly, "she's nowhere near to being your niece. She's Cliff's niece, she's Beth's niece, she isn't your niece at all and never will be."

"Don't take it wrong, Cliffie," said Poppa. "I don't mind if a person has had a drink or two, or even three or four, but I'm not havin' anyone near my kids who's three sheets to the wind."

"Ah, hey, Al!" Cliff sounded as if he was ready to weep. "You know I wouldn't. Man, I wouldn't –"

Poppa put Christie back to bed, pulled the covers to her chin and stroked her cheek as he talked to Uncle Cliffie. "You're Jenny's brother, and I honour that," he said. "More than that, you've been a good friend to me, and that's important in my eyes. But when you're drinkin', man, you're just another goddamn drunk as far as I'm concerned. And I won't have a drunk goin' near my kids when they're in bed."

"Alex, I wouldn't –"

"Right." Poppa straightened. "And since you won't, it won't insult you or interfere in any way if I make goddamn good and sure they're safe."

The look between them held for a long long time, then Uncle Cliff nodded and stuck out his hand. Alex Fraser took it briefly. Christie felt sleep coming on her again, and let herself dive into it, slice into that dark warm deep place where there was nothing could find you or scare you. In the morning Cliff and his friend were gone, and nobody spoke about it.

One day a man followed her home from school, and the next day he followed her again. "I don't know who he is," Christie told Jenny, "he just keeps smiling at me." Jenny told her he had probably mistaken her for someone else. "Everybody has a double or two somewhere," she smiled.

The next day, less than a third of the way home, the man called to her. Christie quickened her steps and the man moved forward, ready to run. And Poppa stepped from the bush, his Lee-Enfield .303 held almost casually in his hand. "You'll die, mister," he said softly. The man whirled and pelted back down the road. Poppa fell in step beside Christie, draped an arm around her shoulder, smiled, and asked, "How was school today, sweetheart?"

"Why aren't you at work?" she blurted.

"Hadda sight in the gun," he said. "Hunting season opens soon. So, how was school?"

Later, after supper, when she was doing the dishes and starting to feel scared about what might have happened, Poppa brought in his teacup and said, "Anybody ever bothers you, you just tell me, darlin', and the bastard'll wind up in a crab trap."

She knew he meant it. He would protect her against God himself. The knowledge did not make her feel safe. His fury only frightened her more than the threat of the nameless gorm on the road. Somehow she was certain she could have saved herself, given the chance. If the gorms of the world were a threat, Alex was a bigger one. But she just nodded and told herself over and over again that Alex loved her.

E L E V E N

There were times you'd wonder if Freud couldn't have written two shelf-loads of case histories just from your own family circle. Without having to make up a thing. Never mind that Buttercup had become so religious she might be willing to throw on a robe and tighten the thumbscrews to assist in a new Inquisition. Except that she wasn't Catholic and would probably have paid for the chance to bomb the Vatican, especially if the pope was inside. Simon says just a baby step to the right and Jo-Beth would be standing alongside the grand dragon of the KKK. Her letters read like handouts for the Aryan Nation. Who would have dared imagine that organ transplants were a plot devised by the coloured and the inferior to pollute the white gene pool? Who would have thought the thousands of children believed to be abducted by parents who did not agree with custody orders, had not been snatched by a mommy or a daddy but by Others who then drugged them, opened them from stem to stern and hauled out bits and pieces and parts of vital organs which they sold on the black market (what other colour would it be?) to ruthless mid-dlemen, who supplied the enormous drug companies (and we know who owns and controls *them*, don't we), who manufac-tured drugs to counteract diseases particular to coloureds, Jews and queers? Would you believe, could you believe, dare you believe that abortion clinics were a plot to reduce the population of whites while flooding the country with swarms of Others? The pill, for example – who invented that, and why? Wasn't it true and easily proven that it had led to many fewer white births, but that Those Others didn't use it, they just kept having more and more and more and more children, the darker the better, and going on welfare with them all (here Buttercup preferred to overlook the source of most of her own meals as a child)? It was just another devious way to undermine the economy of the country, more and more money going into illegitimate bastards and less and less of it into proper defences against the real threat to Our Way of Life, a Way of Life based on the doctrines and teachings of Our One True Saviour and Lord. But it's never too late to repent, Christ loves us all and so do I.

Never mind, either, that young Scott thought the way to solve all problems was to increase security, institute a national draft and a return to such time-honoured solutions as the lash and capital punishment. Well, at least he didn't disguise his nutsiness in religion, he just held forth about more jobs for people who were already citizens and a closed door to those who weren't. Most of Scott's solutions involved more, bigger, better battleships, bombers and nuclear-powered Everything from scooters for the kids to intercontinental guided missiles. Never mind diplomacy – nobody ever managed to veto a neutron bomb in his back yard.

And if that pair weren't barmy enough for a chapter or two by Freud, you could look closer to home.

Robbie lived with Alicia, who was more than ten years older than he was. Now what did that tell you about the way he had grown up or the imprinting he had chosen? Ten years. When Robbie was born Alicia was already trying on her mother's pantyhose and experimenting with lipstick. By the time he learned to walk she was babysitting the neighbour's kids. The question was not why a woman would want a younger man. That's pretty obvious: after age thirty their hair starts to fall out and their bellies hang over their belt buckles. The question was why a young man would want a woman ten years older, with a couple of kids and an ex-husband who paid no child support at all.

"Good," Robbie laughed, "that way we don't have to put up with the bugger."

But they did have to put up with him. Any time he took it into his head to drive Alicia halfway up the wall he just got in his car and drove over, ostensibly to see his kids. Then he sat on

Robbie's sofa in Robbie's living room drinking Robbie's coffee from Robbie's cup while Robbie worked like a dog to pay for it.

And Alicia had decided her children were entitled to things they had never had before Robbie began picking up the tab. Their own rooms, their own walk-in closets full of clothes with the right labels, a playroom, if you please, with every toy manufactured by every company that the kids could see on the tube. Dance lessons. Piano lessons, and a piano for them to practise on, which they seldom did. Robbie headed off to camp, decimating the rain forest and sending money to Alicia because, he said, he was no good with money. It was true. But neither was Alicia, who spent a lot of it on those foil-wrapped dinners you can pop into the nuke and call hot food. Little bitty packages of this and teeny weeny parcels of that, more damn wrapping and packaging than you could believe, and the kids living on sandwiches and sugar.

Before Alicia, Robbie had sent chunks of money to Fran, and when Robbie and Alicia got together Fran had almost made the mistake of giving it back to him for a so-to-speak wedding present. Thank God something had made her think twice about it, wait until things were more settled. She had never told Robbie just how much was sitting in the bank, the term deposits coming due and flipping automatically into whichever term was offering the highest interest, adding up all this time. If she'd followed her first impulse they would have made a down payment on a house, half of which would have become the legal property of someone who had two cheeky liabilities, an ex-husband who couldn't hold a job, and a bad habit of wasting money.

"You know what's going to happen?" She poured more tea for Liz, who was looking like hell these days, all dark circles under the eyes and her skin pale as someone with a case of flu. "The way it's going, before you and I are buried every man in the country is going to be supporting someone else's kids while his own are somewhere else being looked after and fed by someone else. It's like Musical Chairs, only instead of racing for a place to sit when the music stops, you shuffle the short ones around and make sure they don't have the slightest idea of what's going on or whose loyalty they can expect."

Small wonder Robbie drank more than was good for him. A lot more than was good for anybody. And Alicia, instead of trying to do something about it, just smiled her damn lifeless smile and talked about Robbie's needs. "Robbie seems to need these little acts of defiance," she said, or "Robbie seems to need periods of what seem to be independence." What Robbie needed was a few weeks in a treatment centre and maybe a brain transplant.

And Nancy. Well, really. You'd think someone with her education and training would have picked up the ability to think somewhere along the line. But no, there she was, working on the burn unit and looking as if she had waked up in a nightmare from which there was no escape. Just try to tell her, though. Just try.

"Momma," she sighed, "most people can't take it for more than a couple of shifts, let alone a couple of weeks or months. And if I quit, who else will there be?"

"Nobody is indispensable," Fran argued. "At least take a month or two off. You look as if you've been burned yourself, on the inside instead of the outside."

But you'd get further if you talked to your umbrella. Isn't it odd how people who aren't even any real blood relation can wind up reminding you of each other? There wasn't a drop of shared blood between Nancy and Wilma and yet they would have got on equally well in the Roman Empire. In the old days, with their need to be martyrs, they could have converted to Christianity and been thrown to the lions and gone out in glory, instead of this dreary whatever-it-was they were living, one with her strawberry tea brigade, the other with her damn burn ward.

"Sure, someone has to do it," she argued with Liz, "but does it have to be the same one all the time?"

"Well, she must like it."

"Oh, don't be silly! How could anyone like it? Have you seen what some of those people look like after they've been cured? What must they look like during treatment?"

"I don't like to think about it. Let's change the subject."

"You can't spend your entire life changing the subject."

But of course she could, and she would, and what's more, she did.

"Worrying yourself sick over it won't change it, either. And if Nancy is going to drink, she's going to drink whether she works the burn unit or not."

"Maybe. But if stress is why she's drinking –"

"That might be the excuse, but take it away and she'll just invent another. Drinkers drink, Fran. You know that."

So we come to Brandy. Brandy, who couldn't be harder to get along with if she took a course in bloodymindedness. She no sooner finishes high school than she's off to some drippy job in Banff, glorified waitress for the not-as-rich-as-they-like-you-to-believe and the not-as-beautiful-as-they-think-they-are. Hotel management training, Brandy called it, but no closer to that than Liz's old job in the fish'n'chips shop. Next thing you know it's months later and she shows up with this man in tow, nice enough seeming, but it's hard to like or trust a guy who tells you with a wide smile on his face that the reason he is attracted to your daughter is that she's built so much like a boy. "Tidy," he said.

Tidy? Apparently that's what Brandy was, especially after she got into all the Banff-y stuff, tennis and skiing and mountain climbing and riding bicycles up cliffs or whatever they did with themselves in the name of a good time. Not an ounce of fat on her, not that there ever had been. Muscles, though. If you mentioned to her that maybe she was getting a bit, well, overdone, she just laughed and said her aim in life was to have a forearm like Martina Navritalova.

"Why stop there?" Fran asked. "Why not go that last little bit and have a forearm like Mike Tyson while you're at it?"

"Becauthe I'm afraid I'd get the lithp, too," Brandy answered, her voice easy, her eyes just a little bit slanty, and with Brandy that was a sure sign you were in for more than you bargained for if you didn't shape up.

The man who was attracted to her tidiness didn't shape up fast enough. Brandy off-loaded him after they had lived together only a few weeks. "I don't do well with living together," she decided. "Maybe I had to live with too many other people coming and going for too long or something. I like my own space."

Just as well she did. Imagine how upset you'd be if you were in bed sound asleep and naked when the police arrived to arrest your bed partner for getting too fancy with the grade four boys he taught.

"I didn't know what it was," she sobbed, "but something about it just didn't seem right. I only said I needed my space because I didn't know what I was feeling so weird about. And I still don't, but whatever it is, it's awful, Momma, just *awful!*"

"Take a page from your aunt Liz's book," Fran told her. "Just don't think about it."

And Liz did her damnedest not to think about anything. Even when she did get forced to look at something that was bothering her, she managed to look at anything but that one. Like this racism stuff. Wasn't she off on a great old tangent with that. Give her another week or two and she'd be organizing her own branch of the enn-double-ay-cee-pee. The way she held forth all the time you'd think she was the first person to pinpoint it and name it.

"Do you know," she lectured, "that Indians pay much higher insurance rates simply because they are Indians? Someone with a brand new car, someone exactly the same as you or me, someone who just happens to be Indian, they have to pay more simply because they are Indians. That's racism!"

"Just try to do anything about insurance rates for anyone, let alone something like that. You're banging your head against a brick wall."

"If we'd all said that, nobody would have signed the Magna Carta."

"And what good did that do? Chopped off some king's head, but other than that, do you see any huge improvement in our lives? Every damn government we get takes a swing at those so-called rights. They're just slicker now than they were then."

"And you accept that?"

"Read the AA literature. Give me the power to change what I can and the strength to accept what I can't, or something. Smarten up and accept your limitations. Otherwise you're going to get an ulcer."

She probably already had one. Or was giving one to everyone else in the family. Pictures of Sojourner Truth on the wall in the entrance hallway, pictures of Angela Davis over the sink in the kitchen, and what was Angela doing in there with the soap suds and scouring pads?

"Might be a touch of racism in *that*, darlin'," Fran had teased. But you can't tease Dizzy Lizzie, she went into orbit.

"I want my girls to have some other role model than Betty Crocker! And I want them to know doing dishes is not as upscale as they can get! And –"

It wasn't doing the girls much good. Marti was so sick and

tired of it all that she hardly tried to talk to Liz about anything any more, and Reba had joined Liz in her silliness.

"You call me Corby again," she told the coach, "and you can look for another goalie."

He gaped.

"I don't want to be called Corby! I am *not* a crow. I am *not* a blackbird. I'm a goalie."

"Hey, easy," he soothed.

"I'll be easy, just as long as you don't call me anything but my name. No crow, no blackbird, no Corby, okay?"

He must have been really stuck for a goalie because he just nodded. The whole thing had very little to do with racism. What it had to do with was that someone had made a racist crack and then tied it in with a crack about the Harrises. That's what had Liz spewing fire. Fran knew. Fran had heard the crack. But Liz had decided it was racism, and Liz was off on a crusade. Suddenly there were explosions about Aunt Jemima and about companies that used Native art work in advertising without the express permission of Native people, as if you'd get all of them to agree on any one thing.

"Why should they pay property tax?" Liz demanded. "They don't own property. All that reserve land they tell you is Indian land is owned by the federal government. You don't pay tax on land you don't use, why should they?"

"If my roof leaks I have to find a way to pay to get it fixed. If their roof leaks they get it fixed by the taxpayers. I'm a taxpayer. So I have to pay for my roof, and I have to pay for theirs too."

"They don't own the houses. If you were renting and your roof leaked, your landlord would have to get the roof fixed. The government owns their houses, the government is us. We're the landlords, we fix the roofs."

"Most landlords *get* rent, Liz. They don't pay rent."

"And the natural resources we never paid them for? That isn't rent? Damn high rent?"

"Can we talk about something else? This isn't a conversation, it's a very long and very boring temper tantrum. You aren't an Indian. The stuff you've got your shirt in a knot about isn't any of your business anyway."

"Not my business? If the government is us, and the government is doing something disgusting, then we are doing something disgusting, and I refuse to do it!"

"You don't know what the government is doing. The government makes sure we don't know what's going on until it's way too late anyway."

"And you accept that?"

"No. I don't accept that. I don't even bother voting for the bastards."

"You don't vote?"

"I haven't voted in years. It doesn't matter. No matter which party gets the most votes, the system wins and the guys in suits just keep on running things and we never get to vote for the bureaucracy so it continues unchanged."

"That's awful. Fran, you've *got* to vote."

"No, I don't got to vote! They can't make me vote. That's democracy!"

MARGARET ANNE

My aunt Flora was possibly the most beautiful woman ever born on the Island. When she smiled you knew nothing else in the world would ever make you feel that good. She wasn't tall, she wasn't short, she wasn't heavy, she wasn't thin, she was just right. Just Right. Clear white skin, eyes as blue as the summer sea, eyes so blue they jumped across the room at you, and blonde curly hair that made you think the sun was caught in there and shining out at you.

When she was nearly fifteen my grandfather MacDonald said she was to marry. Grandfather MacDonald had agreed to the marriage, agreed to the size of the dowry, agreed she would leave school and leave her mother's house and marry someone she hadn't even seen.

The man who wanted to marry my aunt had seen her walking to town with her mother and decided he wanted this lovely young girl for his wife, so he found out her name, went to her father and discussed the matter, and it was settled. He lived in a half-built house miles out of town and he raised chickens, selling eggs and meat and telling everyone who would listen that in his own country his family had been royalty, his family owned a castle, or a palace, they had servants and acres of good farmland and . . .

Everyone called him Count No-Account.

She was fifteen, she had never spent a single night away from home and she had been raised to be totally obedient. She didn't want to quit school, she didn't want to marry anybody, let alone Count No-Account, but she had been raised to do what her father told her to do. Ag and Jen both invited her to live with them, instead, but Flora was afraid to defy the old man. "Honour thy father and mother," Colin yelled, "that thy days on this earth be long. And if you defy me, my bonny lassie, your days on this earth will not be long!" And Flora's mother, well, she just sat shaking her head and staring holes in the floor, even when Ag yelled at her and called her every kind of fool in the world.

Count No-Account tried. He wanted the big-eyed frightened-looking child to like him, he wanted her to learn to love him. She was so beautiful his breath caught in his throat, she was so delicate he felt enormous beside her frail beauty. He bought her nice clothes. Not too nice – he wanted her beauty to be his and his alone – but nicer than anything she had at home. But she came to the marriage bed trembling, the veins in her throat pulsing, her blue eyes filled with tears. She was so frightened she could not speak, she just lay there trembling with terror, making him feel like a beast.

When her older brother Niall came out to visit and Count No-Account saw how her face lit up, how she moved freely toward Niall, not frightened, not trembling, how she put her arms around her brother as she never put her arms around her husband, how she put her face against Niall's chest as she never did with him, the jealousy grew. And later, when he came in from the hen house and found Niall and Flora dancing together in the kitchen to the music from the radio, Count No-Account stood amazed, watching the two golden ones dance in the still-unfinished kitchen of the house he was slowly building for Flora.

"I didn't know you could dance," he muttered.

"I taught her," Niall laughed. "She learns good, eh, hen?"

"I can learn anything you can think to teach me," she said flippantly, tossing her head, behaving as the Count had never seen her behave.

"I had no idea." He waited, wanting her to dance some more.

"If you didn't keep her locked away in this grey old house," Niall smiled, so that Count No-Account couldn't get angry with him, "if you ever took her anywhere, you'd find out any number of things."

"She never asked."

"Och, man," Niall laughed again, "she never asked to marry you, either, but here we all are."

"Now, Niall!" Flora's smile was suddenly sharp-edged, the way it usually was, and the shadows were coming around her eyes again. The Count knew she was afraid he would tell her brother to hit the road, and he knew she was afraid of him, the one who loved her so much.

"You want to go dancing, Flora? I'll take you dancing," and his palms were damp, if she said no it would be one more rejection, one more attempt to make her smile that died under the weight of her fear.

"Would you really?" She was smiling. At him. Smiling and for the first time not looking as if she is afraid of every move he makes.

"Sure, I'll take you dancing."

"They've got a dance tomorrow night," Niall said quickly. No vague promises for him, put up or shut up.

"Then we go to the dance," he nodded firmly, as if it was all his idea.

Flora darted forward and kissed him on the cheek, and he had to turn away quickly before her brother saw the tears in his eyes. It was the first time Flora had voluntarily kissed him, and he wanted more of her smiles.

At the dance she moved in his arms like a princess at a state ball, and he could forget this was a dance band of fishermen, farmers and dirty coal miners. He could forget that this wasn't the old country, with ladies and gentlemen moving decorously, forget the injustices that had brought him to this backward place, reduced him to raising chickens. For a while he was who he ought to have been, and he was dancing with his wife.

"Having fun, Flora?"

"Oh, yes," and her smile was only for him. All those others could see was that Flora was dancing with that old fart of a husband of hers, but in her smile he thought he saw that given time, Flora would have chosen him over any of these others. She wasn't smiling for them, she was smiling for him. Only for him.

Flora smiled until they got home and he reached for her in bed. Then, as sure as cold wind coming through a broken window, the smile vanished, the laughter withered, she stiffened and the breath caught in her throat as she lay afraid, repelled, disgusted.

Flora kept the house spotlessly clean, kept his clothes washed, ironed, patched. She cooked good meals and was always asking for recipes, always trying to please him. Still, he knew, it was when he wasn't in the house she relaxed, it was when she thought he was in the hen house she sang in the kitchen, took the broom and danced with it, briefly joyous. And when he walked in she stopped dead, lowered the broom and stood there, frightened.

"There's a dance on Saturday." He felt his mouth go dry when her face lit up and her smile almost dared to show. "You want to go?"

"Oh, yes! Yes, please."

"You be nice to me . . ." He slipped his galluses from his shoulders, let them dangle in half loops below his hips. Her spontaneous smile died, giving way to the dutiful one he hated so much. She walked toward him, something in her eyes mocking him, shaming him, making him want to hit her, making him want some honest reaction, not this practised coolness. She pressed against him, her lips on his, not because she loved him or wanted him or was no longer afraid of him but because if she was nice to him she could go to the dance. Train up a child in the way in which she is to go and when she is old she will not depart from it . . .

But there were no children. No sons, no daughters, and he didn't dare ask if she was doing something (what?) to stop the children. At the dances he did not allow her to dance with anyone else except her brother, and when others tried to cut in he growled "Go away," so the young men realized how much it bothered him and out of spite, one after the other, they tried to cut in, tried to touch Flora, tried to get a rise out of Count No-Account.

"You smiled at him!"

"No. No, I didn't. Honest, I didn't –"

"You did!"

"No! I'm your wife, I wouldn't –"

"Prove it." She moved toward him with the practised smile and he closed his eyes, pretending this seventeen-year-old girl wanted him, wanted him to touch her, wanted to touch him.

"You going to take me to the dance on Saturday?" She bent over the back of his chair, breathing on his neck, playing with his hair, rubbing her fingers slowly, teasingly around the rim of the bald spot which now covered most of the top of his scalp.

"No."

"Why not?"

"You flirt with other men."

He wanted to make her desperate to go dancing, wanted to make her so hungry for dancing, so hungry for music, so hungry for laughter and the youth she had never had that she'd forget she didn't like his touch, forget she didn't like to touch him.

Instead, he made her so desperate she went out the window and walked to the dance hall. He heard her at four in the morning, giggling as Niall lifted her up to the window so she could sneak back into the house. Count No-Account waited until Niall had left and Flora was in bed.

"Where you been?"

"The outhouse."

"Bitch!" He reached out, grabbed a handful of her lovely golden hair. "You lie to me and I'll break your neck."

"I met my brother," she said defiantly, "and we went to the dance."

"I said *no!*" he yelled. And he hit her.

Hitting her did no good at all. She had been hit before, she had been beaten since childhood by a short Scot with a barrel chest and arms like young trees, and when Count No-Account hit her he just proved to her that he was every ugly thing she had always suspected. More and more often he woke up at night to find himself alone in bed. And more and more often he beat her, trying to keep her at home, with him.

"You bastard!" Niall dragged him from bed and punched him three times before his feet touched the floor. "You ever lay a hand on her again and I'll make you pay for it!"

"Get off me!"

"I'll drag you out to your hen house and ram a week's worth of chickenshit down your scrawny throat if you so much as think of hitting her!"

After that, Count No-Account made sure he left no marks.

The man's name was Scott McPhail and he was too beautiful to be believed. Golden hair like Flora's, like Niall's, and blue eyes, crinkled at the corners from laughing. Not tall, but built the way men ought to be built, with broad shoulders and deep chests, but not barrel-chested and thick-armed like her father.

"Flor, this is my buddy Scott. Scott, my sister Flora. She's married, though, so you behave yourself," and it was out in the open, understood from the first moment. Scott nodded, smiled, then turned from Niall to Flora. "And would you honour me with a dance, Miss Married-Sister Flora?"

He danced almost as well as Niall, moving surely and smoothly, the arm around her waist as hard as rock, as gentle as a dream. The golden hair at his throat threw the overhead light back at itself, the fine blue veins in his throat showing pale against his clear white skin. He had once been a professional boxer, on his way to a chance at the title. "Ah, but that's a goon's game," he laughed, "and what would I get from it but a wee bit of money and my brains scrambled? Besides, if I hadn't put that aside I'd be in training right now, and if I was in training I wouldn't be here, and I wouldn't have met you, and I'd sooner dance with you, Miss Married-Sister Flora, than be champion of this world and the next."

"Oh, and listen to you!" she laughed. "Another oatmeal savage with a tongue to charm birds from their nests." But it was nice to hear after so many growled orders, and the soft burr of his speech, so like her mother's own accent, was like music after her husband's harsh broken English.

She learned that Scott worked sometimes as a singer with a dance band, "but there I'd be, up with the music-makers, singing my throat dry, and all the fun and dancing happening without me," he laughed.

"If you're not fighting and not singing, what do you do?" she dared.

"You'll never believe me but I'll tell you anyway. I travel with a circus. I'm the strong man, and I bend spikes with my teeth."

"You *what?*"

"Oh, it's all tricks, of course, bending nails with your fingers, ripping phone books, driving spikes into hunks of wood with your knuckles. All tricks. But if the audience can't do the tricks I still look impressive. It doesn't pay much, but oh, my hen, such things as I've seen! In Montreal they speak French and it's one night club after another, dancing in the streets, and even the nuns and priests sing at carnival time. And the prairies! So flat you can see company coming a week before they arrive. The sea smells the same in the Maritimes and the people make me feel I never left home. Bagpipes, kilts, and Florrie your eyes are so blue they remind me of sapphires."

"Don't talk like that, I'm married."

"Was that my doing? Was it my idea?"

"It wasn't my idea either."

When she got home that night the Count was waiting, his leather belt wrapped twice around his hand, and he hit her with the dangling tail, leaving welts on her back, her buttocks. She lay curled on the floor, protecting her breasts with her arms, wondering if Scotty had left yet, on his way first to Duncan, then to Victoria, then a week in Vancouver and then down to the States, he said, with the winter off in Florida.

Mid-week, the Count in the henhouse busy with his chickens, there was a rap on the door. Flora answered, and Scotty stood there smiling.

"You'll get me killed!" she blurted.

"Killed, is it?" His eyes narrowed. "If he hurts you it's him will die, the egg-sucking bastard."

"You have to leave, Scotty! You have to go!"

"Come with me, Flora."

She stared, not sure whether to believe the words coming from this gorgeous stranger.

"Come with me. I'll never hit you, my life on it. There are flamingoes in Florida, henny, with long legs and pink feathers. Come with me."

"But I don't even know you –"

"Och," he laughed softly, "and ye dinna know him, either. If you don't come, Flora, it's a damn shame what you'll do to us both."

He waited on the front steps while she ran into the house. She didn't have a suitcase, so she used a cardboard box, and into it she put a picture of her mother and brother taken on the front steps of her father's house, the hairbrush and comb set Niall gave her for her birthday, and the few clothes she owned. And she was gone.

Scotty put the box under his arm and grabbed her hand, and they ran together down the driveway to the dusty road, and along the road to the highway. Scotty stuck out his thumb and they had a ride, and when they were let off on the far side of town they thumbed another ride, and another, until they were in Victoria. That night Flora stood in the audience, amazed, as Scott McPhail, billed as the Strongest Man In The World, took what looked like an ordinary nail, bent it in his teeth until it formed a rough circle, then leaned over and dropped it in Flora's hand. Later, when she had the money, she took the nail to a jeweller and had it made into a ring which she wore on the third finger of her left hand.

My grandfather spat in the dust and glared at my grandmother as if it were all her fault, as if she had made some dreadful mistake or passed on some terrible genetic fault. And she just looked away, so calm-faced his words of blame died in his throat.

Sometimes, when they were all drinking and laughing and telling stories of d'ya-mind-the-time-when, someone would call up the memory of my grandmother and the errant rooster, and how The Old Fart had heaved a hammer. "Whack, alongside the head, and the damn thing just flopped, dead as dead can be," and my grandmother had acted as if a problem had been solved. "Butter wouldn't melt in her mouth she was so cool, and we never had a mean bugger of a cock again, she got them young and hand-fed them." "Oh, and mind the time she was expecting, and he went into a fury over watering the garden and she just stepped in front of him so he couldn't start pounding on us," and I would wonder what had happened to her. Where did all that spunk go? Why had she been willing to risk hurt to protect the ones who weren't even her own sons, but let Flora be married off to a man almost as old as her father? When I asked, they looked at me as if I'd committed a grievous social error, then continued their conversation as if I hadn't spoken at all. Once my mother said, "Ah, well, after a while you just get tired of the ongoing fuss," and once one of my uncles, Crazy Tamas, told me to mind my own business. "One of these days you might understand, although I hope to God you never do," he said.

When they came back again they had a little girl, with dark hair and serious blue eyes, a little girl who smiles and laughs, but never with her eyes, and who can sing all the songs her mother sings. They went away again, moving from place to place, both of them chasing rainbows, chasing them together, laughing and singing and dancing like gypsy people, "bad as a couple of bloody Cairds," the uncles laughed, "just a pair of diddycoys," and I wasn't very old before I knew that Flora was doing more than following her dream, she was chasing my uncles' dreams too.

"See this, Maggy?" Uncle Scotty laughed. "We end our shows like this," and he put his hand flat against the small of Aunt Flora's back. She leaned against his hand, bending her back until her head touched the floor. Then, with no apparent effort, Uncle Scotty lifted her up and held her over his head, balanced on his one hand. "Looks easy, huh?" he grinned. "Well, we dare any man in the audience to do it, but it'll cost 'em twenty bucks if she falls. And she always falls, eh, Flora?" And like that she fell from his hand. He hadn't wobbled, or shaken, or lost his balance, she just fell, and I knew she had done it and made it look like he couldn't hold her. "It's tricks, see," Uncle Scotty said, "and it's all to make 'em think Strongman McPhail can do things they'll never do in their lives."

"Strong, maybe," Uncle Cliff grumbles, but not when Uncle Scotty is near, "but the bugger's never held down a day's real work in his life. Wouldn't last half an hour with a coal pick in his hand."

"Wouldn't go down into the hole in the first place," my dad laughs. "He's no mug!"

Aunt Flora dances, not just in the circus. The circus is a holiday, a sham, a silliness she does just so she can be part of the act, which he does only so they can travel around, see the world and get fed and paid for doing it. "What you do, Mags, you find something you always wanted to do anyway, then get so good at it others pay you to keep on doing it. Like us, travelling, seeing Niagara Falls, the Miramichi River . . . Ah, now, the Miramichi, lass, there's a river that is a river and all of a river, at that."

She dances in the wintertime when the circus is shut down, she dances in fancy nightclubs, in theatres, and not just burlesque, she dances real dances, too, with costumes and an orchestra in fancy black suits and white shirts. "Well, and Adele Astaire has nothing on our Flora, let me tell you. If things were fair, it would be Flora on the silver screen, but it's just luck, and we weren't in the right place at the right time, is all."

They moved back home, finally. I don't remember where all they'd been or what all they'd done, they just moved into my life like bright rainbows. "Time to put down a root or two," Scotty said. "Can't go dragging kids all over the place or it'll get to be so ordinary they'll never get a thrill out of it later on, eh, Flora?"

"Neither you nor I got to travel when we were little and it's still all bright and new for us. But . . ." She looked over at her daughter and shrugged, as if more could be said with silence than with words.

My dark-haired cousin was named after Fred Astaire's sister, but you couldn't get Adele McPhail up on her feet to dance if you put dynamite under her ass. She knew the words and the tunes to more songs than most people could remember, but when she sang, something vital was missing, something more than laughter or smiles. Once she told me her real father was a Count, which was, she explained, almost a prince. "I didn't always live in old trailers and travel with a circus," she bragged, "I lived in a great big house, and we had a piano."

"Ah, g'wan, you never had no big house nor no piano, neither."

"I guess I'd know where I lived."

"I guess you wouldn't. Bein' as how you don't even know who your dad is. Are you sure you know your mother? Bet you don't! They prob'ly found you on the side of the road and felt so sorry for you they took you home and fed you, like a lost puppy."

Of course she pounded on me until I started to cry.

"Now, now," my mother soothed, washing my face and wiping my tears. "Just don't argue with her and she won't hammer on you."

"She said her dad was a Count and she lived in a big house and that's *lies.*"

"Sometimes when we don't like how things are, we pretend they're how we want them to be."

There never was a woman sang better than my mother. Auntie Flora was good, but even she said she couldn't hold a candle to my mother. Beth Sutherland had been expected to Go On In School. There wasn't a girl, or a boy, either, could beat her in spelling or mathematics. She had only to close her eyes, as if picturing the word or the question on the inside of her eyelids, then smile gently and give the correct answer. Once a month her school competed against all the other schools in the district and from first grade on through high school, Beth Sutherland invariably won her class and her grade. When she was in grade eight, her teacher challenged the other schools, all grades, to come up with a student who could beat Beth Sutherland. And Beth stood on the stage in the assembly hall of the high school and answered correctly for three hours. One by one the other students made mistakes and were withdrawn, until only my mother stood there, smiling happily.

And it all stopped when she met my dad, Niall MacDonald. Instead of going on to university, she went for a walk along the river. Instead of getting her teacher's training, she got pregnant. She quit choir and chorale and glee club, and instead of singing at concerts she wound up singing lullabies to a child with a voice like a crow. I would lie on the floor on my belly, my chin in my hands, elbows pressing into the linoleum, watching, and inside my head I was singing. But I was only mouthing the words, whispering the songs, because as soon as I started to sing, the others laughed. Sometimes my second cousin Johnny McManus would sing with the grown-ups, only thirteen, they said, and already a voice to stop traffic, and he could soar clear to the high notes with the women or down to the low notes with the men, no rules for Johnny McManus, he sings all over the scale, each note pure and true and Uncle Scotty McPhail would sing with him, smiling, as proud as if Johnny were his own son. They sang all the old songs, Scots and Irish and English, the music floating on the twilight, and even when I'd given up and gone to bed, even then I could hear the songs.

By the time I was ten I knew not to try to sing along, and by the time I was twelve I saw the cracks in the amber in which the dreams were trapped. I had grown too old to see gypsies and free spirits all the time. My eyes were no longer happy with things the way they seemed to be, I was always poking into the background, trying to find out how things really are, and why.

"Och, Flora, hen, will you find peace for yourself."

"I'll have peace when I'm dead and buried, Scotty!"

Sometimes, when all the other women were drinking tea, Aunt Flora was laughing a bit too loud, bursting with energy, smoking one cigarette after another, and when the men brought out the bottle Flora held out her cup and turned her tea into toddy. Sometimes, on their way to a dance on Saturday night, they would stop off at the house to pick up my father and mother, and already Aunt Flora smelled of gin. Sometimes it wasn't even Saturday and she'd say she felt a cold coming on, or her sinuses were bothering her. "Must be this damn eternal rain," she would mourn, "I never had sinus trouble in Arizona."

Fran figured if Liz wasn't careful she was going to have trouble on the home front, big trouble. Bert was starting to look like someone who had wakened up one day and discovered that the glow had gone. Four or five nights a week he had supper with his family, the kids started the dishes and Liz watched the news on TV, then started getting ready for work. She gave everyone a big kiss on the cheek and off she went to smile smile smile and pretend to be having the time of her life doing what she had done every night for years, pretending to be involved in the party when she was not part of it at all. When the place closed she put her fiddle in its case and drove home again to crawl into bed beside someone who had been asleep for hours and would soon be getting up to go to work. Talk about meet where they touch!

It was getting like that all over the map. Jerry came out of grade twelve with the old high school diploma and headed off to take marine diesel mechanics, then got a job in Victoria, which you would think was two miles to the west of Beirut for all the visiting home he did. The bus came up-island four times a day, seven days a week, but he might as well have had to transfer to dog team for all you saw of him.

When it came to some others, you wish they would hie themselves off to Victoria and vanish into the diesel fumes. Ritchie seemed to have fallen in love with the ghost of James Dean. Slouching around the house all sulky-faced and pouty-mouthed and mumbling. If you heard what he said, he acted as if you shouldn't have, and if you didn't, he acted as if you should have. Garnet had to go zooming off in another direction, of course. He was into the checked lumberjack shirt, black tee shirt, black jeans and those ugly, expensive clumpy boots that were nothing more than an open invitation to a fight, right now, down and dirty. His entire vocabulary seemed to have reduced itself to "yeah." Yeah. Yeah? Yeah! For a change he went Rambo: Yo. That and the CB influence – negatory instead of no thank you – and if you said anything about it he just glowered. Well, one thing was for sure. The less said, the less regretted. They were all working overtime to get a rise out of her and the less she rose, the better for all concerned.

Something happened when their hormones got out of balance. Not only did they start to smell like an old potato sack left too long in a musty corner, they got nasty, too. There ought to be an antidote for testosterone poisoning. Could they do what they did with venomous snakes, catch them, milk them and use the poison as serum against the actual bite? Pull the little darlings' fangs as fast as they got them, haul out their eye teeth, so that when the testosterone started pumping and they went for your throat you had some chance of fighting them off?

God, she was starting to think like Erma Bombeck. Well, Erma made a fortune doing the I'm-a-martyr-ha-ha routine. How many other women read Erma and wanted to vomit? Dear Erma, my family is inconsiderate. One after the other they go into the bathroom and stay there for three-quarters of an hour and I never get to take a bath or use the toilet. When I complain they ignore me. When I get angry they laugh. What should I do? Dear Constipated in Alberta: Take a bucket into the basement and shit in that. Don't worry about your family, the turds belong in the bathroom anyway, ha ha.

And the bringing home half the lost and lonely of the town. Excuse me, do I know you? I'm Garnet's friend. Oh, really? Yeah. Garnet, who is your friend? Uh, I think his name is Kevin. Well, *of course* his name is Kevin. That's the year all the little boys were called Kevin. Except for the ones called Shawn. The Justins and Jordans came two years later, and three years after that it was Matthew and Mark. But for now we have huge Kevins, massive Shawns, whiskers sprouting, chest hairs bursting up from the necks of their raggedy smelly tee shirts and every one of them living out of dumpsters and sleeping any place they can lie down undiscovered. The question is not how bad is it for them in the alleys and garbage cans, but what was it at home that was so dreadful the back alleys, streets and garbage cans are preferable?

"Why do you put up with it?" Liz asked.

"Put up with it? Jesus, Liz, don't you ever wonder? If they aren't sprawled in a sleeping bag on my living room floor, where are they and what do they have to do to stay alive?"

"One of these days you'll wake up raped and killed in your own bed."

"I blame my refrigerator. Something about it lures them in off the street. If there's a scrap in there, even an orange peel or a dried-up withered dill pickle, there's a homeless kid with his big bony knees poking out of what's left of his jeans, moving hopefully in the direction of the kitchen."

"You can put a stop to it if you want to."

"I know that. The Adult Children of Alcoholics group has explained all that very clearly. What they haven't explained is what I do with my feelings once I've locked the door. Because whatever I decide to do about it, those kids will still be out there cold, hungry and half the time sick."

"Why do you go to that group anyway? They can't be doing much for you if you're still going! I mean, really, sitting around in a circle telling old horror stories. You should put it all behind you instead of picking scabs."

"I'm trying to put it all behind me, Liz. That's why I go. You should come, too."

"Catch me dead there! Anyway, it *is* behind me."

"No, it's not. You've never dealt with any of it."

"Let sleeping dogs lie, I say."

"You might say it but you don't do it, darling. You're still trying to run away from Gowan."

"I am not!"

"Yes, you are. Look at your life. You're classic ACOA. Workaholic. Need to control. Afraid to trust. Always expecting things to be taken away from you . . . Believe me, I'm an expert. I've been there. I still *am* there!"

"Some people get religion one way, other people get it another way, but either way it's still the same thing."

"And some people decide to tilt at windmills and take on racism singlehandedly."

"Eat it, Fran."

"Eat it yourself, Liz."

Liz didn't take the computer printout with her because she hadn't finished reading the story, which was horrible. She went to Fran's place unannounced but knowing her visit was expected. Fran wasn't exactly sitting on the top step with a look of anticipation on her face, but she was quick to answer the doorbell. She didn't smile, she just nodded and held the door open.

They didn't say anything until the tea was poured, and Fran waited.

"You can't do this," Liz said firmly.

"Yes, I can. And I have."

"But it's not fair, Fran. It isn't even all true!"

"It isn't supposed to be true. It's a story. It will be published, advertised and sold as a novel. Fiction. Make-believe."

"Well, it is *not!*"

"Where does one end and the other start? Do writers write about things which have happened, or things which might possibly happen? And if a thing can be imagined, can it not be done?"

"What in the name of Christ are you talking about? *Who* is Tannis Stuart?"

"Why, she's nobody. She's everybody. She's an invented person. She's me. She's . . . who do you think she is?"

"Why are you pretending to write someone else's autobiography?"

"Maybe I'm not pretending."

"Then why change the name?"

"It's a story, Lizzie, that's all."

"It jumps all over everywhere."

"What doesn't? Could *you* sit down and write your life without jumping around from past to present? Hell, you can't even sit down and drink your way through a pot of tea without remembering something someone said or did sometime. Everything that was affects everything that is and everything that one day will be."

"That's just you trying to sound meaningful and profound and someone you aren't!"

"Boy, you really are mad, aren't you?"

"You're damn right I'm mad! You've got no right making wild guesses and putting it down as if it was gospel truth! You're just doing it to be shocking, to have some kind of angle, some kind of hook so they'll publish your damn lousy story and you can pretend to be somebody you aren't!"

/ / /

What it is, you see, is I don't know where reality stops and invention begins. For years, one way or the other, I have danced around the maypole with my ribbon, attempting to weave and failing because I never really looked at the pole itself.

I have tiptoed toward some glimpse of truth then darted away from it, afraid to look at the very thing which obsesses me. I've made jokes about my life being one aborted chapter after another, and in the joke lay the truth with which I was afraid to grapple.

And I do not know if I am Liz or Fran or Margaret Anne or Anne Elizabeth or someone else, or if I am all of them, or if I am none of them or even if I am.

Truth is stranger than fiction. Well, isn't that profound? For some of us fiction *is* truth. There is no line between the two; truth has become fiction, fiction has become truth and neither is real.

But it has to stop somewhere, with someone. Somehow. The gift that goes on giving, that's how they advertise diamonds. And dysfunction is the curse that goes on cursing, generation after generation of children fucked up, fucked over, fucked around and fucked until they no longer know the truth, until what is seems to be what isn't, and what isn't seems to be what is, so you do it again, perhaps in a different way, but what is done is done and too often done over again.

And I do not know if I am Liz or Fran or Margaret Anne or Anne Elizabeth or someone else, or if I am all of them, or if I am none of them or even if I am.

/ / /

But what Fran discovered when she looked at Adlerian theory wasn't far from whatever it is they call truth. You tell a story and in the telling, even if you run away from the truth, you see it and expose it, not only for yourself but for others.

"I guess nothing I say is going to make much difference."

"No."

"I guess they'll publish it whether I write a letter of protest or not."

"Yes."

"I guess you know the whole family is going to go into absolute fits."

"Yeah."

"Don't you care?"

"Hey, will it be the first time? Will it be something I haven't already lived through several times?"

"But *why*, Frannie? Can't you think of something nice to write about? I mean, if the world is so full of ugliness, why not do something to take people's minds off the ugliness, even just for a minute or two?"

"Is that why you go to bars, never drink a drop of alcohol, and play somebody-done-somebody-wrong songs? To take people's minds off ugliness? Or to take your own mind off the things you can't stand to have rattling around and demanding your attention as soon as you aren't busy?"

"What do you mean?"

"You know what I mean. You might not drink alcohol, Lizzie, but you've got all the behaviour patterns of a drunk. I know, because so do I."

"Oh, you think you know so much! You've always thought you know more than you do!"

"Hey, dipper, I've always known more than I dared admit to myself I knew, okay?"

"Momma is going to be so angry!" And then Liz was sobbing. "I can't stand it when she's angry! I feel as if every time she gets angry it's my fault."

"Oh, baby. Don't cry like that. Don't cry because you're afraid to make her angry, cry because you're afraid to let her know that you *are* angry. Angry at her. And for good reason, too."

"I don't know what you mean," Liz said, stifling her sobs.

Fran grinned, shook her head and reached for their teacups. She took them to the sink, poured the cold tea down the drain, rinsed the cups, refilled the kettle. The silence stretched, broken only by Liz's occasional sniffle. Fran stood quietly, waiting for the water to boil. When it did she rinsed the pot with boiling water and began to make the tea.

"One time," Liz admitted, "one time we were doing a dance in Victoria and I got in touch with Aunt Phoebe and told her I'd be down there, and I'd like to visit her. She's real old now, but she still manages to look like a million dollars. You know how some people's hair goes kind of yellowy when they get old? Well, hers is like dandelion fluff. I mean even platinum blondes can't get that colour! She wears it pulled back in this enormous bun on the nape of her neck. She weighs more now than she ever did before, and it suits her, that angular look is gone from her face, and she looks softer and actually younger than she did when she was forty-five or fifty. She showed up for the dance looking like someone out of a magazine, I couldn't believe it. Nobody ever looked so good to me. And she danced! Jesus, if she couldn't get someone to go up and dance with her she danced by herself, and just made sure she had one helluva good time. And afterward, instead of going to the hotel, I went out for Chinese food with her and then back to her place. Listen, she's got floodlights on the outside wall and she can light up her flower garden in the middle of the night! So we sat there in the dark with tea and she smoked one cigarette after the other until you had to wonder what her lungs looked like, and we talked. And she told me that not long ago my mom had been down to visit her. I was surprised. Mom never mentioned it to me, not one word. They had supper together and talked and had a drink and had another and wound up tying one on. And Aunt Phoebe said that my mom had said that sometimes she felt as if she had had a choice, and that choice was no choice at all. She either had to sacrifice one of her kids or sacrifice all of her kids so she sacrificed one to hold things together for all the others and now she wished she hadn't but she didn't know how to change it or make up for it."

"So she knew."

"I guess she did. I don't know. I'm afraid to find out, Fran. Phoebe said I should talk to her about it but . . . I don't want to. If I talk to her about it I might not like what I hear. What do I do if I lose her? I've spent my whole life hating him like fury, and making sure I did *not* hate her! So if I find out for sure, maybe I'll hate her, and then what do I do?"

"The nice people would say you have to stop hating because it's doing you as much harm as what was done to cause you to hate."

"Oh, fuck the nice people."

"I don't want to," Fran smiled. "I spent years looking for nice people and then fucking them and you want to know something? They aren't so nice!"

"Yeah, but you got nice kids out of it."

"Ah, they're all fucked up. Some drink, some don't, but they're all crazier'n'all get-out." Fran laughed softly. "We should try to get a new law passed, that says kids are like waffles and you're entitled to throw the first one away! Or the whole batch if it comes to that."

"Oh, you *stop* that!" But Liz was laughing, they were both laughing, both knowing everything each had said to the other was as true as anything either of them had ever said, thought or believed, and that things between them were better than they had ever been. "Listen, I'm not buying that damn book of yours when it comes out."

"Nah, I'll give you a free autographed copy."

"Just don't give one to Wilma, that's all. She'll shit."

"Do her good. If some of it comes out of her, maybe she won't be so full of it."

"You'll go to hell, you know that, eh?"

"Been there, done that, no surprises."

/ / /

Actually it wasn't a damn lousy story. If you could make yourself get Your Self out of it and just read the words on the page, it was a reasonably adequate job. Not *Gone With the Wind*, but better than many others which wind up on the shelves.

But it was distracting, upsetting and at times sick-making to find things in it which you remembered, in a different context but still remembered. Things which had seemed tacky or terrifying suddenly were set down in such a way they seemed important, things Liz thought she had put behind her were suddenly hammering on the inside of her head, demanding attention. Instead of being a crazy bastard, Gowan – under a totally different name – seemed bigger, uglier, more evil, and Liz wasn't sure how to deal with that. He wasn't evil. Evil is important, and Gowan wasn't important. He was nothing more than a spoiled selfish brat who had never had to take responsibility. He was just an overgrown four-year-old. Evil is something else, isn't it? Something almost inspired. If it isn't, then good can't be much, either!

She hated everything about the story, hated it so much she didn't even talk to anyone about it. There'd be enough talking to do when the damn thing hit the bookstores. Unless she was suddenly luckier than she'd ever been in her life and nobody bought it. Maybe the reviewers would ignore it. She knew she could walk into a bookstore and look at six thousand books and not have heard a whisper about any of them. Maybe Fran's book would be one of those, the ones the publishers must put out just to get the tax write-off.

Could you believe it? Fran, of all people. Sitting in that big grey house with her stupid damn computer, pretending she was learning how to do office work, being so overly casual about it all, even going so far as to say she was just in there playing games like the ones the kids played in video arcades, playing PacMan rather than Solitaire. And all the time it wasn't PacMan at all. What's more, she'd had other things published and said nothing about it. Used another name. Well, and if that wasn't Fran all over again! She'd been using other people's names all her life; each time she took up with some guy she suddenly became Fran whatever-his-last-name-was, as if they'd gotten married or something.

"Why?" Fran laughed, not a particularly nice little laugh. "Why? Because I knew this would be the reaction. Because as long as someone else is doing it, it's fine, but as soon as someone we know starts doing it, we all get paranoid. Because it was easier. Because I wanted to. Because I wasn't anywhere near ready to let all and sundry know."

"But you are now, is that it? You write three hundred pages of slander and all of a sudden it's okay to let everyone know you're writing about *us?*"

"Don't be silly. Nobody is going to put two and two together, they're all too busy protecting their own asses."

Then the book came out. And thank God it didn't hit the all-time bestseller list – it was hard enough to deal with when it was a temporary local storm.

"You should have done something to stop her!" Wilma raged.

"What would you suggest, Momma? I should have tied her up in the basement, then forged a letter saying she had changed her mind and didn't want the thing published? Who am I, Momma? Suddenly God retires and I get put in charge? Go yell at Fran!"

"It wouldn't do any good. And anyway she'd just go home, write down everything I said to her and use it in her next piece of trash! I won't give her the satisfaction."

"Then give me some, and get off my case! I didn't even see the thing until it had already been accepted. Why don't you, for a change, just hold me responsible for what I do and not for what everybody else in the world does."

"What are you talking about? Who do you think you're talking to?"

"I'm talking to you! And I'm telling you I'm sick and tired of it. I'm not the one wrote this book and I'm not the one going to wear it, okay?"

"Don't you dare talk to me like that!"

"You're mad at Gowan? Go take it out on Gowan, but I'm not the reason Gowan did whatever he did to make you mad! You're mad at Gavin for wasting his damn life, go stomp on his foot but stay off mine. And it's not my fault Billy was just good enough as a boxer to go up against professionals but not good enough to keep them from rattling his goddamn brains loose until all he's good for is standing in a ditch with a shovel! I'm not the reason Louise hasn't been seen in town for fifteen years! Gowan isn't the only one won't take responsibility for the way things are. You could take some, too. Because I'm *not* taking it. I was a kid, remember? I was a kid for about all of two years," she ended bitterly.

Then she got up and walked out of Wilma's kitchen without

even saying goodbye. Because one more minute – no, one more second – of spewing her anger and she'd lose control totally, and Liz didn't dare do that. She might wind up breaking her own mother's neck.

It was easier and safer to go home, scour the kitchen, scrub the floor, clean the bathroom, vacuum the bedrooms. No use banging your head on a brick wall. If you positively have to bang your head, choose something that won't give you lumps and a headache. And once the house looks as if it's going to be photographed for Small Town Beautiful, get busy cooking everyone's favourites for supper. Tell yourself Wilma will get over it. Tell yourself you'll get over it. Tell yourself it's all a tempest in a teapot, nothing very important at all. Talk, smile, listen, nod, look at whichever of your nearest and dearest is talking to you about whatever it is they're talking about, and no matter what is going on inside, keep it calm and level outside. One two three four, that's what control is for.

And a good thing you have your control firmly locked in place because no sooner had he finished eating the meat loaf and started in on the double chocolate cake, than Bert dropped his bombshell.

"I'm going on steady nights," he said, looking directly at Liz.

She felt her head cock to one side, as if she hadn't heard him.

"I'm going on steady nights," he repeated, and already he was dug in, stubborn, inflexible, defiant.

"Why?"

"Because if I go on steady nights I don't have to do this same goddamn boring rotten shit job I've been doing for twenty years." He was defending before there was an attack, and that told Liz she had plenty of reason to raise a stink.

"I didn't know you thought your job was rotten," she commented, deliberately casual. She passed a slice of cake to Marti, who smiled her thanks. Then she calmly cut a slice for Reba.

"Well I do! And it is! It's a stinking go-nowhere job and I've never liked anything about it! So I can move up if I go on straight nights and I'm going!"

"Why are you arguing?" She handed Ronnie his cake, then cut some for herself. "I'm not arguing."

"You will," he predicted. "And I'm letting you know right up front that I'm doing this."

"And who is going to be home with the kids?"

"What 'be home with the kids'?"

"If you're going on straight nights you'll start at eleven-thirty. So you'll have to leave here before eleven. I don't get home until nearly two."

"Are they two years old?" he glared. "They can't sleep without someone helping them? Other people pay these kids to look after *their* kids, for God's sake."

"Stop yelling, Bert, you're just trying to pick a fight so you'll feel better about what you've done."

"What have I done?"

"Made a decision without talking to us about it, even though it will affect everyone else's life. Not said a thing to us about it until it's done."

"What do you care?" he said bitterly. "You're never fuckin' home anyway!"

"Oh, why did I know that whatever it was, it would turn out to be my fault?" She laughed and shook her head, mocking him. "I've never even seen the inside of that pollution factory but all of a sudden everything about it is my fault. You want to work nights, work nights. You want to work weekends, work weekends."

"Might as well, for all I'd be missed."

"Oh, poor baby. Poor poor iddle-diddums." She took her cake into the living room and sat in the big chair to watch the news on the tube. She tried hard not to hear the silence in the kitchen, tried hard not to hear when the kids, one by one, pushed their chairs from the table and started doing the dishes. But every sound came to her as clearly as if she was straining her ears to listen.

After a while Bert came in and sat down to watch the news. She knew what he really wanted was round two but she'd go to hell in a barrel before she'd give him the opening.

"You want a cup of tea?" she asked, getting up from her chair.

"No thank you," he said stiffly.

She got her tea and went back to the living room. Bert was sitting in the big chair. She sat where he had been sitting before she left the room. He said nothing. Liz said nothing. The TV dominated the room, and they both sat watching yet another war in yet another far-off corner of the globe, with yet another fifteen civilians dead for every military casualty.

When the news ended and the sports came on Liz took her teacup to the kitchen, rinsed it and put it on the drainboard, then went to her bedroom, put on her terrycloth wrap and went to the bathroom. It was occupied. She leaned against the wall in the hallway and waited. Several minutes later she rapped on the door.

"What!" Reba snapped.

"Hey, don't take up residence in there, okay?"

"I'm fixing my hair!"

"Go fix it in your bedroom. I need the shower."

"Oh *great!*" Reba flung open the door. "Don't pay any attention to what I want, Mother, just move to the front of the line!"

"Hey, you!" And the anger boiled over. "Every night at this time I have to get ready for work. Double-yew oh ahr kay. Okay? And you know that. I don't hog the bathroom to make you late for school or soccer or whatever else! You want to fix your hair, go fix it in your bedroom! This is the only shower in the house."

"Sure, Mom, sure. Whatever *you* want."

That's when Liz saw her hand flash and connect with the side of Reba's face. Her own shock was as great as the shock she saw registered on her daughter. Deep inside her someone was sobbing and screaming, but all Liz said was, "And if you talk to me like that again, this will be nothing but a down payment on what you'll get." Then she grabbed Reba by the shoulder and spun her out of the doorway and into the hallway.

Fifteen minutes later she left the bathroom and went to her bedroom to dress for work. Bert was already there, sitting on the bed with a pillow behind him, watching as Liz chose her clothes for the night.

Finally he spoke. "What's the problem with you and Reba?"

"I slapped her face for being cheeky once too often."

"What did she do?" He was quiet, his dark eyes watching her every move.

So she told him. He nodded a few times, and sighed.

"What does that mean? That big sigh."

"Sometimes you're kind of hard on them."

"Hard on them? Bert, they're spoiled rotten!"

"Sure they are," he agreed, "but they didn't spoil themselves. We did it. Made them the assholes they are today, so we'll just have to live with it."

"Stuff that." She was in no mood to be charmed. "If we made it we can unmake it."

"Is it worth it? She's mad as a wet hen."

"Tell someone who gives a shit, Bert. Reba is mad at something or someone every minute of every day. Bitch bitch bitch, nag nag nag and as far as she's concerned it's her way or no way at all."

"Well, she comes by that honestly enough. You'll have your way or know the reason why. I, of course," he grinned again, "am the soul of co-operation, tact and uncomplaining diplomacy."

"Oh, go eat something sharp," she laughed.

"You left a mark on her face."

"Tough. I'll leave marks all over her if she doesn't shape up in one hell of a hurry."

"No," he said firmly, "you won't."

Liz turned slowly and stared at Bert. He stared back at her, as calm as any person could be. "What did you say?"

"I said you won't leave marks on her. We've never done that, and it's not going to start now."

"Then *you* sit her down and *you* explain to her that she'd better learn how to behave. You might not mind if a sixteen-year-old snippet talks to you as if she had *BOSS* written on her forehead, but I mind, and I mind a lot. *You* get the message to her, and if you can't, I will."

"You leave marks on her, I'll leave marks on you." There was no smile on Bert's face or in his voice.

"You ever lay a finger on me," Liz answered, her voice shaking with fury, "and you'll be sitting in jail so goddamn fast you'll think the archangel Gabriel put you there. I'll press charges on you, Bert. All the goddamn way to and through divorce court, I'll press charges."

"So it's okay for you to hit someone but not okay for you to be hit?"

"You eat her shit if you want. I won't! Nor yours, either."

"Then you keep your fuckin' hands to yourself, lady. Or I'll press charges against *you*."

"Fuckin' try, mister. They'll laugh you right out of court."

"Goddamn it, I won't have my kids knocked around the way I was knocked around! Not even by their supposedly ever-lovin' mother!"

"You really do want to have a fight tonight, don't you? And if you can't get one going at the table, you'll get one going in the living room, and if that doesn't work, you'll come in the bedroom and start one. Anywhere will do and any excuse will do, as long as Bert gets the chance to throw his weight around. Okay, Bert, throw it around. See who you can impress with it. Because it won't be me."

"No, it won't be you! You'll walk out the door and go to work just like you always do. Then you'll stand on the fringe of a party every drunk in town is having and you'll smile, smile, smile your empty smile. Smile smile smile while they party party party, but you're never part of it, are you, Liz? You're apart from everything at work, and you're above everything at home. You're so fuckin' detached from everything it's a wonder you even remember to shit once in a while!"

"The empty can makes the most noise, Bert." Liz pulled on her three-hundred-dollar cowboy boots and reached for her jacket. "Some people," she sighed, picking up her violin, "think all you need to have a conversation is a goddamn mouth."

When she got home he was asleep in bed, or at least lying there with his eyes closed. She didn't bother to find out which. She just tiptoed into the bedroom, got her robe, and tiptoed out again.

The bed in the spare room was all made up and waiting. Liz stripped off her clothes and crawled between the crisp sheets naked. She thought she'd have trouble getting to sleep, but it was as if her pillow was a hole. She put her head on it and fell into soft blackness.

Her inner clock wakened her at the usual time in the morning. She got up, pulled on her robe and padded barefoot up the steps to the kitchen. The coffee maker was burbling and burping. She poured and doctored two cups, kept one beside her and put the other on the table for him, then started breakfast. Bert first. A cholesterol-laden thumb-in-the-eye to all the health food fads. Bacon, crisp but not dark, eggs over easy, toast. Some mornings she switched to sausage and scrambled eggs, some mornings poached eggs with cheese sauce drizzled over them, but mostly she gave Bert what he wanted: bacon, eggs, toast and coffee.

He came into the kitchen quietly, sat in his place at the head of the table and sipped his coffee, and when she put his plate in front of him he nodded as politely as if she was a waitress he'd never seen before. Liz said nothing, she just refilled her coffee mug and began packing his lunch. Then she made lunches for the three kids. Just about the time their brown bags were packed, Bert had finished eating. She refilled his coffee cup and topped up her own. As she turned to put the pot back on the hot plate, Bert spoke.

"You sleep in your own bed tonight," he said evenly.

"I beg your pardon?" There had been other nights when one of them had slept in the spare room. Everyone needed some space. Better to sleep by yourself than lie stiff with unresolved anger beside someone who was just as stiff and just as angry.

"I said you sleep in your own bed tonight," he repeated. "Because if you don't sleep there tonight, don't bother sleeping there any other night of your life."

"Whatever you say. Master." Liz left her coffee mug where it stood and walked from the kitchen.

Whatever it was all about, it wasn't about her sleeping in the spare room or even about her slapping Reba's face. She'd been caught in enough power trips in her life to know they were like violent sea storms and the best way to deal with them was to get your boat out of the other person's choppy water. All she had planned to do was ignore the whole thing, just do what she had intended to do from the moment her eyes opened: make up the bed in the spare room and put the episode behind them.

But not now. Nobody was going to lay down dictum like it had been carved in stone and wait for Liz to obey. Fuck that shit! Don't bother sleeping in it any other night of your life, indeed! Harrumph, harrumph. Ave Caesar. Yes sir, yes sir, three bags full.

He left for work and she watched from the upstairs window as he drove away, then she walked to the bedroom doors, knocking loudly, waking the junior contingent before going downstairs to set out their cereal and start their toast.

The kids were subdued. Did they know she'd slept downstairs? And what business was it of theirs, anyway? They surely hadn't heard Bert's ultimatum. Left to their own devices, not one of them would willingly open an eye before suppertime. Maybe people really did give off auras and vibrations, maybe she was even now sparking bright reds and oranges with some psychic equivalent of smoke coming from her ears.

She made a new pot of coffee, poured a cup and sat at the table, not quite yawning. After a minute or two she got up, went to the spare room, fished in her jacket pocket for her cigarettes, lit one and went back to her coffee with it.

Her kids stared.

"Mom," Marti said. "What are you doing?"

"What does it look like I'm doing?"

"But Mom . . . you don't smoke."

"Shows what you know, doesn't it."

"When did you start?"

"Oh, I don't know. Years and years ago, I guess."

"How come we never saw you do it before?"

"Because I don't do it around here. Anyway I'm not really a smoker. It's just that sometimes I really enjoy having one."

"You look like a different person." Marti stared. "I don't think I like it."

"Then don't you do it," Liz answered.

"Does Dad know?" Reba asked.

"I don't know. Probably. Why? What is the big deal?"

"And he lets you?"

"What's this 'lets'? I know I look young, innocent, beautiful and all that, but I *am* over the age of consent! That's nineteen, by the way, and not one of you is over it yet."

"Oh, give me a year or two," Marti grinned, "and I'll be consenting to the most unbelievable stuff!"

"The kids at school say things about Auntie Fran's book," Reba blurted.

Liz looked at her. "They probably haven't even read the book," she said easily. "So anything they say is probably something they think they heard someone else say, and didn't understand."

"Is it a good book?"

"It's about average. I've read better, but I've read worse."

"The kids say she only wrote it to hog the attention for a while."

"What attention? Is this the literary capital of the country?" They all laughed. "Hell, to get any attention in this town you'd have to walk into the bar at night with a chain saw and cut everyone's legs off above the knee. But writing a book?"

"They say it's a dirty book. You know, pornography."

"Maybe pornography is in the mind of the beholder. I didn't think it was anything special. Mind you, it doesn't make this town look like a place jammed with nice people! They're probably just ticked off they didn't find their own name, or their own life, or something."

"They say she's writing about us." Reba's eyes filled with tears. "And if it's a trash book, then she's saying we are trash."

"She's not saying any such thing," Liz lied. "What she's saying is that usually people don't know other people anywhere near as well as they think they do. That under every roof is a secret. That's all she's saying. And if anyone says anything to you about it just ask them how long it took them to read the entire book. I'll bet they haven't even bought a copy of it!"

"Naw," Ronnie agreed, "they're waiting for the comic book version to come out so they can look at all the little pictures!" They all laughed again, and Ronnie reached for another piece of toast. "It's like what they say about Uncle Billy getting his brains bashed out. I just say yeah, and he made a lot of money while he was getting stupid, but you, you dumb shit, you were born an idiot for free."

"Ronnie!" Liz was dutifully disapproving. Ronnie laughed, hearing the admiration and not-quite-shock in her voice.

"Don't they try to clean your clock?" Reba asked.

"Naw," Ronnie shrugged. "They know Uncle Billy taught me how to fight. He says I'm even better'n he was when he was my age. He says I could go professional if I wanted to."

"Are you going to?" Liz felt as if she would vomit.

"Hey, a bit of credit from the folks at home, eh? There's enough people in the world willing to bash out someone's brains, I don't have to be one of them. Besides, I'm too pretty to risk a bop in the beak. I'm a lover, not a fighter."

"Wear a raincoat," they all chimed, "you never know when there's going to be a squall."

"Yeah, yeah, yeah." He finished his toast and managed to grin while chewing with his mouth shut. Liz figured it took a high level of physical co-ordination to pull that one off.

She straightened the house and did the laundry. Then, still trembling with adrenalin and dread, she drove to the supermarket and shopped as if she had the inside tip there was going to be a worldwide depression. She wrote a cheque, knowing it wouldn't bounce, and took the first cartload out to the car to off-load it. Then she did a second cartload, and a third. She drove it all home and made more trips than she thought possible to unload all the bags. She put the groceries away and folded up the bags. And all the time what she was really doing had little to do with the motions of her hands and body.

Whatever was happening was too similar to other things that had already happened, if not to her, then not far away. How many times had she heard the sound of Gowan's voice, cold and demanding, cutting through Wilma's soft, already defeated voice. And how many times had she lain rigid while the creaking of bed springs came through the wall separating the bedrooms? When Gowan said lie down, Wilma lay down. When Gowan said spread, Wilma spread. And if what Bert was demanding wasn't exactly the same thing, it sprang from the same place, a place Liz flatly refused to occupy. Even when she had been small, and powerless, and it had been Gowan pushing her around, she hadn't accepted it. She had fought back or she had disappeared. Somehow she had not accepted it, not accepted anything, partic-ularly not his right to get rough.

Nobody had the right to tell her where to lay down her bones! And nobody had the right to bounce on her bones, either! Not even Bert could speak to her like that, as if she had no mind, no brain, no ideas, no thoughts, no will, no rights at all.

Liz did more than toss a salad, she flung it together. And she did more than mix the dressing, she beat the bloody devil out of it. Then she arrived at the decision she had already made hours earlier. She went to what had been her and Bert's bedroom and took her things out of the closet, moved them down to the spare room and put them in the guest closet, pissing on all the posts, making the room hers and hers alone, leaving what had been their room to be his and his alone.

She knew she was angry. She knew why she was angry. She did not know she was focussing her anger on the only place in the world it would be safe.

/ / /

The file was already on her desk when Anna arrived at work. She stared at it, took off her jacket, hung it on the hook by the door, then moved to her desk and sat down, willing herself to be calm. Whatever it was, it wasn't good. Whatever it was, it had got the supervisor to work a half hour early, going through files, checking to see which worker had handled which case.

Anna reached out, opened the file folder and stared at the top page. Peter Baxter. Oh God, what now.

Anna remembered the first time she had seen him.

Four years old, his hair hanging shaggy and uncombed past his shoulders, his face thin and smudged with several days' dirt and tears, his clothes smelly and unwashed, too small for him, his overalls held up with pins where the snaps were gone. He was barefoot and when they stripped him down to give him a bath they found a filthy diaper ripped from what had once been a crib sheet. His scrawny buttocks were covered with diaper rash, deep-pitted pustules amid hot red chafed skin, and his penis swollen with ammonia burns, the head of the penis raw, the shaft pimpled and oozing. When they sat him in a bathtub he wept with pain. His feet had been thick with callus, his legs flaky with dry skin she thought was eczema. The doctor said no, it was poor diet, dirt, and probably dehydration. They soaked him in the tub, then washed him with strong green soap even though he wept, scrubbed the pustules even though they bled, and washed his hair to get rid of the lice. When the rinse water cascaded over his face, he quit sobbing and looked amazed, even tried to grin.

By the time Peter was six he had been in nine foster homes. He regularly wet the bed at night and he had sudden unexplained temper tantrums. His mother had not visited him once in the years since his apprehension. She was currently serving a three-year sentence for prostitution and trafficking in narcotics. Peter's father had abandoned the family when Peter was two and a half years old. The government had made many efforts to reach Ken Baxter after Peter was taken into care, and had finally found him in jail, doing three years for narcotics and living off the avails of prostitution. He expressed no interest at all in his son.

And now Peter's file was waiting on Anna's desk. The last time Peter's file had been waiting on her desk, Peter had escaped from the juvenile holding facility where he had been placed after starting a series of fires, one of which had destroyed an elementary school. No. Not true. The last time Peter's file had been waiting on her desk, Peter had been found by the police and returned to the facility. They all wound up in court because Mr. Seward, whom Peter called "Grandpa," and Mr. Thomas, who answered to "Uncle," had made application for custody of the boy, who they said had become a welcome and loving member of their family.

But men so old they can no longer remember their age, men who cannot speak and have no gainful employment, who live in a small unpainted dwelling which could only be called a shack, without electricity, running water or even a separate bedroom for the boy, do not qualify as foster parents.

"Are you suggesting the boy should be placed with Mr. Seward and Mr. Thomas?" the judge had asked her.

"We've been totally unable to find an answer for Peter's problems," Anna had replied honestly, "and I feel that possibly Peter has found an answer for himself. If it was up to me I would have no hesitation in placing him with his grandpa and his uncle."

The judge stared down at everyone for a while, and he checked some notes he had made. "No society," he said slowly, "can call itself civilized unless in its dealings with people it has both mercy and compassion. As a society we must at all times work toward a better life for those most helpless of our citizens. As has already been pointed out in testimony, we were unable to find any answer for Peter, and so he was forced to take matters into his own hands. I recommend that both Mr. Seward and Mr. Thomas be given the same rights and considerations as would be granted to natural parents in such a case. I further recommend that they be given full assistance in regard to transportation and accommodation so they may be included as fully as possible in all future treatment for Peter. They will be given every opportunity to visit Peter at the facility and it is to be hoped that treatment will be so structured as to include such things as overnight and weekend visits . . ."

Peter had started screaming. Anna envied him the freedom to scream, the energy to scream protest at what was so obviously nothing but hot air. The same rights and considerations as would be granted to natural parents – no rights, and no considerations.

A child comes to the attention of the court and only the court has rights, even if the child has committed no crime. Just coming to the attention of the court is enough.

Anna's supervisor came into the office, gently pushed the door shut with her foot, placed two mugs of coffee on Anna's desk and sat down.

"What's Peter done now?" Anna said, suddenly past tired and all the way to exhausted.

"You'd better get ready," the supervisor said gently. "I've got a heavy one to drop on you."

"I'm not ready," Anna blurted. The supervisor brought out her cigarettes and held out the package to Anna. They smoked together and sipped their coffee, and finally Anna nodded. "Okay," she said. "Drop it."

/ / /

Fran's book was published and they all survived, some more noisily than others. Wilma pitched fits the way some people pitch horseshoes – wildly, energetically, aimed only somewhere in the vicinity of a ringer. She raised hell with Liz, she raised hell with Bill, she raised hell with Gowan and with Gavin. She even phoned Louise and raised hell with her. She did not raise hell with Fran. Most of the time Wilma behaved as if Fran had never been born, and when forced to confront her niece's existence, she behaved as if Fran had only ten minutes earlier come into her life, and as if she was suffering from an identity delusion.

Phoebe amazed everyone by ordering a huge flowering azalea from the most expensive florist in town and having it delivered to Fran's door. The card read simply, "You're doing okay, kiddo. Love you, Auntie."

"Well! And wouldn't it be Phoebe would do a thing like that!" Wilma raged. "As if she didn't have just as many skeletons in the closet as anyone else!"

"Give it a rest, Momma," Liz said wearily. "Either that or go over and have it out with Fran. This other thing is going to drive me to a rubber room."

"Did you know about this ahead of time?"

"Not in time to put a stop to it."

"And you didn't say anything?"

"What was I to say, Momma? Why am I the one catching shit for this? Have I written a book? Have I told stories to the world? What have I done that is so bad you have to get on my case like this? *What awful, ugly thing have I done?*"

The go-through they had already gone through had to be gone through again, even harder and louder.

"I've always known that no matter what I did it wouldn't be good enough for you. If I learned how to stand on my head in the corner and spit silver dollars you'd ask why I hadn't learned how to spit them faster. All my life it's been like that. I bring home a B, you want to know why it wasn't an A. I'm not the one who did anything wrong, Momma! All I did was try to do what you seemed to want. And you didn't give two hoots in hell! I could win an international award for country and western fiddling, you'd want to know why it took me so long! I could win the big lottery, you'd want to know why I hadn't won the bigger one!" She took a breath and plunged on. "All I ever did was babysit your kids, wash your floors, help with your housework, get a job, give you my paycheque, go to school . . . I never borrowed money from you, I never phoned in the middle of the night from the police station, I never once shit in the middle of your life or your face. So what is it I did that was so goddamn unforgivable that *every single thing that picks your ass turns out to be my fault?*"

Liz had never shouted so loudly at anyone in her life. She amazed herself. She shocked herself. And when it was over she sat down and gave herself long, hard lectures. She almost managed to kick her own arse, but she had to admit that while she was doing it, there had been a thrill. She had slammed the door and hoped that it would spring the hinges and the whole riggin's need replaced.

The worst part of it was there was nobody she could talk to about it. Fran would just shrug and ask, "Why do you even care, Lizzie old girl? Why do you go on hoping and hoping and hoping when you've got absolutely no reason to hope?"

And she couldn't talk to Bert about anything any more. Bert, who read Fran's book and then burst out laughing.

"It's not funny," Liz said quietly.

"Oh but it is, my darling," he answered, still smiling, but not happily. "I grew up without knowing anything at all about my family. For all I knew I never had one. I could be the kid in the joke, the one whose father was a tramp who jacked off on a hot train rail and then it hatched in the sun. My mother could be nobody at all or every hooker in the country, I don't know. And I grew up in nobody's family, I grew up dreaming every day-dream anyone ever has, that I was really the son of Edward and Wallis and had been put out for adoption so I'd grow up under-standing The People and become the first Real Democratic Ruler. I dreamed that some rich people would drive up in a Caddy and say *That one,* and take me off to someplace with horses and room to ride them, or that I was the direct descendant of Louis Riel and had to be placed for adoption so they wouldn't recog-nize me. That somehow it was all a big mistake, I was never dis-carded with the garbage. And then there you were and you had so many goddamn relations they were coming out of the crack of your ass! Cousins, second cousins, second cousin once removed, third cousin, aunts – Christ you had more aunts than a picnic! And I thought wow, a family!" He picked up the book and looked at the cover, then shook his head and grinned again. "Holy lord liftin' baldy," he sighed. "If this is family, my parents deserve a pat on the back."

They were polite. Oh God, they were polite. They were so polite each please and thank you was like a stab in the heart.

"Would you like poached egg on toast for breakfast?"

"That would be very nice, thank you."

They'd always had red-hot rows, then kissed, made up and gone on happily until the next row. This time there was no row, no kiss, no make-up, no going on happily. Hard head hit hard head and the horns locked. Do-it-my-way-or-else met Don't-boss-me-around, and they stayed in their separate rooms and nobody mentioned it, not even the kids. Especially not the kids.

A hundred times or more Liz came within the doing it of mov-ing her stuff back into the big bedroom. Each time she hesitated because each time she had a mental movie of Bert coming home, finding her things in the room, and very quietly packing up his own things and moving down to the guest room. She would die if he did that. So she didn't move anything back into their room, especially not herself.

She had her story ready, though, in case anyone should ask. She would just smile that smile like the one Wilma had smiled for years, like the one Fran had smiled for years, and she would say Oh, Bert's working straight nights now, you know how it is with shift work, one disturbance and you don't get your sleep . . . Everyone would know it was bullshit, but so what? Who wrote the rule? Who put flaming letters across the sky saying people had to share a bed with other people? *Who said so?*

"I thought I'd take the kids camping for the weekend, leave right after school on Friday and come back in time for bed on Sunday. Would you have any objections?"

"I think they'd enjoy that. Would you like me to cook up some stew or something, put it in the Tupperware and freeze it? All you'd have to do is put it on to warm while you're putting up the tent and stuff and you'd have a good hot supper in no time."

"Would you? That would be nice. Be great, in fact. Thanks."

So she made stew, and two quarts of her killer spaghetti sauce. She made sure they had garlic bread to warm beside the campfire, she set out the sleeping bags and prepared boxes of groceries. She did everything except go camping with them – everything except *want* to go camping with them. How could she, anyway? She played on Friday and Saturday nights.

The book sold enough copies to pay its way, enough the publisher said she wanted another book, even if it wasn't *War and Peace*, even if nobody was banging down Fran's door for the movie rights. And then the second book came out and actually got some reviews. They were lukewarm, and probably did nothing to either help or hinder sales, but at least the work got noticed.

Liz was almost afraid to read the copy Fran gave her. She waited until she knew she'd be alone for a few days before she sat down and opened the paperback. She was amazed how much she enjoyed it.

"I like it," she said, feeling very shy.

Fran's face lit up, and she gave that little giggle that always made Liz feel as if they were both in grade school again.

"Really? Thank you. I'm glad!"

"Yeah. I like it."

Liz didn't ask Wilma if she'd even seen the book, let alone read the first page. And Wilma made no mention of it.

So much was still unsaid. So many things nobody mentioned to anyone else. Liz almost neglected to mention to her husband

and children that she had been asked to play fiddle with a group which would be seen on TV, in one half-hour show per week.

"Really?" Marti grinned, impressed.

"You're kiddin'!" Ronnie blurted. "I didn't know you were *good*. I mean, I thought you – I mean – I guess I didn't know what you did," he finished, blushing.

"I'm not the best," Liz said calmly, "but there's lots who are worse. It's going to mean I have to go over to the city for a couple of days every week. We have to rehearse, then they have to film it and make it look as if we all just sort of drifted by, dead casual, and Oh by the way do you have your instrument with you. Maybe three days a week. So I'm not sure if I'm going to say yes, or not."

"Why not?" Reba demanded. "You think we can't survive without you? Hey, you are not indispensable around here, okay."

"We'll get by," Bert agreed. "Sounds like a good thing to me."

"Yeah." Marti turned away, but her tone was pleasant. "We'll get to see you on TV."

"You mean even if you don't get to see me?"

"Touchy touchy," Marti answered easily. "I didn't say that, you did. All I said was, and I quote, We'll get to see you on TV, endquote. The wicked flee when no one pursueth."

"And now we've got the church alive and well in the kitchen," Bert marvelled. "Next thing you know we'll all be taking vows. Chastity, poverty, obedience –"

"Scrap the obedience part," Liz demanded. "I've had it with obedience."

"Toss out poverty, no poverty for me!" Ronnie agreed.

"And *fuck chastity*," they all shouted, laughing.

"If your grandmother hears you talking like that she'll have a conniption."

"Who cares? She's always griping anyway. Let her have a conniption, maybe it'll improve her cardiovascular," Reba grumbled.

"Honest to God, I don't know what's wrong with most of the people in this family. If they aren't down in the dumps about one thing, they're down in the dumps about another. You'd think this was rehearsal instead of the only damn chance you get."

"She's had a hard time of things," Liz sidestepped.

"After a while a person begins to wonder if maybe people like that don't somehow enjoy a hard time," Reba said evenly. Liz stared. "I mean, maybe there was a time she had to eat shit, okay, I'll buy that. Even if nobody comes out and says it, everyone seems to agree Grandma had to eat a lot of shit. So fine. That was then. This is now. So why is she still sitting at the table loading up her own plate with it unless she enjoys the taste? And why does she keep on trying to feed it to the rest of us?"

"Ah, honey, if only it was that easy."

"I know, I know, things are different now, I shouldn't make judgments until I've had to make some of those tough choices myself, and all that other stuff. I know I'm spoiled, I know things are easier for me than they were for other people. I know all that, and I don't care. I am sick and tired of the fault finding and the whining and the nagging and the complaining, and somehow no matter what it is either we are to blame for it, or we are to blame for not keeping her safe from it. She could move on if she wanted." Reba pointed at her father. "Is *he* storming around ninety miles an hour making the rest of us pay because he didn't have a birthday party until he was sixteen? Does *he* ruin every birthday party anyone else has by reminding us all that he didn't have one?" Now Reba was pointing at Liz. "For that matter what about you? Life couldn't have been lots of fun with them for parents. I'm so sick of being careful not to cause Grandma to have a conniption! Maybe it's up to *her* to make sure she doesn't take one!"

Liz went to cuddle Reba, but didn't get the chance. Marti and Ronnie got there first. And they seemed to know what to do and what to say to take the pain away. Liz had never known how to do that. She stood watching the three of them, feeling more left out than she ever had in her life, feeling a mixture of regret and relief so strong and so confusing she could only shake her head and wonder why she couldn't cry, too.

Liz turned down the TV offer. Not only were they going to be shooting in the studio in Vancouver, but some producer had come up with the great idea that they travel around to small towns with hilarious names and do shows from Pouce Coupe and Likely and Horsefly and Clo-oose, and give the residents free soft drinks as an incentive to come down, watch the show and add some local colour. Great idea, except it meant they'd be gone for longer than Liz was prepared to be gone.

"Ah, poop!" Ron wrinkled his face. "And I thought we'd get to see you on TV."

"I could go downtown and get arrested, would that do?"

"Oh *sure!*" Reba shouted, whirling, and for a moment Liz thought her daughter really was steaming with fury. "And isn't that just like you! Go get arrested in town! You never get arrested right here at home where we can watch! Go get arrested where everyone else will have a chance to see and we'll still be the last to know!"

"Jesus Christ, you scared me," Liz gasped. "I thought you were serious."

"One day maybe I will be, but not yet."

And Liz continued to sleep in her room, and Bert in what had undeniably become his room.

"Too bad about that," he said one morning, having breakfast in the quiet of a house with the kids already off to school. He'd been working all night and looked tired, but not yet sleepy. His face was dark with whisker shadow, and his work clothes were faded where he pulled his coverall over them.

"About what?" Liz was having coffee and mentally planning her day.

"The TV thing. Might have worked into something for you."

"Probably not much, except a lot of stress."

"I know you brush it off and say things like that. Oh-pooh no-big-deal sort of stuff, but, well . . . seems like you've worked so hard at it and I guess I don't understand why you turned it down."

She looked at Bert and for one horrible moment she didn't know who he was. Some kind stranger who expressed interest, maybe even concern, but why would he? Then he was Bert again and they had a huge bulk of shared history between them.

"I told you. If they'd stayed with the plan of shooting in the studio in Vancouver I'd have done it. But to go to every one-dog town up and down the coast? Uh uh, not me, thanks. I've *been* to every one-dog town, and believe me, the dog is no screaming hell. You could see better ones in any pound in town."

"What I don't understand is just exactly that." He was pushing it, and she began to feel as if Wilma was nagging her again. "I thought you liked to meet people. I thought you liked travelling and –"

"Bert, give your head a shake, please. There are only two ways to travel up and down this coast. Either you fly in itty-bitty

airplanes belonging to fly-by-night companies with names like
Scare BC and Panic Western, with pilots who are seventeen and
fresh out of school or seventy and never been to school, or you
drive. If you go Scare BC you've got more chance of winding up
in the chuck than where they said you were going. If you drive . . .
have you ever driven to Tahsis? Let me give you a hint. The road
might be there, but probably not, or not for long. Besides, I kind
of like my kids, eh? I mean, I live here, too, okay?"

"We can get along on our own."

"Yeah? That's nice. Independence is a great thing." She was
working overtime to keep her voice light, but then she took a
deep breath and decided fuck it, you might as well jump in as
stand shivering on the diving board. "I'm trying to tell you something, Bert. You and I might not exactly be living as the
Honeymooners, and I might not be Beaver's mom, and this might
not be Nuclear Family Harmonious, but I'm not the least bit interested in trading it in for a suitcase and a chance to get carsick
with a bunch of people I don't know."

"Easy, easy, Liz, I'm only asking!"

"And I'm only telling, Bert. I said no because I wanted to say
no. I like my kids better than I like your average drummer, and
I'd rather have coffee with you of a morning than wake up in the
Tacky Town Motel, have a shower, get dressed and go down to
the coffee shop where some bubblegum-chewing grade ten
dropout is reigning over the frozen waffles and edible-oil-product
whipped cream. And the pay? Squirrel shit." Bert was laughing
and for a few moments they were almost in that place where they
had been for so many years, when things were easier between
them, when they were less deliberately polite and much more
honest. "People think that life is one huge party for the gang in
the band," she continued. "We're separated from the peasants,
right, up on stage, and while everyone is warming up, we're
working. While the first jokes are told, we're sweating like hell to
set the mood and get the quote-unquote ambience happening.
Other people are loosening up, we're starting to get tired.
Everybody's been sipping suds and we're dyin' of thirst. Then we
take a break, go back to the cubbyhole, change shirts, sponge
down, put on some more of that armpit juice that fights oh-
m'god-body-odour. Suck some ice, but even if you're dead of
thirst don't drink because you have to go back out and stay there

without a bladder break until the next time they loosen your chain. And out we go and everyone has been drinking at top speed because who wants to dance to canned music? And another set is underway and we are not part of the party, we're the trained bears, we're the dog and pony. And then, once the whole shiterooni is finished the choices become enormous. Either you agree to go to a house party where everyone else's old man is going to try to tap on you, or you go back to your motel room or the phone booth or wherever in hell they've reserved cockroach space for you, and you lock your door and put the chain in place and look up the number for the police because as sure as shit some drunk is going to knock on your door."

Bert had stopped laughing. "Are you kidding?"

"No," she said wearily. "It's no fun, Bert. We're isolated, separated, on the fringes, and I am much much fonder of my life as it is than I am of any of that other cow cack."

"Then why do you do it?"

"It's what I've always done. It was better than anything else I could do when I started, and –" she spread her hands, feeling helpless to communicate with anybody in the whole world. "Why do you work at the pulp mill? You hate your job. You hate what the papers are saying about the pollution and crap and corruption and acid rain and ya-da-da-da. You know all the stuff about how there was no link between dioxins and cancer in workers, and how they didn't bother saying that was only for the first year, then the parts per buhzillion skyrocketed and twelve or twenty years later it's drop-like-flies. I bet you're scared shitless. I am! But you go to work every night. You put on your grubbies and you take the lunch kit and thermos and off you go, hi ho hi ho, and no Snow White with the apple, just you and your coveralls and steel-toed boots," and she was sobbing, and her hands were shaking, "and you just head off in the old car, stop at the stop signs because we have to pay attention to fucking safety, Bert, and you wonder why I don't want to go on tour to Gumboot and Mosquito Point and Blackfly and Ulcer Gulch?"

"Easy on, old girl," he said firmly.

Liz sniffed and wiped her eyes with the backs of her hands, then with the palms.

"What it is," he winked, "is I watched too many movies when

I was a kid. Courage . . . bravery . . . guts . . . and it takes real grit to thumb your nose at cancer, right?"

"Oh, you fuckin' fool."

He rose from his chair, took his plate and mug to the sink, then stared for a minute out the window while Liz sat sniffling and wiping at her eyes. Bert kissed the back of her neck before he went to the bathroom to have his long soak in a steaming hot tub. Liz could have walked into the bathroom and offered to wash his back, and everything would have been easy, unembarrassed, back to the way it had always been possible for it to be. But by the time she figured that one out, the chance was gone. And she wondered why it's so much easier to do the mating dance in public, to tap on a stranger, than it is to just be vulnerable with the other half.

Fran locked the front door behind her and headed down the wide front steps to the cracked walkway leading to her gate. The air was chilly and she was glad she was wearing Ritchie's old team jacket made of melton cloth and leather. The neighbours probably thought she looked nuts in it, especially since Ritchie's number had been 10, and Fran wasn't a 10 and never had been, but she liked the jacket. It was warm and it fit, and it didn't bunch up in your armpits or pull across your shoulders or flatten your tits or make them stand out like you were a figurehead on a four-masted schooner.

The neighbours didn't like her high-top sneakers, either. And probably had a lot to say behind their fibreglass drapes about her jeans and sweatshirts, too. But what was it Andrea had said? "Oh hell, Mom, right up their old gee-gees, too." Yeah. Up the old gee-gee.

The Irish setter at the corner wanted to come with her. She shooed it back three times and each time it went back obediently, climbed its front steps and sat on the porch. Until Fran turned to walk down the hill, then the dog zipped back down and raced to catch up to her. You'd think if people are going to go out and spend six hundred dollars on a two-month-old puppy, then pour on the fifty-dollar-a-bag dog food and the seventy-dollar immunization shots and the hundred-and-fifty-dollar surgical sterilization, not to mention the monthly twenty-five-dollar shampoo, clip, trim, brush and getting its little toenails filed, or the thirteen-dollar-sixty-three-cent collar plus all the little incidentals, they'd find some way of keeping the bugger out from under the wheels of cars and transport trucks, safe from discarded chicken bones and rat poison, while they were out at work. You'd think so. But no, the dog roamed around as if it belonged to nobody at all or to everybody on the street. And it loved to follow Fran.

"Okay, Scarlett O'Hairy," she said, "here we are again, trip trap trip trap just like the Billy Goats Gruff, down the hill together, all the same as if we belonged to each other." The dog, whose owners did not call it Scarlett O'Hairy, heeled obediently, which meant they'd also poured money into obedience school. Then they headed off to work at eight in the morning and left the dog to its own devices until six at night, at which time they put expensive food on the porch for it.

Well, it didn't matter. Fran wasn't going to town anyway, she was just going for a walk. Although God knows there was hardly any place left to walk! What is it about memory, anyway? Why could she overlook the plywood mill and the mess around it and still see the foreshore as it had been all those years ago when the water lapped at the rocks and sand, berries ripened on bushes in the sun and blue herons stood on one leg looking like feather dusters dropped by accident? Why did she think of the lakes as they had been and never think of them as they now were, with enormous parking lots carved out where there had once been Douglas fir, and crowds of sunburned pot-bellies where once there had been mallards and wood ducks? What was it made her see the entire place as it had been, and refuse absolutely to see what it had become?

She turned and headed west, back toward the old neighbourhood, knowing there was no good reason to go there. Nobody she knew lived there any more. Nobody she knew seemed to live within a hundred miles of the place. All those people she'd known in school, scores and scads of people, and if you went from house to house, up and down the streets and avenues and roads, you might find fifteen of them and they'd be people you wouldn't want to spend time with. Who were all these other people? Who were these come-lately types who moved in and six months later were getting other come-latelys to vote them onto city council so they could turn parks into car washes?

Someone in a passing car tooted the horn and Fran waved, putting a smile on her face even though she had no idea who was honking. How can you tell with the sun reflecting off the windows? Oh well, costs nothing, wave and smile wave and smile and think of the poor Queen who has to wave and smile eight hours a day. I wonder if she can wash her hair, just comb it into something that doesn't look as if it belongs on a pomeranian, haul on a sweatsuit and go for a walk and not have people screaming and shoving flowers up her nose?

Liz and Bert's house looked funny now that the new people had changed so much of it. Funny, that. Not funny that the new people had changed so much – everybody did that, you buy a place, move in and start in on a very expensive process of post pissing. Funny that Liz and Bert had split, and done it so amicably.

How could that be? *Amicably.* You might read that in a yuppy glossy but how can you after all those years just shake hands and smile and say Listen, if you're ever out my way drop in for coffee? How could two people pull that off and actually mean it?

And isn't it weird, Bert, who grew up somewhere else and only came here because his job brought him, chooses to stay, and Liz, who was raised here, born here, conceived here for crying out loud, stuffs her gear in some black plastic garbage bags and moves so far away it would take half a day to drive there and visit! You'd think she'd be the one to stay.

Although I have to tell you, if Wilma was my mother I'd be more than a few hours away. "Scarlett O'Hairy, you might be lucky. Puppies are born and then either they wander off on their own after a while or they get run over by garbage trucks or motorcycles. They don't wind up having to lick momma-dog's ass for her."

Oh yeah, said the dog, and what about your own self? Why in hell did you move back if not to try to find the bosom of the family and crawl in close and behave like someone who was never weaned? And what did you get out of that if not the same dry tit you got the first time you tried?

"Shut up, Scarlett O'Hairy," Fran said aloud. "Dogs don't talk, not even in horrible novels."

Well, said the dog, you'd be the expert on horrible novels. Just ask anyone in town. They still haven't gotten over the third one you wrote. Highest reported incidence of sexual abuse and incest in the English-speaking world, you wrote. Made all the neighbours feel kindly toward you, didn't it? And wasn't the family just about as thrilled as they could be? You could move tomorrow and they'd heave a huge sigh of relief. You could move yesterday and they'd relax.

"And where in hell to, dog?"

The dog lay on the grass and sighed deeply. Fran sat next to her, looking at the old neighbourhood. There wasn't a vacant lot left. Where once there had been fields there were now houses, townhouses, condos and apartments. There was probably even a bylaw which said nobody was allowed to sit on the grassy strip between the road and the sidewalk! Look, Scarlett O'Hairy said, sighing again, there you are in that great bloody grey mausoleum, and you're almost as good as all-by-your-damn-lonesome. Andrea will be heading off soon, if you let her. That kid isn't interested in grade eleven grade twelve college and career, she wants to get involved and change things. Already been arrested with Greenpeace for going out in her scuba suit and painting *BANG* on the side of the Yankee warboats parked in the harbour! Only reason she ever comes home for a bath and a good sleep is that she's concerned you'll get sick worrying about her. That place is big enough you could break it into apartments, rent each of them out for five hundred a month and live off your income.

"Where?" she repeated, silently this time. People already thought she was several crates short of a full shipment, why add to it? The dog wagged her tail. "Anyway, can you imagine what a fucking horror it would be to pack? Those books! Those damn books! Up to and including the very first Dr. Seuss, and that was Melissa's book, so how many years ago was that? Thirty, anyway. God, is Dr. Seuss that old? Is the Grinch a grandfather by now?"

Fran was a grandmother. Any number of times. So many of them she had started to sound like those old Scotswomen she remembered from her childhood, with their hyphenated explanations. Sally-who-was-Jen-McGee's-second-now-married-on-Ellen-McGaw's-Ewen, and Fat-Alice's-youngest-Norah and our-Jen-as-was-first-married-on-the-McPhail-reddy-haired-one-Colin. Only for Fran it was Melissa's-oldest-girl-Tiffany or Robbie's-wife's-oldest, which neatly separated that one from Robbie's-own.

All those kids and their kids and the kids of the people they took up with kept Fran awake at night. Just when you think you've got past the worst of it, by God doesn't it leap up and bite you on the nose. And aren't its terrible little fangs just as long and as sharp as ever, and you find out you can't deal with it or protect yourself from it any better now than when you were twelve and cowering under that goddamn hut waiting for the yelling and hoo-rahing to die down a bit, so you could stretch out and catch some sleep before it was time to saunter home as if you didn't know every eyeball in the neighbourhood was turned your way and all the tongues going tsk tsk tsk poor thing poor thing.

"Okay, dog, my bum is getting damp and numb. For April it sure does seem close to October, I tell you!"

Maybe that was the greenhouse effect they were always going on about on radio and TV. Winters seemed so much longer and colder, and summer, when it finally arrived, burned down until you wondered when the bedouins were going to show up with their tents and goats. It will have to be goats, reports are that most of the camels have syphilis. Now wouldn't that just about make you wonder? How big was the box that joker had to stand on to do it? Which brings one to AIDS and the many and varied stories we are fed about it. No, really, it's merely an adaptation of a virus found to be widespread among green monkeys in Africa. Green monkeys? Right. And purple cows, too, anything you say, Clyde, anything you say. The question here is, who was fucking the monkeys? Please, would you just stop this bullshit?

You think none of us know the topsoil in the North American breadbasket is blowing away at something like thirty metric tons a month? You think we can't figure out that means there won't be any before long? So where will the overfed grow their food? Well, not in the Ukraine, that place glows in the dark. And we can't take the South American prairie, or where would we grow our beef? Well then, let's look for another prairie, someplace flat where the computers can send out the tractors and turn on the sprinklers and flood the pesticides and fungicides and herbicides and whaticides without ever needing to pay wages to a human being. And there she is, guys, Africa! Oh, I say, Dr. Livingstone, I presume. Africa! Nobody here has nuclear stockpiles, and besides, they are all black as Toby's ass and you know we don't call them niggers but we still think of them that way. So what can we do? We mustn't appear to be doing it, however. Sneaky Pete, please. There's this virus we've been working on, in the biggest germ warfare experimental station on the face of the earth, even though germ warfare has been forbidden for over forty years! Yessiree bobtail, this is a good one, because by the time they start to drop like flies we'll be able to blame the fuckers themselves.

And there's a big benefit to it. The more concerned people are about an epidemic trying to happen, the less they'll have time to take a good hard look at what's going on in that last big prairie. Riot and counter-riot, revolution and counter-revolution, and the whole time the World Bank and the World Development whatsis and the international do-gooders of America and a whole bunch of others are encouraging them to run up debts they'll never pay off, and before long we'll just foreclose on the mortgage, bury the dead for fertilizer and grow the wheat to grind into flour to send to the baker to turn out more Twinkies. You don't fool me, said the little red hen.

/ / /

You can hire someone to do almost anything at all. You can hire someone to cut and file your fingernails and toenails, you can hire someone to rub oil into your skin, to cut the lawn, to look after the garden, to do the housework, you can even hire someone to come and wash the windows. You can hire someone to spruce up the house, someone else to estimate its value, put it up for sale and even sell it for you. Then you can hire someone to pack up your stuff and haul it off to the place where you've hired someone else to keep it in storage. Just be sure you throw out your garbage or they'll pack that up and store it, too.

The surprise was, Andrea wanted to come too. "Why not?" she teased in her cracked and gravelly voice. "Aren't you as close to a muddah as I've ever known? Or are you tryin' to get rid of me?"

"Yeah, that's it exactly, you wouldn't leave home so I tried."

"Well, it won't do any good, I'm tagging along."

They spent a week in a motel because the packers and movers were expected any day and anyway the people who had signed the papers and bought the place kept showing up for just one more excited look and could we please show Mom and Dad what it's like. And then, one morning, it was all done. The stuff was in storage, the house was empty, the cleaning and scrubbing crew was finished and paid and there was no reason in the world to ask Andrea to drive the rented car over for one last look. It wasn't as if Fran felt the least bit nostalgic or anything. But she asked and Andy agreed and then there they were, parked just up the hill a bit, looking at the place and not saying a word to each other until old Scarlett O'Hairy ambled down the steps and moved slowly toward the car.

"Poor old Red," Andy sighed. "I'm going to miss that dog more than I'm going to miss the house, the hill, or the whole damn town."

"Red? Not very original."

"It's what they called her, though. Big Red."

"Jesus."

"Yeah."

"Could have been worse, I guess, they could have called her Rover."

"I never knew a dog named Rover. Did you?"

"No," Fran laughed softly, "I have never in my half-century of life encountered a dog named Rover. But I did know a dog named Spot and I even met up with someone who had a dog named Tinker. But no Rovers."

"What they ought to call her is *in*, at least once in a while." Andy fished a cigarette from her package and lit it. Fran rolled down her window. "Don't nag," Andy said. "You want me to drive, you put up with the smoke and you put up with it quietly."

"I didn't say a word."

"You rolled down your window."

"I wanted the fresh air."

"Let's take the dog with us."

"Of course." And Fran reached over the back of the front seat, popped the door latch to the back and opened the door. Scarlett O'Hairy climbed in as if she had been waiting six years for the chance. "Imagine, going to jail for dog-napping."

"How come if you steal a kid it's kidnapping, if you steal a dog it's dog-napping but if you take a catnap you're sleeping?"

"Shut up and drive the getaway car."

"They won't even notice she's gone until they see the food didn't get eaten."

"Lie down, damn it!"

"How can I lie down and still drive?"

"The dog!"

"You want me to drive the dog? Or you want the dog to drive the car? Make up your mind here, woman, we don't have all day."

But they did have all day. And they took all day. They stopped at every viewpoint and scenic spot, they drove into and looked around every campground and picnic site, they parked on a shell-covered lot and went into an oyster house for huge oysterburgers and took their leftovers out for O'Hairy. "Better get this dog a leash," Andy suggested. "Then we can tie her if we're going to be somewhere for a while and don't want her dying of heat stroke in the car."

"Heat stroke? It's the end of May! I still need a jacket."

"Global climate change, you've been warned."

"Shut up. *You've* been warned. Not one pollution lecture all day or it's off with your head."

"Don't you get sand up your nose when you bury your head in it?"

They got the leash and O'Hairy hated it. They bought groceries and remembered to get dog food too. At three in the afternoon they were in the lineup for the Little River ferry, and at four-thirty they were driving off it on the other side.

"Well, Christ in heaven," Andy breathed, "and wouldn't it warm the cockles of your fuckin' heart? Talk about the decree of Ozymandius! Once the biggest pulp mill on the face of God's green earth, now somewhat diminished, third or fourth in the world, I suppose, but still the number one polluter in this nation. Fifty tons of contamination comes from that every day and has done since nineteen-oh-eight."

"Oh, shut up."

"And by God, there's scenic attraction number two, not a half mile from the ferry, on the only road I can see that leads into or out of town, and what do we have to our right if not a garbage dump with a smoke-belching incinerator. God, and you don't often get to see them any more. Take a picture of it, Lucy, show the folks back home."

"I said shut up."

"What's next? An abattoir? Open-pit mining? Maybe a toxic waste dump." And she started to sing loudly, "Be kind to your web-footed friends, for a duck may be somebody's muuuuh-ther, be kind to your friends in the swamp –"

"Shut up or you walk!"

"Perish the thought. How far do we go?"

"Oh, how far is there to go, I guess."

It wasn't that far, hardly any time at all, and they were parked in Liz's driveway and she was coming from the house, smiling from ear to ear, to grab Fran and give her a big hug.

"Me, too," Andy shouted, jumping from the car and running. "God *damn* but I missed you."

"Where'd you get the dog?"

"Stole it, of course. How else would a person get a dog? You've got a toilet, right?"

"Yeah, I've got a toilet. And a tub. And a towel or two. And supper will be ready in about half an hour."

"Heaven, I'm in heaven," Andy was acting the total fool, and both Fran and Liz were enjoying it. Fran envied her. Andy had probably never walked down the street past a group of teenagers and assumed, when they all giggled – which teenagers seem to do all the time, for no reason – that the lot of them were laughing at her. Not Andy.

O'Hairy sniffed the tires on Liz's car, then squatted and peed, took three steps and peed again, then went over and peed by the lilac bush. Finally, all her peeing done, she headed for the door as if she had spent her life in a house, spent her life, in fact, in that particular house.

"I'm glad you're here," Liz said, making eye contact. "And before we get one minute deeper into conversation or visiting I want you to know I love you."

"I know you love me," Fran smiled. "And you know I love you, right?"

Liz had chosen one of those houses with roof edges that slant up from the front, both sides, and the back, then meet in a little peaked four-sided attic room.

"Looks like a ship's cabin," Andy said.

"Looks like a great studio," Fran said.

"It's cold in winter and an oven in summer," Liz told them. "I use it for my hell hole."

The rest of the house was just exactly what anybody would expect. A tidy kitchen, a small living room, two bedrooms and a bathroom on the main floor, and in the entrance hall a trap door with steps leading down to the basement. There was enough space in the basement for a whole other floor, and some previous owner had done all the work, subfloor, walls, space turned into rooms, heating ducts hidden by ceiling, the whole thing. And it was empty and unused.

"I don't need the space," Liz shrugged. "There's just me."

"You could rent it out."

"Then I'd have to put up with whoever rented it. They'd expect part of the yard, they'd want a garden, I'd go to water mine and they'd have their hose on the tap, their car parked where I was going to park mine. I'd smell their cooking, they'd be making curry or something obnoxious."

"Doesn't the silence drive you crazy?"

"There's lots would say I was crazy before I moved here. Long before."

After supper Andy headed off with O'Hairy to explore the neighbourhood and see if there were any sights. Liz and Fran sat in the living room, looking out the big window at the rose bushes and the quiet street.

"You know Bert's living with someone?" Fran dared.

"No, I hadn't heard. That's good, he needs to live with someone. Have you met her?"

"Yeah. She's our age, going grey faster than us, probably twenty or thirty pounds heavier than the ladies' magazines would say she should be, got two daughters, both married, both with kids, and she works at a daycare centre. She's nice. Nice enough, anyway," she amended with a little laugh. "I find her kind of . . . oh, I don't know, not exactly dumb, but . . . she's not going to light any fires with her mental leaps."

"They're happy?"

"They're like clams in deep water. They hold hands all the time."

"That's nice," Liz smiled, and Fran realized she meant it. "He deserves some of that."

"Why in hell did you move so far away?"

"I needed to be far away. I felt as if my life was all grooves and furrows, and I was only allowed to go where I'd already gone, do what I'd already been doing most of my life, be who they had decided I should be. I couldn't do it any more. I just felt tired all the time, inside me, no matter how much sleep I got. One day I realized that all I could do was smile, I couldn't laugh. Nobody around me was laughing, either. I sat up all night putting one stick of wood after another into the fire, watching it burn, putting in another stick . . . and then everyone was up and making breakfast and it was almost time for Bert to come home from work and I knew if I didn't make some big changes I was going to put myself in the fire instead of the next stick. I made an appointment to see a lawyer, and then it all happened very quickly."

"You could have talked about it."

"Why? It's just words. We've got words coming at us from the radio and the TV, words in newspapers, magazines, books, advertising flyers, Jesus – words words words, and how much good do they do us? People go to school to get papers covered with words to pin on their walls so they can get rich sitting around listening while other people talk, talk, talk, words, words, words, and the ones with the papers get rich and go to Thailand on holiday and come back and say in words how lovely it all was, when everyone knows Thailand is swarming with children who are sexually exploited by the people who go there on holiday and come back and say how nice it all was!"

"Holy fuck." Fran shook her head in wonderment.

"When I first got here I thought Okay, idiot, nobody knows you, nobody gives a shit, you wanted to do what you hadn't done before. I went to Adult Children of Alcoholics, like you said I should. Well, listen, that didn't last long. People talked. But nobody is allowed to counsel or rebut or argue or . . . you just sit and listen. Two months later they were saying the same things. I had visions of us four years later, every Monday night in the same room, in the same circle, in the same order, still saying the same things, spouting the same catch-words and formula phrases. If I hear one more person talk about enabling behaviour or chronic dysfunction . . . I mean, doesn't that sound like a goddamn bowel disease? Oh, she's got chronic dysfunction, her doctor told her to eat lots of bran!" And they were laughing, far harder than the weak joke deserved. "So I tried Incest Survivors Anonymous," Liz dared. Fran just nodded. "But they let you know early on their whole target is for you to forgive and forget. Should that happen, fine, but don't tell me it's a fucking expectation! And don't bother with the claptrap about how hate hurts me more than the person I hate. Bullshit! I hate because I have reason to hate, I hate because hate was what kept me from jumping off a bridge, I hate because it kept me from becoming a perambulating shithead like him. I've got a lot of respect for my hate! My hate stuck by me when nothing else was there for me. And anyway people can't control what it is they feel. What we have control over, a little bit of control, anyway, is what we do with it. I hate him like fuckin' fury, and what I do with it is use it as fuel to make sure I do better by myself than he ever did by me, and to do better by my kids than was done by me or for me, and to make bloody sure they do better by their kids. Because Frannie, I am just sick and fuckin' tired of all this ugliness."

"Wow," Fran smiled. She reached over and took Liz's hand in hers and squeezed gently. "Way to go, Tiger."

"This thing happened. With Bert." Liz told her cousin about the argument and about moving to the other bedroom. "There was one morning when it would have been so easy to just . . . make a move, patch it up. And I didn't do it. I didn't reach for the patch. Because I didn't *want* to wind up being sexual. I've done that! Sure, it was nice, sometimes it was great, sometimes unbelievable, but it always meant more to the other person than to me. At some point I'd always realize Oh well, might as well try for a good time. Like not really wanting to go to the party, but you can't get out of it so you might as well party hearty. It made me feel crazy as hell. You hit orgasm and hear Peggy Lee singing Is that all there is? And hear yourself say Oh well. And I know it's because of *him*. There wasn't a thing I could do to stop what was coming down, so I just said Oh well, it won't take forever. Oh well, it doesn't hurt like getting beat up hurts. Oh well, he'll finish soon. If you learn to walk by scraping the toes of your left foot, you're going to walk like that all your life."

"No. You can go get your nose fixed, for a start."

"I don't walk on my goddamn nose!"

"No, but each time you look in the mirror you see it."

"If I get it fixed I'll see that, too, and it'll take me years to recognize myself! I don't even know what I would have looked like without this bent beak. Change it and I won't know who I am. It isn't the bend in it, you know, or the cracks in my cheekbones that make my sinuses go nuts. That isn't why I hate. It's that he did it, that it ever got done. And nobody gave a toot. *No-bud-dee.*"

"They'd all go to jail today."

"Would they?" Liz shook her head. "I doubt it. One or two of the most extreme might. Gowan might. Six weeks, sentence to be served on weekends so he can keep his job. And Wilma – all the Wilmas in the world – would yammer on about Look what you did to Daddy and See how you've hurt the family, and nobody will send her to jail. But what choice did she have? Did she even know any better? Or Gowan, what allowed him to be what he is? I mean, what the fuck was in Gavin's head when he went to the welfare and said he'd sue if you kids came back to town? How come none of his kids liked him? How come you never put *that* in your books?"

"I couldn't imagine anything that would make him what he is," Fran admitted. "I think about him and my mind leaps away like a jackrabbit."

"Yeah," Liz nodded. "There he was, showing up and raising hell because he heard my face had been rearranged, and after he'd raised hell, that was it. He went to the welfare to make sure you didn't come back, but he never went to make sure there was no more face rearranging done. Anyway, if you figured out what made him, you'd have to start in on what made that person, and what good does any of it do? Here we sit, you're a mess, I'm a mess, my kids are a mess and probably yours are too, you just haven't found out about it yet."

"Yeah?" Fran winked. "Well, I'm a bigger mess than you are."

"No you aren't."

"Yes I am."

"Are not."

"Are so."

"Are not," and they threw cushions at each other, pretended to slap and kick, chased each other around the room, through the kitchen and out the back door into the yard. Andy came home in time to see Fran grab Liz in a half nelson and pretend to punch, punch, punch. Liz grabbed Fran's leg and heaved, Fran lost her balance, Andy grabbed her before she fell to the lawn.

"Hey, hey," Andy laughed, so they pulled her to the grass and pretended to pound on her, each of them yelling, "Leave my cousin alone!"

"Oh God, the poor neighbours," Liz gasped. "Their noses will be flat against the windows, they'll have one hand on the phone, ready to call the cops. We should tell them it's okay!"

"Go to hell if you tell lies," Andy smiled.

They waited until after dark, then got busy in the kitchen and made a chocolate cake. Hardly waiting for it to cool enough to come out of the pan without breaking into bits, they made icing, with real chocolate melted in a double boiler. Then they sat on the floor in the living room and did their level best to eat as much of the creation as they could.

"I woke up one day," Liz said, "and I realized my kids were so close to being on their own all they had to do was notice it and start packing. And I felt so sad, and so scared, and so . . . at loose ends. Like I'd been waiting for a bus and suddenly realized I was at the wrong corner, there'd been four of them go by two blocks away and I'd missed them, and instead of walking down there to catch the next one, I was going home or something. Like . . . Jesus, did I really want to go to town that badly? And I thought, There, idiot, for the first time in your life you actually finished something you started. They're more equipped than you've ever been or ever will be. And I thought Boy, some people walk toward things and I've spent my whole life running around in circles, telling myself I'm fleeing away from." She shrugged, embarrassed. "Well, whatever it was I was afraid to give it a name. I wanted to talk to Bert about it but it would just break his heart. I didn't want to do that. He deserved better."

"One time," Andrea said, licking chocolate off her bottom lip, "a kid at school started giving me the gears about being a foster." She looked down at her plate, idly wiped more icing off with her fingertip, then licked it clean. "I got all set to fight about it. I knew I could probably pound her flat and make her cry and say she was sorry, and I knew that was just about the last thing I wanted to do. Ho ho ho, she said, they gave you away because they knew you were no good. And I was going to say Nyah nyah your folks were too dumb to find the Welfare and throw you away so they got stuck with you. I'm good at that. I got a lot of practice, early on." She looked over at Fran and smiled apologetically. "Some of the kids, even at home . . ." Fran nodded. "And then I wanted to cry and shout and yell and beg someone to say it wasn't true. And I knew it was."

"No," Fran protested quietly. "I told you. Your mother couldn't –"

"Yeah," Andy nodded, "I know. Nor either of my grandmothers? Nor any of my aunts or uncles or shirttail relatives? Nobody at all? And then I thought Whoa, hold on, if that's what they're like, why would you want them? If on a scale of one to ten they got eight or nine for not wanting, I'd damn well get the whole ten!"

"You could probably find out," Liz said.

"I don't want to find out." Andrea held out her plate for another piece of chocolate sin. "You can flog a dead horse and drag it to water but the most you can do is get it wet. And who wants a wet horse?"

"At first I told them no," said Fran. "Then I said Well, only for a few days, until you find some other placement, and then I said Well, maybe for a month or two, but no longer, and then," she smiled, "and then I told everyone it was because Someone Had To Do It. But that first year or so a lot depended on the cheque that arrived for you. And then, oh, I don't know, the whole thing changed. I almost sent back the cheques. Then I thought, don't be a bloody idiot! But when they told me they had a place to put you, I asked was it going to be long-term and they said no, but there was always the chance of adoption. And I said No there's not, and they didn't argue. I said Just leave her here, because unless she's going on to something better, she's not going on at all."

"Why?" Andrea asked.

Fran took her time, tasted her cake, licked her mouth and swallowed. "Because," she said, "I loved you. Not because you were mine, in the way the others were mine. I wasn't that person any more. I loved you because I'd got used to your funny voice and the smell of you in the house and the little tricks and habits you had and I knew if I did to you what had been done to me I'd make a hole in my life so big and so deep I'd fall into it and drown. And I didn't want to drown. Hell, Andy, I'd only just learned how to swim!"

/ / /

Anna heard her supervisor's words and something inside her chest swelled until it cracked. She pulled the snapshot from the folder and sat looking at the sun-bleached hair, the wide-set blue eyes, the strong, even teeth with the gap between the two front ones. She had teased him, called him her gap-toothed boy. He was smiling, wearing a new shirt, new jeans, new sneakers. Standing with him was an incredibly old, frail Native man whose gnarled hand rested lightly on the boy's shoulder, and behind them both a huge dark-haired man with powerful muscles cording his bare arms. Stamped on the back of the picture was a number and the words "Sidewalk Surprise, duplicates and enlargements available on presentation of identification number."

Her eyes burned, the stupid lettering blurred, and she handed the photograph to her supervisor, advertisement displayed.

"If only it was that easy, eh?" she said bitterly. "Duplicates available on presentation of identification number."

"Easy." The supervisor replaced the photo in the file folder. "Take it easy."

"I don't know if I can."

"Want the rest of the day off? A couple of days?"

"Where is he?"

"At the funeral home."

"Home. Jesus. The kid only ever had one home in his entire life and –"

"Easy."

"Yeah." Anna stood up, stubbing out her cigarette. She left the folder and the photograph on her desk and went to get her jacket.

"Where you going?"

"To the funeral home, of course."

"Want someone to go with you?"

"No." She moved to the door, then remembered her manners. "Thank you."

/ / /

Liz didn't mind having Fran and Andy sharing the house with her. None of the things she was afraid of happened. Nobody parked in her parking spot, there was no fuss over the garden, and Fran didn't like the smell of curry any better than Liz did. It all worked out so easily Liz couldn't help feeling there had to be a flaw in there somewhere. She almost hoped there would be. Maybe the dog would do something disgusting. But Scarlett O'Hairy was so quietly content she did nothing but ingratiate and endear herself. Life was so much better on her assigned blanket in the hallway than it had been out on that porch, and it was so much more fun to go for walks with people than by yourself, that the dog seemed to go around sighing with joy. And it was impossible to gripe about a dog that did what you asked, when you asked. O'Hairy didn't seem to understand she was the dog of the folks in the downstairs suite. Her blanket was down there, but if the upstairs got out of bed first, O'Hairy went padding up there to get the door opened so she could head out to pee. "Doesn't bother me," Liz shrugged. "It's not as if opening the door took all my energy."

It was nice to wake up in the morning and hear soft sounds from downstairs, nice to know you could drink your coffee alone at your own table if you wanted, or you could call down the hot air duct and someone might come up and share the space with you. Or might not, and that was okay, too. Fran spent a lot of time on her own, and days passed without Liz actually seeing her. Andy bopped in and out, especially during those times when Fran was glued to her new word processor.

"What will I get out of school, Auntie Liz? I don't believe ninety percent of the shit they try to ram down our throats. It's not a place of education, it's a place of brainwashing!"

"So you go, you listen, you take notes, you get yourself as qualified as you can possibly be and then you refute everything they say."

"You can't change the system by becoming part of it. By the time you've gone through their bullshit, some of it has stuck to you."

"It doesn't have to," Liz said stubbornly. "You take me as an example. I'm your average voting public. Me. Who am I going to believe? A kid who dropped out of school and then got herself arrested for sitting in a tree yelling insults at the cops, or somebody who can sit quietly while the moneybags tell their lies, then stand up and say Yes, well, unfortunately that's a new version of Alice in Wonderland because their own facts indicate . . . and crucify them. Who will I believe? I'm the kind of person laughs at a joke like this one: so there's this guy down on the beach and he's shooting seagulls, and the cops catch him red-handed and tell him seagulls are protected, there's a big fine and a jail term for killing them. And the guy comes apart, gives them a big sob story, please, my family is starving, I haven't worked in a year, I don't have unemployment and I don't want to go on welfare, please don't send me to jail. The cops say Okay, fine, just don't do it again, and as the guy is walking off one cop says, Hey, listen, before you go . . . What do they taste like, anyway? And the guy says, Taste? Oh, he says, well they taste somewhere between a bald eagle and a spotted owl."

"You laughed?"

"I laughed. I laughed like hell! And I'm one of the ones who knows that this idiocy has to stop, and the only question is does it stop while there's still something left? I know that, Andy. But I don't have what I need even to sit down and write a letter to my MP about it. That's what I need from you and your friends. Information is ammunition, kiddo. And right now, however committed you are, you aren't going to convince me of much."

"I *hate* school! And I hate the goddamn teachers. They are so . . . they are so . . . ."

"Hear yourself? Now what kind of argument is that? It's incoherent. Am I going to believe incoherent?"

"You ever pay attention to teachers when they aren't at work? No, how could you, you're not a teacher. Teachers hang out with teachers, they talk to teachers, they buy houses next door to other teachers, they form bridge clubs with other teachers, they play Trivial Pursuit with other teachers . . . and they're always whining about how broke they are. Well, small wonder, with only two or three rental houses bringing in money to help pay off the Beemer and the ski trips and the holiday to Yucatan and . . . they make my ass ache!"

"So you're going to join the however many thousand other kids in the country who are equipped for nothing more than a pair of thong sandals and a coolie hat? Boy, Andy, the things you're going to accomplish! With a bit of help you'll be able to make a picket sign that reads Prepare your soul, the end is coming. Then people can ignore you altogether."

"So you think I should go back to school."

"Sure. You can still work with Greenpeace. You can still train to scale up buildings and get knocked off them by fire hoses, and get your Zodiac run over by illegal driftnet boats. But you can also learn how to, oh, I don't know, become a lawyer and sue the bastards who blew up the *Rainbow Warrior*. Anyway you don't have to be the one who makes your own voice irrelevant. Hell, everyone else is busy doing that, why help them?"

Fran stayed out of the debate. Maybe Andy would pay more attention to the sound of a new voice. No matter how hard they try, they can't make "Oh, Auntie!" sound as dismissive as "Oh, Mom!"

Whatever her reasons, Andy did go back to school. Not to high school, but to the alternate school, and if she never broke down and confessed she actually liked it, she at least didn't go into hysterics when someone mentioned the place. Fran went on fighting with her computer. And Liz played in the pub four nights a week. The money she made, plus the interest on what she got when she and Bert split, was enough for her to live on, not fast or fat, but comfortable.

At first, neither Liz nor Fran mentioned those places where things were not going well. Liz spoke only of how Martine's two girls seemed to be doing fine, and how Reba had found a job she enjoyed and saved her money so she could take kayak trips and go down whitewater rivers wearing a safety hat and a life pre-server. Ronnie was in university, taking courses in how to keep salmon healthy in floating net pens, which Andy insisted was a total contradiction in terms.

"Don't give me the gears about it," Liz answered tartly. "Get your facts together and present them to your cousin. I don't fig-ure in this war! I'm one of the ones gets ignored, the innocent bystander."

"You don't have to be a *passive* innocent bystander! Those fish farms are disasters waiting for the right day to happen."

"If you can prove that, Ronnie will pay attention. Then you might have a fish expert on your side helping you convince other people, instead of more hot air."

"Jesus," Andy muttered, "I don't know how they overlooked you when they were looking for used car salesmen and invest-ment counsellors and all those other bee-essers."

Fran seemed to have no trouble keeping track of her troop, or remembering which kid was whose. Sometimes Liz looked at the pictures in Fran's Rogues' Gallery and felt overwhelmed by all the grins-minus-baby-teeth, pug noses, shiny neat braids, smile-for-grandma faces.

Bit by bit, though, the cracks began to appear.

Ritchie, the one who had apparently been in love with the ghost of James Dean, was the biggest worry. Now, thank the good lord for small mercies granted, he had given over the sullen and pouty look and taken a rest from blinking often so as to make his eyes seem damp and wounded. He even started to talk like everyone else instead of mumbling as if he had his jockey shorts caught in his throat instead of on his arse. Then, over a period of about three months, James Dean finally died and was replaced by James Caan. Oh, not the mature James Caan, not even the *Cinderella Liberty* James Caan, more like the bit actor who had yet to be groomed into a dependable star. An air of privacy but not gloom, a sudden flash of charming smile, and just the occasional hint of knowing cynicism.

Fran wondered if the day would come when Caan would follow Dean. Maybe if she'd called him James instead of Ritchie he could have got it out of his system while they were potty training. It must be something to do with his name, he was working so hard not to use it. Ritchie aspired to better than Ritchie; he would have liked Stud or Tiny, but little guys don't get names like that. You have to be a fair size to be called Tiny. Ritchie had to stand straight to get within range of five-foot-ten. When he realized he wasn't going to get any taller, he appropriated the bench press and weights that had been left in the basement, and began layering muscle onto his little frame, enough muscle that when he went looking for a job in the bush the rest of the crew didn't fall to the ground laughing.

He went into camp for three months and came out, as they say, a different man. Somewhere in the green he left behind all trace of the pain-in-the-ass teenaged boy, and came out with face, neck, forearms and V-shape at his throat tanned and wind-burned to the colour of leather. He came out with muscles on and around his muscles. He came out much quieter than he'd gone in, and passed hours without saying much of anything. These periods of quiet were punctuated with sudden bursts of humorous monologue which made mealtimes fun. Fran wondered who Ritchie was trying to be now.

And one day he phoned to say he was married.

"What?" Fran blurted. "No wedding invitation, no come watch the show, just —"

"Oh, bit of a rush, for sure," he laughed, "but you know how it is, the old biological clock is just a-tickin' away," he said proudly. The teenaged bride was three and a half months pregnant. "Well, hell," Ritchie drawled, "her dad's about twice the size of me and I didn't much feel like havin' my back bust." Everybody laughed, but Fran had the cold sick feeling Ritchie wasn't joking at all.

The mess lasted through the birth of Gowan, lasted another year and a half through the birth of Gavin and the conception of Emma, but before Emma was born it was all over except the heartache.

"Fuck her!" Ritchie raged. "I'm not sending *her* any of *my* money! She'll just spend it all at the fuckin' bingo hall, anyway. I'll send it to the whoofare and they can hand it out to her. Put her on a goddamn allowance like the fuckin' kid she is!"

"And another generation is off to a stumbling start," Fran said coldly.

"Ah, Mom, you don't understand."

He went back into camp and came out again even less like Ritchie. "Come on," he laughed, "I'm takin' you for supper," and on the way there he pulled over at the florist's, went inside, got Fran a corsage and pinned it to the shoulder of her dress. "There you go," he grinned, "They'll eat their hearts out when they see you."

"It's a good job I don't have the kind of mind can worry about them all at the same time," Fran told Liz. "Or maybe they phone each other and arrange to take turns, she's been worrying about me for six months, it's time for her to get off my case, so why don't *you* do something to add to her grey hair, she hasn't fixated on you for three and a half years."

"Is it that bad?"

"It's more like weary. Don't they ever look ahead past the week after next?"

"Did we?"

"Oh, for crying out loud, Liz, must you always answer a question with another question?"

"Do I do that?"

Fran whirled and ran head-on into Liz's grin. "I give up," she sighed.

"Yes," Liz said, "yes, we all hope you will. Because if you

don't give up you'll write another of those awful goddamn books about it, and while you might be able to get away with writing about the older ones in the family, the kids might pay you back in some grisly fashion."

"There's nothing the least little bit interesting in any of their lives," Fran said.

"There wasn't in my life, either, but that didn't slow you down in the slightest. You took a bit for this one and a dab for that one until I felt like the woman in the old Maidenform ads, the one who went all over the world in her underwear. You stripped us all naked."

"Well, how else was I supposed to understand?"

Why wasn't Fran wailing, or shouting? Instead she was just grinning. She even winked. Since childhood that had meant This Is A Joke, but now it didn't work. Liz knew it wasn't a joke.

"Some things are private," she almost whispered.

"Nothing is private. When a person doesn't know where real stops and not-real starts, everything is fair ball."

Fran kept the corsage in her Ritz cracker can, the one with the not-very-good picture of Fred Astaire dancing with a blonde woman who might be his sister Adele, or might be Ginger Rogers. Ritchie stayed for a few days, then headed off to party. Each time he came out of camp he partied. At first he was sober when he arrived home and worked his way into partying, but somehow it got to where he got home from camp smelling of beer, and worked his way into a glow before he left to party.

"He's going to wind up a drunk," said Fran.

"He *is* a drunk," said Andrea.

And he was. Not an overindulger, not an alcoholic, just a boozer, a drunk, a lush, like any of thousands of others who have spent the best years of their lives in camp, shaving the slopes, exhausting their bodies with demanding work and drinking themselves paralytic.

But the paymaster sent big chunks of money to the whoofare when Ritchie was working, and the bureaucrats stingied it out to his ex, who had moved in with someone so like Ritchie she probably didn't notice the difference. And the kids grew up on welfare, yet another generation learning early about the underbelly. Fran sent parcels of new clothes, she sent school supplies, she sent grocery vouchers, she sent everything except money because not everything Ritchie had said was bull dung.

"If it wasn't the bingo parlour," she mourned, "it would be the pub."

And then Ritchie met Carla. In a bar, of course. "Where else?" Andy shrugged. "You don't meet the Carlas of the world at a peace march." But first he met Lois, Carla's sister. The two of them shacked up for part of a fire season shutdown, but they didn't get along very well. They were so much alike they wound up competing with each other. Ritchie was a fast-mouth, quick to make a joke, quicker with a comeback, and Lois had always been front and centre in the same arena. She couldn't resist topping Ritchie, and if she couldn't top him she'd shoot him down, with an air of savagery that was missing in Ritchie's humour. Eventually he got sick and tired of being topped or shot down. Besides, messing around with Lois was sporadic and depended entirely on how she was getting along with the drunk she sometimes called her roommate. So he switched from Lois to Carla. She'd grown up taking a back seat to her younger sister so was already trained to take a back seat to him when he was doing his monologues and making his jokes. And Carla was nowhere near as smart as Lois.

"When God handed out brains," Ritchie glowered, "she thought He said trains, so she took a slow one."

"Sure," Lois snapped, "and when he said Wit, you thought he said Shit, so you passed on it."

"Did someone rattle your chain, bitch?" he smiled, then deliberately turned his head, erasing her.

Lois glared, then went to sit with her sister, muttering about what a damn asshole Ritchie was. And it started to unroll. Carla sat sipping and smiling, smiling and sipping, until she'd sipped so much her smile slipped. Then just about anything in the world might happen.

"Oh, well," Fran sighed, "at least he goes back into camp before someone kills someone else."

But he didn't stay in camp, and he didn't move on to some other out-of-camp squeezie, either. Time after time after time after time Ritchie wound up back in the same down-spiralling mess.

"Oh, now, take 'er easy, Mom," he grinned, his breath beery. "We're all of us here for a good time, not a long time."

"I liked him better when he was being James Dean," Fran

mourned. "At least he didn't drag all these others into my life, at least he was happy to be a loner. Now I feel like I need a program so I can keep track of who's on first."

"Maybe you can steal it and put it on paper and pretend it's a story."

"Who'd believe it? There's stuff happens every day all over everywhere and if you tried to make a movie about it they'd say you'd gone too far."

But what do you do? You can lock your door against burglars, you can buy deadbolts to keep out the philistines, but what do you do when it's your own? Like the time Ritchie showed up with a kid in tow, a kid not his own, a cheerful enough little slum rat who called Ritchie "Squirt" and who seemed intent on eating anything put in front of him.

Fran didn't say anything incendiary until she and her son were sitting on a bench at the playground, watching the kid clamber on the rope spider web. "To what do I owe the honour?" she asked quietly.

"Wanted to see you. Wanted him to meet someone half-assed normal. His mom's off on a toot right now and when that starts up, well, he's better off not bein' a part of it."

"Christ, Ritchie!" she exploded. "If you pulled out of that damn mess and put some energy into your own kids –"

"My kids are fine! You never mind about my kids! I send money for 'em, don't I? Paid for new bikes and had 'em delivered, didn't I? I see 'em, don't I? Take 'em to the PNE and stuff like that, don't I? You don't worry about my fuckin' kids, Ma, because they're okay. Nobody's shootin' at 'em, nobody's bombin' the house they live in, they got three squares a day and money for a show on the weekend and anytime they get sick of livin' with that bitch, they can just phone and they know it."

"Phone who? You? Half the time nobody knows where you are!"

/ / /

Liz wakened at one-fifteen, as the teasing aroma of fresh coffee rising from the downstairs suite and a light glowing from the hallway at the head of the stairs. She knew if she went down she'd find Fran at her computer, sipping coffee and frowning at the luminous screen. Liz sighed and rolled over, away from the light. But when she lay on her left side she could actually hear the pulse in her left ear, a steady hollow drumming sound that just about drove her up the wall. She'd asked the doctor about it, afraid he'd tell her it was high blood pressure, she was on the verge of a stroke. But he just talked briefly about how the walls of our veins and arteries get as tired as the rest of us, and how after forty-five or fifty the resilience goes from every part of the body, and finally told her that if the sound of her blood pulsing through her slowly hardening arteries bothered her, she should roll over and lie on her other side. Oh doctor, every time I lift my arm the pain is so bad I almost pass out. Well, then, don't lift your arm.

She almost got back to sleep but that thump thump thump in her left ear got louder and louder until she couldn't stand it any more. She rolled over again and lay there another fifteen minutes looking at the light in the hallway, yawning, wishing she could ignore it, knowing if she got out of bed and padded down the hall to close the trap door, Scarlett O'Hairy would take it as an invitation to come and visit. I should evict them, Liz thought, and go back to living alone. It's so much easier to live alone. Then she fell asleep, knowing she had spent too much of her life hiding from the glow in the hallway.

FOURTEEN

The interior of the funeral parlour was dim, the air scented with some kind of floral deodorant. Recorded music came softly from hidden speakers, and there were large boxes of tissues on the tables in the waiting room. Soft grey papered walls, pale grey carpeting on the floor, light lilac-coloured easy chairs and sofas and several handy black leather-bound Bibles completed the ambience of peace and rest. Anna waited with something that seemed like patience, but wasn't, and finally the surprisingly handsome young man came back, smiling gently. You don't expect them to be young, good looking and well built, she realized. You expect something old and bald, with hands gone soft and wrinkled from all the embalming fluid.

She followed him from the waiting room to the viewing room. He said something but she didn't hear him. She shook his gentle hand from her arm and moved forward, her mouth suddenly thick and dry, her own pulse hammering in her ears.

We say such stupid things in the face of death. He looks at peace, He looks as if he's just asleep, He never looked better, He looked as if he would sit up again at any second.

Except he didn't look like that at all. They'd done a good job on him, but it was obviously a job, obviously done. They'd dressed him in a soft cotton turtleneck under a new navy blue blazer, to hide the marks on his skinny little throat. The makeup changed the colour of his skin but couldn't hide the lines of pain cut in his face. There was nothing childlike about Peter. He looked like an adult who had been through the gates of hell.

"Was his neck broken?" she asked calmly.

"No," the young man answered.

"Then . . . he strangled?"

"Miss . . . please. It doesn't do any good to –"

"I'm sorry." He was probably right. Did it really matter one way or the other whether the eleven-year-old boy had died of a broken neck or of strangulation? It wasn't the rope that killed him.

"You did his hair wrong," she whispered, reaching out and ruffling the tidy wave someone had hair-sprayed into place. "It always just flopped forward like baby-chick fluff." She dug in her purse for her comb, stepped forward and fixed his hair the way he had always worn it. The young man stood quietly, watching. She put the comb away and reached out again to touch Peter's face, but it wasn't Peter or anything like Peter, who had been soft and warm, with grubby hands.

Anna wanted to say something, and there was nothing to say, not one word to say in any language.

"Poor little guy," she managed. Then she patted the cold hands clasped falsely across his body, and turned away and left the viewing room.

In the waiting room she was glad of the boxes of tissue, glad of the soft chair. The handsome young man gave her several minutes alone, then walked toward her with a notebook and pen in his hand.

"I wonder," he said softly, deferentially, "if you could assist me with some of the –" He stopped, at a loss for words. "For the service," he began again, "would you be able to give me some idea of prayers, for example, which the deceased particularly –"

"I doubt Peter ever cared one way or the other for prayers. He wasn't a very . . . *holy* little boy. What about . . . what is it, Remember thy creator in the days of thy youth? Something like that."

"Could you suggest a hymn or two?"

"Hymns?" Anna shook her head, feeling almost ready to laugh. "I doubt if Peter ever sang a hymn in his life. But I know his favourite songs."

"Songs?"

"Songs." Anna's voice was suddenly firm. "I think we ought to play his favourite songs."

/ / /

The signs of rebellion and riot were everywhere. The plumbing was still plugged, water draining slowly from the bathrooms to the hallways. Boys with mops pushed the water around, pretending to be cleaning it up, but actually making the mess worse. When they saw Anna they grinned, and one of them pretended to stumble, knocking his bucket over, spilling out the water he had unwillingly collected. "Gosh, ma'am," he said, "I'm sorry I'm so clumsy." Anna knew him slightly and sometimes felt afraid, not of him but of what she knew he could become if something, someone, didn't get through the shell of bitterness. Timothy Ian Pritchard, nickname Tip, but only to his friends, one of which she wasn't.

"Yeah, me too," another echoed, swishing his soaking wet mop so close to Anna's shoes she knew it was deliberate.

"Come on, guys," she said wearily. "Gimme a break, will ya?"

"Break your arm," Tip smiled.

So what do you believe? The smile, the soft tone of voice, or the threat?

"Or your neck," another offered.

Anna smiled, pretending they were joking, knowing in the pit of her stomach it wouldn't take much to set them off again.

The walls in the hallway were scorched with thick smoke, the overhead sprinkler system was smashed, the twisted heads still dripping water to the floor. Buckets and pails had been put down to catch the water, then had been moved by the children who were supposed to be mopping up. The glass around the reception area was smashed and the stuffed chairs ripped open, the stuffing pulled out and discarded. Two of the chairs had been set afire and the plastic upholstery had melted down to the floor and hardened in bubbly black lumps. Clumps of ugly soot hung from the ceiling and were smeared on the floor, thick as old cobwebs. Everything stank of smoke and cold ash, of rage and fear. There wasn't a wall hadn't been hacked at with a fire axe or smashed repeatedly with a piece of metal furniture.

The administration office looked like Belfast after a bad day.

The staff sat exhausted, almost shell-shocked, apparently trying to figure out how to bring order out of such chaos. They looked at Anna, then looked away, each hoping she would ask someone else the inevitable question. Anna looked at John, who had been Peter's counsellor, and who had found his body.

"What happened?" she asked. John tried to answer, and instead began to cry. He wiped at his eyes, his hand shaking. Anna wanted to comfort him, to say something supportive, but instead she heard herself yelling at all of them, particularly John. "What in hell goes on in this place? You take one of my kids and look after him so well he runs away! Then you can't find him for months! When you do, you waltz into court to tell the judge to send him back here because you're the only goddamn hope in the world he has, and no more than a day and a half later he's dead and you're all sitting around feeling sorry for yourselves! Don't you feel guilty on payday?" She knew they were no more at fault than she was and she didn't care. "Have any of you even been down to see him?"

"I saw him!" John stood up, angry and shaking. "I saw him, Anna. I'm the one who cut him down."

"I know that! Where were you while he was ripping his sheet to strips, then braiding and knotting the strips? Where were you when he was pulling his bed from the wall and climbing up on it? Where were you when he was tying that strip of sheeting around his neck? Where in hell were you for the fifteen minutes it took him to strangle to death, John? I thought you got paid to supervise these kids!"

"Putting down a riot," he gritted. "Trying to stop them from killing each other while they wrecked the joint. Or didn't you notice the mess on your way in to be holier-than-thou."

"What I saw," Anna shouted, "is evidence that whatever you're doing around here, you aren't doing it very well! For Christ's sake those are children, not the Dirty Dozen!"

"Take it easy," said the director, standing up and making ineffectual flapping gestures with his hands. "This isn't going to get us anywhere."

"Oh shut up, Cassidy!" John yelled. "That's all you've been saying since eight-thirty last night! Take it easy, take it easy, take it easy! It isn't easy to take, okay!"

Anna had to get a grip on herself. "There are reports to be

made, forms to be filled out," she said to John. "I want them on my desk by three o'clock tomorrow afternoon."

He looked ready to take a swing at her and she really didn't know why he stayed his fist. If anybody had spoken to her the way she had spoken to him, she'd have let fly a good one.

When Anna saw the boys standing in the hallway just outside the office door she knew they had heard every word. She stared at them, defying them to get in her way.

"Right on, lady," Tip said, and for a mad moment she wondered if she had said – *yelled* – what Tip wanted them to hear, what he had been telling them during the riot.

"Clean up the water, son," she sighed. "You don't want to live in this shitty mess, do you?"

He grinned and went back to swishing his dirty string mop aimlessly. Anna knew there would be no clean-up, not yet. As she started toward the door, one of the smaller boys stepped forward, eyes overflowing.

"Did you see him? Peter?"

"Yes." She nodded, reached out and brushed the boy's hair out of his eyes.

"How did he look?" an older boy demanded roughly. "Pete, I mean."

"He looked dead," Anna said firmly. They all looked away, shocked and hurting. "He did a dumb thing," she added, praying none of the others was thinking of imitating him. It happened. One kid slashed his wrist and before the blood was dry twenty others were slashing. A boy in Willingdon drank drain cleaner and before they had him at the hospital three others were at it.

"He got out of this place," one boy muttered.

"Yeah," Anna agreed. "And what's he doing right now? He's lying in a fancy box and he's never going to taste ice cream or go for a ride in a car or play hockey or feel sorry for himself or anything else," and she walked away from them before she started yelling again.

She was out of the door when Tip caught up to her. She stopped and turned to face him. They looked at each other for a moment, then Anna dug in her jacket pocket and pulled out a package of Players. Tip took a cigarette and nodded his thanks. Anna lit them up, then gave Tip the whole package. "They'll cut off my head if I give you the lighter," she said, and pathetic as her attempt was, it did ease something. Not the tension, not the pain, not the fear or the rage, but something.

"He'd'a been okay if they'd'a left him with that old guy, you know."

"Do you know that I argued in court for exactly that? Do you know that for a wild minute or two I thought the court would let him go?"

"So why do you even bother trying?"

"I might seem like a pain-in-the-nuts bureaucrat to you, but I'm trying. Bad as things are, how much better would they be if I quit? What if all of us who really do try were to throw up our hands and walk out because the entire system is fucked? What kind of a system would it become then?"

"You're kiddin' yourself, lady. What difference did you make to Pete? What have you ever done for anybody? But thanks for the smoke, it tastes great."

As he turned to go she wanted to reach out, grab him, hold him, make him understand, make him see how much she cared. But she didn't. He was too close to explosion, too close to God-in-heaven-knew-what for her to say one more word.

/ / /

Anna made good time driving out of the city, although the in-lanes were moving slowly. She couldn't abide the quiet in the car, the little voice in her head repeating the same few things over and over again. She reached out, turned on the radio and found a station playing golden oldies. Peter had teased her about her choice of music, which he called mouldie oldies. And yet he had known the words to some of them, even sang along sometimes.

Everybody had been saying for years the boy needed something but nobody agreed on what the something was. His inability to adapt to school led to meetings with the school nurse, with the school childcare worker, with the boys' counsellor. And when all the resources of the education system had been exhausted, Peter's file went to the public health department where, after a month and a half of something called processing, it was sent on to the mental health clinic. Mental health sent it on to special education, and another round of counsellors, advisors, interviewers, therapists. After remedial reading and language enrichment

Peter's grades were still low, his participation lacking or negative. The file, thicker than ever, was sent back to special education, which sent it back to mental health. At each stop there were meetings, at each stop the file grew still thicker. And finally Peter set fire to his school and the juvenile court judge sent him to a medium security facility for the care and treatment of emotionally disturbed children. A wastepaper basket for kids who fell through the cracks.

Anna tried to concentrate on the music, but the words pushed themselves to the front of her mind and without knowing it she blinked rapidly, trying to dislodge the tears welling in her eyes.

Everybody had been saying for years Peter needed something, and still the bureaucracy went grinding on, all the cogs spinning in mid-air, the educational system not integrated with the special education system, which in turn failed to communicate with the mental health department, and none of them the least bit in touch with Peter.

But you can't stay sane and hate a system without faces, names or personal responsibility. Just because you don't know who or what it is you detest doesn't mean you can stop detesting. And finally, the rage focussed on Peter himself. "You poor dumb little jerk," Anna raged, "and what good will *this* do?"

She took the off-ramp, glad to be off the freeway. The traffic was light and the road curved gently through farmland, fat cows grazing on bright green grass, the colours too vivid, too much like a box of crayons. She turned onto a side road, drove along it for two miles, then veered left and along parallel ruts through the brush and third-growth bush. The elderberry and blackberry whacked at the sides of her car, an alder whip slapped the windshield, and Anna felt as if she was driving slowly through a living green tunnel.

The car bounced, something grated against the bottom, Anna muttered to herself, and then the overhang was gone and the car was moving into the clearing. The shingled cabin had been there for more years than Anna had been alive, and had weathered in tones of soft grey and brown. The area around the cabin was littered with small chips of wood from Thomas's carvings, and some carefully selected blocks were stacked neatly under a small roof butted up against a wall.

She got out of the car and knew immediately something was

wrong. It was too quiet. She could hear crickets, she could hear birds twittering and cheeping in the trees, but there was no sound of mallet against chisel, no sound of country and western on the radio, no old man's soft voice, no sign of the whistle the mute man sounded for attention before he made his signs of communication. And there was a note tacked to the door.

The note just didn't seem right. There was no reason for either of the men to expect anybody to drive up, no need at all to leave a message saying they had gone into town for groceries and would be back soon.

Anna moved stiffly to the door, read the note, then sagged briefly against the wall of the cabin. Written in the large, looped handwriting of Leonard Thomas, the mute, whom Peter had told her was really He Who Would Sing. A few brief lines, enough to chill the blood. Anna moved back to her car, turned in the clearing, then drove back down the small rutted roadway quickly. She pushed her driving skill, sped to the closest gas station, got out with her door still gaping open, and raced into the station office. The mechanic watched, unconcerned, as Anna snatched up the phone and began dialling.

There wasn't time to wait for the RCMP tracking dogs to be helicoptered in from Courtenay, so they brought in Kupernick and his hounds from south of town. The hounds were long-eared, deep-voiced, amazingly gentle dogs who trotted easily across the flattened grass of the unmowed front yard and headed into the bush, packed together, running without leashes, following the tatter-eared old bitch, tracking human instead of cougar scent, and behind them went Kupernick, then the police, and finally one white-faced woman.

The hounds bounded ahead, baying happily, and Anna concentrated on not tripping in the tangle of salal and ground blackberry. They wouldn't have to travel far; Leonard Thomas had been carrying a burden when he left the cabin.

The baying stopped and abruptly became deep, mournful howls, a chorus of undulating sound which made the hair on the back of Anna's neck stand up. Kupernick looked back at her, started to say something, then shrugged and headed off alone, running full speed.

The dogs sat at the edge of a clearing, howling, whining, trembling. Kupernick put the leash on the ragged-eared bitch and spoke softly to her, and she headed off, tail between her legs, quivering but obeying. Nose to the ground, sniffing audibly, she moved to a twisted arbutus tree, sat suddenly, raised her head and began to wail again. Anna lurched forward, almost as if shoved from behind, and looked up at the platform, constructed like a child's treehouse in the large branches of the old tree.

Seward, the old man, the Dreamspeaker, lay on his back, his wispy white hair blowing in the soft breeze. You might have thought him asleep in the sun if the ravens hadn't eaten his eyes, pecked open his face. Leonard Thomas, He Who Would Sing, was slumped beside him, tied to the bole of the massive tree, his powerful body slack, the shotgun fallen from stiff, lifeless hands, his head gone above his bottom jaw.

One of the police officers was explaining how one SSG slug was equivalent to a .22 bullet and each shotgun shell contained at least a dozen. Leonard Thomas had shoved a stick in the trigger guard, pushed it with his feet and sent both shells exploding through the roof of his mouth.

The ravens had fed well. There was no mess of fragments to clean up, just the cawing of the birds, the terrible howling of the hounds, the weird unreality of the ugliness.

Kupernick knelt beside his old bitch, stroking her ears and talking softly. Anna watched, wondering if he was as patient and gentle with his children, as affectionate with his wife.

"Did the dog know him?" she asked stupidly.

"No." He didn't look at her. "But they know."

"They hunt," she said. "They help kill."

"Not like this. This is different. No need for this. Nothing natural about this. Dogs get upset when things aren't natural." He looked at her. "I've known both of 'em for years. And I want you to know, lady, there was no need to break that old man's heart. He might not have been John D. Rockefella, and he might not have had a new suit and a white shirt and a stucco bungalow, but he'd'a been good to that nutcase kid. Was no need at all for what you people did."

She wanted to yell at him, tell him he had no right to blame her, she'd done everything she could do to keep Peter alive, to make him healthy. But she said nothing. What would Kupernick understand anyway? Big moron, spending half his life hunting cougars and raccoons, trailing them through the rain forest, chasing them deeper up the mountains, shooting the old cats who wouldn't get the message and insisted on hunting livestock.

If he wanted to ignore her, that was fine with her. She could ignore him, too. She walked briskly back to the cabin and the police followed behind her, leaving untouched the two bodies on the platform. Kupernick did not wait for the photographer or the ambulance. He loaded his hounds in the back of the pickup and drove off, refusing to look at the RCMP officer or at Anna.

"No need for you to stay, ma'am," the younger Mountie said quietly. Anna shrugged, opened her car door, sat behind the steering wheel and stared wordlessly at the hood of her car. She smoked five cigarettes, one after the other, without knowing what she did.

As soon as the ambulance arrived, she started back toward the arbutus tree. She was waiting, stiff and dry-eyed, staring at the bodies on the burial platform when the attendants and officials took charge. They slid body bags over the stiff forms and lowered them from the platform, then collected the strange assortment of things placed on the dark-stained boards. Wooden carvings. An old vest in blue velvet with appliquéd eagles outlined in sequins and old shell buttons. Carving tools. A small cloth bag. A rattle. A dance cape, a spirit blanket, an unfinished Snipe dancing on one leg. The Mountie carefully made a list, describing each item in boring detail, and Anna had to sign as witness. Everything was photographed at least twice, and through it all the ravens and gulls screeched and railed, feathers glistening in the bright sunlight.

When it was all done the Mounties kicked apart the platform and took even that as evidence. Anna followed them, too numb to take it in. She turned once to look at the twisted arbutus drooping over the bank toward the sea. No sign of the platform now. Except for the flattened grass it looked as if no people had ever been here. Just the gulls and ravens.

Anna went back to the office to attack the mountain of paperwork on her desk. Forms, forms, forms, reports, notes and more forms, and several cups of coffee, and when she could no longer ignore the growling in her stomach, and could no longer pretend she was actually accomplishing something, and could no longer hide herself in her work, she sighed, put the cap on her pen and left her office.

She walked to the parking lot, unlocked her car and drove quickly to her favourite restaurant. There she had to spend another ten minutes looking for a parking spot, and she wound up paying two dollars to leave her car for an hour. Muttering, her nerves tight, she left the car and walked the two blocks back to the restaurant, then had to wait in line for ten minutes before she got in, and even then she had to share the table with two people she did not know and did not care to get to know.

Her companions were no more interested in idle social chatter than she was, and seemed no more pleased to be sharing a space with a stranger. Well, that's what happened when your favourite place became everybody's favourite place. Last year you could come here at any time and have a table to yourself, then the Meandering Gourmet wrote an article about the best Szechuan in town and everybody flocked to this latest "in" spot. Now you were lucky if you only had to wait ten minutes to share a table with two other people.

Anna ate hungrily, and felt better right away. The knot was gone from her belly, her hands weren't shaking and fumbling, and driving home she wasn't as inclined to lean on the horn and yell insults at drivers who cut her off or changed lanes without signalling. She wondered how many homicides had been committed by people with empty stomachs, how many assaults took place because blood sugar levels were low.

She parked in the underground lot and moved toward the security door, fumbling in her purse for her entry key. None of the light bulbs had been replaced. It was dark and gloomy in the concrete cave, the floor littered with papers, tissues, gum wrappers and cigarette butts. For a moment she thought she saw someone sitting in the big van parked near the doorway, but that had to be a trick of the dim light. Why would anybody sit in a van in a darkened parking lot?

She unlocked the security door and went into the building, making sure the door closed behind her. She took the elevator to her floor, unlocked the door to her apartment, went inside, closed the door, slid the deadbolt into place, then fastened the safety chain.

"Put the alligators in the moat," she muttered. "Keep the pagans at bay."

She was too tired even to turn on the television to watch the news. All she wanted to do was have a nice long soak in a hot soapy tub, get into bed and sleep for a century or two. Maybe if she slept long enough she'd waken to a sane world.

And yet, tired as she was, she could not get to sleep. She lay in bed, still smelling the bubble bath, watching her curtains blow gently in the breeze through the screened window. She yawned, she turned, she rolled, she thumped her pillow into fluffiness, and none of it did any good. She could not get to sleep.

So she got out of bed and turned on the television. It was an old movie, men in funny clothes riding in old cars with doors that opened the wrong way, racing up and down steps firing popguns at each other. She had no idea who was the good guy, who the bad guy. She fell asleep in the recliner and didn't wake up until the movie was over and the ear-piercing whine of the off-the-air signal cut through the thick fog. She stumbled from chair to bed, fell on her covers and sank into welcome darkness.

Anna wakened in the morning feeling as if someone had spent the entire night beating her with a stick, and the day did not improve. She got soap in her eye while showering and dropped her toothbrush on the floor, bristle side down. Breakfast was a cup of coffee followed by another, and then she was dressed and rushing to work.

The advertisers had been busy in the underground parking again. She pulled a little leaflet from under the windshield wiper, then unlocked her door, got into her car, closed and locked the door, started it up, fastened her seat belt and dropped the leaflet onto the seat next to her. There really ought to be some kind of regulations. You couldn't open your newspaper without being caught in an avalanche of inserts, and half the time the mail in the mailbox was buried under a pile of bright-coloured Special Reduced Price Giant Economy Jumbo Sized Junk pamphlets.

Someone else was in her space at the pay parking lot, and Anna knew her response to the inconvenience was totally inappropriate. She gripped the steering wheel, wanting to leap out of her car and kick the offending vehicle into a pile of twisted metal. Instead she found a free space, parked, locked her car and headed for the office. It was not a big deal, she told herself, it was nothing, it shouldn't make her so angry. But no matter how she lectured herself she was still furious. People should park their cars in the slot assigned them. All it took was one person in the wrong slot and the whole pay parking lot was fouled up, nobody got the proper place to park. Now she was in someone else's place. Nobody was where they belonged.

The unfinished work, however, was where it belonged – on her desk, waiting. Anna went right to the coffee machine. The pot was empty.

"Who took the last cup of coffee?" she erupted. "And why didn't whoever it was take half a minute to start a fresh pot?"

"Sorry, Anna," a voice called.

"Sorry my foot!" She knew she was being a bulldog and she didn't care. "Every time I come over here for a coffee it's the same thing! Have some consideration for other people. Grow up and join the adult world."

"I said I was sorry!"

"Tell someone who cares! Take that story to someone who'll be impressed with your charming smile and big blue eyes. And next time you take the last cup, put on another pot of coffee."

"Yes, Mother," snapped her office mate from across the room.

Anna rinsed the coffee pot, filled it with water, poured the water in the coffee maker, put in the filter and the coffee, turned on the machine and stood waiting impatiently. "If the cream carton is empty," she blurted, "I'll probably kill you."

"There's cream," he said.

Suddenly the fuss over the coffee seemed less than unimportant, silly and even degrading. She felt her face flush, her eyes burn. "I think I really need this coffee," she managed.

"Hey," said her office mate, smiling down at her. "Hey, you're right, I'm sorry."

"I'm sorry, too," she admitted. "I just . . ."

"Yeah," he nodded, "yeah, it's a hard one, all right. You got the fun part of it, I hear."

"Real fun." She poured herself a coffee and stirred slowly. "It was . . . like one of those awful dreams where you know you're dreaming but can't stop it . . . it felt like . . . like this big snowball . . . you know it's coming . . . you can even see it coming. But you can't stop it, and you can't get out of the way, and . . ." She made herself stop. "It was awful."

"It won't get better for a while," he said.

She nodded again. Then she took the coffee back to her desk and started on the pile of papers.

/ / /

Fran heard Liz padding quietly upstairs, heard Scarlett O'Hairy go up the steps, heard the dog's toenails clicking across the kitchen linoleum, then heard the door open and the dog run into the back yard. She got out of bed, pulled on her terrycloth robe, shoved her feet into her comfortable old plaid foam-soled slippers, and went to the bathroom. Face washed, hair halfway brushed, she joined Liz at the kitchen table.

"I heard you," Liz yawned, flapping one hand at the mug of coffee she had poured for Fran.

"Thank you." Fran sipped. "Sleep well?"

"Just put my head on the pillow and that was that. You?"

"Same thing. Must be the pure life we live." She leaned forward and turned on the little radio on the windowsill. The smooth voice of the CBC announcer oozed from the little plastic box and was followed by the sounds of a fifteen-year-old song. "Mailman come yet?"

"Every morning you ask if the mailman's come yet, and every morning I say no, and every day he shows up between ten and eleven," Liz yawned, pointing at the clock. "Two more hours to wait."

They heard the toilet downstairs flush, looked at each other and half-grinned.

"Andy." Liz got up to get another mug and took it to the table. "She'll be here in a couple of minutes, with her cereal. Which reminds me, I've got about five of your bowls in my cupboard."

"Heh heh heh." Fran refilled their mugs. "Saves me having to wash and dry them. I trained all my kids that way."

Andy came into the kitchen with her bowl of Special K, grinned her good mornings and sat at the table. That's when the music stopped and the morning news broadcast began. First the international, then the national, and finally the regional. The story of Peter's suicide was the first item of regional news.

The three women just stared at each other, then Andy pushed her bowl aside. "Shit," she said clearly.

They were all in the living room, the stereo blaring, and the guy
was dancing with the woman in the pink blouse, but he was
watching Mom and Aunt Lois, and he was grinning. The woman
in the pink blouse hadn't come with him anyway, she was with
the other guy, the one sitting at the table talking to the guy next
door. The dancing guy was just dancing with the woman in the
pink blouse, not paying any attention to her, because he didn't
want any trouble with the guy over at the table. Jackie knew you
didn't make trouble like that unless you wanted real trouble. If
someone came to a party with someone else, you found your
own fun, otherwise the one who came with the woman might get
proddy and then there'd be a fight. If there was a fight, the furniture would get all knocked over and maybe broken, and one
of the neighbours might phone the cops. The landlord phoned
the cops at the first sign of trouble. Not having my place smashed
up, he said. Jackie could understand that. When he was big
nobody was smashing up his place. It was bad enough his model
had been smashed. He and Squirt had spent lots of times putting
that model together. After suppertime and even weekend time,
and when it was all glued together Jackie painted it, with Squirt
watching him. And not one of those snap-together ones, either.
A real one, with glue you had to be careful with, keep the window open and not have any open flames. Open flames were like
what you got if you struck a match, or like the pilot light on the

gas stove. Burn the whole joint flat, that's what Squirt said. You gotta be careful, Jackie, because even if it isn't gasoline it works like that. Stuff gets in the air. Any time you can smell the stink of something you can be sure there's vapours. Mist. Like fog, almost. One spark and poof, burn the whole joint flat to the ground.

Squirt knew. Squirt worked in the bush. Gotta be careful, Squirt told him, working in the bush isn't like anything else. Gotta learn to be careful, Jackie boy, because there's more stuff in the world will hurt you than stuff that won't.

They used a toothpick on some of the little bits. Put the glue on the skinny end of the toothpick and spread it on the edges. No need to use a sledgehammer if you can use a little bitty hammer. Don't want these bits sitting up in the air on a half inch of clear glue. Gonna make 'er right, Jackie.

Made her right. Made her real right. Some of the places Squirt used a bit of sandpaper stuff. Emery board, it was called. Got it all smooth. Then Squirt sat eating peanuts and watching. Open 'er up, guy, he said, and Jackie opened his mouth. Squirt popped in some peanuts and Jackie chewed, both hands busy with the model. Chew 'er up good, Jackie, Squirt told him, or it'll stick in your throat and there you'll be, black in the face and there I'll be yelling for help. Give the neighbours a helluva turn if I was to go rippin' outta here screechin' He's got nuts in his throat! They'd think it was a birth deformity. Jackie laughed hard and almost sprayed chewed-up peanut all over everywhere but he got his hand up in time. And that was so funny they both laughed and when Mom asked why, they couldn't tell her. You're both nuts, she said, and that did it, laughed so hard his belly muscles hurt.

Painted it red, then put flame decals down the sides and bright chrome-looking headlights and stuff. Doors opened, trunk door opened, the steering wheel moved. Front wheels moved, back wheels moved, the radio antenna went up and down like a real one. Put 'er up where she won't get hurt, Squirt said. But there wasn't a place like that so Squirt built a shelf on the wall, up above Jackie's bed. High enough up Jackie wouldn't bump his head, so the only way to get it was to take off your shoes and stand on the bed and stretch. Can't have you bumping the old head, Squirt said. People who bump their heads too often get simple.

And then, when it was all done and looking so good, Squirt

had to go back into camp. Gotta go, Jackie boy, he said, off to the sticks. Gonna make some money, fella, and when I come out, you'n'me's going for Chinese food. Just us. I'm having sweet and sour spareribs. What about you, guy? Jackie wanted peanut chicken. It was hot, it burned your mouth, it made tears come down from your eyes and made your nose run, but it was good.

Only there wouldn't be any. Not with Squirt. Because Squirt was no sooner gone than some other guy was hanging around, and then there was a big fight one night. Yelling and screaming and Mom hollering and crying, and then they were fighting in the bedroom and Jackie scrabbled to the end of the bed, jumped over and hid in the closet. And in the stupid fight the model and shelf got hauled off the wall and that was it, all that work schmucked on the floor. They laughed, too, because Jackie flipped when it happened and screamed swear words and hit and yelled for them to get out of his room and look what they did and what about his model and just wait until Squirt came back and they'd all be sorry.

Well, he wouldn't be back. They never did come back. Not the okay ones, anyway. Sometimes the jerks showed up again. He'd said that to Squirt once, at the beginning, and Squirt laughed and said Hey, get used to it, fella, that's life. You'll always be surrounded by idiots. Doesn't mean you have to be an idiot yourself.

And now they were partying again. And the guy was pretending to be someone he wasn't, bowing, taking the woman in the pink blouse back to a chair. Yeah. Well, you don't fool me, guy, next you'll be asking my mom to dance. She'll dance with you, and Aunt Lois will laugh and dance with someone else. And maybe there won't be a fight, after all.

He chewed the pizza they'd brought home for him and watched through the crack in the door. It was good pizza. Or maybe it wasn't, maybe he was just hungry enough anything would taste good. Supper hadn't been hardly worth opening your mouth for, can of vegetable-and-mystery-meat soup and a couple of pieces of bread. Bread so dry you had to dunk it in the soup juice. Outsiders, Squirt called the crusty pieces on the ends of the loaf. Some stale outsiders and some canned soup. Won't hold ya, was what Squirt said about food like that. Won't hold ya, kid. Pizza probably wouldn't hold ya either, but it was a lot better than watery soup and stale outsiders.

Maybe it was cheque day. There were two cheque days, family 'lowance and then the maintenance cheque. Mom's cheque
wasn't on cheque day, it was on payday. Payday almost covered
the rent, she said, hardly worth getting out of bed for. But she got
out of bed. Most of the time, anyway, except days off. Sometimes
she had lots of days off and then that was layoff. Going to work,
he'd ask? Laid off, she'd say. She was laid off right now. Layoff
was no fun. Not enough money and too much partying and guys
coming in to break Jackie's shelf. When layoff lasted too long,
like this time, they got whoofare. Mom said it was better than
nothing. She said jobs were getting as scarce as rocking horse
poop. Said it was hardly worth getting out of bed and going looking.

He was cold. Well, that's what you get, Squirt said. Never sit
on the bare ground or the bare floor. Get a pillow or a cushion.
Pull up the floor and take a load off your feet, Squirt said. Your
bum gets cold and it goes right up your spine and the next thing
you know you're cold inside and out. Jackie put down his pizza
and went to get a sweater from one of the plastic milk crates
stacked on top of each other in the corner. He pulled on the
sweater, being careful not to get pizza sauce on anything. Aunt
Lois had knit it – for Jeremy, not for Jackie, but Jackie had it now.
The nosepickers had come and taken Jeremy away, and Tiffany
and Brittany, too, but the nosepickers didn't get Jackie. Yet.

Squirt said you had to keep your nose clean. Just don't stick
it in other people's business, Jackie boy, he said. Don't poke your
nose in anybody else's armpit, know what I mean? Keep your
nose where it belongs. Otherwise it'll get dirty, and once your
nose is dirty you start picking at it, and then the next thing you
know, you're a nosepicker and there isn't much worse in the
world than a nosepicker. They both laughed.

The nosepickers got his cousins. Almost got him, too. He was
staying over with them because it was bingo night and that always
meant Mom and Aunt Lois went out right after supper. Sometimes
they came home with lots of Chinese food, laughing and saying we
won, we won, other times they came home and said well, maybe
next time, eh. That night they came home with food and pop and
a whole bunch of other people and there was a party and everyone was laughing and drinking booze and making noise, but
Jackie didn't feel like being there because he had a headache.

Couldn't even eat very much. It was just after Squirt had left, just after the model got smashed, and just before he got measles.

It had been so noisy that night. The light hurt his eyes and his nose kept running and his throat was sore and he ate a little bit then almost threw it all back up again. Jesus, one of the women said, that little guy's sick as a dog. Mom noticed then. Hey, what's wrong, she asked him, but he couldn't say anything, he had all he could do not to barf. Or cry, which was even worse with all those guys standing around grinning and drinking beer. So finally Mom put his jacket on him and got one of the guys to drive them home. Must have been a nice guy because he stayed the night. Mom said it was so there'd be a car handy if they needed to take Jackie to the doctor. But they didn't. She gave him aspirins and tucked him in bed and he went to sleep because it was so nice and quiet, finally.

And then when he woke up, Aunt Lois was there. It was after lunchtime and Aunt Lois was crying and yelling and Mom was crying and Aunt Lois had marks on her face. Jackie wasn't sure what all had happened. A fight, for one thing. Aunt Lois getting decked by some guy, for another thing. And the cops came. And after the cops, the nosepickers.

Jackie was too sick to listen to it all. He drank lots and lots of water, then peed and then went back to bed and slept some more. By the time he felt a bit better he was covered with spots and they had to go out to Aunt Lois's place and clean up. Boy, what a job! Stuff smashed all over the place. Some bozo had taken an axe to the door and did a job all over it. Furniture in all the places it shouldn't be and nothing in the places it should be and broken glass and blood marks on the wall and no sign of Jeremy, Tiffany or Brittany.

Nosepickers.

And when Mom was all finished crying and yelling and drinking and coming into his room at night to lie on the bed and cuddle him and tell him nobody was ever taking him away, when she was finished saying over and over again how it was nobody's business but her own, she went on the wagon. And while Mom was on the wagon Aunt Lois finished knitting the sweater she'd been working on for Jeremy. A big dinosaur on the front. They all called it Dino the dinosaur, but he didn't call it that. Squirt said dinosaurs were first cousins to dragons. Said there used to be a

world full of them and then they were gone. Gone with the uni-
corns. Squirt said there was another world, just like this one only
better. No booze, no fights, no nosepickers, just all the things
you'd really like to see, like boggards and nixies and stuff. Stuff
that got sick and tired of nosepickers and boozers and just
packed 'er up and tally-ho'ed off to that other place. Just tally-ho,
Jackie boy. Just up and tally-ho down the old pike.

No Dino the dinosaur here. All gone. Nothing left but bones
and fossils. So he called the dinosaur on his sweater Squirt. It
wasn't really Squirt, but it made him feel better, and when Squirt
came back he'd know why. He wouldn't say, Why would you
name it after me? He'd know. Anyway, it was his sweater and his
dinosaur and Jeremy wasn't coming back. Nor Brittany. Nor
Tiffany. No more than Squirt was coming back.

You weren't supposed to store food in your room because the
mice and rats would move in. But if you didn't put it where
nobody else knew where it was, some bozo would eat it on you.
And the mice and rats had moved in a long time ago, anyway.
Squirt said not to worry about them. Said rats were every bit as
smart as humans and smarter than some. Rats look after their
own, was what Squirt said. And no bozo was getting the last couple of pieces of pizza because you never knew if there'd be
breakfast or not. Jackie lifted his pillow, slid the pizza box
between the bottom sheet and the mattress, then put his pillow
down again.

Might as well just get into bed and try to go to sleep. It sounded like it was going to last all night and then some. He kept his
socks on because you just never knew. Squirt said don't take off
your socks unless you feel safe, Jackie boy. Nothing makes you
feel less able to look after yourself than trying to hightail 'er in
your bare feet. Only thing worse is hauling on your boots and
racing off only to find you've put them on the wrong feet. Make
a person feel a right total fool. Sleep in your socks, Jackie old
boy, then if you have to run for cover nobody'll see your toes and
step on 'em.

/ / /

Vancouver International Airport isn't far from the city, it just takes
forever to get there. Then you have to park so far from the ter-

minal you have to take a shuttle bus from the lot to the buildings. What was it costing the taxpayers, Anna wondered, to bring Rose Baxter and two RCMP from Kingston to Vancouver by air? Then two hotel rooms for two nights, one for the male and one for the female officer. Plus whatever it costs to keep a person in the remand. And leave us not forget, she thought sourly, the cost of the flight back to Kingston. All so Rose could attend the funeral of a son she hadn't seen or written to in more than six years.

Even before Rose was settled in the back seat, Anna could feel the tension. Both Mounties, particularly the woman, looked ready to explode. And Rose knew it.

"Anybody got any rules against smoking in this car?" she asked defiantly, her voice like sandpaper on porcelain. Without waiting for an answer, she fished her package of cigarettes from her pocket, fumbling because of the handcuffs. Then she laughed in the face of the male Mountie. "Hey, Dudley Do-Right," she mocked, "Howja like a chance to flick your Bic?" The Mountie sighed, brought out a package of paper matches, lit Rose's cigarette, then tried to ignore her.

"You'd think they'd have special flights for smokers," Rose went on loudly. "It's a long enough trip without sitting there in a nic-fit." Nobody said anything and Rose laughed again. "You know," she said, ostensibly to Anna, "the last time I was up in front of the judge he said he was giving me five and a half years in Kingston because a long stretch might do what all the short ones hadn't – rehabilitate me. Well, I tell you, I have walked up and down the streets and alleys in just about every city you'd want to name and I've walked arm-in-arm with hookers, rounders, junkies and deadbeats, but there's nothin' more rehabilitatin' than walking arm-in-arm with a lady pig, handcuffed together like Siamese twins. If ever I get turned loose on an innocent and unsuspecting world, the most rehabilitatin' memory I'll have is of sittin' in that plane tryin' to eat Air Canada food with a stainless steel bracelet locking me to the wrist of a government sow."

"Hey, Rose," the male Mountie said coldly, "why don't you just shut up?"

"Dudley, old man," Rose answered, lighting a second cigarette from the butt of the first, "why don't you bend over, put your head between your knees, and kiss your own backside."

"Put a lid on it," Anna snapped.

"Oh, wow," Rose laughed loudly. "It can talk! Wonder if it can think, too?"

The woman officer spoke, finally. "You want to spend the entire week in remand? Because if you don't, if you want to go to the funeral, clean up your act. There's no law says I have to be nice to you, Rose."

"I wasn't talking to you anyway," Rose said. "You. Up front. Driver. Whatever your name is."

"What?" Anna wasn't going to tell her name to Rose Baxter.

"Anybody think to tell Tommy about this?"

"Who's Tommy?"

"Isn't that just typical," Rose laughed again. "Tommy Dugan, of course. Peter's father."

"His father?" Anna suddenly felt as if she was driving in a city she had never seen before. "Peter's name was Baxter."

"Yeah, I know that. Like mine. Like that loser I married. But it isn't the wedding ring does it, or haven't you got that far in school yet?"

Anna took a deep breath and prepared herself. "Peter's file says his father is –"

"I don't care what the file says. I'm telling you, and I guess I'd know, eh? Baxter was a hype, okay? Good for nothing. Tommy Dugan is Peter's father."

"We've been looking for Baxter." Anna felt stupid, knew she sounded stupid.

"Yeah, well, good luck. Haven't heard a word from him since he took a hike. Not one word. Probably checked all the way out. John Doe. Don't you read the paper? There's an article every week. Body of an unidentified man found rah rah rah."

"Where would we," Anna tried to choose her words carefully, "find Tommy Dugan?"

"Just get on your little computer, lady. Chances are nine to one you'll find Tommy doing time."

"Nice friends you've got, Rose," the male Mountie said.

"Yeah?" Rose smiled widely. "Nice enough to buy bullets for their own guns, not like you guys."

Anna got on her computer and sure enough, Tommy Dugan was doing time. Less than four hours after picking up Rose Baxter at the airport, Anna was on the phone, talking to Dugan.

"No," he said quietly, "no, I guess not. I never got to see him when he was alive, I sure as hell don't want to see him dead."

"You're sure?"

"Sure, I'm sure." He cleared his throat, and Anna knew he was close to tears. "Listen, I've got another kid, okay? A girl. You might tell her, okay? I mean . . . her brother and all."

"Where does she live and what is her name?"

"Jenny. Jenny Dugan. She's out there on the coast some-where, in a foster home."

"Where is her mother?" Anna wasn't sure she had to ask. Everyone connected to Peter was apparently locked up for the protection of the rest of the world.

"Oh, I don't know." Dugan sounded as if he didn't care. "Haven't heard from her since way back before I got busted."

"When was the last time you heard from your daughter?"

"Since before the last time I heard from her mother," he laughed bitterly. "Not much of a one for keeping in touch, know what I mean?"

Anna went back to the computer. There couldn't be that many girls named Jenny Dugan living in foster homes somewhere on the coast. By afternoon coffee break she had the address and phone number, and before she left work she had an appointment to see Jenny Dugan after school the next day.

Anna parked her car in the underground and turned off the headlights. As she reached for her purse and briefcase she noticed the litter on the floor. The ashtray in her back seat stank of cigarette butts, but there was a piece of paper she could use to empty the mess into. Some gum wrappers, some pieces of paper, an empty chocolate milk container, where had that come from? She cleaned up the rubbish, locked the car and made her way to the security door. In her apartment she emptied the mess.

/ / /

The cops came with the nosepickers. Jackie didn't even try to run. Anyway there was nowhere to run to, there was only one door in and out of the place and they were standing in it.

He wanted his mom, but she wasn't home. Hadn't been home yesterday either, or the day before. Not even a phone call. He wanted to fight, he wanted to yell, and all he could do was sit.

He didn't look at them when they spoke to him, he didn't get up when they told him to, he just sat and finally one of the cops picked him up and carried him.

He was afraid they'd take him to the cop shop and put him in a cell, like on TV, but the cop put him in an ordinary-seeming car and two lady nosepickers got in, one to drive, the other to sit between Jackie and the door. He wanted to yell, he wanted to kick and punch and fight and force his way out of the car, but they were big and he wasn't and all he'd do would be get them mad. Squirt taught Jackie the words to a song he used to sing: Never hit seventeen when you play against the dealer, and he taught Jackie how to play the game, how to play Twenty-one, and he told Jackie about stacked decks and about not talking when you oughta be listening, and two against one and pick your own time and place. Just play 'er cool, fella. The wheel will keep on turning and sooner or later it'll be your time and place.

They drove and drove, and Jackie didn't know where he was. But he knew it wasn't his neighbourhood. Looked more like the place where Squirt's mom lived, and for a moment he almost hoped, but then he gave up because there had been no ferry ride, and you had to take a ferry to get to Squirt's mom's place. That had been great. Sometimes he watched it in his head like a movie, and started at the place where Mom had been out beerin' with Aunt Lois and Squirt looked over at him and said Hey, wanna take a trip? Rented a car from Rent-a-Wreck and off they went with pyjamas and toothbrush in a lunch bag. Sometimes he played the whole movie, car ride, boat trip, lunch in the ferry cafeteria, everything. Sometimes he just skipped ahead to when they were finally where they were going. And Squirt's mom was there, and his Auntie, too, and a dog. Just down the street, a playground, with swings and slides and stuff, and everybody so easy with everybody. Of course you can take the dog with you to the playground, Squirt's mom said. And here's a dollar in case you need to get some juice at the store. But he hadn't, because there was a water fountain in the park, and when he handed her back the money she looked at Squirt but didn't say anything. It was Squirt who said, Hey, that's your money, now, fella, for anything you want.

The house they took him to seemed huge. There were swings in the back yard, a basketball hoop on the side of the garage, and a ball to practise with. A fat grey cat lay in the sun, and when Jackie went over to pick him up, the cat began to purr even before Jackie spoke to him.

They let him poke around for a bit while the nosepickers talked to the lady. Then the lady showed him where he was going to sleep, a bottom bunk in a room with hockey player wallpaper. She showed him the room where the TV stayed, and told him the other kids would be home from school soon.

The nosepickers left and the lady put Jackie in her car and drove to Wal-Mart. She got him a whack of stuff, unders and socks and new jeans and more nice tee shirts than he'd ever had at one time in his life. Sneakers, too. High tops, the kind where each time you take a step there's this little light in the heel that flashes. Jeremy'd had some like that, once. Jackie had wanted some for a long time. The lady even got him new pyjamas. They had race cars on them.

When they got back she showed him which drawers were his, and he took all the tags off the clothes and put them away. Then he sat on his bottom bunk, trying to sort out everything he'd heard. Near as he could tell, Mom was in jail, or something. Maybe Aunt Lois, too.

The other kids came home from school and then it was suppertime. Jackie thought he'd be too scared to eat, all these faces, and not one of them the least bit familiar, but he ate, and ate lots. Hamburger patties, with gravy, lots of it, and mashed spuds and salad and pickles and thin-sliced green beans. They even had dessert, ice cream with cookies, chocolate chip ones. The best!

He felt like crying, but he wasn't going to do it if he could help it. At least the other kids didn't ask questions. He watched some TV and then when he started yawning the lady said bathtime and he had a deep warm soak, then dried himself as best he could and got into his race car pyjamas. The lady tucked him into bed and told him he was a good boy, and she left the light on in the hallway so he could find the bathroom if he needed it.

It would be okay, if only he had his mom. It would be real okay, except he didn't know where she was. Squirt was in the bush, cutting sticks. But where was Mom? For that matter, where was he? Well, he was here, in this bunk bed, but where was here? He sure did feel like crying.

/ / /

Rose sat between the two Mounties without handcuffs and nobody in the place had any idea that she wasn't just another of them. Anna worried that Rose would just leap up and rip off, but she also thought So what, she's not a mass murderer. If there's a victim in all this it's Rose herself. But part of Anna wanted Rose chained to the wall. The other victim, one of the other victims, was why everyone was gathered here.

And the other victim, Jenny, sitting beside Anna, looking like a graduate from charm school, cool, calm and collected, but she wasn't any of those things, how could she be and why should she be? She hadn't even known she had a half-brother until she didn't have him any more.

Just before the service started the chapel door opened and the boys from the facility came in, two by two, one older with one younger. Most of the younger boys had been weeping. Their eyes were red, some of them were sniffling and trying not to cry any more.

The older boy at the front was Tip, the one who had spoken to Anna in the hallway. He nodded politely at her. Anna nodded back and even managed a hint of a smile. The smaller boy walking with Tip stumbled and the older boy reached out, steadied the younger one, then took his hand as naturally and easily as if they were siblings.

The service was mercifully brief. No eulogy, no prattling on about a better world than this, no pretence that things were anything other than what they were. Remember thy creator in the days of thy youth, I shall lift up mine eyes unto the hills, yea though I walk through the valley of the shadow of death I shall fear no evil for verily I am the meanest son of a bitch in the whole damn valley.

And then they sang. Tip stood up and moved easily to the front of the chapel. He looked at Peter (and why, name of God, why was it an open coffin?), then turned, faced the mourners and sang, easily and clearly. How did a boy who had had the benefit of singing lessons wind up in juvie? You don't expect that. Singing lessons are supposed to mean something more, something safe.

then sings my soul my saviour lord to thee, how great thou art, how great thou art . . .

The look on the face of the juvie superintendent said that Tip was supposed to sit down now. But he didn't. He smiled, and the juvie boys stood up, some of them defiantly. The superintendent must be getting ready to blow a blood vessel, but rather than make a scene he sat biding his time, his jaw set.

the fox went out on a starry night, prayed for the moon to give him light, I've many a mile to go this night before I reach the town-oh

all of them singing. Anna felt as if she was on the verge of throwing herself to the floor and howling like a gutshot dog. She didn't, but when the boys started to sing "Puff the Magic Dragon," she couldn't hold back her tears. And then Jenny stood up, and something passed between her and Tip. Jenny sang, and Anna stood, tears coursing freely. Rose didn't move. Just as well, had she stood up Jenny might have lost it and knocked her back down again.

The last notes faded. The superintendent stood up and walked from the chapel. The boys followed him, but they had what would do very well for the last word. *Left* right, *left* right, they marched, deliberately slamming their left feet to the carpeted floor. *Left* right, *thump* step, *thump* step . . .

As Tip walked past her, Jenny slid from the pew and fell in step behind him. Anna followed her. The Mounties didn't move, and Rose sat between them staring straight ahead, dry-eyed. Anna didn't envy her one little bit.

Outside, the boys walked *thump* step along the sidewalk and up the few steps to the waiting bus. *Thump* step *thump* step, one older boy, one younger boy, the first ones moving to the very back of the bus, giving an illusion of discipline, of obedience, but the illusion shattered with each *thump* step *thump* step, up your *nose*, step, kiss my *ass*, step, bite mine forever.

/ / /

Just sitting where he was didn't seem to be the way to find his mom. She hadn't phoned, she hadn't come to see him, and even though he dialled her number and waited while the phone rang and rang and rang, she didn't answer. He thought maybe she was at Aunt Lois's place, but nobody answered the phone there, either.

Jackie didn't really think about it or plan it or make up his mind or anything like that. He just woke up, stared at the moonlight where it made a patch on his floor, then got up, pulled on clothes, picked up his shoes and left the house.

The entire backyard was silver-bright, the moon big in the dark night sky, and he could see almost as well as if it were daytime. He put on his sneaks, zipped his windbreaker over his Squirt-the-dragon sweater, and walked to the back gate. The alley looked and felt different than a street. You'd know it was an alley even if you'd never seen it before. No pavement, that was one thing, but it was more. The back walls of sheds, the pungent but pleasant odour of compost bins, different kinds of fences – picket fences, board fences, wire fences, some with gates, some without.

And there, leaning against a back fence, right next to a half-open gate, a bicycle! Someone must be awful rich. No lock chain or anything. Maybe nobody swiped stuff in this neighbourhood. But they must, because there were locks on doors like you wouldn't believe. No lock on this bike, though.

He didn't have any idea where he was going, but at least he wasn't staying in one place. He wished he'd thought to bring some food with him, though. He didn't have any money to buy anything.

/ / /

Tip lay staring at the wall, staring at nothing, looking into the green eyes of the little guy who'd gone out sideways. Sooey-sideways. He wasn't afraid of what Pete had done, but he was shit-scared of why he'd done it. Scared because sometimes Tip thought about it, too. Maybe not hanging, although he knew the kind of knot to use and had gone so far as to figure out the best place to do it. Outside. Shinny up the support pole, tie the end and do a dive over the basketball hoop. No strangling there, you'd break your neck for sure. Maybe rip your head off. That'd be final, God knows.

They were probably sitting around talking about how tragic it all was. Well, it was. But if they thought Pete had done it because he was sad, they had their heads farther up their fundaments than usual. People don't off themselves for sad. You cry for sad. When you go sideways it's because you're so angry, so frustrated, so furious, so fed right up that there's no other way to tell them and be heard.

Tip knew about telling and not being heard. When he tried to tell His Royal Freakfaced Self, he got these man-to-man bullshit lectures on how the pressures of work and the stress of the job and rah rah rah and three bags full. Complete with insincere talk about Just because I can no longer make myself live with your mother it doesn't change anything between me and you, you're my son, you will always be my son, and if you just stick it out, pretty soon, things will work themselves out.

Everything would work itself out a lot better if the cheapskate would just pay his damn child support. Put your face on the milk cartons, deadbeat dad, has the best of everything while his ex-family barely scrapes by. All the bumph and mumph about the dysfunctional this and the co-dependent that, and what it boiled down to is a squeeze not much older than Tip himself. Mom had looked right at him and laughed. She said Oh God, it's so trite and so tacky! Say what you want, find your excuses, it's just another tawdry male menopause crisis. The old man had yelled and hollered, nobody was telling him how to live his life, nobody was telling him he had to work his ass off to make enough money to keep a bunch of bloody parasites fat and happy, he'd spent too many years living by other people's rules but now, by God, he was his own man.

Sure. So while he pretended he was Mel Gibson, Mom headed off every day to her job, and he and Sis went to school, then rushed to part-time minimum wage jobs, and still it was not enough. And after a while it becomes a pain in the face. He tried to talk to his dad about it, man to man, and got told to mind his own business. When he hotly insisted it *was* his business, his dad slapped his face.

So Tip waited. Every now and again, and always for his own reasons, the old man said he wanted to spend the entire weekend with the kids. They'd go to his apartment and the phoney baloney would unwind. Everybody pretending things were exactly as they weren't – fine, just fine. And so, when the silly ass was out selling another house, and Tip was supposed to be reading a book or watching a video or playing in the apartment swimming pool or working out in the apartment gym, Tip had poked through drawers, looked at all the papers in the desk, looked through his father's socks and brand-new underwear, looked and looked until finally he had what he needed. It isn't hard when you're fuelled by hate. All's you need is a bit of luck, and everyone knows you make your own.

He knew he'd get caught at it someday, and he didn't care. If it had been a TV show he'd have been picked up before he got half a block, but TV and reality don't meet. He'd put the money from the cash machine in an envelope and left it on the floor in the hallway where it looked as if it had been shoved through the mail slot. Not too much of it. Mom would have known right away if it had been too much. And as it turned out the old man hadn't noticed for over four months. It must be nice to have so much coming in and so much socked away that the absence of three hundred a month passes without a ripple. And then it was another four months before the inevitable knock on the door and the boys in blue asking Mom if they could come in and talk to her about a slight problem. Come time for someone to ask him why he'd done it, he'd told them. They'd all of them told him time and time again, always tell the truth, dear. So he did.

The old man blew up. Probably not good for his image to have the cops, the probation people and the social worker know all about the unpaid thousands. If he'd said anything else there was a slight chance the old fart wouldn't have pressed charges. But Tip told them, even though he knew the balloon would go up for real. So the walking ego pressed charges. But hard head bumped into hard head and Tip told the judge, and by then the others, especially the social worker, had already started their routine. So maybe Tip wound up in this institute of lower learning, but the old man got hit and hit hard.

Then again, a judgment is nothing if nobody enforces it. Amazing, really. If you bought a car and didn't pay for it, wham, the arm of the law. Try to drive that car without paying for mandatory insurance, wham again, arm of the law. Kiss off your income tax return and see how long it takes them to collect it or slam your ass behind bars. But refuse to pay child support, ignore a court order for payment, and they don't seem to be able to find their arses to wipe them.

The green eyes just stared back at Tip. He wanted to talk to Pete, wanted to tell him . . . what?

It wasn't really Pete he wanted to tell. What he wanted to do was fire the bird right up the old man's nose. Why not? What more could they do? And if a guy could slip out of the joint, why couldn't he slip back in again? A guy could make a strong message, a guy could be heard, especially in the wee small hours, as Mom called them. Over the fence and you're out, over the fence and you're in. Time it right and you could get back over the fence and keep out of sight until the rest of the guys were marching lefty-righty two-by-two over to the mess hall for breakfast, which was always oatmeal porridge, skimmed milk, toast, eggs fried to the consistency of shoe soles, and a mystery meat that acted like bacon but wasn't. He'd like to see John trying to figure it out – not there for dorm roll call but spooning up oatmeal glup with the rest of them. Musta been caught in the can, sir. Been having some stomach problems, if you know what I mean. Sorry about that.

It might work.

And if it didn't? What the hey, eh.

/ / /

Jackie's legs ached. He was so tired he thought he might be sick to his stomach. He stopped often and peed but no matter how much he drained himself, he still felt as if he had to pee, as if at any moment it would come loose and flood down his leg. He wouldn't admit, even to himself, that he was scared stiff.

He didn't know where he was or where he'd been or where he was going, and he had no idea where his mother might be. There were no streetlights ahead of him and the last one was well behind him. Without them he was right in the middle of a black hole, and he didn't know if he was falling down it or flying up it. He couldn't even see where the road was.

He found out where it wasn't, though. With no warning, not even a flutter in his stomach, he was in the ditch. He didn't really get hurt. He'd had worse wipe-outs than this and hardly even blinked. But on top of the fear it was more than he could handle.

He huddled next to the wreck of a bike and sobbed. He wanted to scream but why bother? There wasn't anybody to hear him, and if anyone did, it would only be the cops.

Jackie tried to haul the bike up out of the ditch but the front wheel didn't want to turn. He couldn't even get the handlebars to turn properly. So he just left it where it was and started walking, not up on the road where a guy could wind up falling, but down in the ditch, where the worst that could happen was you'd bang into the bank.

He had no idea how long he walked. Several times he had to climb up out of the ditch and cross roads. It was that or crawl through the culvert and he wasn't going to do that, it was too scary.

And then, ahead of him, he saw what looked like a streetlight. His relief was enormous. He plodded toward it doggedly.

The all-night truck stop was small and the parking lot was huge, with plenty of room for the big eighteen-wheelers. Jackie felt almost happy walking between the huge trucks. It was wonderful to be so close to them, some of them still so new the chrome gleamed and the paint shone brightly under the many layers of buffed wax. Maybe he'd do that someday, drive a big truck. He'd seen a TV movie about a guy who drove a truck. The guy had a little dog that could do all sorts of tricks. And he had a little bunk bed behind the seat of the truck, so all he had to do was park the truck and take off his shoes and he could go to bed. When he got hungry, he stopped and had a hamburger and pie. And the guy met all different kinds of people!

Jackie peeked through the window of the diner. Some people were having coffee, and the waitress was talking to a woman with long curly hair. He wished he had some money so he could go in and buy a hamburger, but he didn't. Not enough, anyway. And he was tired, too tired to eat, probably.

He heard a sound and whirled, almost breaking into tears again. Parked between two of the huge trucks was a pickup truck with an aluminum canopy over the bed. The glass window-thing that closed the space between the tailgate and the roof was open and poking out, and the noise he had heard was coming from a medium-sized black dog. The dog was whining, but it didn't sound like it was sad, more like it was excited.

Jackie moved forward slowly, hand out, half afraid the dog would change its mind and take a chunk out of him. "Hey, dog," he breathed. "Hey, how are you?" The dog licked his hand, then pressed against it. Jackie could see into the canopy-covered space. Some boxes, same as if it was a camping trip. And on the floor of the pickup a slab of foam covered with what looked like a wide-open sleeping bag.

He didn't even think about it, he went up over the tailgate and crawled onto the foamie. He heaved a deep sigh that was more like a sob, and the dog lay beside him, warm against his back, making soft little comforting noises. The glow from the diner faded, and all that was left was the feel of the sleeping bag, the warmth and soft sounds of the dog's voice, the steady tip tip tip tip tip of its tail wagging steadily.

Mira left the diner and walked toward her pickup. Still hours to go, but at least driving at night meant she didn't have to bother with the near-gridlock that choked the highway during the day. "You okay, Dog?" she asked, and the dog whined reply. Mira tapped on the canopy and the dog rumbled, but it was her contentment sound, not a warning or a complaint.

The truck started easily.

/ / /

Getting out of the damn place was easy. All he had to do was what Pete had done. And it was easy to know what Pete had done because there he was, little spook, drifting like dandelion fluff, just out of reach. Tip lectured himself, told himself there was nothing there, Pete was just a piece of his own imagination. But it's hard to ignore the evidence of your own eyes. Well, the probation officer had as good as called Tip crazy, and maybe he was right. Jeez, what a dork that one was. Old Lefty-Righty himself. Why do they figure that just because someone put in thirty years in the Air Force they'd automatically make a first-class probation officer when they retired? Soft touch, though. Get your retirement pension as well as your proby pay. You know how it is, a few thousand here and a few thousand there and the next thing you know you're talking real money. But try as Tip might to distract himself, there it was, just in front of him, feet not touching the floor – Pete. Not the poor thing in the box, but Pete as he'd been before he dove out of this damn place. Tip hoped it hadn't hurt but was quite sure it had. And scared. Poor little bugger, scared like that. It's not right.

There was a big red bell on the wall in the corner, near the door, and wires running to it from a brass-or-something patch set into the doorjamb. Obviously the staff could lock the door and set the alarm, then if anyone opened the door the big old red bell would start clanging. If you ripped the wires loose, the noise would deafen you.

But Pete sort of drifted up and pointed. Tip grabbed a chair and stood on it. He could see where the clanger bar had been bent, then straightened. He grinned, then reached out and yarded on the round knob, bending it away from the red bell. Then, because he was feeling particularly owly, he reefed on it again. Try to straighten the bugger this time and it'll snap off in your hand, John-oh. Old sock, old fart, old pal.

And just like that, it was done. Nothing to it. Down off the chair and turn the deadbolt, yank on it and shove. The door opened. The contact between the brass plate in the door and the matching one in the frame was broken, the clanger bar started vibrating madly but the bent-back knob didn't come near the bell casing and there was no clanging alarm. Laughing softly, Tip headed out into the night. He ran across the dew-damp front lawn, then jumped, his fingers and toes hooking into the diamond-weave wire of the fence, moving quickly, hauling with his arms, shoving with his legs, up the fence. He was ready for the four strands of barbed wire on the top. He had a spare sweatshirt gripped in his teeth and now he chucked it over the wire, covering the barbs. He still snagged his jacket, and sort of hung there for a moment, but then the fabric ripped and he was down, landing on the grass, laughter burbling from his throat.

He headed off down the road, toward the train tracks, and as he jogged, he sang to himself: There was a man in our town and he was wondrous wise, he had a goat with horns, sir, that went right up to the skies, and didn't he ramble, ramble, he rambled till the butcher cut him down. Oh, the ram had two horns made of bone and another one made of brass, the bone came out of his head sir and the brass came out of his foot and didn't he ramble, ramble, he rambled till the butcher cut him down.

Where the tracks cut at right angles across the road, Tip pulled a right and headed toward the bush. If they did find him missing the cops would drive up and down the roads looking for him, but who would think of train tracks? It was as if the more planes they put in the sky the less attention got paid to the trains. No way to hitch a ride, maybe, but he wasn't in that big a rush. Now that the damn place was behind him he didn't feel so interested in trying to break back in again. They wanted him, they'd have to catch him.

SIXTEEN

"Look at them! Just look at them! Now that he's dead they can't get enough of him!" Fran waved at the TV as if it was to blame for the crowd on the sidewalk outside the funeral home. "You watch, tomorrow's paper will have an editorial and a feature on the short life and sad death of Peter Baxter, and the stuffed shirts will stand up in the legislature and demand answers to questions that they ought to have asked ten years ago. The harrumph harrumph minister of social services will stay up late tonight reading the file full of computer print-outs and faxes, and he'll actually lose sleep worrying about all the things that could have been avoided if he'd taken some interest before the fact instead of after. And then, with his ass in the hot seat, he'll pass the buck and dump the whole load on the social worker, who couldn't do his job properly because of policy!"

"Easy there, Frannie –"

"And why should I go easy, Lizzie? Why should I? Where were they when we were hiding under the goddamn floorboards? Where were they when you were getting your face rearranged, or when they took the three of us and put us in three different places and then took my flesh and blood away from me? They changed their names! They turned them into strangers! That little guy took a long cold look at what we call civilization and he killed himself. Well, maybe he did the smartest thing any of us ever did."

Liz couldn't remember when she'd seen Fran look so terrible. A person would think she had some kind of flu, except it had gone on too long. This hour with the TV news was an unusual occurrence. Fran rarely came upstairs even for coffee, and when she did she just sat staring into her mug. Sometimes she got up from the table and headed back to her glowing screen without so much as sipping.

Sometimes Liz made a sandwich, took it down and put it on the desk at Fran's elbow, with a big glass of milk. Sometimes the sandwich got eaten, sometimes it sat there and got dry at the edges and the milk wound up fit only for Scarlett O'Hairy.

"Is she going to come up for supper?"

"Auntie Liz, you have to understand, when she's like this we just have to let her do it. One way or the other she takes care of herself, okay? It might be at four in the morning when the rest of the house is sound asleep, but she takes care of herself."

"But she's hardly eating!"

"Listen, four out of five people on God's green earth endure for years on less nutrition than she's getting. She'll go on one of these marathons and then all of a sudden she'll stop it. She'll have a bath. She'll eat a ton of food. She'll go to bed and sleep fourteen hours, get up, eat like a pig, have another bath, go back to bed and sleep again and then she'll be fine for a week or so, and it's time for another jag."

"Oh, Andy."

"Some people go on drinking binges," Andy shrugged. "Mom does this."

"Has she heard from Ritchie?"

"Yeah. He phoned and she gave him a blast of shit like I haven't heard her give anyone in my life."

Liz could imagine. Fran came from a long line of expert shit-slingers. All she could do was stay out of the way, make sandwiches, take bowls of soup downstairs, and try to not say or do the wrong thing.

And one day Fran pulled away from her computer, just as Andy had predicted. She soaked in a tub of hot water and bubbles, then got dressed and announced she was heading into town.

"Want some company?" Liz asked, almost shyly.

"I'm just going malling," Fran answered.

"Mauling?"

"You know, shopping mall. Today's version of the village square. The unofficial news exchange. The only place you can find out what real people are actually thinking, doing and saying, because the media sure isn't going to tell you."

It promised to be a very heavy expedition, but Liz went anyway. There was a kind of brittleness to Fran that made Liz afraid something would be said or not said, done or not done, and Fran would shatter, like one of those old windows that just give up and turn to dust for no reason anyone can pinpoint.

One section of the mall had been designed as a place to sit down with a cup of coffee or a soft drink and just collect your thoughts. Maybe you were supposed to count your last bit of money before heading off to put yourself in the poorhouse. Fran headed to the sitting-down place as unerringly as a salmon swimming to its spawning bar.

She smoked one cigarette after another, watching people go into and come out of the supermarket. She stared at people's faces, practically eating their images with her eyes, and Liz watched, knowing something else was going on in her cousin's head. Abruptly, Fran got up and headed off. Liz followed, although Fran didn't seem to remember she had company. Or maybe she was just too spacey from all the coffee and cigarettes.

Fran wandered up and down the aisles in the department store, fingering the sleeves of garments she had no intention of wearing, stopping to stare at a display of kids' toys, standing in the electrical section as if she was really contemplating buying a brass-and-cut-glass chandelier to hang in the dining room she didn't have.

They lunched at the fast food outlet in Woolco. Each of them ordered a Fish Platter, little triangles of something which might once have been alive and swimming, dipped in a batter and cooked in a microwave, accompanied by objects supposed to be French fries but as likely to be pieces of cedar shingle as potato. Dessert was something sweet and doughy covered with a whipped topping which had nothing to do with cream. Halfway through it Fran looked up and grinned widely, and for a moment Liz felt as if they were both ten years old again, sitting on a branch of the big cedar tree, telling each other off-colour jokes.

"Ain't science wunnaful?" Fran hissed. "All these calories and not a drop of nourishment anywhere."

"A person could get fat as a pig and die of malnutrition," Liz agreed. "So . . . why come here? I mean, just across the mall is a deli that has great sandwiches, whole grain bread and fresh sprouts and all kinds of good stuff. They make their own soup, and use real ingredients, and we're sitting here?"

"Think about the people who go to the deli, Liz, then look at the people here. Look at the faces, the eyes, the cheekbones. There's something about poor that shows. You look at these people and you know their parents were born to poor people, grew up poor, married poor, and had kids who grew up poor. Over at the deli people might be having a bit of a problem with cash flow but they don't have that look."

"So?"

"So this is where we started out, kiddo. This is where the low rent, the trash and the tacky come. This is where the peripherals and outcasts feel comfortable. Remember how sometimes, on payday, our moms would go into town for groceries? And if we were good, and if it was a fat paycheque, and if, and if, if and if, we might get taken to the Esquire or the Modern? Which they called the Modrun? Remember? And they'd have tea made in those little fat green porcelain-or-something teapots, and we'd get a glass of Orange Crush."

"I don't remember that."

"You don't remember? What's with you? Do you remember the time the old man dipped deep and forked over money and we all got taken down to Bond's Fish'n'Chips and we thought we'd died and gone to heaven?"

"I remember working at a fish'n'chips shop, I don't remember being taken to one to eat."

"Jesus, what a head case. You musta caught one roundhouse right too many on the side of the head." She winked to take the sting out of her words. "I'm told if you get slammed on the left side of the head you go to sleep, but if you get bashed on the right side you go groggy and then you pass out and then when you wake up you're as apt as not to have no memory of getting hit. A bonk on the left side you remember. Or so they say. So he musta done a good job on your right hemisphere."

"What has that got to do with us, here, today, pushing this glorified cardboard down our throats as if we enjoyed it?"

"Probably nothing. Except that when I need to take a peek

from a safe distance, this is how I do it. Remember the five'n'dime? And the long counter."

"Oh, God, yes," Liz laughed softly. "And remember us sitting there having a dish of ice cream and when we looked out through the big front window there was my dad prancing down the sidewalk as if he owned the whole goddamn town, and this woman hanging off his arm like an umbrella?"

"Yeah. And I said if that was *my* dad I'd go out and give his twist a punch in the eye and you said shit, I'd wear out my knuckles, half the town's ladies are his twists."

"Right."

"You know they'd all go to jail for child abuse if it was going on now."

"No. It wasn't that bad."

"Give your fuckin' head a shake, Lizzie! I remember one time, not long ago, you said to me you felt sometimes as if you were going crazy. Well, kiddo, you aren't going crazy. You're just starting to come back from crazy."

"Oh, eat your damn mystery-wotzis," Liz laughed easily, racking the whole thing up to another of Fran's creations.

"She does that," Andy explained that evening, as she and Liz watched "Mary, Queen of Scots" on TV, Glenda Jackson and Vanessa Redgrave locked in emotional combat which probably had nothing to do with real politics or history. "It's like she's a sponge, and she squeezes so much of herself into the keyboard she has to rush off and sit in soak-mode, hauling it back in. She'll come home sometimes and if you ask her what she did, she'll talk about people's hands, how some people have their life history written in the knuckles of their mitts. Other times she can't see anything but all the grossly obese people there are in town, and trying to figure out what that means in a world where four out of five people go to bed hungry at night. She's got this theory that the guilt of knowing that is what makes fat people gorp themselves fatter."

"It was," Liz admitted, "a very . . . *odd* afternoon."

Two days later Fran caught the eight-fifteen bus out of town and went down to the city to spend time with Ritchie's ex-wife and her three kids. She came back six hundred dollars poorer, but somehow calmer.

"I bought them all a bunch of clothes," she explained, shrugging. "They were looking shabby, and I hate to see them looking shabby when there's no excuse for it. They all said they wanted to come up and visit so I told them to wait until I finish this book and then we'll have a holiday. I'll find something so they won't be underfoot. Maybe – oh, I don't know, camping in a motel or something?"

"Bring them here if you want," Liz said quietly. "It's not as if I'm going to put pillows over their heads at night."

"You mustn't worry about me, Busy Lizzie," Fran said softly. "I'm not cracking up, you know. This is how I work stuff out, is all. It's not fatal. Only terminal."

/ / /

Jenny could not believe anybody would have the audacity to never tell her she had a brother. Who had the right to do that? All right, so the names were different. They'd found out fast enough once the poor little sib was dead, why couldn't they take a minute to find out while he was still alive? They asked everything else. Where were you born, what education do you have, who filled your grandmother's back teeth, did your great-grandfather play the fiddle, how high is up? Questions, questions, questions and more questions, but never the ones that counted. If she had known, maybe she could have seen him, they could have visited, maybe she could have picked up the phone and dialled and

"Hi, Pete?"

"Yeah. Jenny?"

"Yeah. Wanna go to the movies?"

"Hey, great! Meet you there?"

"No, I'll come by and pick you up."

"I'll be ready."

and she'd have dressed casual for it, no big deal, just a big sister taking her little brother to a movie. Sneakers, jeans, tee shirt, denim jacket, and she'd ask for a transfer when she got on the bus. Get off at the corner and run to the house where Pete was staying. Maybe one of those big three-storey jobbies in the east end. Ring the doorbell and no waiting, no cooling the heels, the door opens, and there's Pete, with his sun-bleached hair falling over his forehead, his big green eyes sparkling up at her, the grin with the space between the front teeth

"Hi, Jen."

"C'mon, sib, let's go!"

and they'd go off together, not holding hands or anything sappy like that, just moving together down the sidewalk, and people looking at them would know they were brother and sister. Siblings. A family, for Christ's sweet sake!

"How's school."

"Okay. Except for history."

"Yeah? Hey, I'm good in history. Bring your book over to my eff-aitch tomorrow and I'll help you with it."

"Yeah? Thanks," and then a pause. "What's an eff-aitch, Jen?"

"Eff for foster, aitch for home. Foster home."

"Oh. Eff-aitch, huh?"

"Yeah. And a foster mom is an eff-em, and then there's eff-dee, and eff-bees and eff-esses."

"Am I your eff-bee?"

"Naw, you're my sib."

"Yeah!"

and in the movie she'd get him popcorn, and he'd sit beside her eating it and wiping his hands on a paper napkin. After the movie they'd talk about what they'd seen, and she'd take him back to his eff-aitch. They'd stand on the porch and he'd hug her, shy, but glad she'd thought to call him.

"Don't forget now, you bring that history around tomorrow. Come in the afternoon, and after you've learned everything there is to know about everything, we'll go to the park or something."

But they wouldn't go to the park. Not ever. And he'd never had the chance to grab her and give her a hug. She'd had hugs from eff-esses and eff-bees, from little effs whose shoelaces she'd tied and from big effs who'd brushed her hair, but never a hug from her own sib.

Maybe something inside her had known all along she had a sib out there somewhere. Maybe that's why Brucie was so important to her. Brucie was already in the eff-aitch when Jenny was brought in, transferred from an aitch that hadn't worked out for anybody, not the pees, not Jenny herself. For sure not Jenny herself, she'd hated every minute she'd spent in it.

And then they helped her pack her stuff in supermarket shopping bags and she'd ridden to the new place in the worker's car. She was scared. She was always scared in a new aitch. Every new

place was full of new people, and all of them determined to fart
wonders and shit miracles with your life. How many times had
she heard a mom say to a dad about a new kid, "It'll take a while,
and it'll be work, but we'll have him shaped up before you even
know it," or heard a mom say to a neighbour, "Honestly, it would
just make your hair stand on end to know some of the stuff these
kids have seen and heard and had done to them." Yeah, hair,
stand on end!

They looked at you like you were a bug, and then there was
all the stuff about new rules and new ways of doing things, and
no matter how good your table manners were it was Don't eat so
fast or Don't eat so slow, and you got taught all over again at
each place how to get soup from the bowl to your mouth. Make
you feel like they're doing you a big favour and all the time they
get paid for doing it.

But Brucie was at that place. And he'd winked at her right
away. She knew he'd be a friend, knew right away he was a foster, too. Shaggy dark hair, big dark eyes, a chip out of his front
tooth. He told her it was from a fight. Then he told her someone
threw a rock at him. Once he said he fell off his bike. And finally he told her the truth. His dad had punched him out. Well, if
your own dad did a thing like that you'd make up stories about
what happened too.

There were two eff-esses and an eff-bee in the house, and
they were okay, but it was Jenny and Brucie who became a unit.
Once she heard the mom say to the dad they should keep an eye
on "those two" because after all, they were both starting to grow
up and you just never knew, it wasn't as if they were *real* brother and sister.

But it was. Or as close to it as Jenny had ever come. And for
three years, from eleven to fourteen, they'd been in the same foster home. Then it was just like in that mouldie oldie, Here we go
again, I hear the trumpet blow again, on the go again, and she'd
been sent to one place, Brucie to another.

But there was always the phone. And after a while they didn't
even need the phone, each knew where the other would be after
seven at night. Video arcade, here I come! And the eff-bee saying, But Jenny, what is there in that silly place? You go there all
the time. You aren't wasting your allowance on those silly
machines, are you?

Even if she was, which she wasn't, whose goddamn allowance was it, anyway? They didn't have to sweat blood to get the money. There was a cheque every month to pay for her food, her clothes, her share of the hot water and electricity and sheets and everything else. More than enough. Plenty more than enough. And anyway, Jenny had jobs.

One of the best babysitters I ever had, one woman said. The very best, another said. Jenny, they said, you have such a way with children, how do you do it? Oh, she said, I get along good with kids. Why, I used to be one myself! and everyone laughed.

She paid for her own clothes. Bought her own shoes. Bought her own schoolbooks and supplies. So the foster parents could just put all that in their own pockets as if the welfare was paying them. And what about all the times she looked after their kids for them, and the laundry she did on the weekends and the dishes and helping with the tidying-up and making supper? She paid her own way. Nobody could ever say she didn't pay her own way.

Brucie was at the arcade, leaning against the wall, laughing and teasing some other kids. As soon as he saw Jenny he broke away from the others and came over to her, put his arm around her shoulders and gave her a big hug.

"Hey, Jen, what's wrong?" he asked, and she told him. He kept his arm around her shoulder, walked her away from the arcade and the other kids, and listened while she talked about Pete and the awful farce of a funeral and how she'd never even known he was alive and by the time she found out about him, he wasn't alive.

"Hey," Brucie said softly, "you sound like someone who could use a toke."

"You know it, brother!" She blinked rapidly, glad Brucie understood what hadn't been said. They went for a walk along the sea wall and shared two numbers, watching the gulls and ducks at the mouth of the small, grungy river, the traffic tie-up on the bridge, the power boats in the harbour.

Ripped and silly they caught the Townsite bus, and walked from the bus stop to a place where Brucie knew there was a party.

stereo blaring, smoke thick in the room,
beer bottles lined against the wall, all

around the living room, like decorations
two boys arguing in the kitchen
a girl crying in the bathroom
Brucie laughing, snapping the tab off a
can of beer and handing it to her

At two-thirty in the morning they left the party with half a dozen others and walked along the sidewalk, drinking beer from cans, joking, shoving, laughing. A supermarket shopping cart over-turned in the ditch caught Brucie's attention.

"C'mon, Jen," he shouted, "give your feet a rest!" And Jenny climbed in the shopping cart and lay back, laughing, her feet in the air, higher than her head, drinking beer, and then they were racing down the street singing and laughing, pushing Jen in the shopping cart, being silly and having fun

and the police car arrived
Brucie was laughing, pulling at her arm, trying to get her out
of the shopping cart
Police coming from the car

"Run, Brucie!" she said, laughing crazily, pushing at his shoulder. Brucie almost tripped, but he ran off laughing. Jenny tumbled back into the shopping cart, giggling, almost helpless.

"Hi-ho Silver!" Brucie yelled, "awaaaaaaay!"

And awaaaaaaay it was. The police had her before Brucie realized she wasn't following him. He whirled and started back to get her, but Jenny waved him off and he turned and ran.

"Well, hi, guys." Jenny got herself out of the cart, beer can clutched in her hand. One of the cops reached out to take her arm and she spun, heaving the can as hard as she could. It arced through the air and over the bank. She heard it rattling down the rocks but she didn't hear the splash when it went into the chuck.

"Not a good move, kid," one of the cops glared at her.

"Oh, bite my bum." Jenny tried to walk away, pretending she was the Queen of the Universe. But it wasn't that easy. It never is.

At the police station she refused to tell them where she lived, just sat on a chair. The three hash brownies she'd eaten just before they left the house were catching up with her now.

Everything was hilariously funny, even the anger in the eyes of the cops. *Especially* the anger in the eyes of the cops. She knew they'd like to give her a good slap, and that was funny, too.

Except the next thing you know there's the damn social worker coming through the door, looking bleary-eyed and fed up. And not the usual one, not the guy with the jeans, white shirt, tie, suit jacket, acting like he was just people and not a dink.

"This," she was laughing like a fool and couldn't stop, "is an unexpected surprise."

"That makes two of us," Anna agreed. "Come on. Let's go."

"Aaaaah-*right!*" Jenny came off the bench in a hurry, still ripped. "Let's blow this pop stand! Bye bye, guys, don't work too hard."

Anna wasn't smiling or laughing or even very talkative. They found a Smitty's and went in for breakfast, Jenny still giddy and unconcerned.

"Listen," she told Anna, "it's no big deal. There were a dozen of us, right? A dozen kids, none of us with a police record or anything. Just having a party, right? Shoving a shopping cart down the street. Now, do you see eleven sets of heartbroken parents sitting here? Seems to me if eleven of the twelve are still Simon-pure, the twelfth shouldn't be the sinner of all time! What's the difference between nice kid and juvie-d? Getting caught?"

"I didn't call you a juvenile delinquent," Anna protested.

"Ah, lighten up, will ya?"

"It's very hard to lighten up when you've only had a few hours' sleep."

"Yeah? Oughta go to bed at a decent hour, then," Jenny lectured, and Anna started laughing. "That's better! You know what they say, Laugh and the world laughs at you, cry and they all stand around and throw rocks."

They had pancakes and coffee, then Jenny agreed to go back to the eff-aitch.

"You're in no condition to go to school," Anna pointed out.

"Come off it," Jenny laughed. "At any given time one-third of any class is ripped. The ones not ripped on grass are ripped on doctor drugs. And half the teachers are so hungover they wouldn't notice if the seats were full or empty."

Anna went back to her apartment, had a shower and changed out of the jeans and sweatshirt she had pulled on when the phone went off and the official voice asked for the Duty Worker.

One of these days God would add up all her brownie points and reward her by giving her a job where one night a week didn't find her on call. You will be known in heaven for good works done here on earth. And if you keep missing four-hour stretches of what ought to be sleep, you might wind up in heaven one helluva lot sooner than you had planned.

The shower cleared her head but it didn't take the grit out from behind her eyes. She collected her briefcase and the papers she'd worked on the night before, and went down to the underground. No paper under her wiper, no blue van parked where it could give her the heebie-jeebies. She drove to work and even got her own parking place.

But you don't get that much good luck in less than an hour without having to pay for it. Someone had managed to get hold of Jackie's mother, and there she was waiting for Anna, with her sister as backup, and both of them had blood in their eyes.

"Where in hell is my kid!" was the opener.

"We don't know," Anna said quietly. "We've got the police looking for him."

"Those idiots! They can't find their heads to scratch them. You're the smart-ass know-it-alls who took him in the first place! If you'd'a minded your own business, none of this would have happened."

That was the start of it. It went on and on, and got rougher, until finally Anna snapped.

"Everybody else is at fault but you, aren't they?" she said coldly. "It's everyone else's responsibility. If you have nothing constructive to add, no ideas on how to improve the situation, you might take the time to consider that if you had stayed sober, if you had taken proper care of him, the court wouldn't have apprehended him in the first place."

"You got no right to talk to me like that!" the woman yelled.

"Probably not," Anna agreed. "But you don't have any right to talk to me the way you've been talking."

"You're the one snatched him in the first place!"

"No," Anna said clearly. "It was not me, nor any other person in this office. It was the law. The law and the government. And the government, I might remind you, does what the people of the community want done. Which means *nobody* thought you were doing a good enough job with Jackie. And you know yourself it wasn't good enough. He deserves better. He deserves a lot better."

It was true, you weren't supposed to talk to them like that. But what the hell, she thought wearily, who wants this job any more anyway? Let them fire me, maybe I'll get a good night's sleep.

They left, both of them madder than wet hens, and Anna would have bet ten dollars they were heading for the nearest bar to air every grievance, real or imagined, then move on to another bar and rehash it again. Two sisters, and not a brain working between them. Four kids, and all of them in care. No time or money to find out why, no time or money or energy to intervene in an ongoing crisis, no counselling or therapy or support, just snatch the kids and hope. After a while you don't even pray any more, you just hope, with a sort of exhausted habitude, like when you keep chewing gum long after the flavour is gone and your jaw is sore and your tongue is raw. Because you don't know what you'll do if you stop chewing. Maybe you'll blow up the world.

She was ready for bed, walking toward the television set to turn it off, when they flashed on a picture of Jackie, looking almost unbelievably beautiful. The news anchor looked appropriately shocked and appalled. "Almost two weeks ago young Jackie Parker was made a ward of the province, taken from his mother and put in a foster home. Tonight, young Jackie Parker is the subject of an intensive police search, and his mother is demanding answers to some questions." The picture of Jackie disappeared, replaced by a photo of his mother.

"It's a great story," Anna shouted at the television set, "and wouldn't it be greater if you could sober her up long enough to get her on camera! But you can't put her on, because she'll blow the story for you. As soon as she opens her mouth, the question won't be Where is Jackie, it'll be Why should that cow get on TV?"

Disgusted, she turned off the set and went to her bedroom, snapping off the lights with too much force. She flung herself on the bed, buried her face in her pillow, and wept. When weeping wasn't enough, she bawled, and that helped.

/ / /

"Oh my God!" Fran sounded as if she'd been punched in the stomach.

"What?" Liz half-rose from her chair and reached out a hand.

"That's Jackie!" Fran pointed at the TV. "That's the little kid Ritchie . . . that's Ritchie's ex-girlfriend's little boy!"

"You're kidding."

"I'm not kidding. I'm telling you, that's Jackie!"

The visit with Ritchie's ex hadn't been quite as easy a trip as she'd made out to Liz. It had been stiff and awkward, with long pauses in the conversation, pauses during which one or the other of them pried a foot out of her mouth and hoped the other hadn't taken umbrage.

What in hell kind of mind would decide the name given by its parents didn't fit its personality? And what in hell kind of mind would then decide that the name which did fit was "Sugar"? Fran had all she could do not to tell the truth about it. "Oh, I knew some people lived down the street from us and they had a boxer called Sugar. It got hit by a car and was dead before they got to it, so they bought another one and called it SugarToo." That would have ripped it. SugarThree would not have appreciated it at all.

So there sat Sugar, with more hair than a pomeranian, and you knew just looking at it she spent lots and lots of money getting the mane styled, streaked and blow-dried. The end result was the look of someone who'd stuck her head out of the car in a windstorm. More goddamn hair than an angora goat! Fingernails, too. Sugar had the nails of a Chinese mandarin.

She sat with one leg curled under her while she drank enough coffee to buy the plantation barons in Brazil another yacht. Coffee and cigarettes and television, and then the kids came home from school and at some point something called supper got thrown together.

"Would you like to come with me?" Sugar asked pleasantly enough. "It's my bingo night."

"No, thanks. But don't stay home on my account, I'll stay here with the kids. Save you the price of a sitter."

"Oh, they don't need a sitter! They know how to look after themselves," and off she went, her jeans so tight the back seam went into the crack of her ass. You'd think when she sat down it would cut her in two. And what, Jesus, ever convinced some young women jeans were made to be worn with high heels? Pantyhose underneath, skin-tight jeans over top, trippy trippy high heels – what does it all do to your pelvis?

Off she went, buttocks jiggling snugly, the White Trash Princess of All Time, to go sit in the bingo hall and pray that she won the super jackpot, because then maybe she could pull herself out of the other jackpot in which she was stuck.

The kids did know how to look after themselves. No fighting and squabbling, no punching each other out then tattletaling when Mom came back from bingo. Not those three. They'd learned early on that the only ones they had to depend on were each other. When Gowan headed to the kitchen to get a peanut butter and honey sandwich he made three, matter-of-factly, and brought them back to the living room. He handed the extras to Gavin and Emma, then looked at Fran and almost did a double-take. "This one is yours," he said, handing it to her and going back to make a fourth for himself.

"Thank you," she smiled, and ate the sandwich.

Then she asked the kids if they would be okay alone for ten minutes or so. They nodded, amazed that she would even ask. She hurried to the corner store and brought home two bags of chips, cheezies and soda pop. "Join me?" she invited. That did something to break down the curtain of uneasiness between them.

At nine-thirty they went to bed. No needing to be told, no ditzing around, just up and off they went. Unfortunately not one of them thought to brush their teeth. Fran said nothing. Why confuse them? She cleaned up the chip bags and empty pop cans and sat watching the tube until Sugar came in, long, *long* after every bingo game in the western hemisphere had closed. She brought with her some fugitive from the tar pits who looked as if he'd had one nourishing meal in his life and it had stuck in his throat, leaving a big lump.

"This is my friend," Sugar said. "And this is my ex-husband's mother."

"Fran," she nodded.

"Hi," he said.

Sugar didn't ask how the kids were, or whether they had been good. She cranked open a couple of beer, handed one to Him With No Name, perched in her chair and turned her baby blues to the TV. Fran finished her pop, excused herself and headed off to climb into bed with Emma. In the morning No Name was still there. Ah well, to each her own.

No Name either didn't have a job or was on a good stretch of days off. He came and went whenever the mood struck him. He and Sugar headed off every night right after supper, not always saying they were going to bingo. Fran began to suspect Sugar seldom made it to the bingo hall. Well, why should she? And what was wrong with her going out, anyway? The father of those kids wasn't exactly going to any trouble to look after them twenty-four hours a day.

"He's okay," Gowan said. "He gets nasty sometimes but all he does is snarl some, it's not like he hits or anything."

"Danny did," Emma glared. "Danny was always hitting."

"He was a goof," Gavin agreed. "But he didn't hang around for long. He kept having car trouble," and the kids howled with laughter.

"Gavin did it," Emma whispered, snuggling against Fran. "He put something in the gas tank. Danny had to take his car to the garage and drain out all the gas and get his tank fixed."

"Show him, I guess," Gavin cackled.

Saturday Fran headed off with the three little toughies and spent most of the day in the children's clothing section of a couple of department stores. Then they went for pizza. There was something stiff and almost defiant about Sugar when they got home loaded down with packages, the kids grinning and laughing and reeking of pizza.

"That's nice of you," she said, and for a moment Fran got a glimpse of what it was like to be Sugar. "They don't get a lot of new stuff."

"There's no excuse for that," Fran said. "I'll try to do better."

"You shouldn't have to do it," Sugar snapped. "I'd like to see those goddamn judges raise a kid on a hundred bucks a month!"

"I'd like to see even one goddamn judge raise a kid."

A look passed between them, and in the brief time the look was alive, Fran felt she knew Sugar. It was almost as if she had *been* Sugar at several points in her life.

She wanted to say Listen, I thought I had raised him to know better, I thought I had raised him to do better. I didn't think Ritchie would bop off and leave his kids in a pickle, I'm sorry, I thought I'd done a better job . . . But she couldn't say it. She *had* raised him to know better. If he didn't know, it was because he didn't want to know.

"It's as if somewhere along the line they got things confused with a bloody hockey game," she said to Andy and Liz when she got home, "and someone has to lose so someone else can win. Ritchie's convinced any money he sends goes into her pocket, or right into bingo. But bingo hasn't got anything to do with it. If the poor stupid thing stayed home all the time he'd find some other reason to punish her. Because if she wins anything at all, even a fifty-dollar jackpot at bingo, he thinks he has lost."

"Oh, Mom," Andy said. "Why don't you just face facts?"

"What facts?"

"There's nothing wrong with their situation. There must be twenty thousand other kids in exactly the same setup! There's a lot of people would think that was normal. I mean, just because it isn't what you would do, doesn't mean there's anything wrong with it. So it's not the Waltons, so what? You know that whole thing about carefree childhood, best years of our lives, and all that is just a big crock of poop. What are you really getting yourself tied up in knots about?"

"Have you got your homework done?" Fran glared.

"Never you mind about my homework. If it's not done it's my lookout, not yours. So they didn't brush their teeth. There's worse things. At least nobody knocked their teeth outta their heads, okay?"

"I liked you better when you went to bed at seven o'clock at night and didn't give me lectures all the time."

"No you didn't."

"Yes I did."

"No you didn't."

"I'm going to my hell hole," Fran said firmly. "Anyone who disturbs me is taking their life in their hands."

"Atta girl," Andy agreed. "Crawl into your hole and block the entryway with a rock. Best thing to do. Get to work, make some money, keep me in the style to which I intend to become accustomed. About time!"

And when Fran was gone Andy looked at Liz and almost jumped into her lap, so quickly Liz was caught off guard, and snuggled up tight, trembling. Liz put her arms around the kid and hugged, and stroked Andy's back while she wept.

"There, there," Liz soothed, "there, darling, I know. I know, and it's okay, Andy, please try to believe that."

"It's *not* okay," Andy sobbed.

"No, it's not. It never has been. That's okay, baby. You cry. Because I don't know if I can."

/ / /

Tip reached out, turned on the car radio, cranked the volume and drove his father's pride and joy down the freeway with the sounds of an old-fashioned New Orleans jazz band belting out "Old Rugged Cross," swinging it the way no Sunday school Tip had ever had to attend had done it.

Pity. Maybe if they had, more people would go to Sunday school.

Nothing to it. No thing to it. There's no problem getting into a building no matter how secure the owner says it is. No problem. And a blind quadriplegic could have jimmied the lock on the old fart's door.

It was so easy. He simply slid open the panel on the phone, popped and pocketed the batteries, closed it up and put the phone back, useless as tits on a teddy bear. Then into his father's bedroom and search every pocket in every pair of expensive pants, every stylish jacket. And when the money and all, and all, and all was in his pocket, out with the tubes of Krazy Glue and just see how long it takes to get these expensive rags off the hangers, and when you do, see how much good they are.

All those years! All those pinch-penny watch-the-budget years! Going to the Sally Ann for clothes, eating brown rice. Look at this place. Bigger than the place Mom, Ange and Tip all lived in together. Why? Because the old fart didn't pay his child maintenance, is why. Into court for another order to pay and back home again with the court order and you could use it to wipe your butt because he just did not pay. And the clerk tsk-tsking and saying Well, if we put him in jail we have to feed him, and it might ruin his career.

Thanks, old fart. From closet to big fancy waterbed. A tube of glue here, a tube of glue there, and the sheets are firm to the mattress, the blankets tight to the fancy dark wood frame.

In the bathroom he glued the faucets so they wouldn't turn, glued the plug so it couldn't be removed from the tub and glued the shower lever so it would never turn on again.

He went through every drawer, taking whatever struck his fancy, and gluing the rest into a solid glob of expensive fabric. Every pair of leather shoes was Krazy Glued to the floor, won't go far in them now, my paternal parental unit. He rifled the jewellery box, took a watch and some things he knew he could pawn, slipped a gold set tiger's-eye ring on his finger and grinned when it almost fit. Then he pocketed the spare set of car keys, and after that it was so easy he almost blew it by laughing himself helpless.

He waited in the fire stairwell, watching the elevator through a small crack in the barely-opened door. Who uses the fire stairs? Who would notice if the door was open a tiny crack? Nobody, that's who.

When his father went into the apartment, Tip hurried to the door, shoving the little pointed cap-spout of the Krazy Glue into the keyhole and emptying the tube into the lock mechanism.

Then he took the elevator down to the underground parking lot, crossed to the car, the beloved car, the all-important car, the ego-demonstration car, and got in, and the rest was strawberry shortcake. Jesus, wouldn't it just about burn their little butts if he drove up in front of the facility, tooted the horn and the joint emptied, kids pouring from everywhere, piling into the car, and then they all drove off and had a total blast?

He stopped on a side street long enough to search the car and find the travel card hidden in the most obvious place in the world, the glove compartment. Come on, Dad, I'd hoped for better from you.

Oh, Tip, I had such hopes for you . . .

Or maybe he should just drive up, park the chrome boat next to John's cheesy little old Volks, walk right up and through the main door, and turn himself in so he could howl with laughter even as they closed the Green Room door behind him. Might be some satisfaction in that one, because sooner or later it's the Green Room. All roads lead to the Green Room.

So there you are, sir. Home from work, sir.

What will you do first, sir?

Change your clothes, sir?

And then what? Do you head for the door first, or do you grab up the phone? Oh, there he is in his boxer shorts, face grim, eyes slitted with rage, trying to get the cops on the scene. And the phone doesn't work! Ha ha ha ha. So back to the bedroom, grab up the clothes he'd just taken off, pull them back on and head for the door.

And then what, sir?

It won't open, sir.

Oh, Tip, I had such hopes for you.

Sooner or later he'd figure it out. Sooner or later he'd realize all he had to do was take a face cloth or a tea towel or his own hair, if he wanted to, light it with a match and hold it under the smoke alarm.

And how long was it before it occurred to you, sir, to wake up the whole building with the smoke alarm?

Oh, sir, I had such hopes for you.

Maybe he should drive back, park the car close by and sit in a nice restaurant eating steak and fries and watching out the window for the fire trucks. No, they'd call the cops on him. A guy who's a cool dude doesn't suddenly start braying with laughter and falling face-first into his strawberry shortcake for no reason.

He gassed up, had the oil checked, put it all on the travel card, then found a good steak house and pigged out, courtesy the old man's plastic. Then, so full he couldn't even manage an after-dinner mint, he was back in the fancy car, driving through the gathering night, wearing jeans, one of his father's good shirts and a soft black leather jacket which must have set the old boy back a fistful.

He switched off the radio, and began to sing loudly.

oh the sons of the prophets are brave men and bold
and quite unaccustomed to fear

but the bravest of all was a man by the name
of Abdullah Bulbul Emir

Good old Lord Baden-Powell and his little short pants brigade.
Learn to tie your knots, Tip, learn your woods lore, Tip, get your
picture taken in your uniform, Tip, and sing around the campfire
with Akela. When they needed a man to encourage the van or
harass the foe from the rear, storm fort or redoubt they had only
to shout for Abdullah Bulbul Emir. What in hell is a redoubt?
Some kind of foxhole? The sword-and-dagger version of a
machine gun?

Probation, they said. Good old Akela, who most of the time
was cleverly disguised as a heavy-duty mechanic, showing up in
court to tell the judge about the fatherless boy who had done so
well in his pack. This badge, that badge, the next badge, always
helpful, always courteous, why, this boy, sir, leads little old
ladies across the street. Whether they want to go or not, sir!
Probation, the judge said, frowning. And twenty hours community work.

Have to learn, my boy, have to learn respect for other people's property.
Oh yassuh, boss! Fo' *Sho*, boss!
up to the Society for the Prevention of Cruelty to Animals
good old Ess Pee Cee Ay
Gimme an Ess gimme a Pee gimme an SPCA. Yaaaay
Wishbone
clean the cages, shovel the mess into a red bucket
originally designed to hold sand near a fire hose
check the water dishes
empty the stale water, rinse out the dishes, make sure
all the slime and grunge is off them
refill with fresh water
feed the dogs every day
German shepherd dogs
dobies
spaniels
cock-a-poo, peke-a-poo, cocka-peeka-poo
sad-eyed basset, big furry mutt
little wriggly puppy

every dog has his day
three days at the SPCA
then
give me liberty or give me death
gimme adoption or gimme
the box
the hot box
just put 'em in, close the lid, and
stand back
sizzle crackle not even a yelp
just the awful stink from the fur
wait for the noise to stop
the scratch scratch of the toenails to stop
then
lift 'em out
drop 'em in the shopping cart
and when it's full
take it to the incinerator
in sin for sure
and dump in the dogs, pour on the fuel oil
light the match, ignite the paper
and leave before you puke
twenty hours of community service
Ah-keh-la we'll do our best to do our duty to God and our
country
There are many brave men come from near and from far to
fight in the ranks of the Tsar, but the greatest of all was a man
by the name of Ivan Skavinsky Skivar.

No Akela next time. Just Mom. Waiting in the hallway with the
other moms and even a dad or two. And the judge still glaring.
Some weenie standing up and reading off the piece of paper.
Called to the parking lot behind the theatre and there did find a
fight in progress between the accused and one Jeremy Nordling.
When the officer attempted to stop the fight the accused attacked
him and used his knee to deliver a blow to the groin that inca-
pacitated the officer. The accused was apprehended by a second
officer and taken to cells. Nordling was taken to hospital and
received six stitches to his eyebrow.

Six months probation. Another twenty-five hours community

work, not the SPCA this time, no sir, you only get one chance at a really good job like that. Go to such'n'such an address my boy and the lady will give you a shovel and you can dig up the leaking sewer pipe of the group home. Except she didn't care for my company. Wonder why?

So down to the cop shop and wash, wax and polish the pigpens. Yessir nosir three bags full sir. Shine your door, clean your windshield, want me to wash it off inside, too, sir, gee I'm sorry, sir, I seem to have spilled the bucket, sir.

Tip stopped briefly to buy a big bottle of blue windshield cleaner, and while the attendant was working under the hood, Tip went inside and picked up several music tapes so he didn't have to listen to that unmitigated crap the old man had in his tape box. Celine Dion, for shit's sake!

He took out a five he'd swiped from the bedroom, got change from the attendant and called.

"Hi, Mom?"

"Tip!"

"Listen, Mom, I can't talk long, okay."

"I know, they've been here."

"Sorry about that. Listen, Mom, don't worry, okay? Everything is fine. I've got some money, I've eaten, I'm warm, and there's nothing heavy coming down, okay?"

"Tip – "

"Mom, it's okay. I just got . . . fed up in there, is all. I figured better to take a hike than freak, know what I mean? It's okay. I'll go back in a couple of days. I just had to . . ." He laughed softly. "Hey, it's okay. They'll add a week or two and it's worth it. I had to take a hike, Mom."

"Has this got anything to do with the boy who – "

"Yeah, Mom. It's been heavy in there. But I'm fine."

We'll just drive us down the highway to a provincial campsite and park under the trees. We'll lock all the doors and wrap ourself in the near-new wool blanket SuperStud just happens to have draped casually over the back seat, and we'll burp our garlic steak, bleu cheese dressing and strawberry shortcake, then close our baby blues and off we'll go with Winken, Blinken and Nod one night sailed off in a wooden shoe, what comes after that, Tip – oh, off to a land of pure delight where all our dreams come true?

Something like that. Winken and Blinken are two little eyes and Nod is a little head and the wooden shoe in which they sailed is Tippy's little bed. Sure, Mom, sure.

> Hey, Pete, you still with me, fella?
> we should have done this together
> should have taken off with you the minute
> they hauled you back in
> should have just tucked you under my arm
> and said Come on, Petie, I know where we
> can score us some clothes and a car and
> just
> just eff oh . . .

/ / /

Jackie and Mira stayed four days at the campsite, puddling in the lake, picking berries, lying in the sun, prowling the woods looking for birds' nests and bits of eggshell.

"See," she said, pointing, and by squinting Jackie could make out the little bundle of twigs, moss and grass in the fork of the maple tree. "And if you look carefully you'll find bits of shell. When the baby comes out of the shell the mother bird picks up the pieces and takes them from the nest. Some birds drop them on the ground, other birds fly off with them and drop them a distance from the nest, to fool the animals that otherwise might climb the tree and eat the babies."

"Eat them?" Jackie felt a twinge of disgust. "Eat little babies?"

"Everything lives off everything else," Mira said. "And the cat or weasel or whatever it is climbs the tree to steal the babies has babies of her own back at her nest, and they have to eat, too. It all balances."

"But eat the babies?"

"Yes," and she reached down and took his hand. "You eat eggs, don't you? I do. And if we didn't eat the eggs they might hatch into little chickens. We eat carrots and peas and cabbages and if we didn't, they'd make seeds. But if we eat them, they can't make seeds. Even lettuce is alive, and when we cut it or pull it from the ground, we kill it."

"Oh . . ."

"If we didn't do that, Jackie, we'd die. It's how it's supposed to be. The animal eats the grass, we eat the animal, and when we die, our bodies go back to the earth and feed the grass."

"You mean rot, don't you?"

"Yes."

"Aunt Lois used to sing a song, about how the worms would gobble you up. She said there was no heaven and no angels and no nothing but worms, worms, worms. When she said it, my mom got mad at her."

"Well, there you have it. Worms, worms, worms for the meat of us and who knows what for the other part, because we're more than just meat and bones, Jackie. But I wouldn't be the one to tell you about that part of it."

The morning of the fifth day Jackie wakened to the sound of rain pattering on the roof of the aluminum canopy. He sat up, yawning, and looked out the back flap. The leaves were heavy with rain, the ground was dark and muddy, and the people with the fancy tent were packing up, grumbling to each other. Mira stirred, sat up and stretched her arms sideways.

"Ah, a nice drink for the trees," she yawned.

"Everybody is leaving."

"Does that mean you want to leave?"

"Maybe I could phone my mom?"

"Do you know the number?"

"Yeah. And I know the address, too. I just didn't know how to get there."

"Well then, why don't we find out? We'll just pack our stuff, tidy up the site and off we'll go, to find a phone."

Mira had expected this. She was fully prepared for it. She hadn't suggested it, however, because she wanted Jackie to make his own decisions, not to feel pushed into anything. She'd been pushed, she knew how it felt. Mira had been pushed right up until the day she pushed back. There was satisfaction in knowing she'd been able to push back, but regret that it had been necessary.

Jackie did his own dialling and waited hopefully. Then a voice from the phone said, "The number you have dialled is not in service." Jackie just stared, then replaced the receiver. "A man said . . . the number was . . ." He shrugged, feeling helpless and lost. Mira lifted the phone and dialled the number, and the same voice told her the same thing.

"Do you think she moved?" she said.

"Maybe she's at my aunt's place."

Mira asked him his aunt's name and the address, got a number, then dialled and waited, listening to the phone ringing, ringing, ringing. Finally she replaced the receiver. "Well then, we'll try again later," she smiled.

He nodded and turned toward the truck, ignoring the puddles, slopping through them, splashing.

Mira drove with Dog sitting next to her and Jackie slumped against the other door. The miles slipped under the wheels of the pickup, and soon Jackie was talking and laughing again. They drove out of the rain, into miles of highway under an overcast sky, then away from that, too, and soon they were in sunshine again.

"We need money," Mira told him. "The price of gas is going up all the time."

"Will we rob a bank?" he teased.

"Better than that," she promised, "we'll get a job."

The sign was a weather-greyed piece of plywood with "Pickers Wanted" painted on it in sloppy letters. An arrow directed them down a dirt road, past fields of strawberries. Mira drove carefully, missing as many of the potholes as she could. She registered at the weigh booth, drove toward the long unpainted sheds and parked her truck in the beaten-down grass between the wire fence and the pickers' quarters. They were entitled to a cubicle, but one look at it and Mira knew they would continue to live in the truck.

"It's pretty awful," Jackie whispered.

"It's ghastly," she agreed.

And it was. You didn't have to look very hard to see the bug holes in the board floor that lay on the ground. Two steps on it and you'd go through, although you wouldn't go far. Up above, against the two-by-fours of the roof, were wasp nests and mud-dauber nests and empty swallow nests. There was no inside wall, just two-by-four supports with plywood nailed over them, and not even good plywood. It curled and buckled, warped and twisted. Big sections of it had pulled away from the nails. The windows were filthy and ill fitting, with many broken panes. No attempt had been made to repair them or cover the holes to keep out the rain and wind.

But people had moved their stuff into the shed. There were little places all along the wall where they had spread sleeping bags or pallets, put out their few pots and bowls and a box or two of clothes. Several small children crawled on the floor, watched over by a few older children who stared at Jackie and Mira with wide, frightened eyes.

Jackie looked at Mira and she looked at him, then put her hand on his shoulder and led him back to the truck. "I can get in four or five hours of picking before dark," she said quietly. "The sooner I get picking the sooner we've got our gas money and the sooner we're gone from here."

"I can help," he offered.

"No." She tried to smile. "I need you to look after Dog, otherwise I'll have to tie her in the truck." Jackie knew that wasn't true, Dog would stay where she was told to stay. "They use poison on the berries," she told him, "to kill the bugs. And the poison gets in the dirt. And it isn't good for you. So I don't want you out there in it."

"There's other kids out there."

"Yes. And nothing I can do about that. But you . . ." She rumpled his hair. "You I can do something about. You go exploring with Dog. There's a bridge down the road a ways, and a stream. Don't drink the water from the tap. Use our water, always. And if you get hungry, eat the food we've got in the truck, don't eat any of these berries unless you scrub them good with our own water."

"Okay," he nodded.

Mira put on old clothes and a scarf to pull up over her mouth and nose so she wouldn't breathe in any of the bug poison. Then she went into the fields to pick and Jackie walked off with Dog.

Funny how Mira had almost lied to him, then told him the truth. Lots of people lied. Aunt Lois, for one. She lied about stuff. Told the man at the bank someone had swiped her purse with her cheque in it so she wouldn't be able to make her payment until her next pay, in a couple of weeks. All of it lies. But then she and Mom went off to bingo and won a jackpot, so it all evened out. She went down with jackpot money and made her deposit. Told the bank man she had asked her boss for a drag, whatever that was, because she felt so bad about being late with the deposit. He believed her. She laughed about it at home. Laughed and said she'd told him she'd work some overtime to try to make up for it. And all the time the cheque wasn't stolen at all. They just partied it away, was all.

There was all this stuff to snoop around at along the banks of the stream. Wrigglers and tadpoles, some of them had stubs of legs, some of them were almost turned to frogs already, just a bit of tail still poking out, not enough to really call a tail. Sticklety-backs, and some minnows, and spiders that could walk on water. Mira said they had air bubbles under their feet. Something to think about, walking on air bubbles. Good trick if you could learn it. Who ate who? Sticklety-backs probably ate the spiders and maybe the wrigglers. Maybe even the tadpoles. Some kind of stinky yellow flower thing, he'd never seen it before. The yellow part of it, the part that stank the worst, had bugs all over it, all kinds of bugs, ants and everything. Maybe they liked the stink. Good for them if they liked it, there was lots to go around. An old stroller frame all rusty in the water. He hauled it out and dumped it in the blackberry tangle. More stuff up there to look at. Some kind of flowers floating on the water and something living in the bank. He didn't get to see it, it moved so fast. When he went toward the hole it lived in, Dog grumbled so Jackie moved away. Dog didn't grumble often, but when she did, Mira said to pay attention.

A guy could spend a lot of time just poking around this creek, maybe swing from that rope hanging from the branch. It wasn't very warm, not warm enough to go swimming, but not so cold it would be nasty if you got wet. He could take off his clothes and leave them on the bank, then swing on the rope and if he fell off, well, he'd get wet but he'd have dry clothes to put back on. Be fun. Saw kids on TV doing that one time. Could be real fun. And maybe after supper they could go phone Mom.

When he got back to the berry farm, back to the pickup truck and the little almost-house under the canopy, there were other people parked on either side. Several kids, some his own age, some younger, some older, were playing in the grass, kicking an old soccer ball around, except for the kid with the big tobacco can of crayons and pencil stubs and the big tablet of paper for drawing. Jackie moved self-consciously to the truck, clambered over the tailgate and sat under the canopy, watching the other kids through the canvas flap.

"Hi," he said finally.

The kid with the crayons looked up, smiled, then spoke, but Jackie didn't understand a word of it. The kid spoke again, and from the tone of voice Jackie knew he'd been asked a question.

"I don't know what you're saying," he answered.

The soccer game stopped. The kids looked at him, then at each other, then at Dog. "What you sittin' in that truck for?" one asked.

"Because I live here," Jackie answered, already proddy.

"That's Mira's truck."

"I know whose truck it is. Don't need you to tell me whose truck it is."

"She's not your mom."

"Don't need you to tell me that, either. I know who my mom is. Mira's a friend of mine."

"Yeah? Then how come you only talk English?"

"Why would I want to talk anything else?"

They ignored him for a while, then the ball came bouncing his way and Jackie jumped out of the truck, retrieved the ball and kicked it back to the group of kids. They stared at him for a moment. "Wanna play?" one of them asked. Jackie grinned. One of the girls kicked the ball to him, he passed it to the boy who'd spoken to him, and within moments he was as much a part of the game as any of the others.

They played happily until one of the older kids looked at the sky, then whistled, and walked from the area of trampled grass to an old Travelall with bright curtains on the windows. One by one the other kids drifted away, and Jackie stood watching.

"What you doing?" he finally asked.

"They'll be home soon," the red-headed boy said. "We have to start supper for them. They'll be tired."

"Oh." He hadn't thought about that. Hadn't thought about Mira working while he was having fun. Jackie went back to the truck, climbed over the tailgate and went to look at the boxes of groceries stored under the tarp.

When Mira got home Jackie had a sort-of supper ready; slices of bread spread with margarine and a small plate with irregularly cut slices of cheese.

"I couldn't make tea," he confessed, "because I didn't have no hot water. They say we can't make a fire here."

She laughed, gave him a hug and showed him how the little stove worked.

Jackie eyed it doubtfully. "Does it blow up or anything?" he asked.

"It might," she admitted.

She got the stove going and the water boiling, and made tea, then sprawled on the flattened grass eating her cheese sandwich and sipping tea and honey.

"These are my friends," she told Jackie. "We move around more or less together most of the time. Not always, but sooner or later we meet up with each other again. Those poor souls," she gestured with her head toward the ugly big shack the farmer called accommodation, "they have no choice, you see. They live like this because they're poor. We live like this because this is how we prefer to live. There's a big difference there, Jackie. Anything you have to do isn't as good for you as something you've chosen to do."

"Why'd you choose it?"

"Because we come from families who have always travelled. That's what they used to call us, travelling people. Not quite the same as the Roms, but close enough you couldn't tell the difference in the dark. Some of us will pick strawberries here, then move on somewhere else and maybe do, oh, lettuce. By the time it's winter here, we're down in Florida, or sometimes Mexico. Sometimes I stay here for the start of the bad weather and pick mushrooms. Pine mushrooms, chanterelles. A good shroomer can make hundreds of dollars a day. And no taxes."

"Don't you ever just . . . stay somewhere?"

"If we want. I have a sister stays pretty much in one place. She makes jewellery and it's easier to sell it if she stays put. So she does that until she just can't put up with it any more, then she joins us for a while. Then . . . sooner or later she'll see someplace she thinks she likes, and she'll put down a couple of roots and stay a while. One place she stayed three years. I," she grinned, "have never stayed anywhere longer than a year."

"Gypsies," Jackie guessed.

"Not quite," Mira said. "But close. We're just the travelling people, is all."

"I never heard of them."

"No," she laughed, "I daresay you haven't. They like to pretend we don't exist."

The people in the big shed washed their dishes in the cold

water from the tap beside the wall, but not one of the travelling people went over with a bucket for water. They all had their own containers of water, and Jackie knew without asking that the water was as clean as that in Mira's own big jug.

"How come they use that water and we don't?" he finally asked.

"We are very particular about water," Mira answered. "Water is a precious thing."

"Water?"

"Water," she said firmly. "Without it we die. In the four main directions of this earth, there is water. Above us and below us, water. We are surrounded by it, and it is inside our very bodies. And the sacred places we hold dear are beside clean springs, or clean lakes, or clean rivers, or clean streams. Always beside water, and always clean water."

Some of the soccer players came over and stretched on the grass, watching Mira's face, smiling eagerly. One of them spoke in the language Jackie could not understand and Mira laughed.

"They want a story," she explained.

"Great!" he agreed.

"I'll tell it in English for the Scaldie," she suggested to them, "and if anyone can't understand, one of the others could translate."

"Tell it to us and let someone translate for the Scaldie," the redhead objected.

"Now, would that be polite, do you think?" Mira smiled. "He's had no chance to learn our speech and we've had every chance to learn his." She winked at Jackie and started the story. "So there were two friends went out in a boat and each of them took an oar. They rowed to deep water and shipped their oars, then each of them baited a hook and dropped it over the side. They were handlining, and as you all know, when you're handlining it isn't like fishing with a rod. As soon as the fish takes the bait, it feels as if something has just lain down on your hook, not pulling, not striking. That's when you have to give a great jerk, and sink the hook in firm or you'll lose your bait. So the two are out fishing and one says Something lay down on my bait, and the other says Same for me, and both of them gave a good jerk.

"Such a time they had, first one would be nearly pulled over the side by the fish he had caught, then he'd get control of his fish and the next thing you knew the other would nearly be over the side fighting, and it went on like that up and down and back and forth and the water whipped to a foam and suddenly there's one fish in the bottom of the boat and two hooks in it. One hook is in the front of the jaw, the other in the corner of the mouth. It's my fish, says the first friend, my hook is at the – Oh no, says the other, its my fish, my hook is more firmly set. Such an argument, and the whole time the dogfish is lying in the bottom of the boat flapping and dying. Well, they argued and argued and argued and finally said each to the other I'll have the law on you. And so it was. They rowed back to land still arguing fiercely, and went to see the po-liss. Well, said the po-liss, this can't be easily settled, we'll have to get the magistrate. So they waited until they could see the magistrate and he said Oh, he said, this is far too complex for me, we'll have to bring in a judge. And we'll need an expert on dogfish, and an expert on hooks and an expert on lines and an expert on boats, and on bait and on tides and currents as well.

"They waited for all that and finally the judge arrived and after him all the experts, and they heard all the evidence and the lawyers talked and the experts talked and everybody talked and then the judge he had to go think about it all. So the whole world was sitting waiting for the judgment and one little child said There's an awful smell coming from the evidence. And that was a true thing! In all the time they'd been arguing and yelling and bringing experts and doing all that, the dogfish had solved the problem her own way, she rotted to such a horrible condition she was no good to anyone. Well, when the whole world saw that, they decided the dogfish was smarter than the judge who was still off thinking. And what is mightier than a judge if it isn't a king? And to this day in some places they still call the dogfish the Dallag, or the king fish, for being smarter than the judge. 'Dogfish' is as close as the Scaldies can get to Dallag; the fish has nothing at all to do with dogs."

/ / /

As soon as the gas station attendant checked the credit card number against the list, Tip knew he was in trouble. Just a flicker of the attendant's eyes, that's all it took, and Tip knew. He grabbed a small propping stick from the windowsill and rammed it into the small of the old man's back, freezing him. "Just put the list down, Pops," Tip said gently, "and you won't get hurt."

"Why do you want to do this, son?" said the old guy. "You're just hurting yourself."

"Sure, Pops, sure," said Tip, reaching for a length of rope. He tied the knots firmly, but not so tightly as to hurt the guy, and took the credit card with him. Anything to slow them down, even for a few hours. Maybe the old guy wouldn't remember anything except that it was a hot card. But Tip knew time was running out. The guy had seen the car, seen him, would describe them both, might even remember a name, or part of a name.

In for a dime, in for a dollar. He filled a bag with cigarettes, chocolate bars, peanuts and chips, not because he wanted them, but because it was part of the game.

He drove east until the tank was empty, found a side road and left the highway, and found the ideal place. It was the last little shred of luck before it all dribbled away. Tip spent an hour wiping prints off the car, remembering things he hadn't known he remembered. Mom coming home from work tired and borderline crabby, finding supper almost ready, him and Ange both grinning. And Mom smiled. Not a tired smile or a patient smile, a real honest-to-God smile, and plopped in a chair, and said Just call me Queenie. And I bet she isn't smiling and feeling like Queenie right now, you dumb jerk.

Oh, Tip, please, just tell me why . . .

He cursed, sent the shining car over the bank into the river; then, with no expression on his face at all, he walked back toward the highway, the pillowslip full of clothes slung over his shoulder, the bag of stolen goodies standing beside the logging road, unwanted, untouched.

Days later he was in a police station, laughing in their faces, refusing to answer questions. He hadn't stayed away as long as Peter had, but he'd covered a lot more ground, eaten a lot of steak and ice cream, and enjoyed most of it.

When the social worker arrived he was lying on the torture rack they called a bunk, singing. Young man, quote Bulbul, has your life grown so dull, that you're anxious to end your career? Foul infidel know, you have trod on the toe, of Abdullah Bulbul Emir.

"Well, fancy seeing you here," Anna said.

"Hey, what's a nice girl like you doing in a place like this?"

"Can you tell me what you want, Tip? Without BS, can you tell me what it is will satisfy you so you won't wind up going from here to the next place? Because you are so close to a real jail, it scares me."

He'd been in jail all his life anyway, what difference would it make? But he thought of his mom, and of Ange, and he had to blink to keep from bawling like a small sib. He opened his mouth to make a wisecrack and the next thing he knew it was all tumbling out, the anger, the contempt, all of it.

"And he charges me with theft? He's been stealing from Mom, from me, and from Ange for years!"

"So sue him."

"You're kiddin'! Fat chance I'd have."

"You've got no chance at all the way you've been going about it."

He thought about that. It was just off-the-wall enough that someone might want to put it in the paper. And if you're out there all gussied up in your nice expensive clothes, trying to grease the way so people will buy something and you'll get a nice big fat cut, the last thing you want is your name in the papers, being sued for being a lying cheapskate.

"They're still going to throw the book at me," he grumbled.

"Lot of difference between a juvenile minimum security forestry camp and a year and a half in jail with guys who think your bum is as beautiful as Marilyn Monroe's face."

"Forestry camp," he snorted.

"Regular visiting on the weekends. There's one close enough for your mom to get up to see you. You never know," she grinned, "you might learn a useful trade. Like making shingles or something. Then I could teach you the logger's hymn."

"You? Teach me?" and he was laughing, and so was she. And there they stood, two people grinning and touching fingers through a set of bars, singing I see that you're a logger and not just a common bum, nobody but a logger stirs his coffee with his thumb.

/ / /

Mira drove from the berry farm to a provincial campsite three miles up the highway from the turnoff. They parked with the other travelling people and joined what seemed to Jackie to be the next best thing to a party. And in the morning everyone woke up at the same time.

The workers got breakfast made for them, then they left, crammed together in two cars, laughing, and the pregnant lady directed the cleanup of dishes and breakfast for the non-pickers, mostly kids. The whole day was games and swimming and hide'n'seek in the bush, it was fishing and even catching some, it was being just the same as the others, and nobody staring at your ratty old sneaks or making remarks about your clothes or asking how come your cousins didn't come to school any more. And if you were hungry you went back to camp and got something to eat.

The lady blew a whistle when it was time to go back and help get supper ready for the pickers. Jackie got to wash salad stuff and slice up tomatoes, he got to stir the big pot of stew and help scrub the potatoes. And then Mira was back, and he went with her to the lake where she jumped into the water, clothes and all, everything except her sneakers, and then they walked back, her clothes dripping on the path. He waited for her to hand him her wet clothes from inside the camper, and he hung them over the little line to drip and dry.

Mira came out in clean clothes and they joined the others for a big supper, everyone laughing and joking, and even if they talked that language Jackie didn't understand, it didn't matter. He'd learned some words. Words for food, and for yes and no and coming and thank you and fish, and the word for Dog.

Everyone chipped in for food and the pregnant lady did the cooking. One night they all piled off into town to go shopping and Mira got him ice cream. He sat in the back of someone else's van eating a big cone with all the other kids eating their big cones, and everyone laughing.

Most nights there was singing, and storytelling, and Mira whispered the story in his ear in English. Knights and dragons, and castles and towers, and a talking head that led an army. And dancing. Someone would start to sing and someone else would play an instrument and people would jump up and start to dance, like no dance Jackie had seen anybody do, and if he fell asleep it was okay, someone always moved him and he always woke up in the morning safe in the back of the truck, with Dog curled against him, and he could phone his mom if he wanted but she probably wasn't home, but he'd phone again soon.

The neighbourhood was dark, not even a patch of odd-coloured glow from a television screen issued from any of the windows. Somewhere a large dog barked with boring regularity, but the canine communication system wasn't answering. The downstairs light shone in the Billings house, and then the side door opened and a slender figure hurried out, pulling on a zip-front jacket. Jenny headed for the carport, a set of keys dangling from her hand. She unlocked the car door, got in and started up the engine, then backed out in a series of erratic jerks, the engine roaring and the car nearly stalling. The upstairs hall light snapped on as the car lurched onto the street, jerked from reverse to forward, and rolled toward the corner. The front door opened and Jenny's foster father stood on the porch in his jeans, glaring after his departing car. He swore loudly and padded back in the house, his bare feet shrinking from the cold floor. He picked up the phone to call the police.

Jenny didn't look for Brucie or anyone else. She had no idea where she was going or what she was going to do when she got there, but she did know she wasn't staying where she was for one more minute. Take university and stuff it. Take the whole entire pissin' world and stuff it.

what is it about me makes them think they can come on like that?

smile smile wanna play Monopoly? smile smile wanna learn
to drive? smile smile smile
and then sooner or later, usually sooner
Why you savin' it, kid
Who you savin' it for, kid
Don't be so hard to get along with
I've been nice to you, now you be nice to me
Oh yeah, and who'd believe *you?*
You don't fool me
Who are you givin' it to
some kid I bet
that Brucie I suppose

And what do you do? Sit down with Mrs. Billings over a nice
chummy cup of tea and say By the way, there's something I've
been wanting to discuss with you, would you mind suggesting to
your husband that I'd just as soon he not come into my bedroom?
Would it be at all possible for you to suggest to him that I don't
exactly appreciate his fatherly little hugs and pats? And could you
also drop the hint that this brushing of the arm with the fingertips is just a bit creepy? Me telling him hasn't done any good, he
goes all innocent and injured good intentions, and says Jenny,
you've got a filthy mind.
     And what has the eff-em ever done to get that dumped on
her head? And who ever decided it was up to her to run herd
on her husband? Why should Mrs. have to monitor the behaviour of Mr.? When does he have to learn how to behave
properly?

     nip nip nip nip the red and blue
     lights flashed circles on top of
     the dark blue and white car
     well, shit!
     you are never going to outrun them, Jenny.
     Jenny-you-idiot you can barely steer this pig
     at low speed
     Well, putz, eh!

When Anna arrived at the police station, a full-scale high-decibel
argument was in progress. Jenny, partially restrained by a police-

woman, was yelling insults at the good-looking truck driver who
was her most recent foster father, and he was roaring back.

"I want this little twist charged, you hear!"

"There isn't a scratch on your lousy car," Jenny screeched. "All
I did was borrow it!"

"You stole it!"

"Up your nose! You could never make the payments on it if
it wasn't for the welfare cheque!"

The duty officer was more than happy to have Jenny taken to
a small room to meet with Anna. For the first ten minutes they
just sat in silence, then Anna lit herself a cigarette and slid the
package across the table to Jenny.

"So, what kind of foster home do you want this time?" she
sighed.

For the first time in all the years of dealing with and being
dealt with by social workers, Jenny saw a person. A tired person.
"You okay?" she said. "You sound tired."

"Yeah. I'm tired."

"I don't want a foster home," Jenny blurted. "I want to live on
my own."

"What a great idea," Anna yawned. "Do you have any idea
the mountain of paperwork it would involve? I need a reason.
Not some BS excuse, a real live honest-to-God reason."

"I am tired of being pawed," Jenny said clearly.

"Oh Christ," Anna said, her body sagging. "I am so tired of
being ineffectual."

"Hey." Jenny drew back, uncertain.

"I'm supposed to provide certain things for you. And if you
don't know it, I haven't been doing my job."

"Oh," Jenny's voice hardened. "Your job."

"My job," said Anna. "Not only as a social worker but as
someone who breathes the same air as you. Do you think I
approve of someone being pawed? Do you think I think it's just
normal? I cannot believe you are so stupid!"

"I am *not* stupid!" Jenny shouted. "And I'm tired of everyone
thinking I am!"

"Then stop acting stupid. Tell, Jen."

"And who would listen?"

"Me," Anna answered. She stood up and stubbed out her cigarette. "Wait here."

Billings just stared defiantly. "Forget about laying charges?" he sneered. "And why would I want to do that"

"Because if you don't, you're going to jail for at least three years, more likely five."

"She's lying!" His face paled.

"About what, Mr. Billings? I haven't even said what it is you'd be charged with. What's the lie?"

/ / /

It wasn't the Green Room, after all. The Green Room is for ankle-biters. When you start messing around with robbery, stolen cars, fraudulent use of credit cards, you are no longer an ankle-biter. And when they find you guilty, as they inevitably do, you do not go to a facility for emotionally disturbed children, you go to the Young Offenders Unit. If you're lucky, you are transferred out of the Young Offenders Unit to a minimum security forestry camp, but not if they think you'll go over the fence, like you did at Kiddy Camp. Well, maybe if he stopped thinking of the welfare broad as a welfare broad, and started being real . . . a forestry camp might not be all that bad. Better than the Young Offenders Unit and the buttfuckers.

"Hello?"

"Hello . . . Mom?"

"Jackie! Baby! Where are you?"

"I'm okay, Mom. Where were you? I phoned and phoned but nobody answered."

"Where are you, Jackie? I'll come and get you."

"I'll be home soon, Mom."

"Where are you?"

"I don't know. Some park. Mom? Who's that talking to you? Mom? Who's that guy?"

"Just a friend. Jackie, listen, tell me where you are and we'll come and get you."

"Is it Squirt?"

"Who?"

"Squirt. Is the guy Squirt?"

"No. Jackie, where are you?"

"Is he a cop?"

"Jackie, baby, just tell me where –"

Jackie hung up the phone. Nosepickers. Everywhere you went, nosepickers.

"You okay, Jackie?"

"Yeah."

"If you want to go home now, I'll drive you."

"Nosepickers," he managed, and then he was crying.

Mira let him cry. She waited until he lifted his face and looked at her. Then she knelt, gathered him against her body, closed her arms around him, and just held on.

"Easy old man," she whispered. "Easy there, now."

He lay wrapped in a blanket, his head on Mira's lap, watching the men dancing in a circle, holding long sticks in their hands, slamming the sticks on the ground as if it were a drum. Some of them had funny hats on their heads, with feathers or flowers stuck in the bands, some of them had bells tied just below their knees with leather thongs, dingling and jingling with each step. Some of them had vests or jackets with old pearl or shell buttons sewn on in designs Jackie could not recognize, and even though Mira translated the songs into English, some of them made no sense at all.

"Maybe," she whispered, "maybe Morriss means Moorish from the Moors who were part of the Roman army. Maybe it means Moorish because the travelling people lived on the Moors. Nobody knows. We don't think it matters. Some Morriss dancers are Scaldie, some are English, some don't even know there are still travelling people. It doesn't matter. We all do things we don't know the reason for. Cross our fingers for luck, sneeze if we look into the sun, yawn just because someone else yawned. The dance is what is important."

"He has a horse head on his stick."

"Yes. And that's a dog carved on that stick."

"Why?"

"Because," she laughed softly, "because his family has always danced with a stick like that."

"Why?"

"Why not?"

"What are they singing?"

"They sing about us. About how everything is part of everything else. If you destroy the water you destroy the fish living in the water, and the reeds and the water lilies and the frogs and the birds who live by eating the frogs. You destroy the water and the rain is gone, and without the rain there is no grass. Without the grass the deer and cows and horses and others who live on the grass die, and without them, the wolves and cougars and coyotes are gone. Without the grass the mice and rats are gone, and without them there is nothing for the hawks and falcons and young eagles. Destroy the cows, and the deer and the flies and ticks and horseflies and such are gone, and without them the birds who feed on them. You cannot destroy one thing without destroying everything. If the wild deer, mice, rats and squirrels are gone, the predators will have to move against the cows and sheep and pigs and chickens, and if they go, people will starve. If you cut down all the trees, where do the birds nest, where do the marten live, and without them, what will occupy their space in the weave of creation? Without the trees the rain will wash away the soil and where will the berries and grass grow? And without berries and grass what will the birds and bears and deer and other things eat? If the soil washes into the stream, what of the fish?"

She said more, but the words no longer made sense, not even in English. Jackie could only hear the rhythm of her voice. He yawned and snuggled closer, his eyelids fluttering. The bells, the ribbons, even the rhythmically pounding sticks faded and blurred, his thumb moved toward his mouth, and Mira touched his hand to stop the movement. He sighed, and slept.

/ / /

Anna explained it all, and Jenny nodded calmly. They discussed their options, and both agreed it only made sense for Jenny to go to the group home until she had finished school.

"It'll take a day or so to make the arrangements. Until then you stay with me."

"You sure?"

"I'm sure. And you'll only be in the group home until the end of the school year. That's just a couple of weeks."

"Yeah."

"After graduation we can figure out something better," Anna promised.

"Sure," Jenny smiled. "Sure. That sounds good."

Anna drove Jenny to school, and stopped in the parking lot. "So you've got your key, right? And I'll come right home from work. We'll go over to see Billings together. Get your stuff, take it over, then we'll go for pizza and maybe a show."

"Sure. Great."

"You feel okay about this?"

"Fine. You'd better get a move on or you'll be late for work."

"Right. See you later."

She wasn't surprised when she got home to an empty apartment. Not surprised at all. If Jackie had phoned his mother, Jenny would phone Anna. Sooner or later. All you had to do was tough it out and make sure you didn't go insane worrying about all the dangers waiting for them.

Anna searched in her purse, found what she needed, and went to the telephone standing on the small table beside her big recliner.

/ / /

Jenny could hardly believe how easy it had been. Almost too easy. All she'd had to do was ask and she had the names of her father's next-of-kin. Anna didn't seem surprised, just checked the file and handed over a piece of paper and that was that. All Jenny had to do was wait until it felt like Time, and when all the talk started about group home and graduation and all that good stuff, it felt like Time.

She walked away from the school and took a city bus down to the bus depot, and as easily as if the angels had been arranging it, she had her ticket and only fifteen minutes to wait before the bus left.

She waited until everyone else got on the bus, then found an empty seat. She slid over by the window and put her jacket and schoolbooks on the vacant space beside her. If the bus filled up she'd have to move her stuff to the overhead rack, but until then she had some privacy.

The highway cut through scenery she had only seen in travel brochures and books. Mountains and gorges, miles of open valley already yellow with hay, men on huge machines already cutting the first crop. Other valleys with cattle grazing or standing in the shade of small groves of trees, staring across barbed-wire fences at the highway and the traffic moving steadily to someplace else.

She got off at a bus depot and walked to the closest Chinese restaurant. If you liked the taste of fried rice there wasn't a town in Canada where you couldn't find a passable supper. There wasn't much variation from one Golden Lotus to the other, maybe they got it in big bins, like the bulk food in the supermarket. Just add water and soy sauce and stir twice.

She read the local paper while she ate, trying to get some sense of where she was and what people did in this dozey little hole. Not much, from the looks of things. Logging, obviously, and some farming or ranching. An article about the construction of a five-mile section of highway, an editorial about graduation and the decision of the grad class to have dry grad. Yeah, right.

She paid for her meal and the paper, then walked up one side of the street and down the other. Within fifteen minutes she'd seen the main drag, and found the cab stand.

Four-fifty for the cab. Worth it at twice the price, my man. She paid, put her change in her pocket and watched the cab move off down the quiet street.

The house was small, tidy and stucco-covered, the lawn freshly trimmed and raked, the flowers lining the concrete walk so well tended they hardly looked like flowers. Not a withered or faded bloom in the whole collection. Jenny walked to the wide front stairs, and then the front door was opening and a strong-bodied square-faced woman with grey hair was looking her right in the eye.

"You're Jenny," she said, no question in her voice.

"Yes, ma'am," Jenny said, feeling no impulse to smile.

"Come in." The woman stepped aside, holding the door open, and Jenny Dugan walked into her grandparents' house.

Whatever she had been expecting or not expecting, she didn't find it.

"Have you had supper?"

"Yes, ma'am, I ate in town."

"We saved some in case you hadn't. Would you like some pie and a cup of tea?"

"Thank you, yes."

The man, the grandfather, sat with his arms folded on the oil-cloth table cover, watching her face with eyes as blue as her own.

"You look like him," he said finally.

"Do I?"

"You do."

"He's in the Maritimes." The grandmother spoke from the counter where she was slicing pie and putting it on plates. "In jail."

"They told me."

"Good place for him," his father gritted. "Best place for him."

"Harden not your heart," his wife chided gently. "Judge not that ye be not judged."

"Thou shalt not steal," he answered with a kind of easiness that told Jenny this exchange had happened often.

The pie was good, the crust flaky. But so were they. Flaky. They stopped just short of putting an extra plate on the table for God.

"Do you attend church?" he asked.

"No, sir," she answered.

"You should," he said. "And will, while you're here."

"Yes, sir," and how long will it take to get back to the bus depot?

But she didn't leave. She sat at the table looking through old photo albums. She couldn't remember ever seeing him, although she must have when she was little. But she knew him even before they pointed him out to her. Not just because he looked so much like her, but because she had seen Peter. Pictures of Peter, and Peter at the funeral home, but don't think about that or you'll start screeching.

a boy in old-fashioned crew cut and jeans, with a striped tee shirt and black canvas sneakers, holding his fishing rod proudly, a black and white pointer-type dog sitting at his feet, looking up at him, the dog's mouth open, tongue lolling, as if the animal, dead now how many years, was laughing

the same boy with a bike and a carrier full of newspapers

and either of them looked more like Peter must have looked than that poor cold little guy in the box.

"Did you know about Peter?" she asked.

There was a long silence.

"Suicide is a sin," the woman said firmly.

"He was just a little boy!" Jenny wanted to yell, but her voice came out all soft and gentle. "And nobody even told me about him until . . . after."

"I blame Tommy for that, too," her grandfather said angrily, but he was more than angry, he was something else. Jenny was sure it was sorrow. "No excuse for that."

"Do you know where my mother is?" she dared.

"No," the grandfather shook his head. "No. Haven't heard from her in years."

"Did you know where I was?"

"Knew the welfare had you," he answered.

The silence stretched.

"It hurt too much," her grandmother said.

"Always trouble," her grandfather sighed. "Nothing but trouble."

"But . . . Peter . . ." She swallowed, blinked the tears from her eyes. "He was just a little boy —"

"No good, either of them!" the grandfather roared. "What can you expect? Drugs! Both of them. And both of them married to someone else!"

"And finally, I just told them all, Tommy, the police, everyone, I just said *leave me alone*. I can't take any more of it. Leave me alone. So they did."

"And me?" Jenny sobbed. "What did I do wrong? I was a good little kid. And I didn't even know I had a brother."

"One day you'll understand," her grandmother said stiffly. "Everything looks so easy to the young. It all seems so black and white. But you don't know until later, and sometimes you can never know. He was stealing when he was seven years old! And by the time he was thirteen . . . I was so tired. I still am tired."

Jenny stayed two more days, knowing there was nothing there for her. These people did not want to know her, and finally she admitted she did not want to know them. Even if she had grown up living next door to them they would still be strangers. Maybe that was why Tommy was in so much trouble. Maybe he felt like a stranger, too.

She took the bus back to the city and phoned Anna from the bus depot.

"You okay?" Anna asked.

"I'm fine," Jenny said, but then she was sobbing, hanging onto the phone and almost choking with grief and loneliness.

/ / /

Mira and Dog stayed in the truck. Jackie went up the stairs eagerly, toward the familiar smells, the sound of the risers creaking under his weight. He didn't knock, he just opened the door and walked into the little apartment. She stared at him, then he was running to her and she was gathering him up, cuddling him, and sobbing.

"You're back," she said over and over and over again.

"Mom," he said. It was all he could say. "Mom."

He was sitting at the table eating ice cream and feeling so good to be home, feeling safe and certain nothing the nosepickers tried would ever split them up again, when he heard the stairs creaking.

"Someone coming," he grinned. Wait until Mom and Mira met each other! Wait until Mira came in and saw him at his own table, with his own spoon and his own bowl. Wait until she sat there having tea and telling jokes. Mom would laugh. They'd all laugh.

Mom opened the door and it wasn't Mira at all.

"No!" he screamed, jumping from the chair, throwing the ice cream, bowl and all. "No! *Mom!*"

"Jackie, I had no choice. It's the law, now. But we'll go to court and we'll fight and we'll win."

"*No!*"

But there was nothing much he could do. They carried him down the stairs, his mother following, sobbing and begging him to understand. And when they got to the street and put him in the back of the police car, there was no sign of the pickup truck, no sign of Mira, no sign of Dog.

He sat in the police station for what seemed like forever before a man came and got him. Another car ride, and the man carried him from the car to the house. Jackie couldn't stop crying. He didn't want to, he didn't mean to, but he couldn't stop crying.

The man took him to a bedroom and lay him on the bed, then Jackie was alone. The lady came in later, after the man was gone, and tried to talk to him. But he didn't want to listen, and he still couldn't stop crying. It was his own fault. Whose big bright idea had it been, anyway? Mira had looked at him and said Are you sure? and he had said Sure I'm sure.

It wasn't supposed to happen like that. Mira was supposed to wait. Half an hour, she said. I'll give you half an hour to get your welcome homes done and then I'll come up and meet her. But she didn't. And how had they known? Did they have someone watching the house? Or did Mom phone when she went into the kitchen for the ice cream? But why would she? It wasn't supposed to be like this at all.

The man and the lady came in and stripped off his clothes, washed his hands and face, gave him a big spoonful of cough syrup or something, and put pyjamas on him. Tucked him in bed. Stroked his forehead and said Sleep now, Jackie, it will all seem better in the morning.

It wouldn't, either! And he couldn't sleep. He just kept crying. Cried and yawned and yawned and cried, and then someone was lying down on the bed beside him, putting her arms around him, pulling him close.

"Ssssshhhh, little sib," she whispered. "You're okay. You're going to be just fine."

"No," he managed, "you don't know."

"Oh, yes I do," Jenny whispered. "I know exactly."

She whispered to him and cuddled him until the syrup caught up with him and he fell asleep. The eff-pees came to the door and asked if she was all right and Jenny smiled as if something like this happened every day of the week, and who knew? Maybe it did.

"It's okay," she said. "I'll stay with him."

In the morning she showed him the bathroom and waited until he came out, face washed, teeth brushed, eyes still swollen and bloodshot. She waited in the hall while he got dressed, then walked with him to the kitchen and helped him with the bowl-cereal-milk trip.

"Eat it up," she urged. "It won't make you feel any better, but it'll keep you from feeling worse."

"My mom doesn't want me."

"You're lucky you've got one."

"You don't?"

"Nope."

"What happened?"

"I don't know."

"How'd the nosepickers get you?"

"The who?" she laughed.

"Nosepickers," Jackie repeated, and explained.

"Just my luck," Jenny said. "You know how it is, if it wasn't for bad luck some of us wouldn't have any luck at all."

"Mira says you can make your own luck."

"Who's Mira?"

He almost didn't tell. He knew the nosepickers would make trouble for Mira if they got the chance. But something inside told him Jenny wasn't a nosepicker. So he told.

/ / /

Mira waited in the truck, giving Jackie time to get past the first flush of joy. Then, just as she was about to go up the stairs to meet the legendary Mom, the police car pulled up in front of the apartment building.

Mira sat absolutely still, across the street from the blue and white. A moment of discussion, then they left the car and, as her heart sank, they turned into the tired old apartment building. She knew they were going for Jackie. She started the pickup, turned it around and went back the way she had come, parking on the side of the street, where she could see the apartment building and the police car parked in front of it.

She put her hand on Dog's neck and shushed her several times, but she had all she could do to keep Dog from going out the open window when they brought the screaming Jackie from the building, put him in the car and drove off with him.

It is one of the easiest things in the world to follow a police car. All roads lead to Rome, all police cars go to the police station. Mira sat and waited. They couldn't keep the boy in a cell forever. After a couple of hours a young man came from the building carrying Jackie. He was easy to follow, too.

Now all she had to do was keep an eye on the house. The days of maidens in towers and kidnapped princesses in dungeons were gone, there were no dragons guarding prisons, no moats full of alligators. Mira waited.

/ / /

Anna drove through traffic that had snarled and slowed to a crawl. People leaned from their open windows, screaming invective, drowning out their own words by blowing their horns. The exhaust hung at lung height, turning the air a thick blue-grey, through which the blinking lights of the police cars cut murky streaks.

The Operation Rescue zealots were out picketing the abortion clinic again, massed in front of the door, some kneeling, others pressing little plastic models of fetuses against the lenses of the television cameras. The police were removing them, with a gentleness seldom shown to union strikers or protestors who want to stop clearcuts. No fire hoses here, no billy clubs to the side of the head. No yanking of arms or grabbing of hair or accidental dropping in mud as they dragged them away, no, these protestors got lifted onto stretchers and carried quickly to paddy wagons.

A young cop was trying to divert traffic through a detour, but was hampered by more demonstrators who had shown up to support the ones volunteering to be arrested. They sang hymns and engulfed the young officer like a smiling, righteous wave.

The driver in the sand-coloured Firefly in front of her suddenly swung open the door and jumped out of the car.

"Why don't you just mind your own fuckin' business, lady, and let me get where I'm going!"

"God said Thou Shalt Not Kill," the demonstrator smiled.

"Then write a letter to your Member of Parliament!"

"And nobody has any right to terminate the life of a baby."

"Baby my ass! We aren't talking baby, we're talking blood clot! And it's none of your business anyway!"

A policewoman moved forward, put her hand gently on the arm of the driver and spoke quietly. He got back into his car and slammed the door. The policewoman stood between the line of traffic and the demonstrator, ignoring whatever the woman with the plastic fetus pinned to her lapel was saying to her.

More police cars were arriving, and the detour signs were finally in place, but half a block behind her. Anna was stuck in the snarl in front of the clinic, waiting for the police to clear the road of singing, chanting zealots.

She had heard it all. The Right to Life, the Sanctity of Life, the Protection of the Unborn. Who says? What would it mean to someone born on a garbage dump in Calcutta? What would it mean to a child born in Somalia, or Ethiopia, or on the poor side of Washington DC? What sanctity is there and what is sacred?

Why are the unborn so precious, and the ones already here so easily discounted and discarded? If life is so sacred to these people, why do they vote and pay taxes to support an army, which is a group of trained killers? Protect the unborn, so they can be born to mothers who never wanted them, whose own mothers never wanted them either, and fathers who disappear over the horizon claiming a man's gotta do what a man's gotta do. What then?

Every hour of every day of every week of every month of every year the industrialized western nations use thirty times as much of the world's resources for military purposes than we would need to feed, clothe and educate every child on the face of the earth for its lifetime. Sanctity of life?

And what could one person, one tired and half-hysterical woman, do about it? Anna had more than seven hundred "clients," as the ministry called them, seven hundred people she was supposed to help. From the very young to the very old. She was supposed to take care of them in forty hours a week, four weeks a month. One hundred sixty hours. Divide that into seven hundred plus and how much time did she have for these people she was supposed to help? Who was she going to help and how was she going to help them in thirteen-point-seven minutes?

> oh God, please, let things work out for Jenny and Jackie.
> I can't take another Peter
> I can't take another kick in the teeth
> I can't take
> much of anything these days

Anna had no trouble understanding why Jackie's mother had phoned the police and told them Jackie was at her place, eating ice cream in her kitchen. Nobody wants to admit she can't cope. Nobody wants to admit it is all just too much, the job too hard, the wages too low, the life too grim and the stress too great. Nobody wants to say I can't do it, take him away.

> but
> once it's done and the first noise is over
> the relief is enormous
> no more worry about food

or clothes
or shoes
or medical
or dental
or child care
or glasses
or
anything
and on the weekends you can visit, see him all dressed up in decent clothes, with decent sneakers on his feet and no more toothache because the trip to the dentist didn't have to wait until there was money. You can go for hamburgers, or fish'n'chips or pizza or Kentucky Fried. You can go to a movie, or to Playland or someplace fun.
no worry about hydro
or telephone
or heat
or fuel
or why there's no hot water for a bath
or food for supper
or

and then back you go to deliver him to the people the government pays to look after him properly. Pay more than you could make at your minimum wage job. Pay more to split you up than help you stay together.

kisses and hugs and promises
next week for sure, darling, give Mommy a kiss
will you phone me?
of course I'll phone you
and you'll phone me
I love you Mom
I love you Jackie

and she does. Anna has never had a doubt in her mind about the love. We are not talking a lack of love here, we are talking a lack of ability to cope

with poverty

lack of choice
miserable housing
grinding despair
fear

We are talking hopelessness. We are talking lack of education. We are talking about the walking wounded trying to raise another generation who will wind up walking wounded, we are talking bundles of emotional scars making more emotional scars.

Of course she loves him. Enough to reach for the phone and call the police so her son won't have to listen to the sounds of desperate people who drink to forget what their lives really are. Enough to send him away

to good food
warm bed
decent clothes
some chance of something

Enough to dial even though she knows she will have to hear him screaming no Mom no Mom no Mom no Mom no Mom. Enough to do for him what nobody ever did for her.

But God, how to explain that to Jackie?

Nosepickers
he screamed it as if the pain and fear inside him was
bigger than an elephant
bigger than a whale
bigger than a schooner
in full sail
bigger than Jack's giant
bigger than Dumbo's ears
bigger
than the moon itself

Seven hundred clients, forty hours a week, thirteen-point-seven minutes each. It's barely enough time to sign the damn form which releases the inadequate welfare cheque. How do I explain anything to Jackie in thirteen-point-seven minutes?

And Jenny?

You might have seen more bizarre setups in your life, God, but I'm not sure I have, and I know I don't want to see any more. What are we having here, a fire sale on kids? Oh, no thank you, they might be smoke or water damaged, I'd prefer a perfect specimen. No thank you, the last one I had got into trouble and I can't discomfit myself again. No thank you, after all, this is a no-deposit no-return disposable society and I'd just as soon dispose of this problem, thank you.

God, if you will please just give me a break here, I'll be good. I will. I'll stop smoking, I'll donate to good causes. I'll stop lying on my bed crying. I'll smarten up, I'll get it together, I'll cook proper meals, I'll go on a diet, I'll be a good girl, I promise. I'm tired. Are you? Is that's what's wrong, God? Are you tired? A bit of Celestial burnout?

The supervisor hadn't gone for the idea of Jenny living with Anna, but if you sit down with a pot of tea and take a minute to think of what the rules, regulations and policies are intended to do, instead of what they say, if you look at the flesh and blood instead of the subsections and clauses, if you admit to yourself that we are wasting our time if we cannot relate to each other from the heart, then you can probably find something that works. What do we all need? How can some of us, at least, get some of what it is we all need? And how far will the rest of us go to ensure that happens?

/ / /

Liz knew the worst was over when she wakened in the middle of the night and smelled the unmistakable aroma of Campbell's vegetable soup. The light from downstairs shone in her hallway. She pulled on her blue terrycloth robe and made her way down to Fran's suite.

"Grab a bowl," Fran invited her.

"You look like the wrath of God."

"Is that all? I feel like the vengeance of the living dead."

"Well, a bowl of soup is a start. I think I will join you, after all."

"It's my comfort food. What's yours? When you really need to suck your thumb."

"Macaroni and cheese. With lots of cheese sauce, and some hard-boiled eggs chopped into it. Lots of onion. Baked in the oven. And once in a while, if I'm really up against the damn wall, I cook some spaghetti, boil up some eggs, peel them, chop them, put them in with the spaghetti and then throw on a can of chicken noodle soup. Starch overload! It does me more good than all the cathedrals of Europe."

"Yeah, well, this is just a minor crisis so Campbell's vegetable soup will handle it. If I was in real shit, up to my eyebrows and with no visible exit sign flashing red and comforting in the gloom, I'd be eating chow mein."

"Why chow mein?"

"Because if they came home with take-out cartons of chow mein it meant they were in a good mood and there wasn't going to be another fuckin' donnybrook."

"What *was* donnybrook?"

"Some battle the Irish won, I think. Or convinced themselves they won. Or lost valiantly and gloriously. Or maybe Scottish, I don't know. If they came home dancing and singing and laughing and had chow mein with them it usually meant the whole weekend would be fine. If we were real lucky nothing would happen. Sometimes I'd smell it even before I was awake, it was like being wrapped up in a warm blanket. I don't particularly like the taste of chow mein, but Jesus, I do like the smell."

"You know what they say, you're stuck with your family, but thank God you can pick your friends."

"I think we can pick our family, too. How many cousins, second cousins and shirttail cousins do you suppose we have? Fifty? Sixty? And how many do I see in a year? Three? Out of the whole pack you're about the only one I really know. That's pretty choosy. And Andy. She and I picked each other, right? And then you two picked each other. So we're building up the crowd, bit by bit."

"You got any crackers? It isn't real soup unless we have crackers with lots of margarine smeared on top."

"Margarine! I wouldn't have that crap in the house! You want margarine you go up and get some out of your own fridge. All I have is butter."

"If that's all you have I'll make do. It always tastes so weird, and greasy."

"There you go betraying your low-rent origins again," Fran laughed. "You probably still think caviar is fish eggs in a jar."

/ / /

It was better than a group home, better than the Billingses, better than most of the places Jenny had been in. They even seemed to understand why Jackie was so important to her.

They kept a close eye on him, though. Someone was with him all the time, and at night the red syrup zonked him out so there was no chance of another trip out the back door into the wide wide world.

Jenny tucked him in bed and lay beside him, holding his hand, listening to him talk about camping out and people who talked different, and lived different, danced and sang and never sent their kids to school.

"It's a secret, okay?" he asked repeatedly.

"Not one word, sib, I promise."

"I had a dog, Jen. Black."

"Lucky you."

"They were teaching me to dance with the stick."

"Time to go to sleep, Jackie boy."

"Why, Jen?"

"I don't know, sib. Life's a bitch and then you're dead, I guess."

Only after he was asleep, only after she had tucked his blankets around his body and kissed his forehead, did she leave the room. Only when she knew he wasn't going to wake up all alone in the darkness did she go to the phone and reach for her own lifeline.

"You're sure you're okay?"

"Yeah. Well, not A-okay but I'm going to be fine. I'm head-tripped, is all. I keep trying to make sense of it, and at the same time I'm telling myself it isn't ever going to make sense."

"You want I should come over for a while?"

"No, it's okay. I just needed to hear your voice, is all."

"You wanna hear my voice?" He laughed. "Hey, Jen babe, old sib, old eff-ess, old girl, want I should sing for you? 'My Wild Irish Rose,' maybe? My granddad used to sing that. He'd get all juiced up and the next thing you know he'd be caterwauling away, the

sweetest flower that grows, and you'd think he was the happiest
son of a bun in the entire world. Two minutes later he'd be sitting on the floor crying like a baby. Just pop, and he'd go from
happy as a lark to sobbing his guts out. Oh, he'd say, oh but
where are all my people gone and why am I left alone? I'm standing in front of him, bawling right along with him and screaming
I'm here, I'm *here*, and he's wailing away because he's got
nobody. When I was real little I thought it meant he couldn't see
me because I'd disappeared, the way the world does when you
shut your eyes. I'm *here*, Grandpa, right *here* . . . But I learned
that song if you want to hear it."

"Why do they try to pretend what isn't is? Mom and Dad and
two-point-three happy little kids, the steady job, the station
wagon, the poodle and all that good shit."

"Don't let it get you bummed out, Jen. Some of the most
famous people in the world were foster kids like us."

"Yeah, sure, Brucie. Get real!"

"Sure," he laughed. "Moses was a foster kid, wasn't he? King
Arthur? And what about *Superman!*" She couldn't stop the giggle.
"Probably Wonder Woman, too," he said. "And what about Mary
Marvel?"

"You think Robin is Bruce Wayne's foster kid?"

"Or they're faggots. How many fosters do you know wear
coloured panty hose?"

"Thanks, Brucie. Maybe when he's in better shape I'll bring
Jackie with me and we can meet at the park, or something. He
really needs some sib stuff."

"Sure. You tell him Brucie said to hang on, okay?"

"Okay. Love you, Brucie."

"Love you, Jen."

"You really know how to sing that song?"

"You may search everywhere, but none can compare, to my
wild Irish rose!" And then the mockery was gone from his voice
and Brucie was singing from an open throat, his voice rich, each
note on key. Jenny leaned against the wall in the hallway of the
foster home, listening and smiling, hearing more than the song,
hearing and accepting what Bruce was trying wholeheartedly to
give to her.

Dumb song, stupid song, pathetic song, almost as stupid as that
stupid thing stupid Anna had them play at that stupid funeral. Puff

the magic dragon, frolicking in the autumn mist with the wild Irish rose.

Jackie was watching when she stopped at the door and waved goodbye each morning, and when she came home from school in the afternoon, and she could tell whether it had been a good day or a bad one by looking at his eyes. A bad day and the syrup made his eyes glassy. A good day and his eyes were swollen and bloodshot from crying.

"If you keep crying," she warned, "you'll make yourself sick."

"I don't mean to. I just do."

"Okay, sib. Will you eat your supper tonight? For me?"

"Yeah."

"Good. And tomorrow's Saturday. We're going grocery shopping. I've got money from babysitting. What would you like me to buy you?"

"Strawberries?" he looked hopeful. "Would they have strawberries?"

/ / /

Liz sat on the top step, a cup of tea resting on her knee, her fatigue so deep she imagined it visible, like a huge pulsing grey jellyfish, coming from her belly button and circling her, holding her in its middle, turned on itself, coming from her inside, wrapping her outside so she wound up inside, spiralled and looped, wrapped and enclosed. She heard Fran come from the kitchen to join her, not sure she wanted company but not sure she didn't, either.

The computer printout lay on the second step down, between her feet, the soft breeze, scented with nicotiana, riffling the edges of the pages.

They'd all shit bricks. Those who hadn't been able to find the time to visit would suddenly appear, hoping they could prod her into Finally Managing To Do Something About Fran. As if she could. As if she would, even if she could.

"It's not all true," she said softly.

"What is? All. What is? True."

"Why did you mix what did happen with what didn't?"

"I don't know what actually did happen, Lizzie. I don't know what didn't happen. Things which are, sometimes aren't as real as things which aren't, okay? Things which have never happened are more real and more true and more believable than things other people tell me did happen! All I do is write 'em. I'm like a fuckin' onion, all right? I try to peel the onion and only some of the layers, you know how an onion comes in layers, well, some of them aren't mine. I didn't grow 'em, they were grafted onto me or something."

"You aren't making any sense. I don't even know which story I'm supposed to be reading, for Chrissakes! You start things and don't finish them and you —" She started to weep. "It's like a crazy story, Fran, it's like you wrote it and went crazy."

"Nah, I went crazy first, then I wrote it. I hate to tell you this, Lizzie, but you're never gonna get a job as a book critic."

"And you're going to let them publish it?"

"Sure. They want to."

"And . . ." What about me, she wanted to ask. What about all the stuff my mother is going to say when she hears about this? How do I defend you, how do I explain to her, how do I defend her, how do I explain to you and *why always me?*

"I'm going down to the city day after tomorrow, to see Sugar and the kids. Want to come?"

"To see *Sugar?*"

"I know, but if I don't see her I don't see them and if I don't see them . . ." She shrugged. "Then I start to feel the way I did when nobody came to see me."

"Andy comin'?"

"No. So I need someone to run herd on me."

"Count me out. I mean it. Count me out. It's none of my business."

"So you going to wear your red shirt? I ironed it for you."

"Well, if it's ironed I might as well wear it." She leaned to one side, put her head on Fran's shoulder and laughed softly. "Such bullshit. I mean it. Really."

/ / /

The eff-pees thought it would do Jackie good to go with them, get him out, get him some fresh air, take his mind off things. "Just keep a close eye on him," they told each other, and they did.

Up one aisle and down the other, filling shopping carts with milk and cream, cereal and eggs, margarine, butter, sour cream for the baked potatoes, cottage cheese and farmer's cheese and everything you need to feed two adults, three teenagers and one small boy for a week.

"Strawberries, Jackie!" Jenny helped him pick out two pounds of the biggest, firmest and nicest. "With whipped cream?"

He nodded, and held the plastic bag of berries against his chest as if the treasure of the Andes was stored inside. "Maybe," he whispered, "maybe Mira picked them."

"Probably did," she agreed. "Definitely she did. And you know what? When you're feeling better, and when you can talk without crying again, you and I are going to go see a friend of mine. His name is Brucie, and he's more than just a friend, he's my sib. If you're lucky, maybe he'll be your sib too. And he is going to come with us and we'll go see another friend of mine, and after we've seen her, things are going to get better for everyone, Jack-oh."

"Yeah?"

"Yeah. You'll see."

"You're not just saying that?"

"Jack-oh, would I try to sell you a used car?"

Jenny was pushing one of the loaded carts across the crowded parking lot toward the van when suddenly there was a middle-sized gleaming black dog, leaping in the air and yapping

and Jackie screaming and running
the eff-pee made a grab for Jackie
the dog charged underfoot
the eff-pee hit the ground
a shopping cart tipped

"I'll get him!" Jenny yelled, taking off after the sib and the dog she knew was Dog.

The eff-em was helping the eff-pee up. The knee of his pants was torn and blood poured from his knee; either he'd skinned it when he landed or Dog had taken a good chomp. And then he was running after Jenny, who was running after Jackie, who was running after Dog. Only the eff-pee was limping and losing ground with every hobbled step.

Across the parking lot and down an alley Jackie ran, full-tilt boogie, the bag of strawberries swinging from one hand. The dog turned a corner, Jackie turned the corner, Jenny skidded, almost fell, turned the corner, and there was Jackie scrambling up the tailgate of a pickup truck

Jenny reached out
her hands closed on Jackie's butt
and suddenly
she was staring down at a face so much like her own
she knew right away what they said was true
SIB!
Hi Jen
Hi sib
Don't do it Jen don't do it Jen don't do it Jen

Her hands tightened, don't do it Jen, she pushed up, heaving his weight, do it Jen, Jackie went over the tailgate into the back of the pickup and Jenny threw herself after him. Did 'er, Jen, did 'er! The tires screeched, the engine roared, the truck raced down the alley and did a right into the traffic and headed through town toward the freeway. That's my sib, Jen. Oh, Jesus, Petey, if I'd known it might have been different. Fine the way it is, Jen, I'm okay.

"It's okay, Jackie boy, it's okay, don't cry, we're fine."

"All the berries is squished."

"*Are* squished, goofball."

EIGHTEEN

Anna came out of the shower so tired she didn't know if she'd been punched, bored, pinned, folded, stapled or mutilated, and she didn't much care. Her eyes burned, her mouth felt fuzzy and all she wanted to do was crawl into a hole and stay there. She knew depression was nothing but anger turned inward, and the knowledge did nothing to overcome the depression, it just fed the anger and made her feel even more tired. Or maybe the fatigue came from knowing she'd gone out on a limb and now that limb was about to crash to the ground, along with the tree it grew from.

She sat in her recliner and leaned back, the soggy towel on her head already beginning to feel uncomfortable. But if she went to bed she'd just lie there, fighting the need to cry. Maybe if she stayed here she would at least catch a nap.

The sudden ringing of the phone jarred her, almost kicked off a panic reaction.

"Anna? It's me. Jen."

"Are you okay?"

"We're fine. You heard, I guess, huh?"

"I heard. I guess I heard! You're sure you're fine? Does he need his medication?"

"You sound like you need some."

"Ah, babe, I've been worried sick. Every cop in the country is going to be out looking for him."

"Anna, can you do something? He'll go nuts, you know that. He's just about as goofy as an outhouse rat already. I bet he's worse than Pete was!"

"Are you okay for tonight? I mean, you know, a warm place to sleep, good food to eat, stuff like that?"

"We're fine. I promise. But if he has to go back he's going to . . . I don't know what he'll do. It's all such bullshit! I mean it is just such fuckin' bullshit! I'm in one place, Brucie's in another place, we're like those little hunks of wood they play checkers with, hop it here and jump over there and move this and wow I won and I've got a king, now I can move any old which way I want."

"Jen. Please. Hang on just a bit longer, okay? I'd tell you to come to my place but I know that's asking too much, and I understand that. I know there's a limit to how much you can trust anyone and –"

"Oh, fuck, Anna, we're right around the corner from your place!" Jenny managed a small laugh. "Put on the kettle, okay?"

The water was boiling and the table set with mugs and sandwich fixings by the time the doorbell rang. Anna opened the door and stepped aside to let Dog in first. Jackie stood pressed tight against Jen's leg, his hand gripping Mira's. He watched Dog as if she represented everything safe and wonderful.

"Come on in," Anna invited. "And don't worry about Dog, there's nothing here she can hurt."

They came in and she closed the door, then knelt and looked at Jackie. Nothing the least little bit like Peter; hair colour different, skin colour different, shape of face, chin, nose different, no gap between his front teeth. But for a moment, for one wild moment when she wondered if she'd snapped her twig, she thought she saw Peter. Not the way he'd been in his coffin, not the way he'd been when she first met him and he was pathetic, half starved, all wild. She saw Peter suntanned and calm, his eyes blue and gentle, the expression on his face expectant, and she knew she would do anything at all to keep from letting him down again.

"Hey, boy," she whispered. "Do you like ham sandwiches?"

/ / /

Anna got to work early and had the paperwork done before her supervisor arrived. With even a little bit of luck she'd pull this one off. She remembered someone saying I'm not even asking for good luck, just for an absence of bad luck.

The supervisor blinked. "At *your* place?"

"It seemed the quickest and easiest stop-gap. The foster father was upset. He'd said we should find another place, that Jackie was just too disruptive. And separating them at that time would have been about the worst possible thing to do. And," she smiled what she hoped looked like an apologetic smile, "I was wiped out totally. I think it would work, and I think it's best for everyone if, instead of straight foster care, we arrange Child in the Home of a Relative status. We're pretty well out of foster options, anyhow."

/ / /

The car pulled into the driveway, the pickup following. The door of the house opened and two women stepped onto the porch and started down the stairs. Andy came around the side of the house with Scarlett O'Hairy trotting behind her. A black bitch leaped from the pickup and for one startling moment it almost looked like a dog fight was about to happen.

"Your manners, bitch," Mira said quietly. Dog relaxed.

"Hi," Andy smiled.

"Hello." Jenny looked less than trusting.

"Hey, sib." Andy reached for Jackie's supermarket bag of clothes. "I remember you. 'Member me? When you came to visit that time?"

"With Squirt," the boy said. Andy looked over the top of his head and nodded at Jenny. "How's it going?" she smiled.

"Oh, you know how it is," Jenny answered.

"Sure do. Hope you don't mind, but you get to share my room."

"Fine by me."

"You're out of your goddamn mind," Liz hissed.

"Yeah? How would you know? When have you ever been sane?"

They walked the beach at twilight, the western sky streaked with the last glory of sunset, the waves lapping against the barnacle-encrusted rocks.

"So you see," Mira said softly, her hand clasping Jackie's, "now I know just exactly where you are, and an address and everything, and can come visit. And summer holidays and such we'll travel and all."

"And my mom?"

"She knows where you are. She has the phone number and she'll be up to visit as often as she can. It's not perfect, Jackie boy, but it's better than a poke in the eye with a sharp old stick, now, isn't it?"

"I wish –" he blurted, his eyes threatening to brim over again. He shook his head, blinking rapidly.

"Oh, we all do. If wishes were horses, beggars would ride. But they're not, so we don't, we just take it one step at a time."

"Down the old pike, right?" He wiped his eyes. "Squirt says one step at a time, down the old pike."

Liz sat on a rock, watching the sunset, watching Mira and Jackie strolling the beach. Fran came and sat beside her, lit a cigarette, and inhaled deeply. "Andy comin'?"

"No, Andy's with Jenny and I think they're going out to get themselves arrested."

"Arrested?"

"Yeah. I think they're taking spray cans to the statue of the Queen, soap in the courthouse fountain, some kind of demonstration. Going to confront the right-to-lifers or invade the offices of the multinationals."

"God, they're all going to the dogs."

"Right. So I need someone to run herd on me. Gotta meet with Jackie's mom at some point."

"Shit! Count me out. I mean it, count me out! I have nothing to say to her, not one word, nor to Sugar, either. Not me. It's none of my business."

"I know, you're the embodiment of the middle class voting public."

"I don't see why you can't go down there, get those kids and bring them up here! I mean, school's out for the summer soon, why should they have to swim in a chlorinated pool instead of here?"

"The basement's going to wind up absolutely jam-packed full."

"There are, after all, bigger houses than that one."

"You sure? You'd have to get involved, and that's not very middle class."

"One day I'm going to slap you, I should have done it long ago."

"Slap you back if you do."

"Pull off your arm and hit you with the wet end of it." Liz laughed suddenly, her face fuller, softer, younger. "I looked it up. It wasn't a battle."

"What wasn't?"

"Donnybrook. It's Irish, what else, eh? It's a fair, they have it every year. I don't know if it's a fall fair or a spring fair or . . . but everybody gets together for a really great old time, and it always winds up in fistfights and brawls! Year after year, probably for centuries, Grandma and Grandpa, Mom and Dad and all the little children pack a lunch twice as big as they'll need, put on their best clothes and head off for a good time they know is going to wind up a riot. We could start one right here. Call in the rest of the family. Call in the neighbours, old and new. I'm sure everyone would have a very good reason to leap in and get themselves punched and punching."

"Bigger house, huh?" Fran got off the rock and headed slowly down the beach. "You're really nuts this time, Lizzie. It's been bad before, but this time . . . right around the bend."

"Yeah? Change the words to the song. Are you going to donnybrook fair? Bring your brass knuckles, your clubs and your knives . . ."

Liz watched as Fran picked her way past the seaweed-covered rocks and walked toward the others on the beach. Everyone knew you didn't step on those rocks, you were almost guaranteed to slip, fall off and wind up badly hurt. It was like watching herself walk away from herself, but of course that was impossible. Liz sat still as a heron stood in the shallows, first on one foot, then on the other, paying attention to her own vision of reality and nothing else. Only the very last light of day was left by the time Fran reached Mira, Jackie and Dog at the edge of the water.